The Mastig

Brian R Hill

Copyright © Brian R Hill 2017

*The moral right of Brian R Hill to be
identified as the author of this work has been asserted.*

This novel is a work of fiction. Names, characters, places, and incidents are the product of the author's imagination. Any resemblance to actual events, locales, or persons, living or dead, is coincidental.

All rights reserved. No part of this publication may be reproduced, stored, or transmitted in any form or by any means, electronic, mechanical, photocopying, recording, scanning, or otherwise without written permission from the publisher. It is illegal to copy this book, post it to a website, or distribute it by any other means without permission.

ISBN-13: 978-1543139037
ISBN-10: 1543139035

*Brandywine Font by The Scriptorium
Cover Art by Ruth Stevens*

Novels by Brian R Hill

Genre — Fantasy
The Shintae (Second Edition)
Shadows from a Time Long Past
The Mastig

Genre — Thriller
Love, Lies and Treachery

The Mastig

Prologue

With a start, Ryce came out of his reverie. For too long he had been sitting, head in hands, his thoughts trapped in the darkness of his mind. Blinded by grief, he had failed to notice something. Silence! The childish shrieks, chatter and endless questions from which he had taken refuge, had fallen silent. It was much too quiet. He hastened towards the doorway.

To one side of the walled garden, he could see his daughter. This week she had celebrated her third birthday. From over her eyes, she flicked away a strand of long dark hair. Her usual happy smiling face was, instead, a study in concentration. Something in her right hand held her attention. Ryce went cold. He realised what the object was — a dagger. Terrified to shout in case she panicked, he knew one slip and her injuries could be severe.

Ryce kept his pace steady as he moved towards her. Not wanting her to think she was in trouble, he forced a smile. The knife was one he recognised; it was razor-sharp. It belonged to her older brother, Peter. Once again, the lad had failed to keep dangerous weaponry out of his sister's reach. Five paces from his daughter was a target, mounted onto the stump of a tree. Earlier, Peter had been using it to hone his knife-throwing skills.

Before Ryce could reach or speak to her, she looked up and smiled at him. It was an impish smile, which cut straight to his heart. It reminded him so much of her mother.

"Look Dada," she called.

She turned away, holding the weapon near to its wicked point. The child was too quick for him. Her arm moved. There was a flash as the sun's rays caught the steel blade. It hurtled through the air. Thud! The knife quivered as it plunged into the centre of the target. She clapped her hands in delight.

"Kariwyn cwever! Kariwyn cwever! Isn't she Dada?" she said, as Ryce reached down and scooped her into his arms.

"Oh! Yes, you are," he said, holding her to his chest, his heart racing.

There was no denying it, Karilyn was smart, too damned smart. It thrilled and saddened him at the same time. He had hoped the legacy would pass to his son. At thirteen, Peter was already big and strong. Soon, he would become a man. To be *the* one — that required something extra. When first Ryce thought of training Peter, in the skills needed to carry out the duties of the Bearer of the Scraufin, he had decided to wait a little longer. As Ryce had only the one child, it was a strange decision to make. Later, when he and his wife believed that fate would not allow then to conceive again, he continued to prevaricate.

Born a few months after Peter's tenth birthday, Karilyn had been a much-cherished surprise. Within eighteen months, her gifts were apparent. Quick and bright, her strength and agility were unusual for one so young. She displayed all the potential he had hoped for in Peter. Ryce's affection for his son remained undiminished; it was Karilyn who was something else, something special. She was the one who had inherited the traits to continue her father's calling.

Five weeks ago, her mother had taken ill with a fever. A week later, Ryce had buried her. Since then, locked in a mire of despair, he had spent hours on his own, mourning her loss. Because of this, Ryce had no knowledge of how long Karilyn had been playing with the weapon. A rickety stool stood beside the target. It terrified him to think how often she must have thrown the knife, each time clambering onto the precarious platform to retrieve the weapon. Thoughts of the consequences, had she had slipped and fallen onto the blade, made him shudder.

It would have been his fault. Karilyn's nurse was ill in bed. Ryce had promised to watch the child until she recovered. Instead, he had allowed his own misery to put her precious life in danger. He must never let that happen again. It was unfair to blame Peter. He had been irresponsible with the knife — Ryce would speak to him — but the boy was not the one elected to keep watch over his sister.

"Again, Dada," Karilyn said, struggling in his arms.

Ryce walked across to retrieve the dagger. With gentle hands, he placed her on the ground. He taught her the correct way to hold the weapon, then worked on her stance and throwing technique. She was a quick learner. Soon, Karilyn could hit the centre from many angles. Her age and strength limited the distance from which she could throw, but, within her range, the child was deadly.

Her brother had practised for many months to reach the level of proficiency his sister now displayed. This would be something best kept to themselves, Ryce told her. He wanted Peter kept in ignorance of how adept his sister was. If possible, Ryce would prefer her talents to stay hidden from everyone. Karilyn nodded. Handle first, she handed him the dagger. Her wooden dolls were nearby. She skipped over to play with them.

There were no doubts in Ryce's mind she would keep silent about the matter. The ability to keep a secret was another one of her inherent qualities. Whenever she displayed something that demonstrated her rapid development — talents that Ryce considered best kept from others — he had only to warn her once to keep them private. Even her brother could not bully information from her.

Her duty was something Karilyn would grow into and bear until her dying day. For her to achieve some level of normality in life, and keep safe, her special talents must stay hidden from outsiders. If called upon to perform her duty, so be it. Ryce prayed fate would spare her from this destiny.

With tenderness, he gazed towards his daughter. As he watched her play, his heart filled with pain. He knew nothing about rearing children. How would he cope without his wife? Karilyn looked up at him. She seemed to sense his inner turmoil. With her dolls abandoned, she walked round the garden and took his hand.

"Come, Dada," she said. "Kariwyn show you how make daisy chain."

Chapter One

Despite the lateness of the afternoon, the sun's rays remained intense, burning into Amron's back. Distant objects danced and flickered in the haze. The hot air sapped his energy and dried his throat. Throughout the day, the breeze had been absent. For a moment, he stopped work. He leaned on his pitchfork. In contrast to the glorious weather, his sour expression was an ideal match for the darkness of his mood.

After another day's hard toil in his father's fields, the young man's resentment at the unfairness of his life was close to breaking point. While he laboured, others prepared to celebrate the end of harvest. That night, his friends would be having a riotous time in the tavern. He swore as he kicked the ground in frustration. For Amron, there would be many more days of labour before his harvesting was at an end — much longer if the period of settled weather ended.

Awareness of why Tamin, his father, refused to take on extra help, intensified Amron's temper. Tamin's interference in Amron's life was deliberate. Although unable to put a complete stop to Amron's association with his drinking companions, his father put as many difficulties in the boy's way as he could.

Had Tamin been capable of easing Amron's workload, the boy's grievance about the lack of seasonal help might have been less. Sometime before his son's birth, Tamin had suffered a serious injury. With age, his body had weakened. This affliction compelled him to leave most of the heavier work to Amron. His mother was little better. Her body, twisted by arthritis, meant she struggled now to move around the house.

An only child, Amron looked forward to his evenings away from the farm, drinking and womanising. He had no wish to spend his whole life tilling the soil, as had his parents, or so he believed them to have done. They had never mentioned any other former lifestyle. On an evening, his parents retired early to their bed, leaving him to sit alone. With only the fumes and dull light of a tallow lamp for company, such time alone afforded him little pleasure.

Amron yearned for companionship and excitement. He wanted a life, yet his parents insisted on putting obstacles in his way, the most recent of which was to ban his friends from visiting the farm. 'Idle troublemakers' was one of his father's more repeatable descriptions of the gang of youths and young men, who, most evenings, used to ride to the door. It was Tamin's belief, several of these 'friends' were behind a spate of petty thefts in the area. Two, who were newcomers to the district and somewhat older than the others, always had a regular supply of gold and silver coins with which to impress his son. It was strange that, since the pair's arrival, neither of them had done a day's work.

Amron's father had great sympathy with his son's aspirations. The old man had come late to farming, only after an eventful earlier life. Trapped in the hills, working the land alone, while looking after infirm parents, was no life for a nineteen-year-old. Although it was doubtful Amron ever noticed, Tamin did what he could to help. He was aware his son needed the company of people his own age — apart from the group of wastrels who frequented the tavern.

Tamin was no fool. He knew why they sought-out his son. Over the years, rumours had spread that the family had hidden wealth. Stories persisted that, somewhere on their land, treasure lay buried. Denials did nothing to stop the gossip. Instead, to many, they served as confirmation. If he and his family maintained their simple life, Tamin hoped the tales would die. This was not because they were lies, rather because they had some foundation.

Despite his hoard, Tamin was no miser. Neither did the treasure consist, in its entirety, of the precious goods that others so desired. The reality was much more dangerous than most people could have imagined. This was not knowledge he was ready to entrust to his son. If there was one thing Tamin had in common with his son's friends, it was his belief that Amron, when drunk, was incapable of keeping a secret.

Amron stabbed a bale of hay with his pitchfork. He tossed it high onto the back of the wagon. This time, he misjudged the angle. The bale bounced off, to hit him full in the face. He went sprawling to the ground. In fury, he threw off the bundle. As he sat up, he spat out a mouthful of dried grass. His pride hurt more than his body. He stood, spluttering and coughing, the slight taste of blood salty on his tongue. Angered, he lashed out with his boot at the bale. He abandoned his task for the day, swearing and cursing; although few bales remained to stack on the wagon.

Many of the village girls considered Amron handsome. Six feet in height, his tanned, muscular body carried no excess fat. His long flaxen hair, bleached paler by the summer's sun, had a covering of hay from the bale. He shook his head, then brushed away the debris. As usual, his face, flushed with anger, carried a petulant expression. Dust from the bale stung his blue eyes, making them water. He rubbed them, only to wince as he caught the bridge of his long nose, made tender by the blow.

Still swearing, Amron pulled on his tunic. The rough material chaffed against his broad back. The tavern beckoned him, as did the folk within. Amron blushed as a feeling of guilt came over him. Back at the farmhouse, his mother would be warming a meal over the coals. Tamin would be standing in the doorway, waiting for the first sight of his wayward son. Amron could picture the disappointment in his father's expression as, once more, he realised he was waiting in vain. His body would slump and his head appear to sink lower into his shoulders. Tamin needed no telling where his offspring might be.

The village glowed in the warm, reddish light, which emanated from the setting sun. Amron approached along the winding dirt track towards the tavern. He pushed hard against its weathered door. Leather hinges creaked. He ducked his head as he stepped through the low entrance, onto a straw-covered, stone-slabbed floor. Acrid smoke, rising from the many lamps placed at random round the room, filled the air. The fumes stung his eyes. The tavern was full. Inebriated, villagers and local farmers jostled, laughed and shouted over the clamour as they celebrated the bringing-in of the harvest.

Amron wove his way through the crowd, tables and packed benches. The floor was awash with beer and mead, spilt from a large array of overflowing drinking horns and glass vessels. Loud cheers erupted from his friends when they spotted him. Within minutes, he was quaffing from a horn filled to the brim with ale. He had let down his father again; the knowledge filled him with shame. This spurred on his drinking until, for the moment, he cared no longer. He became drunk, much drunker than anyone could remember. Urged on by his companions, he sang and drank away the evening. His tankard never seemed to be empty.

Much later, as the party became more raucous, Amron became unwell. He collapsed onto the end of a nearby bench. As he tried to steady himself, his free hand grabbed for the nearest tabletop. He missed. His balance gone, he crashed to the floor where he retched, much to the amusement of his friends. Their mocking laughter attracted the tavern-keeper's attention. His attempts to throw out Amron met with determined opposition from the boisterous group. Tonight, they wanted him near them.

Such intervention was unusual. Most nights, they would have relished his humiliation. They would embellish details of such an incident, then use them to embarrass him at every opportunity. Amron was too drunk to care. He passed out. The tavern-keeper shrugged his shoulders. His friends were spending good money, ordering flagons of beer by the dozen. To upset the group might have an adverse affect on his takings? Let the lad sleep it off under the table. The tavern-keeper sent a serving maid, with a bucket of water and another of sawdust, to clean up the mess.

After she forced her way back through the crowd, towards the bar, Amron regained consciousness. He was lying on the floor, his head beside a pool of foul smelling slime created by the mop. Now he did feel ill. He struggled to focus. The room revolved, ever faster. Underneath tables, benches and between people's legs, he crawled towards the edge of the room. Nearby, a stick propped open a small side-door.

Unnoticed, Amron crept along the wall-side towards the gap. Once outside, as the cool night air hit him, he vomited again and again as his body rejected the drink. This was worse than anything he had experienced. With the aid of a wall, Amron pulled himself to his feet. He staggered along the road, away from the tavern and its commotion. For the moment, nobody realised he had gone. A thin layer of cloud filled the sky. Without the stars to guide him, and his senses befuddled by drink, Amron lost all sense of direction. Confused, he took the wrong road.

Outside the village, Amron fell over a low hedge into a hayfield. He clutched his stomach. A spasm caused him to double-up in agony. The pain eased. He stood. With eyes half-closed, he wandered across the open ground. A dip in the land caused him to lose his balance. Head first, he stumbled into a hayrick. On hands and knees, he crawled round it. He made contact with a ladder that rested against its side. Somehow, without toppling, he clambered up the rungs.

He climbed above the height of the stack. The balance of the ladder shifted. Its base slid away. Amron fell. As he landed on the mound, his legs knocked the ladder sideways. With a thud, it hit the ground. His body sank into the hay. He stretched-out. Within seconds, he was unconscious.

Sometime afterwards, a large party of horsemen rode by, on the road into the village. In the early hours of the morning, from the direction of the settlement, came sounds of a violent struggle. Frightful screams floated across the night air. Amron stirred but didn't waken. He slept, too, as the smell of burning drifted across the land.

Dawn broke. Still he slumbered. Mid-morning and the sound of horses, moving towards him, brought him to semi-consciousness. Amron tried to move. His head pounded as his hangover took hold. He sank back into his bed of hay. His stumbling gait of the night before was over sun-baked ground and stubble. He had left no tracks for anyone to find.

Bridles jingled as the noise of the hooves grew louder. The sound of voices reached Amron. He was too ill to pay attention. He wanted to be alone, allowed to die in peace. Nearby, the horses halted. A man spoke, his voice sharp and loud. The speaker was someone Amron knew, his friend Talon, the elder of the newcomers against whom Tamin had warned.

Before Amron could call out, something in the tone of the rider's voice cautioned him to stay silent. There was a chilling edge to the man's words. He spoke with an air of authority and command. Such traits, Amron had never associated with Talon. The man had worked hard to give everyone the impression he was a happy-go-lucky wastrel. An instinct for self-preservation caused Amron to bury himself deeper into the hay.

"Where the hell's that pathetic, drunken idiot gone?" Talon said in frustration.

"I don't know, Captain." The new speaker was on the defensive.

Since when had anyone addressed Talon as captain?

"We've accounted for everyone else," the speaker continued. "There's no-one left alive in the village, nor in the surrounding area. We've scoured the land around the village. In the state he was in when he disappeared, he can't have wandered far."

It was a moment before Amron realised the second speaker was Egesa, Talon's friend and fellow newcomer. He too had thrown off his casual persona.

"He's a loose end." Talon sounded angry. "I hate those. We've no idea how much he knows. I would prefer to be certain of the boy's death. The amount of poison I slipped into his last drink would have killed a horse, but he threw up most of it inside the tavern. Now we have what we came for, we can't stay here much longer. If the stupid oaf's father had told us where the object we sought was, he might have saved himself a few hours of grief.

"I still can't believe how big a fool the boy was. So eager to please and fit in, like a child, he fell for everything we said. He told us all we needed to know about his parents and their routines. His father! He showed true courage. His wife threw him a sword and, despite his lameness, he held three of our men at bay with it. He killed two of them, and would have done the same to the third if the rest of us had not arrived to overwhelm him. We questioned him for half the night, without learning anything useful. It's a pity the men killed his wife when she attacked them. We might have been able to use her to persuade him."

"Is he dead?" Egesa asked.

"He should be by now," Talon said. "Nobody could survive what we did to him. Once we found the casket, we left. I suppose, I should have killed him outright. With the courage he displayed, he'd earned a quick death, but, in the excitement, I forgot he was there."

"Where did you find the casket?" Egesa sounded excited. "I was elsewhere. By the time I arrived you were already leaving."

"We tore apart the house and outbuildings but found nothing. Then I remembered, years ago, soon after he'd taken flight, we traced the old man to Sumrania. He'd lived there for a while, before he disappeared after a fight with our men. It's taken Betlic all these years to find him. There is a Sumranian trick, where they set loose stones into the linings of their wells, with a cut-out behind to store their treasures. We lowered Slean into the old man's well, where he found such a place, a few bricks above water level. The casket was inside the opening."

"Did you open it? Was the object there?" Egesa said, his voice rising with excitement.

"Yes, it was in the box. We can go home at last. Our master will reward us well for these past few months' work."

"Soon, Betlic will rule the world. He'll reward us well for our part. Everyone will acclaim us as the men who brought him the final piece.

Because of our efforts, he will become Master of the Talisman of Grebarta."

"You fool, never mention that name again," Talon snapped, "not until the casket's back safe with Betlic. No-one must know what it contains. The men believe we've been seeking a trinket that Betlic coverts. If they find out its true worth, they'd slit our throats and try to ransom it."

"Forgive me," Egesa said, chastened. "I won't mention it again."

"If you do, believe me, I'll be the one who slits your throat."

"Is it possible the boy tried to cross the river by the stepping-stones?" Egesa was quick to change the subject. "He's fallen in before, several times. He uses them most nights as a shortcut home from the tavern. The bridge is out of his way, it adds too much distance to his journey. Unlike here, the mountains have seen plenty of rain this past week. The water's running deep and the current's treacherous. There might have been too little poison left inside his body to kill, but, combined with the drink, it must have left him confused and unsteady. If he slipped, there's every chance the current swept him away. He has to have drowned."

"It might explain why we can't find him," Talon said. "Although I would have preferred to see a body, we don't have time to search downstream, it could take days before the remains come to the surface. We have to move out. Round up the men, we leave as soon as possible."

There was a moment's silence. Amron sank deeper into the hay. He struggled to comprehend everything he had heard. His stomach knotted in agony, the after effects of the night before combined with a deep sense of fear. He must have misheard them. The village, and everyone in it, could not have gone. The tavern had been full last night, filled with dozens of happy villagers as they celebrated another fine harvest.

This idiot boy they were talking about, who was he? From out of his addled senses, his random thoughts came together. A chill ran through Amron. It was he. He was the target of their search. It was he they had tried to poison and now wanted to find and kill.

Everything became clear to Amron. The old man and woman Talon and Egesa had discussed were his parents. If Talon had spoken the truth, then his men had killed them both. His father tortured. For what? A casket, what casket? Amron had no memory of his father mentioning such an item. A hiding place in the lining of the well was news to Amron, too.

Guilt overtook him again. If only he had taken the time to listen to his father. In recent years, whenever Tamin tried to talk, Amron ignored him. Because he expected to receive another lecture on his lifestyle, he would turn away. It was sad, but Amron knew little about his father's past. He was a simple farmer. Yet, Talon had said, with a sword passed to him by his wife, Tamin killed two of his attackers. What sword? Amron had never seen one at his home. When did it come into his mother's possession and, of greater importance, when had his father learned to use it?

Amron felt a violent urge to leap from the hayrick and kill his murderous 'friends'. Self-preservation dictated he refrained from such action. He was no match for the pair. They talked in the manner of seasoned warriors, skilled fighting men. Amron had no experience of war and, apart from a small knife, neither did he carry a weapon.

The sound of horses, moving away, was a relief. He remained where he was, frightened and forlorn. Many times he was ill, until he could retch no more. This was much more than a hangover. The small amount of poison he had absorbed was still enough to affect Amron. It was fortunate for him that its symptoms were short-lived. Tears rolled down his face. Tormented by his thoughts and fears, he dared not make a move until nightfall.

The clouds cleared and, after a final flare of brilliance, the sun faded. Darkness spread over the land. It was time for Amron to leave his hiding place. Several hours earlier, a large party of horsemen had ridden along the roadway at the edge of the field. Since that event, apart from the overwhelming sound of carrion crows as they descended on the village, and the wind blowing through the hay, there had been little noise.

Amron clawed away the layer of stalks that concealed him. Moments later he slid down the side the hayrick, to land with some force on the warm earth. He stank of stale ale and vomit. Pain pounded behind his eyes, he felt dizzy and his mouth was dry. By the light of the three-quarter moon, he worked out his position. He headed towards a nearby spring. With cupped hands, he scooped the cold water. He splashed it over his face, then drank a capacious amount. After he had slaked his thirst, he stripped and washed before soaking his soiled garments. The wet clothes were icy cold when he pulled them on again. He shivered. Hesitant and fearful at what he might find, he turned towards the road that led back to the village.

Chapter Two

By moonlight, the village was an eerie sight. The inferno that destroyed it had died away to nothing. A few roof beams and several crumbling lengths of stone-built wall were all that survived. With their thatched roofs and timber-frames, the buildings had stood no chance against the flames.

The charred remains of human flesh, twisted into grotesque shapes, horrified Amron. These were people he knew, people with whom he had talked, shared jokes, worked and drunk. To some he had made love. He imagined strange creatures and spirits were creeping up on him. Amron knew such thoughts were foolish, but this knowledge did not prevent him from casting nervous glances into the shadows.

In places, the heat remained intense. Areas of rubble glowed with an unearthly redness. Sparks flickered as ashes settled. A thought came into his mind. Could he have brought this upon the village and everyone he knew? No, a voice said inside his head, his father's secret had done that.

In a daze, Amron wandered through the ruins. With tears running down his cheeks, he made a solemn, boyish, promise. He would develop the skills needed to defeat Talon and his ilk. Amron would avenge his parents and the people of the village.

Shame, too, clouded his thoughts. If only he could have found it within him to treat his father and mother as he ought. He had been too concerned with his own desires to consider those around him. His problems, which had towered above everything else, now seemed so trivial. Somehow, before he could atone, he must discover more about the casket, and what made its contents so significant. What they had to do with this talisman of Grebarta, he could not imagine. Who was Betlic, the person who, so it appeared, was responsible for the slaughter? For that crime, Amron would bring him to account. First, though, the young man would find his parents' remains, and bury them.

Nearby, in the darkness, something moved. For an instant, Amron thought the killers had returned to finish their work. A soft whimpering came to him. His heart slowed its pounding beat. Careful where he stepped among the smouldering ruins, he moved towards the sound.

After a quick search, he found the source of the noise. A brute of a dog lay half buried beneath the remains of a fallen wall. How the animal had survived the flames was a mystery, unless the stonework's collapse had ensnared the beast afterwards. Amron talked to the dog as he knelt down beside it. He stroked its head. Had circumstances been different, it looked as though it might savage anyone who came too close. In its present situation, it appreciated the company.

Amron's expected the dog's injuries to be so severe, he would have to put it out of its misery. As he felt around its body, he realised the animal was uninjured, but trapped at the bottom of a drainage channel, across which a beam had fallen. The wooden joist had protected the dog from falling rubble, but had left too small a gap for it to squeeze back out into the open.

Amron worked fast to clear the debris that held down the beam. He stopped from time to time to stroke the animal and comfort it. With the wood free of rubble, Amron took a firm grip. After several deep breaths, he used his powerful legs to push hard. For a second nothing happened. The beam creaked as it came loose. It moved a mere hand's height. Amron called to the dog. It scrambled and clawed its way through the enlarged gap. It cleared the opening as Amron lost his grip on the joist. The animal ran off, into the night. Amron sank to the ground, exhausted.

He remained seated for a minute or two while his breathing eased. From out of the shadows, a large shape leapt out at him. Afraid the beast meant to savage him, Amron covered his face and throat. To his amazement, the huge animal landed on his legs. A pair of colossal paws, thumped down onto his chest. Moments later, a large wet tongue slobbered all over Amron's hands and the few exposed parts of his face. He had made a friend.

The dog lay down at his side. Amron eased its heavy head away from his lap. He stood. As far as he could recall, the hound was unknown to him. There was none to match the size of this one in the district, so where it had come from was a mystery. A name occurred to him. He would call it Heardwine. Amron turned and moved away. He looked back, then called the animal by the name he had given it. It pricked-up its ears, then ran to the side of its new master. There it remained, at heel, as they walked towards Amron's home.

To fear something, then have that fear realised, as the young man was soon to discover, were two disparate things. Despite what he had seen and heard, he somehow expected to find his father, waiting for him at the door to their home. Sometime later, as he stood on the slope overlooking the farm, a lump came into his throat. He found it difficult to breathe as his chest constricted.

The remains of his home were stark in the moonlight. They smouldered still. He could make out two shapes, lying together, near to the front of the ruins. One was dark, the other dressed in flowing white. To be at his wife's side, his father must have survived long enough to drag himself there.

Amron took a deep breath, then moved down the hillside. The soft padding of the dog's paws kept pace with him. Without warning, it dashed ahead to examine the area. Amron watched as the animal moved among the ruins, sniffing and smelling the air. For a while, it disappeared from sight. From behind the building, it came back into view. It sniffed the remains. For a moment, it froze beside Tamin's body.

The dog lifted its head to the sky and howled. Seconds later, it raced back up the path. Before Amron could react, the beast clamped its jaws round his arm. It dragged him towards his father. Unable to resist the strength of the animal, Amron was running by the time they reached the lower ground. The hound released him. Amron saw a slight movement in his father's body. He was alive. Amron hurried across, to drop to his knees at Tamin's side.

"Father, wake up," Amron cried as he cradled Tamin's head.

Tamin opened his eyes. In the pale light, he looked up. He lifted his free hand (his other clasped that of Rowena, his wife) and rested it on Amron's face. Tamin tried to speak. After a whole day spent outdoors in the sun, his throat was too dry. There was movement nearby. Amron turned to see Heardwine carrying something in its mouth. Amazed, Amron took the dripping leather-canteen from the dog. He poured some of its contents, a few drops at a time, between his father's lips. He swallowed. Amron continued. After a while, Tamin spluttered and shook his head. He had drunk enough for the moment.

A spasm caused his legs to move. His face creased in agony, but, apart from a slight moan, he neither cried out nor spoke. Dozens of burn marks covered the old man's body, as did countless bruises from the blows he had received. Of Tamin's injuries, the worst of the pain came from his lower limbs. In their attempts to elicit information, Talon's men had broken them.

Amron gazed at his father with fresh eyes. He remembered what Talon had said about him. Those things, which had led Amron to hero-worship his exciting and sophisticated friends, were fantasies built on lies. This crippled human being, lying in his arms, was a real hero, a man of courage. Here was the person up to whom Amron should have looked. Instead, he had ridiculed him, sometimes to his face but most often to others. Amron was ashamed.

"Oh! I'm so sorry," he said. "Please, please don't die. I've been so stupid. If only I'd listened to you about Talon and Egesa, I would have been here to protect you and Mama. I'll make it up to you, I promise. I know it's been years since I said so, but I do love you."

"Shh! It's all right. We always knew you did, your mother and me." Tamin's voice was more a croak than a whisper. "There is much I must tell you, but later, when I'm stronger. There's no need to look so worried," he added. "I'm not going to die. I've suffered worse at the hands of others. These men have little skill. First, you must set my legs. If I'm lucky, when they heal, I may be able to hobble. If you do nothing, I'll never walk again."

"I can't do that, you're much too weak. The shock will kill you."

"You must. You helped set Jontive's leg when he fell down the cliff last year. This time, you must do it on your own, with the dog's help if necessary."

"Heardwine!" Amron said. His father's injuries must have affected his mind.

"You called him Heardwine?" Tamin said. "I didn't think you'd remember. You were a child then."

This conversation was becoming weirder by the moment. 'Remember what?' Amron wanted to say. His father had turned his attention towards the dog. It cocked its head to one side and lifted an ear as Tamin spoke.

"Heardwine, in the wall at the edge of the field, there's a loose stone in the corner. Push it over and bring me the bag hidden beneath it. Go, fetch it."

The hound bounded off, to leave Amron unsure whether it was his father's mind or his own that was wandering. The animal had understood everything. It returned a few minutes later. A bag, dangling from its mouth, rattled as pot jars rolled against each other. Amron opened one. He caught the strong smell of spirits. At Tamin's insistence, Amron lifted it to his father's lips and poured the contents, a mouthful at a time. It took a little while, but Tamin managed swallow half of the spirit, coughing as the fiery liquid burnt his throat.

"Use what's in the spare pots to cleanse my wounds," Tamin said. "What's left in this jar should numb my senses while you work. I'll need a branch to bite on when you begin. With luck, I'll pass out. Please, help me finish this jar. Once the drink's worked, you must act without delay. Have courage, you can do it."

When the jar was almost empty and Tamin's eyes had glazed over, Amron knew it was time to start. He laid Tamin on his back. By some miracle, the wood-store had escaped destruction. Amron stepped over to it. He snapped four of the supporting poles, which he carried over to where his father lay. In the wreckage of an outbuilding, Amron found several lengths of rope and, in a basket, a bundle of old clothes and rags. When he returned with these, Tamin was singing a bawdy song, the likes of which, from the mouth of his father, were new to Amron.

Soon, the alcohol was in full control of Tamin's body. He was drunk, his singing reduced to an incoherent ramble. Amron could put off setting his father's legs no longer. When Amron fetched the stick, despite the drink, Tamin knew what was coming. He clamped his jaw shut to hold the wood, tight between his teeth. Amron ripped open what remained of Tamin's breeches. With a firm hold on his left ankle, Amron pulled hard.

With difficulty, he manoeuvred the fractured bone back into place. An unnatural sound came from Tamin's lips as he fainted. Amron grabbed two poles, placed them on either side of the leg. He bound them with lengths of rope and strips torn from items taken from the basket. After a moment's pause, he repeated the procedure on the other leg. Both breaks looked to be clean. Neither had splintered through the skin. From the appearance of Tamin's body, Talon's men had tried beatings and burning first. They must have found the casket before turning their attention to the damaged legs.

While Tamin remained unconscious, Amron stripped the last remnants of torn clothing from him. The old man was a mass of fresh welts, bruises. Whip marks showed red across his back. There were several deep cuts on his chest, which, when inflicted, must have bled profusely. Amron started at the sound of movement. He turned to discover Heardwine had brought a bucket of water from the stream. The dog placed the pail in front of Amron before padding into the dark again. The animal was unusual, although he felt no threat from it.

While he cleaned the dirt and blood from Tamin, Amron discovered numerous ancient scars, puncture wounds and marks left by what could only have been the slashing blades of swords. This was a revelation. The old man never bared his chest in front of his son. Who was this man he called father?

Amron poured the remaining spirit over the injuries. When finished, he covered Tamin with horse-blankets. For now, Amron could do no more. He left his father for a while. Among the remains of the stables, the young man found a spade. At the rear of the house lay a fenced-off area where an older, stillborn sibling lay buried. Amron spent the rest of the night alongside his brother's grave, where he dug a large hole. Long before dawn, the moon disappeared over the horizon. In darkness, he completed the task. Alone and in silence, he buried his mother. The weather was warm; it was over a day since she had died, and the flies were taking full advantage. If the situation had been otherwise, he would have waited until Tamin awoke.

Despite his grief, the lateness of the hour and his exhaustion, Amron felt better in himself than at any time since he had awakened in the hayrick. He stumbled back to the house. Hard work and drinking plenty of water must have cleared the last of the poison from his body. He sat beside his father. Amron's intention was to stay awake until Tamin regained consciousness. Instead, his eyes closed and his head fell forward.

Dawn broke. Amron slid to the ground. Heardwine returned to his new master for a moment. Reassured everything was all right, the dog ambled away to the highest area of land nearby. The beast stretched, then fell asleep. At the faintest of noises, its ears twitched, its senses ready to awaken it at the first sound of danger.

Chapter Three

It was mid-morning before Tamin stirred. His head was pounding. He groaned as a wave of nausea hit him. Although his legs were painful, splints held them firm. The whole of the man's body ached. The spirit poured onto his cuts had removed the dirt and cleansed any infection. Although uncomfortable, they were not as painful. He could not say the same about his burns, which felt still to be on fire.

His lips were dry and cracked, his throat parched. Amron had refilled the water-carrier and placed it near to his right hand. Tamin stretched-out, but his grasp was too weak to hold onto the bottle. It tipped over and its contents spilled. Tamin muttered something that, had Amron heard, he would have blushed. His father had not used such language in front of his son.

Tamin lay back. His head was resting on a rolled-up horse-blanket. A thin layer of high cloud covered the sun. The air was cooler. It would rain before nightfall. Before the weather broke, they must find shelter, but the thought of moving filled him with dread. He needed to rest for a while, to build-up his strength. He moved his hand, further out from his side. There was no-one there. Rowena, his wife of many years, lay beside him no more.

Tamin looked across at Amron, at the mud covering his son's hands and clothes. Abandoned nearby was a dirty spade. For the first time since Talon tore his world apart, Tamin shed a tear. It grieved him not to have said goodbye to Rowena. The boy had done the right thing. Tamin knew his son would have had little choice other than to bury her. It must have taken most of the night. No wonder he had overslept. Desperate as Tamin was for a drink, he left Amron to sleep.

Heardwine had no such compassion. The dog wandered down from its watch point as it had done many times. Once it realised Tamin was awake, it sat beside him for a moment to lick his face. The animal then moved over to Amron. It ignored Tamin's whispered commands for it to leave, as it tugged and pulled at Amron's sleeve.

"What...What's wrong?" Amron stuttered in alarm.

Startled, he leapt to his feet. Was he under attack? Everything was quiet. His gaze came to rest on the ruins of the house. Memories of the day before flooded back, the village, the dog, his father's legs and the burial of his mother! Father! Was he all right? Amron looked down to see Tamin staring up at him. Amron knelt. With head bent, he strained to hear his father's faint, croaking words. 'Water' was all Amron understood. In haste, he went to refill the water bottle, then helped Tamin to hold it while he drank.

"Thank you. I needed that," Tamin said, his voice was stronger and much clearer. "I fear rain's on its way. Before nightfall, we must find shelter and something to eat."

Amron looked at the thickening cloud. The air was becoming cooler and the breeze gaining in strength. To move Tamin in his present condition could prove fatal, of that Amron was certain. Not that he could think of anywhere to take him. He knew, from the conversation he had overheard between Talon and Egesa, their men had destroyed all the local farms and murdered their occupants.

An idea came to him. The hay wagon and horses he had abandoned the other day, might they still be where he had left them? They were on the eastern border of Tamin's land, grazing in a secluded hollow. No-one lived less than a day's ride beyond that line. Because Talon knew the area was unoccupied, he would not have wasted his raiders' energies by sending them that far. It was worth a journey to find out. Amron explained to Tamin where he was going. Heardwine made as if to follow. Amron ordered the dog to stay, he wanted it to keep watch. Although unhappy, the hound obeyed his command.

Within the hour, Amron reached the hay field. Everything was as he had left it. He hitched up the horses, leapt onto the front of the carrier and drove it back to Tamin. Heardwine bounded over as soon as Amron came into view. Barking, the dog jumped onto the driver's seat beside its master. Heardwine's wagging tail banged against the wagon's side as the animal licked Amron's face.

Tamin was asleep so Amron did not disturb him. He unhitched the horses and put them to graze in a small enclosure. On his return, he unloaded the hay bales. Careful to avoid catching his father with the wheels, Amron positioned the empty cart over Tamin to form a roof. During his absence, the cloud had thickened, and the sky darkened. Dust and debris was swirling around the farmyard in the breeze. Without delay, Amron stacked the bales round the wagon. He pushed them tight against each other, so they would keep out the elements. The result was a shelter that was warm and dry. Tamin continued to sleep. His face was pale and drawn. Amron doubted his father would survive much longer without food.

Nearby, a horse whinnied. Mindful of danger, Amron crawled out through the narrow opening he had left between the bales. He looked around in trepidation. To his relief, he found the source of the noise was his father's horse. It was grazing close to the enclosure. Despite its taste of freedom, the animal, which had escaped during the raid, had returned to familiar territory. Amron called to it. The horse pricked-up its ears at the sound of a familiar voice. It moved nearer to nuzzle him, then bent its head to feed from an unused hay bale.

Only the house had been set on fire. From the tracks that surrounded the ruins of the outbuildings, it appeared the marauders had used ropes, tied to their horses, to pull down their wooden walls. Amron turned his attention to these remains. He rummaged through the wreckage until he found a saddle and tackle. Once Amron saddled the horse, he left it for a moment, to see if his father was awake. His eyes were open, but he remained weak, and in great pain.

"I'm going for supplies," Amron said. "I won't be long. Farmer Dag built a cold room in the woods behind his house last year. I doubt Talon's men found it. Dag's wife kept meat and produce there. I'm sure there'll be something in there we can use."

"Please hurry, but be careful," Tamin warned.

He felt unwell. Lack of food, as well as his injuries, made him lightheaded. As Amron ducked out of the opening, Tamin lay back. His son had worked hard. In his younger days, Tamin had slept in places far worse than this. The wagon would provide shelter from the rain, and the hay would keep out the wind. What more could anyone want?

The horse needed no urging to increase its pace. As ever, its response to the slightest command was instant. How had his father afforded such a powerful animal? This had been a puzzle to Amron. It was rare for them to have any spare money for clothes, or tools for the farm. Yet, one day, Tamin had visited a horse fair, from which he returned with this magnificent animal.

His mother's reaction, too, was uncharacteristic. Her attention to detail, particularly with money, was the source of much local humour. For someone who watched every coin she spent, this expensive purchase seemed to pass her by; she had never mentioned it in Amron's hearing.

Farmer Dag's farm was a short ride away. At the entrance, rough-hewn log-gates hung askew from leather hinges. Heardwine, who accompanied Amron, ran ahead, along the narrow cart track. The dog paused from time to time, to sniff the air or at the tracks that covered the ground. The flames had long-since died, to leave behind a strong smell of charred timber. There were no bodies outside the blackened heap. Amron decided against examining the rubble.

Throughout the district, there would be many similar sights, too many for him to search for victims. Amron said a short prayer, then dug his knees into the horse's flanks. Travellers would discover the carnage in the village and, before too long, word would reach the ears of the king's agents. They would be quick to investigate. Let them make the burial arrangements — it would do them good to earn some of the money they stole in taxes.

What further action they could take, with no firsthand accounts, was hard to imagine. By such times, with his father, Amron hoped to have journeyed far from the area. Whatever Tamin had kept hidden, Amron suspected the secrecy that surrounded its details should remain in force. Because they were the sole survivors, they would come under intense scrutiny. If blame was to attach to them, they could find themselves incarcerated or worse. Authority always seemed to want to hold someone to account, proof of guilt an unnecessary complication.

In the woods, behind the ruins, Amron dismounted. He tethered the horse to the broken branch of a nearby tree. Ahead of him was a steep-sided mound. At its base, a recessed doorway led into a yellow clay-brick surround. He drew back a bolt then pushed the heavy door. It screeched as its wood panels scraped across the floor. When he stepped inside, cool air wafted against his face. A spring of ice-cold water bubbled at the centre of a large circular, vaulted room, lined with more yellow bricks. Channelled in a spiral pattern around the chamber's floor, the water drained away through an opening at the rear. The temperature was low enough to preserve the food, which lay stacked on tables, and in wooden frames that rested against the walls.

From a peg, near to the entrance, a variety of empty sacks were hanging. Amron took one. He filled it with vegetables. In another sack, he placed salted and smoked meats. He had enough food to last for several days. At the back of the chamber where it was coldest, ham shanks hung from hooks. He took the largest for Heardwine. Amron could return for the others later if needed. He shivered in the chill air outside as, to keep out the wildlife, he closed and bolted the door behind him.

Tamin was awake when Amron returned. A worried expression lifted from the patient's face when he identified the rider. Dark grey clouds filled the sky. Raindrops, large and few at first, hit the ground. Amron unsaddled the horse and left it in the enclosure, with the carthorses. Heardwine was already inside the shelter. After greeting Tamin with a lick, it shook itself. By the entrance, it lay down to await Amron's arrival.

Rain was falling by the time Amron crawled out of the wet. It was too damp outside to light a fire. Beneath the wagon, the hay was tinder-dry. It would be foolish to start a blaze here. The cart was his only means of transporting his father. They would have to be content with a cold meal. The water bottle was empty. Amron dashed to the stream to refill it. Once back, he removed his wet, outer garments, and hung them over the wagon's axles to dry.

Tamin was too weak to feed himself. Amron cut a chunk of the cooked meat into small pieces then fed them to his father. When he could eat no more, Amron attended to himself. The food, cold fare that it was, fuelled Tamin's body. From the inside, he warmed. In pain and discomfort, he drifted in and out of sleep.

Amron ate in silence. Earlier, when he opened the sacks, he had given Heardwine the joint of meat. The animal must have found a dry comfortable place to eat because he had not seen it afterwards. Overcast skies brought darkness early that night. Both men were soon asleep. Although Tamin woke several times, he had sufficient strength to hold the water bottle. With no reason to awaken Amron, Tamin let his son sleep late into the following morning.

Chapter Four

On the hillside, down which Amron had walked two nights earlier, wet grass glistened in the sunlight. Careful not to disturb Tamin, who slept close by, Amron crawled from under the wagon. He stretched to ease the stiffness in his back. High on the hill, beyond the farm, he could see Heardwine. The dog barked a greeting, but remained on watch.

The rainstorm had blown clear. Large puddles bore evidence to its passing. The woodpile, unstable after the removal of its supports, had collapsed in last night's winds. Amron pulled a few dryer ones from the middle of the heap. Back at the shelter, he built a fire, using small shards of wood and a handful of straw for kindling. His father carried a spare tinderbox in his saddlebags. Once Amron retrieved it, he wasted no time in starting a blaze. What the pair needed most was a hot meal. That would happen later. For now, he cut a slab of cooked meat into small pieces for his father, who was now awake.

This morning, Tamin looked and felt better. Although gaunt and wracked with pain, much of the deathly pallor had left him. For the first time since Amron found him, he smiled.

"Sit with me," Tamin said, once Amron finished eating. "We have much to discuss. No recriminations," he added in haste as Amron apologised again. "What's past is over and forgotten. Many of our problems were due to my stubbornness; I should have handled matters better these past few years."

"What is this casket I overheard Talon discussing?" Amron wanted to know more. "He spoke of a talisman, and a man called Betlic."

"The talisman is the 'Talisman of Grebarta', an object of great antiquity. It's a magical device, desired by many, but much too dangerous for mortal use. Without the Mantle of Agetha, the talisman has, for generations, remained dormant, a mere curiosity. That, I'm sorry to tell you, is about to change. The casket, stolen by Talon, contained the mantle. His master, Betlic, the person who ordered it stolen, already possesses the talisman."

"But who is this Betlic? What has he to do with us?"

"He rules over a distant land, Xicalima. Before he seized power, bands of marauders targeted the country. Although I have no proof, I believe they were Betlic's men in disguise, sent to create havoc. After many months of constant fighting, the Xicaliman forces were no closer to vanquishing the raiders than when they started. The king was weary of the struggle. His subjects longed for peace. One day, Betlic arrived at the Royal Court. Outside the castle a band of warriors, several hundred strong, awaited his return.

"His majesty was grateful to accept Betlic's proposal to rid the land of the scourge. What was curious was the lack of monetary demands by the visitor for his services. All he required, he said, was one tiny item. Stored away, in the depths of the castle, was an ancient bauble, a talisman — an object of little value. This trinket would be his reward. The king's reaction was that it was a small price to pay. The talisman's powers were unknown in Xicalima. For centuries, it had remained hidden. How Betlic came to hear of it, or its whereabouts — unless by other magic — is not known. Within weeks the raids stopped. It was time for Betlic to demand his prize.

"His majesty was not naive. If Betlic wanted the talisman and nothing else, it must be of greater importance than he had led his highness to believe. He ordered it brought to him, together with any documents of relevance. An elderly man, with knowledge of the object, worked in the archives. For generations, his family had been custodians of both it and the mantle — an arrangement that now seems unwise. While he disclosed nothing about the mantle to the king, the archivist revealed much of the talisman's history.

"Its magic was too powerful for human hands to wield. It corrupted all who tried, no matter how honourable their intentions. Then, the talisman had its malevolence constrained within a stone jar of unknown origin. If someone were to release it from the container's binding properties, it would begin its evil again. The king gave the matter great consideration. He was a man born with a divine right to rule, or so he believed. The talisman was his property, to keep and use as he wished. It took a long and impassioned entreaty by the archivist, to convince his majesty that the dangers of using the object far outweighed those posed by Betlic. With reluctance, the king agreed to send it far away. He was too late."

Tamin paused a moment for a drink of water. Amron was impatient for his father to continue. After making himself comfortable, Tamin resumed his tale.

"Betlic was a young man, proud, arrogant and sure of himself. He brought his army to the gates of the castle. His original band had grown to number several thousand — most likely the groups of bandits and marauders who had rejoined his forces. The king ordered the drawbridge raised, and the gates closed. Betlic had anticipated this. A group of his men, masquerading as peasants, were already inside the castle. With their disguises thrown off to reveal the chain-mail and black leather uniform of their master's army, they drew their swords. They were ruthless, beyond anything the defenders had seen. The castle guards offered little effective resistance. Those who survived the initial slaughter, surrendered command of the gatehouse and fled. When reinforcements arrived, it was too late. Betlic's main army was already swarming across the drawbridge.

"In triumph, Betlic rode into the castle. The captain of the king's guard had failed in his attempt to carry the talisman to safety. Betlic had his new plaything. Despite his spells, the object remained dormant. In his rage, he had the king, and the surviving members of the royal family, tortured. The inquisitor's attempts were in vain. They were unable to uncover the reasons behind Betlic's failure to make the talisman respond to his enchantments. The prisoners knew nothing, the only person who did was the archivist, and he'd disappeared. Within the castle walls were many secret chambers. Inside these, he kept himself and his son safe from Betlic's men. In a desperate search for information, the usurper's scribes ransacked the archive's vast collection of scrolls."

Tamin halted again. He had drunk all his water. Amron went outside to refill the container. He hurried back and put the canteen within easy reach of Tamin.

"Please go on. What happened then?" Amron pleaded as he sat beside his father.

"Did I mention that the old man and his son were not alone? No! I thought not," Tamin said when Amron shook his head. "The king's niece, a feisty young woman, was in the library when Betlic attacked. She went to change into an outfit more appropriate to that of a warrior than a lady of royal birth.

"Better able than most men in the use of a sword, she fought alongside the archivist's son. When it became apparent that defeat was inevitable, he led her to safety in one of his father's secret places. From there, they worked their way through the castle to rejoin the archivist. The three then waited to see what would happen.

"Once Betlic accepted that neither the royal family nor their advisors possessed the information he desired, he had them killed. The king's niece was now queen, although in name only. The fugitives knew it was too dangerous for them to stay at the castle. Each day they feared discovery. The old man, too frail to travel any great distance, was aware he would hinder his son and the queen apparent. They refused to leave him to his fate. For a short while, they remained at an impasse.

"From their secret places, they listened in to conversations between Betlic's scribes inside the library. Through them, the fugitives discovered someone had divulged the archivist's part in the king's decision to keep the talisman safe. The following day, the news was bleaker. Betlic had discovered the existence of the mantle, and its relevance to the talisman. It was not long before he connected all these pieces of information to the archive's curator. With great urgency, Betlic started a hunt for the custodian."

"Betlic would have ripped the castle apart until he found the archivist, so the old man gave his son and the queen an ultimatum. Unless they left that night, he would take poison. Without him, they would have no reason to stay. Although they were vehement in their protests, the old man convinced them his words were no idle threat.

"It was then he told them everything about the talisman, and the danger it posed when combined with the mantle. If Betlic gained possession of both objects, he would bring the world into a time of darkness and sorrow. It was the son's duty to escort the mantle and the queen to safety. The archivist's arguments were compelling. He had one more piece of information, which he passed on to them, more a curiosity than a fact.

"In an ancient text was mention of a Mastig, but no description of what it might be. The writings said that, once the talisman and the mantle had come together, only the Mastig could thwart their evil. Without corroboration, the old man gave little credence to the script. When the castle fell, he destroyed the manuscript. If the story was true, and Betlic gained possession of the mantle, the archivist thought it wiser for the enemy to remain ignorant of an object that rendered his powers impotent."

Amron sat motionless. His eyes were wide and his mouth open as he listened. After a moment's pause, Tamin continued.

"The archivist assured the others that, whatever happened, Betlic's men would never take him alive. The poison, which he carried with him always, was swift. Without Betlic's intervention, it had been long overdue for him to pass-on to his son the mantle, and his knowledge of the talisman.

"That afternoon the archivist led them to a spiral staircase, which took them deep underground. For more than a league they walked, along dank and foul stone-lined tunnels. The trio's journey ended at a gap, smothered by undergrowth, concealed beneath a rocky outcrop. They squeezed their way through, to emerge into the evening light at the base of a scar. The castle lay behind a line of hills. A gentle slope, in front of the trio, overlooked a cottage beside a stream. The vale, unknown to the residents of the castle, was small and secluded.

"An elderly man greeted the archivist at the cottage door. They exchanged a few whispered comments. The man disappeared round the back of his home. A short while afterwards, he returned, leading two saddled horses. He left them with the young couple while he entered his home. A few moments later, he re-emerged, with saddlebags that bulged with supplies. How he knew they would come for them, was a mystery.

"The archivist could have stayed there, in relative safety, as the others' wished. But, he realised it was not possible, the longer he remained free, the wider Betlic would extend his search. The fleeing pair would be at a greater risk of capture in the hue and cry that followed. If the archivist returned, once Betlic found the old man he would call-off the hunt. At that time, Betlic was unaware of the son's existence. After a long absence, he had returned for a short visit. Not until the fighting started did he venture from his father's rooms. In the mêlée, no-one recognised him. Once out of the area, the couple would be safe."

"What about the queen?" Amron wanted to know. "They must have looked for her too? I imagine Betlic would want to rid himself of any possible claimant for the throne."

"There was a young woman, killed during the fighting, whose build and hair was similar to the queen's. The injuries to her face were so severe; she was beyond recognition. With the body dressed in some of the queen's clothing and jewellery, Betlic believed her to be the real one, therefore no longer a threat."

"What happened then? Did they escape? Was the archivist found?"

"A few days later, when Betlic's men broke into his hiding place, the old man took his poison. The young couple made good their escape. During their long journey, they fell in love, married and settled for a while in Sumrania. Within the year, Betlic learned about the archivist's son, his visit and then his disappearance, along with the genuine queen. The tyrant set about tracing their whereabouts.

"Taken by surprise, the couple overcame their attackers, but not before the husband received severe wounds. To cover their trail, they journeyed through many countries as they made their way north. In the end, they settled here. Within weeks of their arrival, their first son was stillborn. A stray dog, similar to your new friend, had followed them from Sumrania. It stayed with them until, a few years after the birth of their second son, it disappeared. That animal, too, they called Heardwine."

For a while Amron was silent as his mind absorbed everything he had heard. Until the final part, he had believed the tale to be one about strangers. The significance of the mantle being under his father's protection had escaped him. With the mention of Sumrania, the truth became clearer. His father was the young man in the tale. It was no 'accident' that had crippled him. The elderly archivist, Amron realised, was his grandfather. If this was correct, Amron's mother was the queen. That caring but firm lady, who had wiped his nose as a child and sung him to sleep, had been the feisty young woman. Therefore, if his mother had been queen, what did that make him? A prince! Never! He was a simple farm boy. He must have misunderstood. Amron turned to speak. He was too late. Exhausted, Tamin had fallen asleep.

Chapter Five

While Tamin slept, Amron sifted through the charred remains of the farmhouse. Last night's rain had dampened and cooled the area. He soon realised there was little left to salvage. One discovery was an old iron cooking pot, lying near to where the door had been. Talon's men must have tossed the vessel there when they ransacked the building. After cleaning out the dirt and ashes, Amron half filled it with water, then added salted meat.

His mind was racing. Was his understanding of what he had heard correct? He had thought so. The marks he had seen on his father's body pointed to a past life less peaceful than one of a farmer; but marriage to a lady of royal birth? That was beyond belief. Amron had great difficulty picturing his mother as a dynamic young woman, far more wielding a sword. His main memories of her were of a white-haired woman, aged prematurely by the onset of arthritis. As did most young people, Amron thought of his parents as being old — as such, he supposed, they must be both in their mid to late fifties, to him ancient.

Amron resumed his search, now among the outbuildings. Apart from several bowls, he discovered little else of use in the wreckage. The damage to most items was beyond repair. In one of the smaller ruins, he found a stockpile of cured meat, which he stored inside the shelter for safekeeping.

It was early afternoon before Tamin woke. A few hours of sleep, after the food he had eaten earlier, had led to a noticeable improvement in his condition. His face had filled out and the dark shadows around his eyes had faded.

"Hungry?" Amron asked after Tamin called out to him.

Through the opening in the hay bales, he had watched his son work.

"Yes, but something hot, if possible."

"In that case, you'll have to wait a little while," Amron said, pleased at the returning strength in the invalid's voice.

Earlier, he had built up the fire and pushed the cooking pot into the embers at the edge of the blaze. To the meat, which had been simmering for a while, he added vegetables to make a broth. Once the food was ready, he filled a bowl for his father.

With care, Amron eased Tamin into a sitting position. He was strong enough to feed himself. Afterwards, Amron cleaned his father's wounds. Everything appeared to be healing without complication. They sat back, in companionable silence. Neither could remember when last this had happened. For the first time since he had awakened in the hayrick, Amron put aside his worries. His curiosity still ran high. Unable to keep silent any longer, he asked the question foremost on his mind.

"Father, I didn't misunderstand you, did I? You are the archivist's son and Mother was the king's niece?"

"No, you didn't. Your mother was the uncrowned queen of Xicalima."

"But what am I, a prince?"

Tamin thought for a few seconds. "No!" he said, his tone firm.

Amron experienced a twinge of disappointment, although he half expected a negative answer.

"No," his father repeated. "Not any longer. You were a prince, but, now you've inherited the crown of Xicalima. Please don't take offence if I neither stand nor bow to you, your Majesty," he added.

"King!" Shocked, Amron's mouth fell open. "Me, a king? Now you're making fun of me. Aren't you?"

"No, although I must admit, the thought only occurred to me a moment ago. As far as I know, your mother was the only relative of the old king to survive Betlic's takeover, hence her title of queen. On her death, you, as heir apparent, became king. As you must have realised, your kingdom is under the rule of the usurper Betlic. Despite that, you are the rightful pretender to the throne, King Amron of Xicalima — the king without a country.

"Your mother wished to protect you from this knowledge, and from anything to do with the affairs of that land. Now Betlic has found us, you have a simple choice. Either you attempt to reclaim your birthright, or go into hiding for the rest of your life.

"By leading a modest life here, she hoped to fade into obscurity. Few knew your mother had survived. No-one here wore a sword, so we put away ours. She decided not to teach you how to use one, in case it drew unwelcome attention. To keep you safe, your mother rejected any thoughts of attempting to take back her country. She hoped you would settle into farming and need never know the truth. It was a foolish dream, one, to some extent, we both shared. Because of your bloodline, the possibility that events might draw you into a future conflict has crossed my mind, more than once."

"I cannot recapture a country," Amron said, stunned. "Who would follow me? I've no idea how to rule over people. I'm no king, it must be a mistake. I've never touched a sword. How can I lead an army?"

"You'll learn," Tamin promised. "You still do the exercises I showed you as a child. I know, because I watch you sometimes. You're swift on your feet and your reactions are excellent. These are exercises taught to your mother and me, by well-respected teachers. Already you know the correct moves and stances. All you need is training in how to perform them while holding a sword. That will be a start."

Amron had never thought these exercises anything other than to keep his body strong and supple. Such attributes had won him much favour with certain girls of the village which, in turn, had motivated him to continue the daily routine. As he thought about his father's words, he imagined doing the exercises with a sword. He was quick to realise he could combine the two things with ease.

Tamin continued, "But first, before I can turn you into a warrior, we must move on from here. Time grows short. Soon news of the massacre will reach the ears of King Grogant's agents. If they find us in the district, we'll have too many questions to answer."

"It would be better for us to leave," Amron agreed. "But we can't go until you're well enough to travel."

"My fitness is of no account. We leave tomorrow. Before then, you must make a bed of hay for me on the wagon. Pack it deep, it will absorb much of the impact of the trail. We've a long way to travel."

"Where are we going? Not to Xicalima?" Amron sounded worried.

He had no desire to be anywhere near that land. The more he thought about it, the more certain he became it was a place he never wanted to visit.

"No, it's too dangerous there for you. Betlic will have the mantle within months. Once he has mastered its use with the talisman, he'll start to spread his empire. We go west, to the Mogallean Mountains."

"What, that inhospitable place? If half the tales I've heard are true, we'll die from hunger and thirst."

"There's game and water, if you know where to look. I've an old friend who lives there. He'll find somewhere for us to live. From him you'll learn much."

"Who's he?" Amron said.

He was curious. His father had never mentioned any old comrades outside the area. In and around the village, Tamin had been sociable, without encouraging any close friendships.

"His name's Hafter," Tamin said. "He's much revered as a sage, and a fellow refugee from Xicalima. We'll be safe with him, providing Betlic does not use the Eye of the talisman to find us."

"What's that?" Amron asked. Every time his father spoke, he seemed to mention something unfamiliar.

"The Eye's the object that lies at the centre of the talisman," Tamin explained. "Once Betlic puts on the mantle, he'll be able to make use of the Eye to call up visions of anyone he seeks, and their surroundings. The Eye shows the general direction of the location, but does not pin-point it. For Betlic to be certain of finding his target, he would have to make the journey himself, making frequent use of the Eye to keep himself on the right path.

"Your 'friend' Talon will inform his master we are both dead. As the Eye seeks only the living, it's vital Betlic continues to believe that. Unless he learns about our survival, he has no reason to use the Eye against us. From our tracks, King Grogant's agents may suspect someone survived, but, as everyone who knew us is dead, there's no-one's left who can identify us."

For the rest of the day, Amron made preparations for their travels. From bales of hay and layers of straw, he made a secure and comfortable bed for Tamin. Once the work was to Amron's satisfaction, he saddled his father's horse.

With Heardwine beside him, Amron rode into the countryside. Out in the fields, many barns had escaped destruction. Most contained little of use to him. A pile of waterproofed cloths was a welcome find. With an axe, taken from the wall of another barn, and the fabric rolled and tied to the back of his saddle, he returned to the farm. It was time to make a cover for their wagon.

Using the axe, Amron cut down a dozen tall, supple saplings from a small patch of woodland nearby. He used several of the poles to form an arched framework, which he lashed to the wagon's side panels. He tied pieces of waterproofed cloth over this, at the ends of which he left flaps for access. Once he tightened the guy-ropes, the whole frame became rigid. It looked secure. Whether it would stand the rigours of travel would become apparent only when they were on the move.

After the evening meal, Tamin fell asleep. Although Amron wanted to do the same, he had work to do before he could rest. He saddled the horse again, then made several trips to farmer Dag's cold room, each time returning laden with supplies. Satisfied neither he nor his father would go hungry for a while, Amron put the horse to graze inside the corral.

Tamin had not stirred. Careful not to disturb him, Amron crawled under the wagon. Soon he, too, was asleep. Heardwine padded down from his spot on the rise to circle the farm. No danger threatened. Content, the animal returned to the hilltop where it flopped down onto the grass. With its head resting on its front paws, it closed its eyes and relaxed its body. As always, at some level, it remained on guard.

Chapter Six

That night, the pain in Tamin's legs was persistent. Unable to find a position in which he was comfortable, he slept little. When he woke the first time, it was soon after Amron had fallen asleep. Hours passed. Tamin stirred several times. He suffered in silence until the agony became too great for him. With reluctance, he called his son awake. Alarmed by his father's condition, Amron moved to un-wrap the bindings that held the splints in place. Dark purple bruising covered much of both legs. The skin, below the breaks, was warm to the touch, with none of the foul smell of infection, or putrefaction Amron had feared. Relieved, he re-strapped Tamin's splints into place.

Along the riverbank, purple willow grew close to the water's edge. The day after he set Tamin's legs, Amron had cut a quantity of bark for his father. Since then, chewing the substance had done much to ease Tamin's discomfort. Amron looked at where the bundle had been.

"Why didn't you tell me you'd used the last of the bark?" Amron asked, surprised Tamin had not mentioned this.

"It was late in the evening before I realised. You were absent, and I was in little pain. I thought I could last until morning."

"Hmmm!" Amron snorted. "There's a young tree by the stream, I'll go and strip a length of bark for you."

Tamin made to protest. The look on his son's face silenced him. Amron stumbled into the night. The moon was low over the horizon, its glow barely enough to light his way. On his return, Amron broke the bark into smaller pieces. He passed several of them to Tamin. Grateful for the supply, he chewed on the soft strips. His pain would soon ease. Too weary to talk further, Amron lay down. Within minutes he was snoring. Tamin cast a fond glance at his son. Over these last few days the lad had matured. Had she been here, it would have eased his mother's heart to see the change in him. Despite the grief Amron had caused, her faith in him had been steadfast. Tamin prayed he would live long enough to witness his son's coronation. Tamin's agony lessened and his eyes closed. He too fell asleep.

Amron stirred. When he left his bed and stepped outside, it was mid-morning. His father was still sleeping. Amron looked around, then stretched. He made a fuss of Heardwine, who came down to join him. They played for a while before he retrieved a joint of meat for the dog. It trotted off to the crest of the hill to eat. Amron inspected the ropes round the canopy, then stacked the rest of the supplies inside the wagon.

Tamin continued to slumber. Amron decided to delay their start for another day. This would give his father much-needed extra time to improve. Down by the riverside, Amron filled a large sack with bark from the purple willow. He had no way of knowing when they might find further supplies. For some time his father would have need of its pain-relieving properties. The jolting of the wagon, at best, would be unpleasant for him.

Regarding Tamin, Amron had few expectations. The boy knew, because of his father's weakened state, he would be fortunate to survive the journey. Had circumstances been normal, Tamin would have rested until his body healed and his strength returned.

Amron re-entered the shelter, sweat dripping from his face after the long uphill walk, Tamin's eyes were open. After he had helped his father into a sitting position, Amron showed him the sack and its contents.

Tamin smiled, grateful for such a generous supply. "Let's hope I feel much better soon, then I won't need to use it all. When do you think it best to start?" he asked, referring to their impending journey. "Mid-afternoon might be best, when the sun has passed its peak."

"I've decided to wait until tomorrow. After last night, I believe we should wait an extra day. The rest will be beneficial for you."

Tamin's first inclination was to disagree. He thought better of it. Amron was right. An additional night's rest could make all the difference. For once, his son was responsible in his thinking. It would be good for him to become used to making decisions. Tamin resolved to step back and advise only when asked. Whether he could maintain this position when he felt better, was uncertain. Old habits were harder to break than legs. In addition, there was one last task that Amron must perform before they left, the main reason behind Tamin's earlier suggestion they delay until later in the day. He explained to Amron what it was.

"In the field where we keep the horses, at the corner nearest the stream, is the trunk of a dead tree," Tamin said.

"Yes, I know the one."

"Where it faces into the enclosure, there was once a hollow between the roots. Many years ago, I covered it with soil. Hidden, beneath the grass, is a chest. I want you to dig it out before we go. We'll have use of its contents."

"I thought you concealed everything of value down the well?"

"Not everything. It might have been better had I put the mantle under the tree! But I believed it safer where it was."

"What's in the chest?"

"The sooner you start digging, the sooner you'll find out."

Intrigued, Amron picked-up the spade with which he had buried his mother. He walked over to the paddock. It was hard work, labouring beneath the dead tree. Before long, his body was running with sweat. Behind him, excavated soil formed a mound. The deeper he dug, the more he had to widen the hole. When he was waist deep, he was in despair. If a box was here, he should have found it by now.

Weary, he put-down the spade. It was time to see if his father wanted for anything. Tamin reassured Amron that he had buried something there. How far down, Tamin could not recall. The cavity was already in existence when he hid the chest. After a brief shared meal, Amron returned to his task.

For a short while longer, he continued to dig. His spade hit wood. With renewed vigour, he attacked the ground. Soil flew from the blade as he uncovered the box top. It was a while before he freed the sides from the dirt. The chest, made from seasoned oak, was in good condition. Attached to each side were large metal rings. Its length was one and a half times that of Amron's arm, and over half an arm's length in width and depth. He grasped hold of the handles and tried to lift the container. Nothing happened. The combination of its weight, and suction from the earth beneath, proved too much for his tired muscles.

Amron returned to the ruins of the farm where he found a length of rope. Once back in the enclosure, he placed a halter on one of the workhorses. He led it towards the hole. He looped the rope through the metal rings before tying the ends to the strap. Amron coiled the surplus, which he used to slap the side of the horse. For a few moments, the animal pulled hard without effect. With a lurch, it moved forward. There was a loud squelching sound as the box lifted free. Straining, the horse dragged it onto the pasture. Amron brought the animal to a halt.

The chest was on its side. With difficulty, Amron righted it. The container was heavy. Intrigued, he wondered what it might contain. He scraped away as much of the dirt from it as he could, to discover a large keyhole at one side. He hoped his father had the key. Another one of his secrets, Amron supposed. The box tore into the uneven grassy surface as he led the horse across the pasture. They soon reached the shelter. Once the horse was back in the enclosure, Amron turned his attention to the chest.

With a damp cloth, he cleaned the wood. He could find no markings on it. Its timbers, though stained, showed little sign of decay. Several sturdy metal bands around its sides gave it added strength.

"Is there a key for this box?" Amron demanded as he entered the shelter. "Otherwise I'll have to break it open."

"Of course there's a key," Tamin replied. "It's under the paved slab, at the front of the farmhouse where the doorway used to be."

"Oh! No! No more digging, please." The thought of having to excavate another patch of ground was too much for Amron.

"Not this time." Tamin laughed at his son's woeful expression. "The key's hidden under the stone. There's no spadework involved."

"Good!" was Amron's heartfelt response.

Amron levered the slab to one side with a charred piece of timber. Near the centre of the exposed ground was a roll of waxed cloth. With care, Amron unwrapped the package, to reveal a large black key. He had to remove the detritus from inside the keyhole before he could insert the key. A quarter-turn later, the teeth stuck. The years spent underground had caused the mechanism to stiffen. Amron was wary of breaking the shaft. At Tamin's urging, he applied more pressure. A creaking noise came from within the chest, followed by the sound of levers moving with the key.

"Keep going," Tamin advised from inside the shelter. "It opens after the third turn."

At each rotation Amron could hear sounds of movement from more levers. Only after the final complete revolution did the lid lift a little. With his fingers squeezed into the gap, Amron pulled hard. The rusted metal hinges screeched as he forced the top open. He was in at last. A layer of cloth covered the contents. Amron dragged it away.

Lying at the top of the chest, wrapped in waxed tubes, were numerous rolls of parchment. He pulled out several and studied the writing. The documents concerned the Kingdom of Xicalima. Although most of the words were familiar to Amron, the style of writing was not. When he was small, his mother had insisted he learned to read and write. Apart from his parents and the village scribe, no-one else in the area had mastered the skill. Tamin, whose own father had taught him, had done most of the schooling.

"Leave those for now," Tamin said. "They prove your legitimacy as heir to the throne. If anything happens to me, take them to Hafter in the mountains. He knows what to do with them."

Amron returned the scrolls to their tubes before he passed them to Tamin. The object that followed had a black cloth wrapped around it. It was long and lay diagonally across the chest. As soon as Amron picked-up the article, he knew it was a weapon. With care, he unravelled the material to reveal a sword. Inside its scabbard, it looked insignificant. The handle, although crafted with skill, had neither jewels nor semi-precious stones to decorate it. This weapon was no ceremonial object — it was a warrior's tool, designed for killing. Amron drew the double-edged sword out from its cover. Reflected from the patterned surface of the blade, the sun's rays blinded him.

"Ouch!" he cried as he caught one edge. The touch had drawn blood.

"Be careful!" came Tamin's belated warning. "The sword's eastern-made. It'll cut through stone. I know of only one other of its type. That was your mother's — the one I used during the attack. Talon took it. Be wary if you confront him. Apart from the blade being a hand's width shorter, the weapon differs little from this one. You should have no difficulty in recognising it."

Despite the weapon's length and strength, it was lighter than Amron had expected. He tried a few strokes with it. With the sword in his hand, many of the exercises taught to him by his father felt complete. Amron made as if to strap the scabbard to his belt. Tamin, who had been watching, stopped him.

"Until you've received schooling in the weapon's use," he said, "it would be better if you stay unarmed. We've a long way to go. Most people we meet will be friendly; they'll regard us as fellow peasants. If you wear a sword, they'll treat you with suspicion; someone might challenge you. Except in times of trouble, peasants who bear weapons of war have a reputation for being troublemakers, or bandits. Men of importance claim ownership of swords of this quality. People might believe it stolen. If pushed to fight, you may be lucky, only to find victory is the start of your troubles. Those you defeat will have family and friends. They'll want revenge and, in our circumstances, we can't outrun anyone.

"When we're alone, I'll school you in the weapon's use. Hafter, if still able, will teach you more. Although he is better known as a sage now, in his younger days he was a fine swordsman, the greatest teacher in Xicalima. The main reason I survived my early life was because of the skills he taught me."

Amron held the sword a moment longer, before, against his wishes, he returned it to its scabbard. He rested it against the shelter. Back at the chest, he looked to see what other treasures it might contain. A chain-mail vest, which had belonged to his father, fitted Amron well. The vest would protect its wearer from a slashing blade, so Tamin said, but was less secure against a direct thrust. Amron placed it beside the sword. To wear the garment was something else to set people talking.

The next layer was another one of documents. Amron passed them to his father. Many were twice the length of the sets removed earlier. These were maps. Other, smaller ones, were deeds they could study later. Amron pulled away another piece of cloth, covering the contents of the bottom third of the chest. Here, a wooden panel formed a false bottom, fixed in place by wooden wedges jammed into a groove, cut around the inner sides of the chest. Amron twisted the blocks to release the panel. He lifted it clear.

His mouth dropped open. He was speechless. The panel fell from his hands. Stunned, he stared for several moments at what he had uncovered. The reason for the container's weight was now clear. Layers of gold coins filled the base of the compartment. His mouth opened. Still no words came out.

"Are they real?" he asked, when his powers of speech returned.

"Of course they're real. What else would they be?"

"There's a fortune here. Why did you hide it? There's so much you could have done with the money to make life more comfortable for you and Mother," Amron accused.

"It was your mother's fortune, not mine. She insisted we save it for a time of need. Now it forms a part of your inheritance. If you're to be king, you'll have great use for it. There are other, larger hoards hidden in distant places. Loyal followers removed these from Xicalima before Betlic could seize them."

"How do you know all this? I thought you isolated yourselves from everything and everyone, to keep the three of us safe?"

"It's true we hoped to live out our lives here in peace, and that the rebels might allow you to do the same. A tiny and select group of trustworthy people knew we had survived, and where we had settled. They maintained contact with us. Over the years, most of the travellers who stayed here were your mother's subjects. Many of these were people of rank and title.

"They brought news of Xicalima. At first, they expected your mother to join them. She was adamant she wanted nothing to do with the rebel cause. She knew Betlic was too strong. Other countries, wary of antagonising him, offered the rebels little else except sympathy. For them to go against the tyrant alone would have been suicide.

"Over the years, we came to believe Betlic had forgotten about us. Your mother hoped the rebels would do likewise. After your birth, she attempted to renounce her claim to the throne, so the affairs of Xicalima would concern us no more. Those leaders in exile who knew about her made it clear that, if she abdicated, you would become king in her place. They said, until you were of age, you couldn't make any decisions about your future. Your mother was furious. She told them she was going nowhere, and neither were you. They must declare you both dead and choose someone new to lead them.

"Since that time, whenever visitors came to stay, they avoided the subject. Your mother thought she'd won. She was content. If I'd voiced my many reservations, these would have caused her to worry again. I knew the rebels were biding their time. When I was young, I studied Xicaliman law. The rules of succession are clear. Unless you abdicate, the nobles cannot choose a new king while you live.

"Among the rebels no-one, other than Hafter, now survives with knowledge of your existence. Somehow, he has persuaded the leaders against the selection of a new king. He knows your destiny. It is yours by birth, not by choice. There's no other person who can fulfil it.

"Despite everything, I chose to believe you would remain unaffected. Without the aid of the talisman, Betlic was reluctant to incur the risks involved in expanding his territory. Of more importance for your well-being, while he remains too powerful for the rebels to overthrow, your presence with them is not essential. Only if they march against Betlic will they have need of you. I had hoped that Hafter would take your secret to the grave with him. But, knowing him, I'm sure he's made provision to pass the knowledge on to others.

"Now, the future is less certain. Betlic's men have the mantle and, once Talon delivers it to Betlic, he will seek to create his empire. Support for a leader to go against him will become widespread. Despite your mother's wish that you follow a different path, you are the one to whom they will look. You are the rightful King of Xicalima, the leader, so the old scrolls say, who will unite the nations against the evils of the talisman. To you will appear the Mastig."

"How can you say this?" Amron said. "I'm a farmer's son. I can grow crops, till the soil and work around a farm. Of leadership and war, I know nothing. You told me no-one knew anything about the Mastig, and the story was a fable. What makes you believe it exists now and will appear to me? You said your father dismissed the story as unreliable."

"Yes he did. That's true. But, over recent years, Hafter has discovered more, enough to convince him of the tale's veracity. To avoid further upset with your mother, messengers came to me with news of any developments. To you, Amron, the natural and rightful heir to Xicalima, will appear the Mastig. The heir will bring order out of chaos. He, and only he, can defeat the power of the talisman. The writings, so I understand, are in an ancient tongue and difficult to decipher. What Hafter has translated, so far, indicates it could be the heir alone who will succeed."

"What else do the writings foretell?" Amron was anxious to know. "How can the Mastig, whatever it is, help me? What does it do?"

"I don't know, I've no answers. I'm hoping, when we meet with Hafter, we may learn more."

Amron fell silent. He had much to consider — none of which was to his liking. At first, this onerous responsibility was not something he wanted. Yet, another part of him seemed eager to go in this new direction that fate was about to lead him. The more he thought about it, the more confused he became. Beset by conflicting ideas, it would be a long time before he came to understand and embrace his destiny.

Chapter Seven

Tamin and Amron remained at the farm a few days longer. The old man's fragile health left Amron with no other course of action. Once they set off, the first week's travel, as feared, proved a painful experience for the patient. Amron had driven the wagon with as much care as was possible — the rutted tracks they travelled proved less accommodating. The hard-baked ground, riddled with potholes, caused the wagon to sway violently. The willow bark helped to dull Tamin's pain but, over this early period, the distance covered was short. By day's end, the constant movement left him exhausted. By the second week, much to Amron's surprise and relief, his father's health showed an improvement.

They journeyed for several weeks as Tamin recovered from his ordeal. Once he could travel, seated with his legs raised at the front of the wagon, his spirits lifted. In time, using a pair of crutches that his son fashioned for him, he was able to hobble round their nightly campsites. Twice, they stayed at isolated farmhouses, where Amron bartered his farming skills for items they needed.

At first, their most pressing need was fresh clothing. Both men's outfits were in tatters. Tamin's attackers had shredded his clothing, while Amron's tunic and breeches had suffered much after the raid on the village. It was fortunate, in the wreckage of the outbuildings, he found a set of old garments for Tamin. Although threadbare, they were wearable.

A week into their journey, on arrival at the first settlement they came to, the farmer who greeted them was wary of this newcomer dressed in rags. The man stood back, pitchfork in hand. From his bed, Tamin called out to him. The traveller's story about an attack by bandits soon gained the farmer's sympathy. Amron agreed to accept, as payment for two days' labour in the fields, a set of clean, little-worn garments for him and Tamin. The farmer gave them a few old pots and a sack of fresh food.

On an evening, when alone and far from habitation, Tamin coached Amron in the use of the sword. With ease, he learned the different moves and strokes. Whenever it was possible, Tamin took the weapon and demonstrated the technique. Although there was great worth in this work, it was no substitute for intensive sparring against an opponent. If Amron was to survive, he needed tutoring by skilled swordsmen. By itself, knowledge of tactics was a poor substitute for experience.

They were making good time. To Amron, his life on the farm belonged to a different world. Since leaving, they had travelled over a hundred leagues. The hills around their old home had given way to grass-covered plains interspersed with areas of high moorland. Heardwine kept them company. The dog had boundless energy. During the day, it ranged far and wide. Amron came to rely on the animal. Whenever it perceived a threat, it would race back to the wagon, barking loudly. It knew by instinct what posed a risk to the safety of the travellers. When people were nearby, Amron soon learned to interpret the actions of the dog. They avoided those who caused great agitation in the animal.

Early one afternoon the travellers pulled up to rest the horses. It was close to two months since they had left their home. The Mogallean Mountains were within sight. Tamin took advantage of the halt to stretch his strengthening limbs. In the distance, Heardwine was running down the trail, its wagging tail a sign that friendly company was approaching. Therefore, moments later, the large party of hostile horsemen that charged towards the wagon, took the pair by surprise.

With swords drawn, the riders leapt from their horses. Amron tried to speak. A bellowed shout of 'silence' from one of the group stopped his protest. The party's leader, although still a young man, was several years older than Amron. The man's hair was dark-brown. Years of exposure to the sun had weathered a face that was more rugged than handsome. His nose, broken at some time in the past, was crooked; his jaw was strong and covered with stubble. Crows' feet had developed around his green-flecked, blue eyes. His mouth, instead of its more usual smile, was tight-lipped. Tall and well-muscled, he looked tough and agile. Both the leader and his men wore leather breeches and grey tunics. A red flash down the side of his tunic, as opposed to the green on his subordinates' tunics, showed his rank. Amron could hear the sound of troops rifling through the wagon behind him.

A terrible, agonised scream pierced the air. Turning round, Amron saw his father on the ground. He clutched at his right leg, his face contorted in agony. One of the new arrivals leant over him. The soldier's sword rested close to the leg Tamin clasped. Amron, certain his father's fall resulted from a blow, was sure the soldier intended further injury.

A short step behind Amron, his sword lay concealed beneath one of the wagon's side panels. While all attention was on Tamin, Amron stepped backwards and pulled clear the weapon. He raised it and was at his father's side within seconds. Before Amron could strike down Tamin's assailant, the man in charge pushed his way between the pair.

Amron diverted his anger towards the leader. He lashed out at him instead. The man parried the stroke but the power of the blow sent his weapon flying. Amron showed no mercy. He persisted with his attack on his now unarmed opponent, who twisted and turned to avoid the slashing blade. A soldier threw a sword to his leader, who, in the same movement, caught it and dodged another blow. Amron's opponent was quick to realise that, although his young adversary was agile and gifted, he lacked any real experience. Energy and raw anger were a dangerous combination that the leader had the skills to overcome.

The troops backed away, leaving room for the combatants to manoeuvre. As Amron's lack of skill became more telling, he found himself hard-pressed. His opponent kept shouting at him to stop. Amron's rage was too great for him to listen. His adrenaline was flowing. He wanted to destroy. The man nearest to Tamin started a whisper. It spread. The watchers, who until then had been cheering on their leader, fell silent.

Amron's opponent caught his heel on a loose stone. The man fell backwards. His grip on his sword loosened as he hit the ground with force. Amron moved in, the point of his blade wavering close to the fallen man's exposed throat. To kill anything, other than vermin or for the table, was an experience new to Amron. Against a defenceless adversary, he hesitated. The man returned his stare. His eyes showed resignation, not fear. Tamin's voice broke through the rage that clouded his son's mind.

"Stop, Amron! Let him go. I slipped and landed on my knee. This man came to help me. These are Hafter's men."

Amron's muscles relaxed. A faint sigh escaped from his opponent. The two men looked at each other. Both knew that luck alone had brought Amron victory. In a conciliatory move, the victor transferred his sword to his left hand. His opponent's smile was rueful as Amron stooped down to help him to his feet. The smile froze. A stunned look replaced it. The leader had caught sight of his men. All were on one knee, their heads bent in homage towards Amron.

Hafter's agents, when they learned of the massacre at Amron's village, had sent word by carrier pigeon to the sage. The rebel Xicaliman High Council, once over the shock that their queen and her heir still existed, agreed with the sage to limit disclosure of such information. They needed confirmation of the attack and reports of any survivors. In confidence, patrol leaders who operated west of the mountains received the startling news about the royal family. This knowledge came as much a surprise to these men as it had their leaders. As did most Xicalimans, they believed Betlic had murdered the entire royal family, years ago. Hafter maintained the hope that one, or more, might have escaped this latest assault. If so, he believed they would try to seek sanctuary with him and the rebels in the Mogallean Mountains. There was nowhere else for them to go.

The leader of the group who surrounded Amron, had been sceptical when he heard the story. Now, he wished he had given it more credence. A sense of unease filled his mind. Of all the people to become embroiled with in a fight — it should never have been his future king. Once he had seen the travellers close to, he had dismissed any idea they might be Betlic's men in disguise; one was far too elderly. The thought they could be royalty, masquerading as peasants, had not occurred to him.

Before he had the chance to talk to the pair, to greet them in a friendlier manner, the old man had stumbled and fallen. Unlike Amron, the leader had seen the incident. He was aware the younger one acted in defence of his companion. Although the rebel soldier had wanted nothing more than to disarm his adversary, he had enough experience to know a misjudged blow could have killed his king. The man shuddered.

He, too, dropped to his knee, his head bowed. It was Amron's turn to look stunned. Tamin must have alerted the troops to his son's true identity. Embarrassed, Amron realised he had made a fool of himself. His hasty conclusion could have ended someone's life, his own included. He blushed in shame. The rebel band, however, placed a different interpretation on the episode. Here, against overwhelming odds, a mere novice with a sword had leapt to the defence of a companion. His actions showed great courage. Despite Amron's fears, the men had formed a favourable impression of him.

"Please, stand," Amron said, after a few moments hesitation, although it was at a pitch higher than intended.

The men obeyed. Most backed away. Two remained to tend the king's travelling companion — someone they believed to be an old retainer. One of them, with knowledge of wounds, examined Tamin's legs. Amron, assured his father was in good hands, went in search of the group's leader. The man, a worried expression on his face, was standing apart from his men. The members of his patrol shuffled in apprehension. They were unsure what action the king might take against his opponent, or those who followed him. A charge of treason was a possibility.

"Come here, please," Amron beckoned.

"Your Majesty," the man began as he approached.

"Call me Amron."

"Yes, King Amron," he said.

This response was not the one Amron wanted to hear. He found the title unsettling. For the moment, he let it stand. It was another sign his life was changing forever.

"Your Highness," the man said, as he explained his group's initial intrusion, "although rare, Betlic's raiders sometimes operate this far from Xicalima. It wouldn't have been the first time they'd hidden in wagons. I've lost men in the past to such ploys, now I take precautions. Had we known it was you, we would not have approached as we did. Please, accept my apologies for the confusion that resulted from my conduct. I'm the only one to blame. My men share no responsibility, they were under my orders."

"It's already forgotten," Amron said.

He was aware the fault lay with him and not the man in front. Without reservation, Amron accepted the apology. The man's attitude impressed. He had not tried to shirk any possible consequences of his actions. In fact, he had taken full accountability and absolved his men from blame. How different this man was from his former friend, Talon.

"What's your name?" Amron asked

"Orvyn," the rebel leader said.

"Orvyn, perhaps it's I who should thank you. Apart from a few bruises, you left me unscathed. I didn't understand why you held back. Now, I realise it was because you were trying to disarm me. As you can see, I have little experience with the sword, and none of combat — whereas you're a skilled swordsman. I would like you to work with me, to help improve my technique and, if possible, help with other matters too?"

"It would be an honour, your Majesty," Orvyn said, startled at the idea, "but I'm only a captain. Once you cross the mountains, you'll have an army of advisors and generals to take care of you. The High Council will be most insistent any aides to you are at their personal recommendation."

"I'm sure I'll have advisors aplenty, but, besides those, I want someone I can trust," Amron insisted. "Only in recent days have I learned of my rank. I've little understanding of what being king means, nor what my duties might be. How I'll cope with them I can't comprehend. My father," he indicated Tamin, "has explained a little about the intrigues of those who'll surround me. I need someone without an ulterior motive, someone to be my eyes and ears. Will you to be loyal to me alone? Would you swear an oath to this?"

These requests took Orvyn by surprise. At best, he anticipated a flogging or imprisonment — at worst execution. Amron's mention of the old man being his father explained the ferocity of his defence of him.

"Of course, your Majesty," he stuttered. "But, as a captain, I am excluded from the inner circles of our leaders. They'll be wary I shall gain too much influence. I shall find myself redeployed, far away."

"I am the king. That should make a difference. It would be foolish of me to ignore their advice on state affairs, but, I don't intend to become their puppet. They'll have no say in this matter. I doubt you'll be popular. Some will plot and scheme against you. Others will flatter or try to bribe you. They may offer you vast riches in an attempt to subvert your will. Are you strong enough to stand against such temptation? When we reclaim Xicalima, such loyalty will not be without its rewards."

How much of this was possible, or probable, Amron was unsure. Where these thoughts sprang from was a mystery. To him, they sounded as if they were words a king might speak.

"It's an honour to serve you your Majesty. I'll not betray your faith in me."

Orvyn dropped to one knee and bowed his head once more. At once, Amron commanded him to rise. They shook hands. This was an arrangement that appeared to offer much to both parties. Had either the gift to see into the future, the outcome of this meeting might have been much different.

Their conversation was inaudible to the others. When Orvyn went to his knee, his men thought it was the end for him. He had treated them with respect and, as a result, they regarded him well. Unlike some troop commanders, who were less secure in themselves, he led by example from the front, without the necessity to drive his men with threats, sneers nor insults. Several were ready to intercede in defence of Orvyn when, to their relief, they saw their captain stand and the pair shake hands. Heardwine, who had ignored the commotion, came to sit beside Amron. He patted the dog's head.

At the king's command, Orvyn made immediate preparations to escort the royal travellers into the mountains. It would take them a few days to reach the lower reaches. From there, a month or more would pass before the party came within sight of their destination.

Chapter Eight

Ryce was older and, he hoped, wiser, certainly in the ways of bringing up a daughter. Without hesitation, Karilyn would have agreed with the first, perhaps less so the second. A few weeks short of her fourteenth birthday, she was at an age where she thought she knew everything. Despite periods of moodiness, which were incomprehensible to her father, she was loyal and, in matters related to her calling, hardworking. No longer a child, but not yet a woman grown, she kept her father mentally alert. Notwithstanding his fears after losing his wife, Ryce had raised his children with great success.

Once Peter, his son, reached sixteen, he left home. At that time, he had no interest in the running of his father's estates. The boy craved excitement. Before he settled down to country life, he wanted to explore the world and see its sights. From the occasional letter that reached Ryce, he knew his son had become a soldier. As to where he plied his trade, he never revealed. In his younger days, Ryce, too, had fought in various wars. Only when he met his future wife did his priorities change. Within the year, they had married and come to live on the family estate.

Life was hard for the local population. For women, the largest killer was childbirth. The male death-rate was even higher, and often at a young age. Men and women worked long hours, many in the fields, in all weathers and seasons. Accidents, illness and wars took their toll. To others, it seemed strange that Ryce stayed single; there were many suitable widows who lived in the area. Most would welcome, and sought, his attention. But, to Ryce, they were unsuitable. Most had families — children, brothers, sisters and parents who would pry and tittle-tattle. His, and Karilyn's, duty to the Scraufin must remain a secret.

Karilyn had received excellent schooling. It was unusual for country boys to have the chance to learn how to read and write, for a girl this was even more so. Until her death, the year before, Karilyn's former nurse, an elderly aunt of Ryce's late wife, had helped in this work. She was the one person in whom he could confide. With her close attachment to Karilyn, it would have been impossible to hide the special training and extra tutoring from the nurse. The woman's dedication had been total. Without her assistance, in the early years, Ryce had to admit he would have struggled to cope.

Karilyn knew by heart the history of her future charge, and her role if called upon to perform her duty. She spent days, hidden away with her father in a cavern in the hills nearby. Here, she learned how to defend herself, by hand or with a weapon. Ryce honed her natural abilities until she was as near perfect as was possible. She soon mastered a strange code, passed down through her family for generations. The one thing she lacked was confidence in her own ability. A throwback, Ryce believed, to when her brother lived at home.

Peter's jealously over the perceived extra attention his sister received had some basis. Although Ryce had given as much time as he could to his son, Karilyn's extra needs were hard to ignore. When Peter uncovered details of Ryce's secret, he could not understand why, instead of him, Karilyn was the chosen one. Afterwards, he took out his resentment on her. His constant ridicule, and frequent blows, had undermined her self-belief. In time, Ryce knew she would overcome her fears. Until then he must work to advance her skills.

☙ ❧

Although she would not admit to it, Karilyn was excited. She was to leave soon on a trip with her father. For the first time, and for several months, she would be absent from her home territory — with a new horse to ride. Ryce had provided her with one of real worth, one much finer than the lumbering animals she rode around the farm. Large and strong, with great stamina, it would trot for miles and, if necessary, have the speed to carry her clear of danger.

Ryce's neighbours doubted his sanity. The animal was far too powerful for an adult woman to ride. To expect a girl of Karilyn's years to be able to control it was madness. Why was he taking her away? Instead, he should be introducing her to suitable young men. Girls of her age, past their first cycle of womanhood, ought to have marriage on their minds. Did Ryce want his daughter to turn into an old maid? Never anything but courteous, he listened to their well-intentioned words of advice, nodded vaguely then ignored them. Ryce had raised Karilyn to have a mind of her own. Who, when or if she married would be her choice, not his.

Spring had been warm. Ryce's lands were in good condition, his workers well-trained. Without his presence, his overseers were competent to run the estate, for several months if necessary. Satisfied everything was in order, two weeks before the summer solstice, Ryce and Karilyn started on their expedition. With a packhorse laden with supplies, and the addition of any game they caught on the way, they hoped to keep their interaction with people to a minimum. Once clear of their home region, Karilyn took to wearing her sword at all times. Two lone riders burdened with supplies would be a valuable, and tempting, target to outlaws.

For five months they travelled. One of the first places they visited was the one that Karilyn would need to find, should the call come for her to fulfil her duties. They spent many weeks approaching it from various directions, so she could find it from any starting point. She learned how to read a map, and to live off the land. A close bond developed between Father and Daughter. Her training regime Ryce maintained all the while. Karilyn's skills were becoming formidable.

She became used to the nomadic life. On their return home, it took a while for her to adjust to the normality of staying in one place, day after day. Her daily routine of study and practice resumed. The journey had served its purpose. Karilyn better understood her role. To learn where to go was one thing. For her to have intimate knowledge of its location was of much greater value. To have experienced a part of what her duty entailed was beyond price. Being confident of performing it was another matter. Her main anxiety was that, if called upon, she would prove unworthy of the responsibility.

Chapter Nine

Marazin gazed around in horror at the sights that filled his vision. What had the unfortunate people of this isolated village done to deserve such dreadful retribution? He scratched his head in bewilderment. A group of foreign merchants, passing through, had discovered the massacre. For more than two weeks, they rode hard to bring the news to the capital. The authorities treated their story with disbelief; attacks such as the traders described did not happen in their country. So exaggerated was the report believed to be, those who first heard it diluted it so much that, by the time it reached senior figures, it appeared to be nothing more than a local disturbance.

The sovereign, when told the outrageous story, unedited, by one of his servants, was curious to learn why the two accounts differed. He commanded the merchants be brought before him. Their complete sincerity convinced the monarch something was seriously wrong, although he still believed the tale embellished. Under the command of Marazin, a captain in the royal guard, the king dispatched a small troop of soldiers to investigate.

From the bare details relayed to him, Marazin expected to find the bloody aftermath of a neighbourhood dispute. His instructions were to restore order, then bring back the main culprits to stand trial. On arrival, it was obvious to Marazin that his information had been vastly understated — this was much more than a local disagreement. As he looked around, he felt overwhelmed by the size of the task that he and his men faced.

He set his band of men to bury any bodies they could find. Most of his party were new recruits. They had never seen action. Of those who had, few had witnessed such charred and disfigured remains as these. The weather had been hot, the wildlife voracious. The dreadful sights they came across unsettled both their minds and stomachs.

Marazin remounted. He called one of his more experienced followers to accompany him. The man, Sherwyn, needed no urging. In haste, he resaddled his horse and rode over to his leader. The pair had served in the same unit for many years.

"I think we need to widen the search," Marazin said. "I doubt if anyone nearby is alive, but, if we're lucky, we might find something to help us identify the raiders."

"Who could have done such a thing?" Sherwyn asked, as he looked back towards the ruins, shock still evident on his face.

"I can't say for certain," Marazin replied. "In this country, I don't think I've ever heard of an incident as serious as this. It reminds me of Xicalima. My parents escaped the land when Betlic seized power. They left behind my grandparents, several uncles, aunts and numerous cousins. I was there a few years ago, hoping to discover what happened to them."

"Did you find anyone?"

"No. The few people who lived in the area were newcomers, much too frightened to talk. I did make contact with an old man who, for the price of a loaf of bread, spoke to me. He told me my relatives joined a major rebellion against Betlic's rule, but their fate was unknown. In reprisal, the tyrant destroyed every village within five leagues, then massacred those unfortunate enough to have remained.

"My visit had attracted the attention of Betlic's agents. Later that day, the old man risked his life to warn that they were searching for me. I left straight away, evaded my pursuers and escaped to safety."

"So, you believe this is Betlic's work?" Sherwyn sounded surprised.

"It's possible," Marazin said, "although Xicalima is a long way from here. Yet why would Betlic send his men (and there must have been a large number) all this distance to wipe-out one village? It makes no sense. How could such a large group of soldiers travel unnoticed through our lands? There've been no reports of such a party being seen, neither entering nor leaving the country."

"Are there any known feuds or bands of outlaws in this district?"

"No, nothing recorded; the village is many leagues away from its nearest neighbour. Despite how improbable it might seem, I have an uncomfortable feeling Betlic is behind this atrocity. There's something about the ruthlessness of it. If so, to convince the king, we must gather as much evidence as possible. He, and the whole country, will be in grave peril if Betlic is considering expanding his empire this far from home."

Sherwyn saw his captain's unease. It was rare to see him with an expression so grim. It left the younger soldier much unsettled. This mood intensified as he realised his leader was riding across the landscape with ever more caution. Did Marazin suspect the raiders were still in the area? Sherwyn hoped otherwise.

Marazin's eyes never stopped moving as he looked for signs of danger. He kept a hand close to the hilt of his sword, at times easing the blade in its scabbard, ensuring it moved freely. It was an old sword, a family heirloom. As a weapon, it appeared unremarkable. It had seen use in many conflicts. Because of the quality of its blade, it would have commanded a high price if offered for sale. Marazin, despite several good offers to buy it from him, declined to sell. It was his to care for and use until it was time to pass-on to a new generation.

Unlike his men, Marazin was a veteran of several campaigns. Most of which for countries other than the one he now served. A year or two short of thirty, his late teens and early twenties had seen him travel extensively. His skills he had honed on the battlefield. He stopped his horse, to survey the land ahead, before riding into view on top of any high ground. The greater the area they covered, the more relaxed he became. Nowhere were there any fresh tracks. The ground appeared undisturbed since the time of the raid.

"Captain, down here!" Sherwyn called out as he examined a burnt-out farmhouse.

Marazin had been keeping watch from a slope nearby. After a final look, he rode down to join his companion. Sherwyn had dismounted. He was studying the ground. There was evidence someone had been there after the attack. The ruins showed signs of disturbance, both among the ashes and in the remains of the outbuildings. Whether he, she or they had been perpetrators, survivors or later arrivals was hard to determine. Marazin meandered round the ruins and into the nearby fields. The signs of movement, and the abandoned bales of hay, revealed that a temporary shelter might have been set up around a wagon in the farmyard. If the bales had been in place before the raid, they would have burned with the farmhouse.

The charred remains of a campfire were visible, along with tracks made on ground that once had been muddy. These cut deep into the ash-strewn soil. A hard crust had developed afterwards, to preserve the footprints in and around the farmyard. The indentations suggested one person. In among were the paw prints of a huge dog.

Marazin returned to where the shelter had been. Inside were the remains of two beds, made from layers of straw. On one of them, dark stains, he believed to be blood, could be seen. Nearby, in a fenced-off area, was a recent grave. Did it contain the body of the person whose blood was on the straw, or the remains of another person? Old prints covered the ground, some of which matched those of the recent walker. Whatever the answer might be, since the rain, it was impossible to find new tracks belonging to any other. If the injured one still lived, he or she had not walked away. A further mystery lay in the nearby paddock. Someone had dug a huge hole, at the base of a dead tree, from which they had dragged a large object. The tracks surrounding the opening were the same as the ones at the shelter.

The pair stayed for a while longer. They could find little more to help them explain what had happened. The tracks of a laden wagon led away from the farm. Two large workhorses had pulled the cart and, from the superimposed lighter hoof prints, tied to the rear was a saddle horse. The pawprints of the dog were visible among the others. Marazin and his companion followed the trail for some distance. It maintained an easterly course.

The sun was low. The air cool. They turned their horses and rode back, past the burnt-out farmhouse and on towards the village. Marazin knew there was no easy way to break the news to his men, that their work in the village was only the start. In the surrounding district, many more bodies needed burial.

The following morning, Marazin set off, alone, to return to the capital, with news of his discoveries. He left Sherwyn to organise the men in their grisly task. After the third day's ride, Marazin entered more densely populated lowlands. Now, he was able to change horses at regular intervals, it enabled him to ride for most of the days and nights. He stopped only when too exhausted to travel further.

☙ ❧

A week after his departure, tired and dishevelled, Marazin arrived at the Vretlianan capital. He presented himself at the castle where, within the hour, a servant ushered him into a large antechamber, adjacent to the throne room. The dark wood-panelling on the lower walls was part-covered with fine tapestries. Above, shields and crossed swords adorned the white-plastered walls. Several stuffed animal heads, trophies from the king's hunting trips, gazed down upon the assembly. Many candles lit the windowless room, the air heavy with their smoke.

A dozen oak chairs, occupied by the king's chief advisors, were arranged in a semi-circle, spread out from the large central seat upon which King Grogant was sitting. These were people who, for now, had the trust of the monarch. Only one, the head of tax collection, was female. The rest were military or political allies. Because of his service in the king's guard, Marazin knew most of them by sight. His position, as a captain, was of too little importance for him to socialise with them. The king, impatient to hear Marazin's news, indicated that the visitor should start his tale without delay.

Marazin stood with his shoulders back. He looked straight ahead while he gave a detailed description of the carnage he and his men had discovered. He broke off to clarify details whenever asked. At the end of his narrative, he moved back a step, then bowed his head to the king. For a while, nobody spoke, nor moved. Shocked and saddened by the gory facts of the massacre, it was Marazin's suspicion of Betlic's involvement that had shaken them the most. Protocol dictated the king speak first. The silence persisted for some time before he cleared his throat.

"On what do you base this wild idea about Betlic? We know he's a monster, an evil man, yet he has never made a threat against my kingdom. There are many lands between us. They remain free from his tyranny. Why should we fear him now? He appears content to rule within his own borders."

"Your Majesty," Marazin answered. "My parents fled Xicalima before I was born. They told me much about the period when Betlic overthrew their king. In search of relatives, I have ventured inside Xicalima and seen the results of Betlic's rule. The village I left a few days ago could have been any one of many I saw while inside his domain. There was nothing random about these deeds. The attack was well planned and co-ordinated. Ruthless as any bandit raid, it was, but this assault was an exercise in thoroughness and precision. It showed great discipline and military training. I know of no other than Betlic, who would dare to send an expedition so far from home."

Had Marazin stopped there, he could have left with his reputation intact. It was foolish, he knew, but he felt the urge to add more. "Your

Highness," he said, "my father spoke of a mystical object, the Talisman of Grebarta. Betlic acquired this when he deposed the old king. The talisman was the reason behind Betlic's seizure of power. Another object, one that controls the talisman, disappeared from the old king's castle before Betlic could find it. Ever since, he has searched for the item and those who took it away. Should he succeed in his quest, he will become invincible. For his men to have come this far adds credence to my suspicion that someone brought the object to Vretliana, and concealed it in the village. Or so Betlic might believe."

"Ridiculous," one advisor sneered in distain. "This is a fairy tale, mere speculation at best."

"I agree," interrupted another. "If the man believes such wild stories, what credibility can be placed on the rest of his information?"

"The man's a fool," the tax collector said, waving her finger at Marazin, determined to join in with the condemnation. "He should be dismissed from his majesty's guard without delay."

Shouts of agreement followed. The general, who represented the sovereign's armies, leapt to his feet, his face flushed with anger. How dare one of his subordinates embarrass him like this in front of the king?

"Outside, and wait for me there," he roared at Marazin, before muttering, "I'll speak with you later."

Marazin's face reddened at the accusations. He controlled his tongue with difficulty. Stiffly, he bowed towards the king, turned and marched from the room. 'Simpletons', he muttered under his breath. Doubtless, their shortsighted opinions would persuade the king there was nothing to fear.

The huge oak doors slammed shut behind him. Judging by the reaction to his story, Marazin feared reduction to the ranks might be the best result for which he could hope. He paced the stone-flagged floor, his footsteps echoing throughout the chamber. Something Marazin had failed to notice was the king. After his initial comments, he had excluded himself from the pillorying. Instead, he had been listening to one of his advisors who, standing beside him, had been whispering with great urgency into his ear.

Although it was only a short time before the doors re-opened, to Marazin it seemed an age. The king's advisors walked out. Some ignored him, while others sneered. Several laughed aloud when the general strutted towards his red-faced captain.

"His majesty will deal with you himself. I recommended he banishes you for life. If I ever have the misfortune to see you again, it will be too soon," he said in disgust before he stomped away.

Marazin, his face hot with anger, found himself alone. Behind him, someone cleared their throat. Startled, Marazin turned to see a white-haired figure, dressed in a long flowing dark-brown robe. This was the person who had whispered to King Grogant. The man beckoned to him from the doorway. Until that morning, he was someone with whom Marazin had never spoken. The captain swallowed. He took a deep breath. It was time to learn his fate.

"Ignore them," the elderly man said, as Marazin joined him. "The king's not blind to their vain posturing and jostling for position. Follow me; his majesty wishes to speak with you in private, away from those sycophants."

Somewhat less apprehensive now, Marazin followed his guide. They walked through the now empty antechamber, to a doorway at the rear of the room. This led into a narrow corridor. They turned right. Within moments, the pair arrived at an ornately carved door. His guide rapped once on the wooden panels. He gave the door a gentle push. It creaked open. Marazin stepped into a comfortably furnished chamber. He was inside King Grogant's private quarters. The door closed behind Marazin. The king's advisor remained outside in the corridor.

Chapter Ten

The day was cold. Deep within the castle, the temperature was several degrees higher than outside. Inside the confines of the king's private chamber, at the centre of a massive hearth, logs crackled and flames danced. In a continuous stream, the chimney drew smoke and sparks away to the battlements above. Nearby, a large comfortable chair stood, its back turned towards Marazin. An arm dangled at one side, while two feet rested on a small, padded oaken stool.

"Come, sit," the king commanded.

Marazin selected a straight-backed chair, standing against the wall beside him. He placed it to the king's right and at some distance from him. Marazin bowed low before sitting.

"Move closer," the king indicated a point, halfway between them. "I've no intention of savaging you, as did those fools."

Marazin repositioned his chair. While he made himself comfortable again, King Grogant took the time to study his guest. He was tall, a fraction short of six feet in height, broad of shoulder and, under his dusty tunic, his body appeared muscular. His hair was dark and long, circled by a leather band around his head. A tinge of worry marred an otherwise pleasant countenance. Marazin had a strong jaw line, covered with several days' growth of stubble. His deep blue eyes were dark rimmed from lack of sleep. Once his visitor had settled, the king, in a low but firm voice, began to talk.

"The man who showed you in, Garrenar, is my oldest and, by far, the most learned and reliable of my advisors. He confirms your story of the talisman and that, without the Mantle of Agetha, it is powerless. Until you spoke out earlier, I had no awareness of either object."

This was the first time Marazin had heard the name of the other object.

"Your Majesty, what does the mantle do, and how does Garrenar know these things?"

"How the mantle interacts with the talisman is unknown. Garrenar has limited understanding of either. We do not know how he came by the information. He has his own sources and means, which for their protection he keeps to himself. He, too, believes that if Betlic gains control of both items, we are all in danger. You mentioned both your parents were Xicaliman exiles. What do you know of your own history?"

"Very little, your Highness, both my parents died in an accident while I was absent. I do know they were not long married at the time they fled Xicalima. My mother gave birth to me a few months later. They left behind a large number of relatives. It was rare for my father to talk in any detail about his family. When he did, it was more about them as individuals and their personalities. As to what occupation they had, or what position they held, if any, remains a mystery. He concentrated more on Betlic's oppression of the Xicaliman people and the destruction he had inflicted upon the country. Father was aware of the talisman. He warned me about it and its counterpart, although if he ever mentioned that by name, I've forgotten.

"My parents were reluctant to leave Xicalima; they believed it was their duty to fight on. My grandparents insisted. They said it was to preserve the family line. Why this should be so special, I've no knowledge. When I left home, I was little more than a boy. My father said there was something he needed to tell me when I returned. I would be a man then and better able to understand what it was he had to say.

"But I became a soldier. I travelled the world, filling my life with adventure and excitement. I thought I had plenty of time. No sooner did one campaign end when word would reach me of another, and I would go to war again. It was only later, when news reached me of my parents' death, did I return home.

"They had a chest, filled with papers they had brought with them from Xicalima. It burnt in the blaze that killed them. Once I realised these records had gone, I decided to visit my homeland. I wanted to find out more about my relatives, their fates, and why the progeny of my parents was of greater importance than that of the others. Instead, I discovered nothing of use and was fortunate to escape with my life."

"Are you positive the blaze was an accident?" The king asked.

Marazin paused; such an idea was new to him. His parent's neighbours had said the house caught fire overnight. They believed a lamp or candle had overturned. The timber-framed structure was old, the wood dry, and the thatched roof had seen no rain for weeks. It would have been a swift death.

"Considering recent events, your Highness, it's possible the blaze was not an accident," Marazin admitted. "But why would Betlic want my parents dead, after all that time? They were a long way from Xicalima. My parents were not involved in any plots against him. Their lives were content. I doubt if any proof of arson exists now. It's something I will consider."

The king nodded, a possible alternative cause of the fire had been worth considering. He thought it more than probable it was deliberate, and that Betlic had possession of the papers that Marazin believed destroyed.

"What is Xicalima like?" Grogant was curious.

"From a distance, it's a beautiful land. Only when you cross the border, do you see that large areas are laid waste. Betlic's dark-clothed soldiers are everywhere. People are punished for the slightest show of dissent. As a warning, bodies hang from trees, or in gibbets. Many thousands of people are little better than slaves. His armies swell with conscripts. Any recruits who are unwilling, he brutalises until they follow orders without question.

"There are many who embrace Betlic's rule. Those who are most able, rise through the ranks without impediment, some to high levels. The ones with real power, are those commanders who were with Betlic when he overthrew the king. There is not a Xicaliman among them."

"With your experience of the world outside our borders," Grogant asked, "is it your belief that, if Betlic has taken possession of the mantle, he will use the talisman to expand his empire?"

Marazin answered without delay. "If what little we know about the objects is true, your Highness, nothing is more certain. He's held back until now because of the strength of the surrounding nations. Had Betlic attacked, they could have combined their forces and crushed him. If both mantle and talisman are under his control, it's too late. He can crush armies and take other lands whenever he wants. His expansion won't be instant, but it will be relentless. You have some time to prepare before his armies arrive at your borders, a few years if you are lucky. Long before Betlic's arrival, he'll have infiltrated some of his followers, to create dissent and unrest."

"We're sure Betlic already has spies in place," the king admitted. "We believe he has corrupted at least one of my own advisors."

"Cannot you challenge and remove these traitors from your court?"

"No! Both Garrenar and I know their identities. If we remove them, Betlic would corrupt others who might go undiscovered. For now, we control the information they gather. We give them a smattering of the truth, and much that is not. This brings me to the subject I wish to discuss with you.

"As you're aware, Marazin, we have discredited you. News will have spread through the palace. By evening, it will be all over town. With your agreement, we want to ensure the story travels throughout the land. We will issue a proclamation we have sent you into exile as punishment for spreading false rumour."

"But why, your Majesty, what do you want from me?" Marazin was somewhat puzzled. He cared little for what others thought of him. There was no-one to whom he was close. His parents were dead, so nothing could hurt them. He knew the truth of the matter, but, for him to accept such harsh treatment, what justification could there be? He had done his duty, as he saw it, and Garrenar had exonerated him.

"We want you to follow the survivors," the king said, "We believe they can confirm whether Betlic has the mantle. Garrenar believes, as do you, these are the people, or their offspring, who removed the object and guarded it ever since. Had they been ordinary villagers, they would have sought help, not disappeared into countryside that is less populated and more open to ambush.

"We will send more troops to the village. On their return, we shall announce that new evidence proves the outrage was the work of outlaws, nothing at all to do with Betlic. We shall disclose that travellers, who arrived after the raid, made the tracks you found and confirm there were no survivors. Betlic's spies will report this news to him.

"Soon, people will have forgotten both you, and any talk of massacres. This is of vital importance. It's possible those entrusted with the care of the object know of a way to counter its powers. Such an idea is not one with which Betlic would be comfortable. If he learns a custodian of the mantle has survived, it is something he is certain to consider. He would start an immediate hunt. Therefore, while Betlic continues to believe they are dead, they will be in less danger. You, too, will have a much-reduced chance of encountering his men.

"There's something else you may want to take into consideration. Up to now, we have assumed the raiding party found what it sought. What if they failed? The mantle could be in possession of whosoever drove away the wagon. If it is, we want you to assist them in removing it far, far away, beyond Betlic's reach."

"By now, your Highness, the trail will have gone cold. It might be difficult to find."

"Go east," the king said, "in the direction they were travelling. Garrenar has spoken of a large population of Xicaliman exiles who live among the Mogallean Mountains."

"But there's little water there. How could they survive?"

"I suspect there's more to the mountains than is generally known. It's possible the rebels exaggerate such difficulties to keep the land safe for them. Garrenar assures me tens of thousands live there. There is every chance, you'll find news of your missing relatives. Whatever you do with your life, whether you stay with your countrymen or return, we need to know what you discover. We cannot plan for the future without having all the facts at our disposal. The man with you at the village, Sherwyn, can we trust him?"

"I believe so. He has been with my company for some time and is dependable. His father was one of your ambassadors. Sherwyn grew up in foreign courts. He will know how to behave in front of the rebel leaders."

"Good. We want him to accompany you. When you have the information, send Sherwyn back with it. Should you return, we shall reinstate you. We shall announce you were working on my behalf at all times.

"Before you go, Marazin, we have some advice. Be cautious with whom you discuss your past. If Betlic's men murdered your parents, something we consider most probable, you'll be in danger if he finds you're alive. Your family must have been of high standing in Xicalima for him to hunt them down. Among your own people, new leaders and powerful groups will have emerged. They might conclude a possible descendent from one of the old elite families a threat to their ambitions too."

There was a moment's silence. King Grogant indicated the audience was over. Marazin stood and bowed low. He had turned to leave when the king called him back.

"We should finish this meeting in a way that people expect. Along the corridors, we expect courtiers and servants are listening for raised voices. If you walk out without any commotion, it will create talk and suspicion."

At the top of his voice, the king launched into a tirade. It made the one Marazin had received in the antechamber appear innocuous. The monarch had an inventive, colourful and forceful way of expressing his supposed anger. Marazin's face was burning when he left the room. Despite knowing it was an act, he behaved in much the same manner as had the outburst been genuine.

People looked away. Few bothered to disguise their contempt for him. Marazin hurried from the castle. As he neared the gateway, which led out from the courtyard into the market place beyond, a dozen well-armed soldiers blocked his path. Like Marazin, they were members of the king's guard. He knew them well. The leader, a captain too, shuffled his feet in embarrassment. This duty was not to his liking — Marazin had been popular. He was also a good friend.

"I'm sorry Marazin, but I've strict instructions to place you under arrest until we finalise arrangements to escort you to the border. If you give me your word you'll make no attempt to escape, I'm content for you to remain in your own quarters until you leave?"

"Yes, you have it, although my word now appears worthless."

"It's good enough for me, and my men," the captain said.

His troops nodded. Few believed the story behind their orders. Belief was one thing; palace politics were another. The troops might have sympathy for their prisoner, but not sufficient to allow them to deviate from the king's orders. There was no desire among the men to join Marazin in exile.

For several days, he remained confined to his quarters. Marazin spent the time preparing for his journey. In secret, the king provided the supplies Marazin would need, and a packhorse. After a last, long and, for most parts, sleepless night, a knock came at his door. The captain who had escorted him there, entered. It was the morning of the fifth day. It was time to leave.

With fresh eyes, Marazin looked around his home of the past few years. It no longer felt as if it was his. Without his belongings, it had become somewhere a stranger might live. Mentally, he had moved on. He doubted he would ever return. For a while, he had fought an urge to begin a new life, although he would have preferred to have started it under better circumstances. But, a start it was. He would join his countrymen in the Mogallean Mountains. A cold shiver ran down the young warrior's spine. Something else drew him towards the mountains, something far more compelling than the king's assignment. If only he could isolate that feeling, to know what that might be.

Once Betlic started to expand his empire, Marazin would join the struggle against him. It would make little difference whether Sherwyn returned with the information the king wanted. To halt Betlic's ambitions, the rebels would have to take the talisman, or mantle (preferably both) from him. Marazin doubted anything else could prevent the tyrant from fulfilling his aims.

With the captain behind him, Marazin stepped outside. His horse was saddled and waiting. Without delay, soldiers strapped his supplies onto a packhorse. His sword, taken from him at the time of his detention, the captain returned to him. The man made to speak but Marazin held up a hand to stop him.

"There's no need to apologise," Marazin said, "We all have our orders. As such, I bear you no grudge."

"Thank you," the captain said. "The king has decreed Sherwyn shall escort you out of the country. Why? I've no idea. We've sent a rider ahead to warn him. These men will accompany you to the village where the trouble started."

They shook hands with the warmth of friendship past. Marazin mounted and, with his escorts, passed through the palace gateway. The market place was a mass of bustling people, stalls and traders. Jugglers, sword swallowers and other entertainers amused the crowds, drawing them in to part with their money. Marazin kept his face expressionless, his eyes fixed on a distant point. Jeers and insults sounded loud in his ears. As the crowd swayed towards him, Marazin's escorts moved closer to his side. They drew their swords. The sight of the weapons had the desired effect. A way opened for the riders. Despite the show of strength, the abuse persisted, the sounds of which echoed inside his head.

Away from the market place, the group continued through narrow streets. Less busy here, few paid attention to the men on horseback. Of those who did, some swore at Marazin; others looked at him with scorn. No more than a thousand paces to the outer walls, for Marazin, it was the longest ride he had undertaken, ever.

Chapter Eleven

Marazin reined in his horse. Its hooves skidded over the frozen ground as it came to a halt. Autumn was a distant memory, and the air was still and bitter. He wrapped his furs more tightly round him. His face and teeth ached from the cold. It was time to look for somewhere to set up camp. He waited a while until, back down the trail, Sherwyn came into view over the ridge. Because his horse had developed a hot spot on its leg, Sherwyn had been compelled to lead it for most of the day. From this distance, Marazin could see the animal's limp had not improved.

The pair had ridden long through the Mogallean Mountains. The harsh winter was drawing to an end. Deep layers of white smothered the peaks, but here, at lower levels, snowfall had been much lighter. The pass they travelled remained open and safe to cross. Marazin was desperate to reach his destination. Their remaining supplies were meagre. A late, heavy blizzard would bury the tracks they followed and could trap them in the mountains until late spring.

Sherwyn's horse needed time to rest. Time they could ill afford. It might be days, weeks, before it was fit to travel. Marazin, who was leading both packhorses, had a solution. If they combined their dwindling supplies onto one animal, it would leave the other free for Sherwyn to ride. The pack animals were not mounts of choice, but preferable to travelling on foot. The lame horse? Its future was something they could discuss later.

Trees, their naked branches gaunt and twisted, covered the landscape to his left. Marazin followed a faint pathway that weaved between the dark stunted trunks. Soon, he discovered an old shelter in the undergrowth. The refuge was a welcome sight. He dismounted then tethered the pack animals. Back at the trail, he waved his arms to attract Sherwyn's attention. Marazin pointed towards the trees. The distant figure raised his arm to show he understood.

Built from rough-cut heavy logs, the shelter was open at the front. The roof, made from woven branches, had a deep lining of mud. Dead branches littered the surrounding ground. With fuel to spare, Marazin soon had a fire burning in front of the refuge.

It was a while before Sherwyn arrived. He too was limping; his legs ached and his feet were sore. For years, he had done most of his travelling on the back of a horse. As such, he was unaccustomed to walking long distances. He tied his horse next to the others then, with a sigh, slumped onto a log. The smell of meat, roasting over the flames, made him realise how hungry he was.

Marazin smashed a hole through the icy surface of a nearby stream. With fingers stiffened by cold, he filled their canteens. The pair was fortunate to find this supply. Large areas of this region were, as feared, bleak and waterless.

Since entering the mountains, apart from the tracks they followed and the shelter they now enjoyed, the travellers had seen little sign of human activity. Before the frosts set in, the wagon they sought had passed this way. In many places, its wheels had cut deep ruts into the muddy surface. Here, the indentations, frozen in place, were visible with ease.

The people in the wagon were no longer travelling alone. A few weeks earlier, as the trail entered the foothills, the tracks they followed merged with those of others. A large group on horseback had attached themselves to the wagon party. Marazin believed these to be members of a Xicaliman rebel patrol; Betlic's men would have turned south, after killing the wagon's occupants. At places farther along the trail, where the group had made camp, footprints belonging to the original pair of travellers were visible. Both seemed to have been free to move around, without restriction. The one with the pronounced limp appeared to be walking better, although crutch marks were clear.

With somewhere to shelter, the exhausted riders spent a restful night. Overnight, the sky cleared. By morning, there was a significant drop in temperature. Marazin shivered at the prospect of another day riding in the cold. King Grogant had been generous in his supplies for the two men. Their winter clothes were thick and warm. Such layers proved to be an excellent challenge to the chill air, which exploited any opening it could find. Sherwyn welcomed the suggestion about the packhorses. While he repacked their provisions, Marazin stepped into the open. His breath, a cloud of white, swirled round him. Among the trees, frost sparkled in the sun's watery rays. He examined the lame horse. The animal's leg was no better, the swelling more pronounced.

Sherwyn joined him. The horse was unfit to travel. If left behind, it would starve to death on the frozen ground. What grass remained was insufficient to feed the animal for more than a few days. A wolf howled in the distance. The men looked at each other. They had no choice.

"I'll do it," Sherwyn said with regret. "It's my horse, my responsibility."

Marazin nodded as his companion led it out of sight of the camp. Sherwyn was not long absent. When he returned, his eyes were moist as he gazed straight ahead. During the past few months, the animal had served him well.

While Sherwyn threw his saddle over one packhorse, Marazin loaded their supplies onto the remaining animal. It was a sombre pair that rode from the shelter. With the sun ahead of them, the tracks of the wagon marked their path. Hour by hour, the riders climbed deeper into the heart of the mountains.

Later that day, the pair reached the top of the pass. From the summit, they gazed on a wondrous sight. Below them, bathed in the warm light of the afternoon sun, a layer of white cloud covered the land. With majestic grandeur, distant peaks rose through the stratus, their slopes basking in the golden light. By evening, the cloud had risen to meet the travellers. Dank air seeped into their clothes. The damper they became, the more the heat flowed from their bodies. The mist was impenetrable. It was unsafe to continue riding. At the side of the trail, in a small hollow, they made camp.

Marazin considered it the worst night of their journey. If only it could have stayed so. Overnight the mist lifted. The air remained heavy; despite a rise in temperature, it felt no warmer. During the day, they experienced an increasing number of snow showers. To the riders' relief, the rising wind swept clear the path. Overnight, snow fell for several hours. By morning, the trail had disappeared; so too, the clouds.

With the weather bright and sunny, the pair set off in higher spirits. They saw no evidence the wagon had left the valley, nor anywhere where it might have done. With confidence, Marazin and Sherwyn followed the line of least resistance. In places, where the snow drifted clear, they caught glimpses of the ruts. They made good time but, during the afternoon, banks of cloud formed on the horizon.

By evening, the billowing mass was ominously close. As the wind increased, the travellers bowed their heads low into the oncoming gale. The valley opened out. To the rider's left was an abandoned mine, its tunnel entrance dark and forbidding against the surrounding snow. Close to the opening were the remains of a building, its walls formed from layers of turf. The roof, which had collapsed at the front, had a covering of the same material. Light was fading as they crossed the valley floor towards the ruins. The riders would shelter there from what was going to be a stormy night.

A small paddock, its framework in good condition, was to the left of the sod walls. A mound of hay, piled high, filled a corner. Marazin and Sherwyn scraped the layer of snow off part of the stack, then left the horses to graze. Weary from the day's travel, the two men staggered towards the building, their supplies and saddles in their arms. The breeze was growing stronger. Ragged strands of cloud raced overhead. Marazin felt something cold and soft on his face. Flakes of snow were blowing in on the wind.

Beneath the edge of the roof, where it remained sound, someone had taken the time to stack turf to form a new front wall. In the centre was a doorway, its lintel made from an old mine prop. Inside, they discovered a pile of wood and some tallow lamps, still primed with fuel. It was probable a shepherd took residence here during the summer months. After a little work, the pair soon had a fire blazing in the hearth. The lamps, which lit the interior with a dim warm glow, filled it with their acrid fumes.

Leaning against the wall, close to the entrance, was a rough-hewn wooden planked door. Although too large for the current opening, the travellers were able to wedge it over the gap with a plank of wood. The lamps flickered in the draught coming from around the door and ventilation holes left in the sod walls.

All evening, the wind strengthened. It screeched and howled around the walls and roof. Several times objects crashed into the building. Dawn was approaching before the storm eased.

Marazin opened his eyes. It was mid-morning. The fire was almost out, the room starting to chill. Because the lamps had burned out, the only source of light was a faint glow from around the doorway. He threw off his blankets. Sherwyn stirred, yawned and stretched.

"You make breakfast, while I go see if the horses have survived," Marazin said.

He removed the prop from the door, which toppled inwards. He caught it and swung it round to rest against the wall. As he turned away, behind where the door had been, he stepped into a barrier of snow. Startled, he sprang back, spluttering as he wiped the icy crystals from his face.

"Damnation!" he cried.

Sherwyn looked up, startled. "That's a lot of snow," he said, a worried edge to his voice. "I hope it's nothing more than a drift."

"It has to be. It's not possible for the whole valley to be covered to this depth in one night, is it?"

With Sherwyn's help, Marazin pushed his way through the wall of cold white powder. It was only an arm's length at its deepest. Moments later they were outside in the open. Across the valley, a white layer, several inches deep, sparkled in the morning sun. Sherwyn returned inside to rake the ashes. The embers glowed. He added a few twigs, which soon caught hold.

Snow had drifted up the side of the paddock fencing. Within the enclosure, the horses remained secure. They had pushed through the fresh white layer to graze on the hay beneath it. Marazin shivered. He had not thought to put on his furs. Despite the brightness of the sun, he feared there would be no thaw that day. Assured the animals had suffered no harm, he rejoined Sherwyn in the relative warmth of the shelter.

From what they had seen the previous day, the travellers knew the highest part of the range was behind them. In the distance, between jagged gaps in the mountains, the land sloped away towards a basin. With distant peaks rising on the opposite side, the lowland seemed vast and free from snow. If the rebel's base existed, Marazin believed they would find it somewhere on the grassland. If the weather held, he expected to reach the lower ground within days. He felt confident that, below the snowline, the tracks they followed would be visible again. The travellers' quest was nearing its end. A feeling of hope buoyed their spirits.

Chapter Twelve

It was with some regret the riders left the relative comfort of the abandoned mine. The fear that further snowfall might trap them drove them to continue. The first day's ride proved a challenge for the horses. One moment they trotted with ease through a thin layer of snow, minutes later, they struggled through drifts up to their flanks. The occasional marker, driven into the ground, was Marazin and Sherwyn's only indication of the path they followed. The posts towered high above the mounted men, which was a worry. They dreaded to think to what depth the snow might accumulate in this area?

Twice the valley forked. Posts were visible in both directions. At the first junction, Sherwyn scraped the snow from each path, to find the tracks had vanished. Either the wagon had taken a different route, or frost had already hardened the ground when it reached here. Marazin chose the way that seemed to offer the shorter route to the lands below them. The travellers' rate of descent was rapid. By nightfall, they reached an area where snowfall had been light. With insufficient fuel to build a fire, they ate a cold meal. Although they wrapped much of their spare clothing around them, the pair spent most of the long night, shivering. Unable to sleep, at first light, they were already in the saddle.

For much of the day the peaks cast deep shadows over the riders. When glimpsed, through gaps between towering summits, the sun offered little warmth to their bodies. Despite this gloomy prospect, between dawn and dusk there was a marked difference in temperature. At first, the trail was steep, in parts covered by thick layers of ice. Such places were hazardous to descend. Marazin became convinced the wagon must have taken a different route. In summer, many of the descents would have caused difficulties for a cart. In winter, these would be impossible to negotiate.

By noon the snow line was behind them. Riding became easier. As the path wound lower down the mountains, the covering of ice thinned, then disappeared. Overnight, frost formed again, but, by mid-morning it had melted. The wagon-tracks reappeared, joining the trail from a side valley. The rebel guides had known of an easier route.

Across the basin beyond, in the late afternoon sun, snow-capped mountain peaks glowed with a tinge of orange. As the colour faded, Marazin and Sherwyn entered a copse. A hot meal lifted their spirits. Thanks to ample fuel, they stayed warm that night. Under a star-studded sky they slept well, to wake re-energised. With good heart they rode out in the cool morning air. With the trees soon behind them, the riders cantered down an open valley.

By early afternoon, dense woodland lay before them. Seen from higher in the mountains, it reached to the flatlands. Beyond the trees, from what Marazin had discerned, the basin was an area of undulating grassland. This continued northward as far as he could see. Southwards, the mountains curved round into the distance, to join with the lower end of the peaks they had ridden through.

The trail led the riders into the trees, where it cut a steep path as it descended. The ground on either side was soft and spongy. Here, the air was warmer. The valley began to widen and level. As dusk drew nigh, the woodland gave way to ever larger open spaces of grassland.

To the travellers' right, a stag leapt out from the trees. It charged across the glade, straight towards them. In its panic, it was several moments before it noticed the horses. The beast skidded on the wet grass. It righted itself to race over the open ground in front of them. Within seconds, the beast disappeared into the woods on the riders' left. Startled, the horses reared and bucked. No sooner had Marazin and Sherwyn brought them under control when they showed signs of fright again.

A party of horsemen galloped from the trees, close to where the stag first leapt into view. A hunting party, of whom several carried bows, surrounded the travellers. All the newcomers wore swords. Although menacing, at no time did the strangers issue any threats. Marazin was uneasy. Sherwyn's hand moved closer to his sword.

"Don't move!" Marazin whispered. "There're too many of them. Stay calm. Let's wait to see what happens."

For a short while, only the sounds of the horses were audible. Restless, they stamped their hooves and snorted. No-one spoke. A horn sounded from within the woodland. Three riders entered the clearing. Their leader was a young man, dressed in fine attire; his two companions were a little older, their eyes ever watchful. Each carried several weapons. The trio moved towards the group, which parted to allow them passage. The riders, who surrounded the travellers, bowed their heads at the youngest of the newcomers.

"Who are these people?" The leader's voice was sharp. He addressed no-one in particular. "What are they doing here in my hunting grounds?"

"We don't know, your Majesty, we awaited your arrival before questioning them," a rider replied.

Your majesty! This was an unexpected complication. The man appeared little more than a youth. Marazin had expected to find a self-governing region, occupied by Xicaliman exiles. So, Marazin wondered, over which country did this boy king rule, and where were the rebels? Their monarch, and all his line, had perished when Betlic took over, or so he understood. He had heard nothing to contradict this. If these people were his countrymen, whatever claim this person had to its throne must be substantial.

"You," the young king said to Marazin, "who are you? How dare you wander through my forest. You've disrupted my hunt and lost me my prey."

The speaker studied the interlopers. He paid close attention to their dishevelled, travel-stained appearance. Their heavy fur outer garments were unsuitable for lowland weather. It seemed they had come far. That they were poachers, out for a quick meal, he soon discounted.

"How did you reach here, the passes are no longer open?" the king demanded.

He was showing increasing signs of irritation at Marazin's hesitation. It appeared he was used to instant responses to his demands.

"Your Majesty," Marazin spoke at last. "My name is Marazin and my companion, here, is Sherwyn. We come as emissaries of King Grogant of Vretliana, about an unpleasant incident that took place in his country, several months ago. He believes that one or more people made good their escape. Although in no way responsible themselves, King Grogant thinks they possess valuable information concerning this event.

"We're certain they sought refuge with the Xicaliman exiles. His majesty commanded us to contact the rebel forces, to ask for their help in finding these people. For many weeks we've followed the tracks of a wagon, which our king believes has connections to this matter. His highness has concluded the wagon's occupants were victims of the events and fled because of them."

The king glanced up at the snow-covered peaks behind the travellers. Scepticism showed in his eyes.

"The pass was open," Marazin insisted, "but, after a heavy storm a few days ago, I expect the route will be impassable now until later in spring."

The king looked at one of his companions, who nodded in agreement.

"If you go back the way they came," this man said, "you reach a low-level pass that crosses the mountains. It's not unknown for it to remain open for much of the winter."

Satisfied, the king turned back to the intruders. Earlier, his eyes had narrowed at the mention of Vretliana and the wagon. Ever since, his face had remained impassive. Now, he studied Marazin and Sherwyn anew, with a mixture of curiosity and suspicion. 'His majesty knows something,' Marazin thought. He felt a tingle of excitement.

"I am King Amron, of Xicalima. Of this incident, tell me more."

"Of course, your Majesty. Raiders massacred and burned a village, along with all the surrounding population. We believe they were working under the direct orders of the despot, Betlic. We know for certain two people survived. They left the area in the wagon I mentioned. Its tracks have led us here," Marazin pointed to the marks, still visible in the fading light.

For a moment, at the mention of Betlic, the king's face showed real anger. In silence, he indicated that Marazin, who had paused, should resume his explanation.

"King Grogant wants certain questions asked of the survivors, about an object of which they might have been custodians. His majesty fears Betlic is preparing to wage war on his neighbours. As such, the king needs to make preparations. The answers will aid his majesty in his decision making."

"What are you waiting for? Ask the questions," Amron demanded.

"My orders are to put these to the survivors, no-one else," Marazin said, with some hesitation. He was apprehensive as to what Amron's reaction might be. "King Grogant believes neither questions, nor answers, should become common knowledge."

The group that surrounded the travellers outnumbered them. If this King Amron took offence, Marazin knew he and Sherwyn would have little opportunity to defend themselves. The men on either side of his majesty had the appearance of seasoned warriors, by themselves more than able to take on the intruders.

To the speaker's surprise, his reticence provoked no adverse reaction. His earlier suspicions that Amron possessed knowledge of the mantle appeared correct. If so, the king would understand Marazin's reluctance to talk in front of a wider audience.

"Move back," Amron commanded the men surrounding the travellers. "I wish to speak to these people in private. You too," he instructed one of his personal guards.

The other guard, Orvyn, remained. He knew as much about the mantle as did his master. During the long ride, to join the Xicalimans in exile, Amron had confided much in him.

The rebel captain had stayed loyal to his king, as promised at their first meeting. Although Orvyn was thankful his master's earlier demand, that he swear an oath of allegiance, had faded from Amron's memory. The king's shock at the raid on his home and the death of his mother had diminished long ago, along with much of his contriteness. Only bitterness towards Talon, Egesa and Betlic continued unabated. This would never leave him.

Orvyn remained immune to the promises of wealth and influence he received, from those who wished to take advantage of his position with the king. It was regrettable Amron had ignored his own advice. The constant adulation was quick to seduce him. Within days of his arrival at the rebel stronghold, the persona of the arrogant, womanising young man, who drank his life away in taverns, had reasserted itself. Orvyn soon rued his acceptance of the king's offer.

Amron turned his attention back to Marazin. "Well! What is it you wanted to ask of me?"

"What do you know about the people in the wagon?"

"Everything! They were my father and I. After the attack, the raiders left him for dead. I was away from the village on business when it happened."

Amron kept secret the truth about his absence that night. Had it become known he survived only because he was on top of a hayrick, sleeping off a wild night of excessive drinking, his suitability as king would come under greater scrutiny. Already, his lifestyle caused great concern among the staider members of his court.

This admission amazed Marazin. How had Amron lived in Vretliana for so long, without his true identity becoming known? Many related questions entered Marazin's mind. He put them to one side, he would ask only the ones

Grogant had given him. There would be time, he hoped, to satisfy his curiosity later.

"King Grogant wants me to ask these three things. Are you, or were you, custodian of the Mantle of Agetha? Was this the reason for the raid? If so, did the attack succeed?"

Irritated, Amron stirred in the saddle. Dammit. It seemed anyone of any importance in the world was aware of the object's existence. Anyone, except him; only after its loss did he learn of its existence. By now, he had convinced himself that, had he known of it, he could have saved it from the raiders. In truth, in one of his many drunken states, it was probable he would have told Talon everything. Out of petty mindedness, he thought of withholding the information. Orvyn, sensing Amron's hesitation, whispered something to him, which brought a scowl to the royal countenance.

Orvyn was proving to be a huge disappointment to the king. The man was a bore. He lacked a sense of fun. His inclination, too, was to argue against Amron's excesses. As promised, Orvyn had begun to educate the king in the use of the sword, and in the art of unarmed combat. The rebel captain also kept his majesty informed of the day-to-day gossip of his court, but it was always the negative comments people made about the king Orvyn related, none of the positive. Amron discounted the possibility this was because no-one had anything good to say about him.

Amron had spent his childhood and youth working on a farm. Now he was in a position to enjoy himself — he would do so. Hunting, drinking and feasting had become important parts of his life. It was rare for him to be the sole occupant of his bed. Meetings with his advisors, who tried to discuss matters of state, held little interest to Amron. Although he had few problems in his understanding of what they said, he was fearful of making a fool of himself in matters beyond his experience. Despite Hafter's attempts to instil into Amron how important were his royal duties, testing the limits of his power appeared to be his main interest. His advisors and the High Council were there to look after the details.

One task he relished was to sit in judgement, over the many disputes that came before him for adjudication. Many of his decisions were dubious, others, overtly biased. Those with the ability to offer the strongest support to the king, financially or otherwise, tended to be more successful in the outcomes of their petitions.

"Your Majesty, if I may suggest," Orvyn said again, a little louder this time.

"Yes, what is it?" Amron was impatient.

"Your Highness, please give this offer your full consideration. You've a great opportunity here to make a treaty," Orvyn kept his voice low, so only the king could hear him. "We know Betlic has the mantle, along with the talisman, and that war is certain. Before you came to us, without success, we attempted to forge alliances with several kingdoms hostile to Betlic. This is a chance to instigate an accord of your own. It will go down well with your subjects and raise your popularity."

Amron glared at Orvyn, annoyed at his interference. For a moment, there was silence. A few of the words registered with Amron. Raise your popularity! The king was not a complete fool, although he was close to achieving such status; many whisperings against his excesses had reached him. Orvyn's advice, for once, might be of value. If it improved the monarch's standing with his people, it might silence his critics for a while. He nodded at Orvyn before turning back to face Mazarin.

"The answer to all your questions is 'Yes'. Betlic has the mantle to go with the talisman. Over the past year, he has recruited warriors from many regions. Once he has gained mastery of both objects, we believe his territorial expansion will begin. Your King, Grogant, what will he do once he has this information?"

"He will prepare his armies in readiness for conflict. He is aware no country, alone, has the resources to confront Betlic. Grogant wants to make pacts with like-minded rulers, those unwilling to surrender without a struggle. He believes if enough unite, they may prove too strong, even against the magic of the talisman."

"Do you intend to return to Grogant with these answers, once the passes are clear?" Amron wanted to know.

"No, your majesty, my companion Sherwyn bears that duty. My intention is to stay with the rebels. My family came from Xicalima. I wish to discover whether I have any relatives living."

"Do you know who they are?"

"No, I'm afraid my parents never spoke of their time in Xicalima. I think their memories were too painful for them," Marazin said, heeding King Grogant's advice not to reveal too much of his past.

"We shall ride to my camp," Amron said. He had lost interest in Marazin's possible family. The king doubted they would be of sufficient importance to be of value to him. Instead, he turned away from Marazin to address Sherwyn. "Once the mountain passes are clear, I shall provide an escort of troops for your safe return to Vretliana. From me, you will carry an offer of co-operation to present to King Grogant."

As Amron turned away, the handle of Marazin's sword caught his attention. For a moment the king stared, open-mouthed, paralysed with shock. A rage built inside him. Somehow, he kept his emotions under control. He looked Marazin in the face. When Amron spoke, his voice was husky.

"May I see your sword?"

"But of course," Marazin said, puzzled by the sudden interest.

He eased out the weapon. Holding it by the blade, he offered it to Amron. The king took it, his face darkening. He passed the weapon to Orvyn. He, too, found Amron's abrupt change of mood a mystery. In a flash, Amron's own sword was in his hand. He rested its point on Marazin's chest.

"You murdering dog," Amron roared. "You killed my mother. That's her sword. There's no other in the world to match it except this one! Seize him."

Before Marazin could move, hands grabbed hold of him. Yanked from his horse, he hit the ground on his back. Winded, he was unable to defend himself from the kicks and punches that landed on him. Within moments, he lay trussed.

"There's been a mistake," Sherwyn shouted, aware the king's attention would soon turn to him. "I've known Marazin for many years. He's always worn that sword. When he reached manhood, his father gave it to him. It's an old family heirloom from Xicalima."

Amron's sudden move and accusations had taken Orvyn by surprise. The king's advisor was a good judge of character. Marazin's air of bewilderment appeared genuine. It suggested the visitor had nothing to do with the assault on Amron's home. Sherwyn's subsequent comments had carried the directness of truth.

The king had already dismounted, his sword raised high. In a moment, he would execute the bound, shocked and protesting prisoner. Sherwyn, who tried to intervene, received a blow from the hilt of a sword that knocked him senseless to the ground. Most of the men were chanting encouragement to Amron, bloodlust fuelling their eager anticipation of the kill. Orvyn leapt from his horse, to throw himself between Amron and his victim.

"Wait!" he shouted, trying to make himself heard above the clamour.

The roar of disapproval from the men was deafening. They were relentless as they urged the king to kill the prisoner. They pushed and pulled at Orvyn. He stood his ground. With the hilt of Marazin's sword, he hit out to force back the jeering crowd.

"Move away, or you die too," Amron bellowed in frustration.

His eyes were staring. Sweat stood out in beads across his forehead. He was beyond reason. Amron and Orvyn faced each other over the prostrate figure. Orvyn was aware his relationship with the king was at an end. No matter how right he was, he would be lucky to escape this confrontation without the direst of consequences. Amron was desperate to strike down Orvyn but, although his majesty's swordsmanship had improved over the past few weeks, he was no match for his opponent. For several moments, they glared at each other, at an impasse.

In-between the opponents ran the largest dog that Marazin had ever seen. It came to a halt, to stand over the top of him. At first, he thought the beast was about to savage him. He took a deep breath, which he expelled in relief when he realised it, too, was here to shield him. The animal snarled and barked at Amron. His muscles tensed. Rivulets of sweat ran down his face and onto the ground. His grip around his sword handle tightened.

"Out of the way Heardwine," Amron shouted in anger at the dog.

Heardwine growled again, a low rumble deep in its chest, before it snapped and snarled at its master once more. Wary of the beast, Amron stepped back, out of range of its teeth. He looked at Orvyn.

"Give me a reason why I should not have both you and this treacherous beast killed now."

The rest of the group moved closer. At the first sign from the king, they would try to overpower and seize Orvyn.

"Your Highness, I don't believe Marazin had anything to do with the attack on your home, or your mother's murder," Orvyn said. "I admit this sword has the look and feel of your own — the same armourer could have made both — but, if what Sherwyn said is true, it's been in the man's possession for years. Your mother's sword, your father said, was shorter than the one you hold. This one's longer. Why don't we take the prisoners back to court where Tamin can examine the weapon? He'll know whether it belonged to our late queen. If it is your mother's, would you deprive your father the satisfaction of executing one of his wife's killers?"

Furious, Amron glared at Orvyn; but his words had struck home. It was Tamin's right to see justice done. Heads nodded. Amron had no doubt the sword was his mother's. Whether Marazin, along with Talon, had some involvement in her death was something only Tamin could confirm. On their return to court, he would exact full retribution against Orvyn. For now, he would strip him of his responsibilities. One thing was certain, no longer was there a future for him at the court of King Amron. When Tamin confirmed Marazin's guilt, Orvyn would face the severest of punishments.

Amron sheathed his sword as the opponents drew apart. Heardwine kept a close eye on everything. Amron ignored the animal. His own dog had turned against him. As had Orvyn, it had made him look a fool in front of the men. It was time to replace it with a loyal, obedient hound. The dog was huge and clumsy, it no longer suited Amron's new lifestyle. Of even greater importance, the king had heard comments deriding his ability to control it. Amron had no need to concern himself about Heardwine. Now the dog had brought the king through to safety with the rebels, it was time for the beast to attach itself to its true master.

"Leave the prisoner's hands bound. Throw him onto his horse and tie him to it," Amron commanded.

"What shall we do with this one?" a follower pointed towards the unconscious Sherwyn.

"Strap him to his saddle. Until we discover the truth of this matter, I can't trust either of them. Orvyn can ride with them."

There was coldness in Amron's voice. Guarding prisoners was a menial task, a role unbefitting the king's personal advisor. Members of the group sniggered at Orvyn's public humiliation. The reaction did not surprise him. Although popular with the men he had captained, it was the opposite at court. By those who sought to ingratiate themselves with the king, he found himself despised or envied in equal measure.

Chapter Thirteen

As darkness fell, the hunting party reached a well-appointed campsite. Servants, in dark green tunics, scurried everywhere. Inside a huge tent, they hastened to put the finishing-touches to a long trestle table. It overflowed with a variety of dishes. Tallow lamps hung from posts. Groups of candles, which flickered in the draught, stood at regular intervals along the centre of the table. Outside, an ox roasted on a spit over a large fire. To one side, a servant slowly rotated the carcass. Once the king and his companions dismounted, attendants cared for the horses. The royal party moved towards the tent. At Amron's nod of consent, the feasting began.

It was fortunate for Marazin and Sherwyn that the ride, which followed their confrontation with Amron, was of short duration. Strapped across his horse, Sherwyn was stiff and cramped. Soon after the ride commenced he regained consciousness. His head ached. He struggled at first, but a soft word of warning from Marazin had calmed him.

For the moment, there was nothing they could do to improve their situation. Only later, when they reached the rebel stronghold, could they hope to prove their innocence. Marazin hoped there were significant differences between his sword and the one taken by the killers of Amron's mother. The consequences of it being a twin were too appalling to consider.

Orvyn also dismounted but, at a word from Amron, the attendants moved away. They looked embarrassed. Left to tend to his own horse and those of his prisoners, Orvyn shrugged his shoulders in resignation. He led the horses round the camp. In the darkness, beyond the banqueting tent, he lashed the reins to a tree. He took his sword then severed the bindings that held Sherwyn to his horse. Orvyn caught the man as he slid from his saddle. The ropes had cut deep, which made it difficult for Sherwyn to stand. Orvyn helped him to the ground before attending to Marazin.

"If you give me your word that neither of you will try to escape, I'll release you both from your restraints," Orvyn said, as he helped Marazin to dismount from his horse.

"You have it," Marazin said. "Without your intervention, earlier, Amron would have killed me outright. My predicament seems to have cost you dear. I'm sorry for that. We are who we say we are. The sword is mine. To my knowledge, it's been in my family for generations."

"I believe you," Orvyn said. "I cannot say I'm saddened to be no longer an aide to the king. My situation has become somewhat difficult of late. He has, shall we say, failed to live up to the expectations I had of him. Nevertheless, I did hope to leave his service on more amicable terms."

Orvyn whispered the words. For all his relief at being free from the king's employ, the former aide had no wish for his enemies to overhear his true feelings, then report them back to Amron. Orvyn wanted to survive. Heardwine had kept the three disgraced riders company throughout the journey. It appeared strange to Orvyn that the dog had turned against its master. The beast had seemed loyal, despite its recent treatment by Amron. Soon after his arrival in the valley, he had ignored Heardwine and banished it from his rooms.

There was something else Orvyn found peculiar about the newcomers. It concerned the prisoner with the sword. At first, he could not decide what it might be. Marazin appeared straightforward and honest. He had courage. Unlike many in his position, who would be shaking with fear, his attitude was more one of concern than panic. He had seen much action in the past, of this Orvyn was certain — he knew when he was in the presence of a genuine fighting man.

It was the prisoner's looks, Orvyn concluded. At first glance, there were few similarities between Amron and Marazin, none at all if temperament was a factor to consider. There was something, though, in Marazin's face and bearing that, after deeper consideration, reminded him a little of the king. A faint, albeit distant, family resemblance seemed to exist between them. These thoughts, too, the captain thought better kept to himself.

There was the subject of the weapons, too. Orvyn knew the king's sword; both men had sparred together. Such objects were rare. Even more so were people with the skill to craft a blade of such quality. It was probable the same armourer had made both swords and, by inference, that of the late queen. Orvyn needed to speak to Hafter. In the few months since Amron's arrival, Orvyn was aware the sage had found the royal behaviour disappointing. Marazin might prove to be someone of interest to the old man. Among Hafter's papers, too, there could be records of the three swords, and details of how one came to be in Marazin's hands.

It was soon apparent that the trio would have to forage for their own food. Orvyn left his charges to rub some circulation back into their limbs, while he went in search of something they could eat. Light-footed, he skirted round the camp, hidden by the darkness from the raucous group inside the banqueting tent. From there, he could hear laughter and merriment, most of which appeared to be at his expense. He reached the supply wagon unnoticed by all but the cook, who looked round before speaking.

"What happened between you and the king?" he asked, unsure what the response might be. "The gossip round the table is that you attacked his majesty and are lucky to be alive. I've heard it said you're in league with the prisoners, and that they killed his mother and injured his father. Some believe they should have executed all three of you on the spot."

"It was nothing so dramatic," Orvyn said, grimacing at the spreading lies. "Last year, Betlic's men raided the king's home back in Vretliana, during which they murdered his mother and tortured Tamin. The king believes one of the strangers took part in this. On the evidence, I thought it questionable. All I did was prevent his majesty from killing someone who I believe to be innocent of that crime.

"Within a few days, we shall be back at the palace. Tamin is certain to know, either way. I have little doubt he will confirm my belief. That will be of little benefit to me. I shall no longer be welcome at court. For defying his majesty in front of his friends, he will find as many ways as possible to make me suffer. From now on, I shall have to watch my back. Take my advice and keep your involvement to a minimum, you'll live a lot longer."

"I'm sorry." The cook was sympathetic. "I've never known you to be anything but straight with people. If you find yourself in need, I know many across the land who will aid you. For now, I have instructions to turn you away, so I shall go for a short walk. Take what you need while I'm gone. Whenever you want more, make yourself visible nearby and I shall wander off again. Good luck."

Orvyn thanked him. The cook disappeared into the darkness. The newly appointed custodian found sufficient supplies to feed him and his charges for several days. He had no wish to endanger the cook by returning for more.

At dawn, with the servants left to break camp, the royal party began its journey back to the king's court. Amron's face flushed with anger when he realised the prisoners were without restraint. His first impulse was to instigate another confrontation with Orvyn. He decided against it. Their recent altercation had left a less than favourable impression with some who had witnessed it. Although in a minority, not every member of the hunting party was a close ally of the king. Instead, in a loud voice, he stated the prisoners were their keeper's responsibility. If they escaped, Orvyn would be the one held to account. The former aide neither acknowledged the threat, nor made any move to restrain Marazin and Sherwyn. Orvyn had their word. Something, he felt, that was more honourable than that of his highness.

From the start, the royal party shunned Orvyn. With Heardwine for company, the three outcasts travelled, ate and slept by themselves. The dog had found a new friend in Marazin. It was rare for it to stray far from his side. For much of the first day, the members of the hunting party were morose. Last night's over indulgence of ale, wine and rich food had left most of them with sore heads, and irritable digestions.

By the following day they had recovered. They amused themselves by aiming pointed insults and open abuse in Orvyn's direction. He struggled to keep his face from reflecting the anger he felt. His prisoners proved a welcome distraction. He talked long and in depth with them as they rode. Any doubts about their sincerity, he soon dismissed. These men spoke the truth.

By the middle of the first morning, the party were clear of the forest. Lush grasslands opened up in front of them. The Xicaliman rebels and refugees had taken residence throughout much of the vast area enclosed by the mountains. By noon, they had ridden past the first of many farms. The roads along which the party rode soon became well defined. The cultivated ground was criss-crossed with dirt tracks. Cattle and sheep roamed across other areas. Most farms and villages consisted of timber-framed huts, or roundhouses. The nearer they approached the seat of Amron's power, the greater the number of villages they came to. Many were of considerable size, with two-storey structures. It was clear to Marazin the rebels were far more organised and in greater numbers than imagined. He had expected to find a few thousand warriors, housed in a sprawling campsite. Everything seen so far led him to believe they were riding through a settled country.

The riders climbed a low slope. At the brow of the hill, Marazin and Sherwyn caught their first sight of the exiled Xicalimans' capital. The area was vast, covered by a sprawling mass of houses, markets and tradesman's premises. Larger houses, surrounded by grassland, stood apart from those of the masses. Several of these buildings had fortifications. Orvyn explained these homes belonged to those who held sway at court. These were the nobles and generals of the High Council that had ruled the country until Amron's arrival, and who now supported him.

On the opposite side of the town, a house of generous proportions was in the process of enlargement. Similar to other buildings belonging to the nobility, its timber-frame was on a much grander scale.

"That's his majesty' palace," Orvyn replied when questioned by Marazin. "Soon after his arrival, King Amron took up residence in the old part. Lord Acwellen, one of his advisors, presented it to him. When the man lost his wife last year, he moved to a place with fewer memories. The palace extends daily."

"What's that building, over here?" Sherwyn pointed to a large, grim looking single-storey building nearby, surrounded by a high stockade.

"That's where we'll be, if Tamin fails to confirm your story," Orvyn scowled in distaste. "Until his majesty's arrival, it was a secure hut, where drunks slept until they sobered. An occasional rustler or thief spent longer in there. It was unknown for it to be as full as now.

"The king seems determined to criminalise half the people brought before him, those without influence or money in particular. Rich and powerful men can settle scores, or escape justice, with a contribution to the royal coffers. Amron dismissed those who used to sit in judgement of their fellows. He told them that, with his arrival, their positions were redundant. The majority of those were even-handed and fair. They preferred to settle matters amicably, rather than with a huge fine, imprisonment or both. In the short time since his majesty's arrival, it's hard to believe the change that has come over the land."

"The king's popular?" Marazin's tone was heavy with sarcasm.

"With the younger, wilder ones," Orvyn said with a wry smile.

They kicked their horses into motion to follow the royal party down the slope. The supply wagon and servants brought up the rear. Everywhere, men and women bowed their heads as the royal procession meandered its way through the rubbish-strewn streets. The stench in places was overwhelming; a mixture of human waste, sweat and rotting-vegetable matter. To Marazin and Sherwyn, after their many months of travel in the wilds, the odour was foul. Several riders held lavender cloths to their noses.

Surrounding Amron's palace was a moat, wide and deep. By the time the riders reached it, daylight was fading. Encircling the complex, on the opposite side of the water, was a stout barricade made from the trunks of pine trees. They sloped outwards, to the height of a man on horseback. The tip of each trunk angled to a vicious point. A bridge lay across the moat. Without hesitation, the king's party crossed over the wooden platform. Orvyn and his prisoners followed. Marazin held his nose. The water stank. Once the supply wagons had passed through the internal gateway, sentries slammed shut huge planked doors into place. There was a dull thud as a heavy wooden bar slid into position.

No easy way out through there, thought Marazin. He looked back towards the wooden balustrade. Near the top was a ledge built for defenders. The angle at which the builders had set the poles meant, at a run from the inside, they would be easy to climb. It offered potential if matters turned unpleasant. The moat on the opposite side was another prospect. Unless he had exhausted all other possibilities, the human and other waste that floated on its stagnant waters meant it was not something Marazin would contemplate as an escape route of choice.

Ahead of Marazin, the king's party rode towards the main entrance, at the older part of the house. Wooden scaffolding surrounded this, with newer construction spreading around it. Once completed, his majesty's residence would look impressive.

Ushered inside by servants, Amron and his friends disappeared from sight. Stable-hands led away their abandoned horses. One attendant remained outside, a man with whom, on several occasions, Orvyn had disagreed. With a smirk of satisfaction on his face, the servant waited until Orvyn and his charges reined in.

"Once you've stabled the animals, his majesty has decreed you bring the prisoners before him and his father for judgement," he found it impossible to control the glee in his voice.

For a second, the rider's gaze reflected his distaste for the man. Orvyn refrained from comment, instead his expression changed to a broad smile.

An action that, as intended, irritated the attendant. The man stomped off. He would be the one to laugh — at Orvyn's execution. From what the servant had overheard at the doorway, the dreadful man had gone mad and attacked his majesty. Why the king allowed his attacker to roam free without chains, the servant found hard to imagine.

Orvyn led his companions to the stables at the rear of the palace. The stable-hands looked embarrassed but, under strict instructions, ignored the new arrivals. They rubbed down their own animals. Afterward, they placed them in stalls, well supplied with bundles of fresh hay and water. Marazin wondered whether he would see his horse again. It had served him well. With trepidation, the group made their way towards a servant's entrance behind the palace.

Inside, several armed soldiers awaited the trio's arrival. As soon as Orvyn stepped through the door, strong arms grabbed him and threw him to the floor. With his weapons seized, the men bound his hands behind his back, yet another indignity for him to endure. The prisoners, too, had their arms restrained. This was becoming too much, Orvyn decided.

Why had he been such a fool as to allow himself to become involved in royal affairs? Although flattered by the king's offer, Orvyn knew now he should have declined. Hindsight was no substitute for foresight. He had thought the man with whom he made the bargain was honourable. In Orvyn's mind, 'His Majesty' and 'honourable' were words no longer applicable to the same person.

Pushed and jostled, the prisoners were unable to defend themselves. At sword point, the guards forced them towards the great hall. Outside, the three waited, for what seemed an age, before the door creaked open. They were frog-marched through the opening. Inside, on a cold, stone-slabbed floor, powerful hands forced them to their knees. From behind, soldiers grabbed each prisoner by the hair. With guard's knees in the middle of their backs and their heads yanked back, the three found their gazes fixed on Amron. All round, the king's friends roared and taunted them. The feast came to a temporary halt, music stopped. It was time for some real entertainment.

Behind Amron, a door opened. Marazin watched as an elderly man entered. His pace was slow as he hobbled across the room, aided by two sticks. Servants rushed over to ease forward the table in front of the king.

They brought a large, comfortable chair from the side of the hall, which they placed beside his majesty. Amron stood to help the old man into it.

"Your Highness, what's going on? Why have you disturbed me? I was enjoying an evening with friends." The old man looked round the room.

For the first time, he saw the three bound prisoners.

"This is too much, Amron. What's Orvyn done wrong? He's been your loyal aide for months now," the old man complained.

This must be the father, Marazin thought. No-one else would dare talk to the king in this manner.

"He's in league with the other two. I discovered them trying to sneak into our lands. I'm certain they intended to finish what they started when they killed Mother and destroyed our home."

"These men weren't in the party who killed your mother. I've never seen them before."

"Then they must have belonged to the group who burnt the village."

"Why? What have they done to make you suspect that?" Tamin was becoming more confused by the moment.

"This one had mother's sword with him," Amron said with huge satisfaction, a finger pointing in the vague direction of the prisoners. "Only someone who was there could possess it."

Tamin looked startled — Rowena's sword? Possession of that would be damning.

"Talon took that," he said.

"He must have passed it on," Amron countered.

"Talon was an evil, murderous dog, not a fool. No warrior with his experience would give up a sword of that quality."

This discussion was turning into a disaster for Amron. Again, he was looking foolish in front of his friends. Why did his father do this to him? It had been the same back at the farm.

Exasperated, Amron called out to one of his bodyguards, "Jarick, bring out the sword and show it to my father."

This was the one who had ridden beside the king and Orvyn when first Marazin had seen them. The man stepped forward from the back of the room. Hilt first, he presented the weapon to Tamin. The old man took it from the bodyguard. A look of surprise crossed his face, as opposed to the one of anger that Amron expected. Tamin studied the hilt. He progressed to the blade. He peered at a tiny mark stamped into the metal beneath the guard. When he looked up, his left eyebrow had risen in a quizzical expression. Tamin shook his head.

"It's a remarkable sword, but too long to be your mother's. The design on the pommel is different and the pattern on the blade is stronger. It's easy to see how you would be suspicious, with only your own for comparison. The mark on it shows it was made by the same swordsmith."

Open-mouthed, Amron stared. He had convinced himself it was the one stolen from his mother.

"You are sure?" He said after a long pause.

"Of course I am," Tamin said testily, irked by his sons doubts.

The king sat, muttering in annoyance. Tamin ignored him.

"Which one of you owns this sword?" he addressed the prisoners.

"It's mine, your Highness," Marazin answered in discomfort.

A soldier still held onto his hair, a knee pressed into his back.

"Oh! Release them," Tamin said. He sounded annoyed. "I've already told you they'd nothing to do with my wife's death."

The guards looked at Amron for approval. He waved a hand sideways as if he had given up on the situation. Within seconds, with their bindings removed, the prisoners were free.

"Orvyn, introduce them."

"Your Highness, may I present Sherwyn, who comes as an emissary on behalf of King Grogant of Vretliana. He wishes to create an alliance with King Amron. His companion is Marazin, a Xicaliman exile who accompanied him on his journey."

Had one been necessary, the look Amron flashed at Orvyn would be a warning. From now on Orvyn would have to be careful. Both he and Marazin, Orvyn thought, as the king transferred his gaze to the newcomer. Sherwyn, his majesty ignored. This emissary was important; he offered an alliance. As such, he had been at the periphery of the king's rage.

"Come with me," Tamin commanded the former prisoners.

He had caught sight of the glance his son had thrown at them. For the trio's immediate safety, Tamin thought it better if Amron's temper cooled before he met any of them again. It was plain to see he was furious.

"I shall be all right," Tamin said, forestalling his son's comments. "Jarick can escort us if my safety concerns you."

Taking the matter as settled, Tamin offered his arm to Marazin, who stepped forward to help the old man to his feet. With the released men at his side, Tamin, still holding the sword, limped from the room. The sound of the door, closing behind them, echoed round the silent hall. No-one uttered a word. The servants manoeuvred themselves towards their entrances. They wanted to be out of the hall before Amron's rage exploded. Food and drink, enough to supply a small army, covered the tables. It was doubtful the revellers would need the attendants again. As soon as they could, they fled.

Minutes passed. Nobody moved. Amron stared straight ahead, his clenched fists resting on his knees. His muscles became less tense. He smiled. Far from pleasant, it was only a slight step away from a grimace. He indicated one of his companions should pass him his goblet. The king emptied it. Someone rushed to fill it. The others relaxed; they too started to drink.

"Leave me. Take food and drink to your rooms," Amron ordered the group. "Not you," he pointed towards Boden and Tedrick, two of his more ruthless supporters. "Stay and keep me company for a while."

With arms filled with food and pitchers of wine, Amron's other guests departed. Whatever it was the king wanted to discuss with those two, it was something from which the others would prefer to be absent. God help anyone that pair went against.

The king dropped his voice to a whisper. Walls had gaps in them. He had no desire for his words to travel beyond this room. "Orvyn and Marazin," he said. "I want them dead. How is up to you, provided no blame attaches to me. Do you understand?"

Both men nodded. Boden had few scruples; a cold-blooded ambush killer, he relished the task. Tedrick's triumphs, unlike his fellow, had always been in combat. As a fighter, he was tough and ruthless, but he was not an assassin. When he killed, it was in hot blood, not cold. Although he thought it unwise to refuse his king's request, he was uncomfortable with the command.

Since Amron's arrival at court, Orvyn had become a thorn in the side of those who wanted to lead the king astray. His pleas for moderation in royal behaviour had proved irksome. Marazin was a stranger. He had no-one to grieve over his body, nor to seek revenge on his behalf. Yet, were these reasons sufficient to condemn them both to death? Tedrick, unlike Boden, remained unconvinced.

"The one called Sherwyn," the king said, "must suffer no harm. He can be useful to me. I shall make him welcome and see that all doors are open to him. We need an alliance with his king. Over the coming days, I shall build bridges with Orvyn, but not reinstate him. Marazin, I will invite to a meeting with the High Council, where everyone can witness I bear him no ill-will. Once everyone knows and accepts my position towards them, they are yours. Take whatever time you think necessary but, by summer's end, I want them gone."

The meeting broke-up. Amron retired to his room. Alone, instead of satisfaction at his actions, doubts clouded his mind. His temper had cooled; he knew he had been rash. His rise to power had been too quick. He was ill prepared for the responsibility and decisions expected of him. Because he feared to appear weak, Amron knew many of his reactions to situations were irrational. For that reason alone, he was unwilling to call-off the assassins. He needed to look strong in front of them.

His former prisoners, so Amron believed, remained as guests of his father. In truth, only Sherwyn, as a temporary measure, slept in a bed in the old man's quarters. As for Tamin, Marazin and Orvyn, they had slipped away. Without delay, they had ridden from the palace, their destination unknown to all but Tamin. The night guard, without question, opened the gates. The king's father was free to come and go as he pleased. Unlike walking, riding was something the old man could manage with ease.

Chapter Fourteen

The heavy wooden door flew open. With a crash, it slammed behind Karilyn as she stumbled into the house. The sound reverberated throughout the building. Her face was hot and flushed. Embarrassment, as much as anger, clouded her thoughts. A thick layer of dust covered her skirt. She was weary beyond measure, her feet ached and her throat was dry.

At nineteen, Karilyn was now a woman, to many, one of great beauty. Plaited hair, a rich dark-brown in colour, reached to her waist. Her slender, hourglass body, she held stiffly as she rested a hand against a panelled wall. Below dark and narrow eyebrows, her large, angry flashing eyes were brown with long dark lashes. A slim nose was upturned, so slight as to be hardly noticeable. Her lips were full, parted now to show a glimpse of white. High cheekbones were set in a face that was not too wide as to be unattractive, while her chin was short and rounded, her skin without blemish.

Karilyn's cheeks burned as she remembered the events of the afternoon. The day had started so well. Early that morning her close friend, Willa, arrived with an invitation to accompany her on a picnic. She was the daughter of a nearby landowner. The girls were of a similar age and had known each other for as long as either of them could remember.

Whenever Karilyn needed a rest from her studies and training, Ryce would arrange for the pair to meet. Over the years, their relationship had been a mixture of best friends and greatest enemies. As they grew older, their friendship strengthened but, after Willa's marriage, their meetings had become less frequent. In the three years since then, Willa had borne two children, of which only the younger survived.

A fraction shorter than Karilyn, Willa, too, was slim, but her breasts swelled with milk for her infant. Under slightly arched eyebrows, her eyes too were brown, set back over strong cheekbones. She had a pert nose, beneath which her lips were full and plump. Her dark hair, which she wore to her shoulders, highlighted her pale oval face with its softly angled chin. Young and vivacious, she greeted Karilyn with a hug and a kiss on the cheek.

Delighted, Karilyn cancelled her day's arrangements with Ryce. For many weeks, she had been training hard without a break. He gave the venture his blessing. It would be good for his daughter to relax with a friend for a few hours.

Willa had brought food enough for them both, so Karilyn fetched wine for them to drink. Wedged on a shelf beneath the seat of the small horse-drawn carriage, which Willa had driven, was an open box. Wrapped and strapped into this was her young son, Scard. The boy, less than a year old, carried his father's name. Karilyn made appropriate noises. She had limited experience with babies and was not comfortable with them. When her time came, Karilyn believed she would embrace motherhood wholeheartedly. For now, she was more than happy to leave infants to those who knew what to do with them.

There was a place in the foothills, Willa said, which would be perfect for their picnic. Karilyn thought nothing about it, although there were places, much nearer to home, where she would have preferred to spend the day. It was close to noon when they arrived. Willa leapt from the carriage, then passed Scard to Karilyn, to look after while she set out the food. Awkwardly, Karilyn held the boy. He sensed her discomfort and, ready for his mother's milk, he screamed and struggled in her arms.

Karilyn knew enough to realise his reddened cheeks and runny nose was a sign of teething. She put a finger in his mouth. For a moment, he chewed on the digit. He was hungry and difficult to pacify. He squirmed and screamed again. Much to Karilyn's relief, Willa took him back. She pulled down a part of her tunic front and shift. The infant fell silent as against her breast he fed.

Karilyn cast a glance at the blanket spread on the ground, which Willa had covered with a copious selection of food. There seemed to be rather a large amount for the two of them.

"Let's wait a little longer," Willa suggested, as Karilyn leant over to take something from a platter. "I'm not hungry yet," she added, although her stomach rumbled as if to prove her wrong.

Karilyn curbed her impatience. She sat back to wait while Willa finished feeding Scard.

"You know, you looked good with Scard," Willa commented. "You'd make a good mother, you should marry."

Karilyn was wary. It must have been obvious she was ill at ease holding the baby. She glanced again at the amount of food on display. Surely, Willa was not attempting to be an intermediary. No sooner did the thought enter her mind when, over the lip of the hollow they occupied, a rider came into sight. After a few moments Karilyn recognised Halwende, Willa's older cousin. Karilyn remembered him from her childhood, when the three of them shared several childish adventures. Since then, there had been no contact. He was not someone whose company she missed, neither was he a person for whom she harboured any amorous intent.

"This is a surprise," he said as he dismounted. "I thought I heard voices."

"Come and join us," Willa said.

Discretely, she removed Scard from a teat and covered herself.

"I seem to have brought too much food for Karilyn and me. You remember Karilyn, don't you Hal? We used to have such good times together."

Karilyn caught sight of the quick look exchanged between cousins. She cringed. This had the potential to be an awkward interlude.

"Halwende will be far too busy to dally with us," Karilyn interrupted before he could speak. "You oversee much of your father's land now, don't you?" she turned to speak to him. "Work of such great importance must leave little time for idle chatter with womenfolk."

"That's right! I take care of the estate," he said with pride, as he tethered his horse. "But I'm riding the land today, to see if everything is all right. I'm free to spend my time as I feel fit. I'm in charge, so I can do what I want."

He was trying to impress. Instead, he sounded pompous. Willa directed him to Karilyn's side, where he sat, with less than a finger of space between them.

"You should have seen Karilyn with little Scardy a few minutes ago, Hal," she cooed. "I was just saying they looked perfect together. What do you think?" she added, again thrusting the poor child into Karilyn's arms.

'Scardy', who had been content with his mother, looked unhappy. His face pouted. Willa was not prepared to admit defeat. She pushed a wooden comforter into his mouth. Scard, distracted, chewed and sucked on it. He settled and fell silent.

"Oh yes! Perfect!" Halwende said.

He tried to close the tiny gap between him and Karilyn. She moved to take some food. When she sat back down, it was at an arm's length away from him. Karilyn was doing her best to keep her temper under control. On the ride out, she had so looked forward to an hour of two of idle talk, gossip and chatter with her friend. Now she found herself, miles from home, the target of a matchmaking party. Foolishly, she had ridden in the carriage, so was without her own horse.

Each time Halwende inched closer, Karilyn moved away. Exasperated and on the pretext of settling the baby, she stood and walked about the picnic site. He had started to wriggle again. To her surprise, and annoyance, the movement sent him to sleep. The last thing she wanted was for him to slumber, she wanted him to scream, so she could pass him back to his mother.

Scard continued to slumber. Karilyn sat again. This time, she placed herself at the opposite side of the blanket to her unwanted suitor. Halwende was incapable of taking a hint. Within minutes, he moved across to join her. Karilyn was starting to feel trapped. With her training, this bode ill for Halwende's imminent well-being.

The afternoon progressed. Whenever she tried to change the subject, Karilyn found her wishes ignored. Willa seemed determined to bring her friend and cousin together. In time, with the baby passed back to its mother, Karilyn found having a free hand useful. She needed it to keep extricating herself. Halwende had taken to moving closer and, nonchalantly, clasping one of her hands in his as he talked.

Frustrated with the lack of results, Willa gave up inserting subtle, and less than subtle, hints into the conversation. Karilyn, for some reason, was oblivious to them. Willa decided on a more direct approach. It was a while before she brought to a close, a monologue extolling the merits of Halwende. She described at length his importance, his position and his future inheritance. He was an excellent catch. He thought Karilyn was attractive and would look good beside him. She would be stupid, so Willa said, to turn down the offer of marriage he was about to make. Willa was certain Karilyn would come to love him in time.

Karilyn had heard enough. She exploded — verbally. No, she had no intention of accepting a proposal of marriage from Halwende, should Willa allow him the opportunity to speak long enough to make one. Karilyn was sure he would turn some lovely woman into a downtrodden drudge; if that was the life she desired, so be it. Karilyn would never be that person. Marriage to someone, whose main desire was to have a mindless creature that looked good at his side, was not what she wished. It seemed to her that what he wanted was someone who could impress the neighbours when they came to visit? When they left, what would happen to her then? Would he lock her in a cupboard until the next visitors arrived? He might do better with a dog for a companion.

When she married, it would be to a person she wanted to be with, to someone whom she loved, someone who loved her in return. It would not be to some ninny who lacked the courage to come to her door to ask in person, a boy who needed his cousin to do the work for him.

After this outburst, the conversation degenerated rapidly. As the exchanges became more acrimonious, all parties said much they would regret later. Both picnic and friendship were at an end. Karilyn became so incensed she stormed-off. Halwende ran after her. He demanded she stop. It was too far for her to walk home. He would not allow it. She must do as he said and ride with Willa.

Halwende then made the biggest mistake of his day. He grabbed her wrist and tried to force her back. Willa screamed as her cousin landed on his back, his face contorted in agony. For a moment, he believed he had broken his arm. It was impossible, so Willa thought, for Karilyn to be capable of causing such damage. Her cousin must have slipped. Halwende had no idea what had taken place; his landing on the ground had happened too fast for him to comprehend.

As Willa ran over to help her cousin to his feet, Karilyn's glance at the pair was scathing. She turned her back and continued walking. Eyes straight ahead, she kept her distance from the track until, much later, Willa drew near. She pulled up for a moment and called out. Karilyn ignored her. Wiping her eyes, and with her head down, Willa spoke to her horse. The carriage trundled into the distance. It was several hours later, as night was falling, before Karilyn reached home.

Hot tears flowed down her face. Was it her destiny to become a shrivelled old maid, to live out her life on her own, without friends and family? At the end of their heated exchanges, Willa had said that was what would become of her. Willa had accused Karilyn of thinking herself above her station; that she was too good for the local boys. As for love, that came later if you were lucky. Otherwise, there were children to care for and someone to provide for you.

On the long walk home, these thoughts had occupied Karilyn's mind. She agreed, to some extent, that she considered herself different from, but never better than, the people who lived locally. As to marriage to one of the neighbouring boys, none filled her with desire. Some were kind and considerate, a few were bullies. Mostly, they had wandering hands. To a man, they possessed one common trait. Not one had an iota of adventure in them. Karilyn had too much of her parents in her make-up, to accept the ordinary. For now, she lacked the self-confidence to leave home and travel, as had her brother, although there was a part of her that craved it.

Above all, there was the problem of the Scraufin. Whomsoever Karilyn married, it must be someone she could trust to keep her secret. A man who was secure enough in himself and their relationship to accept that, maybe for many months, she might have to leave to travel with a stranger. She would be on a mission, steeped in danger, one from which return might be impossible. Somewhere in the world, such a person must exist. Of one thing she was certain. She would know him when she found him.

Alerted by the noise, Ryce rushed into the room. He saw the dusty state of Karilyn's clothes and the tears running down her face. Concerned, he hastened to her side.

"What's happened? Are you all right? You were so late, I was starting to worry. Where's Willa? Why hasn't she brought you home?"

Through her tears, Karilyn explained the events of the day. When she reached the point in the story where Halwende grabbed hold of her arm, a troubled expression crossed Ryce's face.

"He is all right, isn't he?" Ryce asked.

He knew full well his daughter's power and capabilities. If she had killed the oaf, Ryce would have to make urgent preparations to take her out of the area. The lad had no understanding of what he risked when he tackled Karilyn.

"Of course he is!" Karilyn was indignant. "He'll have a sore arm and a painful back for a few days, nothing more."

Ryce sighed in relief. This was the first time his daughter had used the skills he had taught her, in any situation other than in training. It was a relief to find she neither panicked nor over-reacted, physically. Ryce held her until the tears stopped. She was young and was right to feel upset. Someone she thought she knew well had let her down. Today, Karilyn had learned a valuable lesson in trust.

Had Karilyn been a little older and wiser, she might have been able to laugh off the situation and deflect Halwende's attentions. Ryce hoped the consequences of her outburst would be short-lived. He feared, for a while, her peers might shun her. The humiliation inflicted had not all been one-sided. The duties of the one responsible for the Scraufin could bring with them the curse of loneliness. He hoped isolation would not be a permanent state for his daughter.

Chapter Fifteen

After his meeting with Boden and Tedrick, Amron was true to his devious word. He made it known, out of respect for his father and a desire to catch his mother's killers, he had erred on the side of caution in taking prisoner the strangers. In this version, Amron was the hero. It became accepted that his intervention had saved the travellers from death, at the hands of un-named members of his hunting party.

He praised Orvyn for his assistance. It was soon common knowledge his majesty had released his aide from his duties, to allow him to concentrate on personal matters. The king had cleared Marazin of any involvement in the death of the queen. His majesty, in Marazin's absence, thanked him for helping Sherwyn to reach his destination.

When these proclamations reached Marazin and Orvyn, both raised their eyebrows, then dismissed the details as the lies they were. Wisely, they stayed a long way from the city. In their refuge, at Hafter's summer retreat in the hills, the occasional message from him kept them up-to-date with life at Amron's palace. Otherwise, since their arrival, the fugitives found the days long and slow to pass.

The night the pair fled the palace, Tamin took them across town to Hafter's winter home. Although the king's father refrained from speaking ill of his offspring, he, too, was unhappy at the speed with which his son had fallen back into his old ways. It would have distressed his mother, had she been here to see it, although she would have been better able to council him in the ways of royal conduct and court etiquette.

Tamin had heard many tales about Amron's behaviour. His money for favours and the injustices he meted out, in his so-called courts, were only the beginning. But, sooner rather than later, war was coming. It was rare for the fairest and kindest of leaders to triumph in such events. It was the most ruthless and determined who achieved success. Such qualities, Amron was developing daily. He would need them when he came up against Betlic. Tamin also looked to the future. He lived in hope that, when his son married, his offspring might have a temperament more suited to rule in less tempestuous times.

Tamin's stay that night was brief. He needed to be back at the palace before Amron realised he was absent. Before Tamin left, he had Marazin show Hafter his sword. The sage examined it with interest. His guests, he could see, were hungry and tired, so he held back the many questions that filled his mind. Before Tamin departed, he related the little he knew about what had taken place.

Heardwine had followed them to Hafter's home. The dog stayed with Marazin, reluctant to leave him. The only time it had, since its intervention to help save his life, was at the palace, a place where it was no longer welcome. The dog's constant presence beside the warrior puzzled Hafter.

As had Orvyn, the sage noticed the vague similarity, in both looks and stance, between the stranger and Amron. The man, the sword, the dog, there must be a connection between them and the king. Fate had brought them together at this time. It had to be more than coincidence. Hafter needed to know what and why. The survival of his people might depend on these reasons, and his ability to manoeuvre the right person to the correct place at a time that was auspicious for all.

Once his guests had eaten, despite the lateness of the hour, Hafter quizzed Marazin. What the young man could remember about the history of the sword and his family were the sage's main concerns. Not until the early hours of the morning did he stop. Orvyn had fallen asleep several hours earlier. Marazin struggled to keep awake. Hafter realised he had as much information as his guest could recall at this time. It was possible other details may come back to him later.

"I'm sorry," Hafter turned to Marazin, "but it isn't safe for you here. It'll not be long before Amron learns you left the palace with his father. Amron knows Tamin and I have become good friends, so my house is the logical place for him to bring you. You must be away before dawn. I'll think of something to explain your absence."

Marazin looked dismayed. He was weary, in a strange land, with nowhere to go.

"Have no worries," Hafter said, "I've somewhere in the mountains where you can stay. One of my servants will guide you there. They're completely loyal and trustworthy. No-one else knows you're here tonight."

Marazin nodded his thanks. His eyes closed. Hafter watched a candle burn through two, single hour notches before he shook his guests awake. Soon afterwards, Marazin, Orvyn and their guide were away. Long before first light, the city was far behind them.

Hafter had provided the travellers with fresh mounts, unknown to Amron's men. On little used tracks, and disguised as peasants, they passed unnoticed across the land. After five days, they reached Hafter's summer home. He would join them once the land had warmed. For now, it was too cold in the hills for his old bones.

CB 8O

Spring was several weeks old. In the last few days, Hafter had taken-up residence at his summer retreat. It was in a desolate place. Situated at the top of a ridge, there was no vantage point overlooking it — not one close enough for an observer to make out any details. Whenever strangers were in the area, Marazin and Orvyn remained closeted in their rooms. Otherwise, dressed as peasants, they explored the surrounding hills. At all times, they kept a wary look out for trouble.

News reached them that Boden and Tedrick were seeking them. Despite Amron's public declarations of how much he would like to meet with Orvyn again, or talk with Marazin, they harboured few doubts that the king had instigated the search.

Both hunters paid a visit to Hafter's town house a week after the confrontation at the palace. Over the following weeks, they visited his summer retreat several times. Under various subterfuges, they gained entry. Orvyn and Marazin remained undetected. The entrance to the fugitives' rooms, built into caverns beneath the retreat, the builder had concealed well. The visits convinced Boden that, none other than the housekeeper and her husband was resident. Tedrick was more observant. He noticed several small items the servants had failed to cover-up. Still unhappy with the situation in which he found himself, he kept silent about his observations.

With Hafter's arrival, the house took on new character. The quiet and peaceful atmosphere changed to one of bustle and noise. During the day, visitors arrived in a steady stream. Marazin and Orvyn, much to their frustration, had to spend their days below ground. In the time between their first meeting and his arrival in the mountains, Hafter had learned much. He had brought a variety of scrolls and ancient manuscripts with him. For a few days, he ignored his guests. In-between receiving visitors, he spent his time reading parchments. Only after a week of deep study did Hafter invite Marazin and Orvyn to join him for a meal. The day's final visitor had left an hour earlier.

Seated on comfortable padded seats, around a wooden trestle table, the three men enjoyed an excellent meal. Hafter ate far less than his guests. At his advanced years, he preferred to consume smaller amounts. What his age might be was unknown. If he knew, it was not something he revealed. Thin white hair sprouted over his ears and round the back of his neck, onto his shoulders. Candlelight reflected from the baldness on top. His bushy white eyebrows stood proud over deep-set, pale green eyes. His forehead was deeply lined and his face wrinkled with the creases of his years. As it was spring, he had shaved off his beard. Later in the year, when the days shortened, he would allow it to grow again. Shoulders, rounded after years of study, made Hafter appear shorter than his height of five and a half feet. Slight in build, he was tough and wiry. He could still handle a sword with a skill that would outmanoeuvre most younger men.

Heardwine, for once allowed to join them, slept on a thick rug in a corner of the room. The trio's conversation was congenial as they sampled the many dishes. They discussed the latest gossip from the palace, especially that about Amron's behaviour. It was apparent there was little improvement in his disposition, although he was becoming wiser in his use, or abuse, of power. His attitude had hardened. He was more ruthless. Such traits were advantageous rather than detrimental to his future as rebel leader; a weak king was a liability. Rumours from the south, about Betlic and his expanding empire, were more disturbing. If Amron were to succeed in his bid to build alliances, and defeat the enemy, he would have to take many painful decisions without regret.

Once the meal was over, the servants cleared the remains. The housekeeper and her helpers retired to their quarters. Hafter filled goblets with wine for his guests and himself. They settled down on cushions, beside a roaring fire. After sunset, so high in the mountains, the temperature soon dropped. After one last check that they were alone, Hafter related much of what he had uncovered over the past few months.

"It was your sword that puzzled me most," he said to Marazin. "It's a royal sword, a match to the king's and to the one taken by Betlic's men. When I was young, I taught the king's mother how to use that weapon. She was a mere child then. Her sword was familiar to me. Once you know them, you cannot mistake them for each other. Your sword is of greater length than either hers, or the king's. Each blade bears the mark of the same swordsmith.

"Ancient records show that, several centuries ago, they were a coronation gift to King Aethelmaer of Xicalima from his commanders. For generations, they remained in the family and saw much service. Never meant for show or ceremony, the swords were weapons of war, crafted to be the best."

"If they are the property of the kings of Xicalima, why has one been in my family for several generations? My parents were not royalty," Marazin said, surprised by the unexpected news.

"That's true," Hafter said, "but they were noble. Unlike Amron, you have no legitimate claim to the throne. That's his fate, but your lineage, along with that of his majesty, is traceable to the old kings of Xicalima. Your presence, at this time, is a matter of great importance."

Marazin looked at Hafter in amazement. What, he wondered, had his parents' chest contained? Heardwine opened an eye for a moment, closed it and went back to sleep.

"How do you know all this?" Marazin asked.

"Shortly before you arrived here with the rebels, a messenger brought me an old leather-bound volume, the Book of Gryphrata. He refused to tell me from whom it came; only that it was imperative I read it. After I'd spoken to you, I took time to study the tome. I soon realised that, if its content was correct, many of my assumptions were wrong. It's taken me until now to uncover the whole story, or as much of it as it's possible to find. I had to go back a long way in the records. Even now, the details are sparse, no more than a basic outline of events. There's a copy of a codicil attached to a testament left by your, and Amron's, common great, great grandfather, King Wyman. In it is a bequest leaving the sword to your great grandfather. In a letter, the king explains why.

"The note tells of his misspent youth, before he ascended to the throne, and the much sowing of wild seed. As fate would have it, one of his liaisons bore fruit. At the same time, his parents, after a long search, found him a suitable match in marriage. Although the prince was a wild youth, he had great fondness for this young mistress. He found a place for her to live during her confinement. The poor woman died in childbirth and left him with a baby boy. It was impossible for him to return to the palace with a child. His marriage was weeks away. Neither would his sense of honour allow him to abandon the infant.

"A solution presented itself to the prince. He took it without hesitation. The mother was staying at the home of an impoverished young noble and his wife. The couple, unable to have children themselves, offered to care for the child as if it was their own. A grateful prince agreed. On his return to the capital and, later, when he ascended to the throne he made generous settlements on the family. King Wyman went on to have a legitimate son by his wife, from whom Amron's line descends. The first-born, illegitimate child, also fathered a son, from whose line you are the latest generation."

"If all this is true, then I've no claim to the throne, nor anything else, except a possible title and some land in Xicalima. How can my presence be of significance to anybody?"

"Ah! Because you are the one to whom the Mastig will reveal its secrets. For long I believed it was Amron. Now I know differently. It is his duty to rally his subjects and lead them into battle against Betlic. Your obligation is to take advantage of the chaos, and find the means to defeat the man, his talisman and the mantle."

Orvyn had kept silent throughout the exchange, but he had payed close attention to everything Hafter said.

"What's a Mastig?" he asked.

"Of that I've no direct knowledge," Hafter answered after a moment.

"Could it be Heardwine?" Marazin asked as the dog opened its eyes and stretched. It moved closer to rest its massive head on his foot.

"No, it's an object of some kind rather than a living creature," Hafter said. "I believe the dog is connected, somehow, but only as a protector. It brought Amron through to safety with his subjects, because he was heir to the throne, and of great importance in the battles to come. That strengthened my belief he was the chosen one, but, as you can see, once Marazin arrived, the dog turned its attention to its true master."

"This Mastig, what has it to do with me?" Marazin was curious to know.

"The true line of the heirs to the Mastig, is through the first-born of the present incumbent; male, female, legitimate or otherwise. I had thought it passed always to the monarch or his heir. Only when I delved into Marazin's past, did I realise the truth. With the help of the book, going back further I discovered the line of succession has moved between peasant to noble and back again several times. When it passed to royalty, it was by marriage."

"All this is fascinating, but what does it mean for me?" Marazin asked again.

The thought of responsibility did not daunt him. On the contrary, the story had aroused his interest. It explained, too, why his grandparents sent away his parents from the fighting in Xicalima. His own father had been the previous heir. This was what Marazin was to learn on his return, but his father had died in the fire first.

"Again, I'm unsure," Hafter said. "Before you can fulfil your task, if I'm correct, an element you need is missing. Without it, you'll be unable to find the Mastig. That's why I want Orvyn to undertake a mission for me."

"My pleasure, Hafter," Orvyn became alert. His confinement inside the house had been too long. He craved a change from the monotony of his daily life.

"Somewhere, south of the mountains, between here and Xicalima, are people who guard this element. Who these persons are, I cannot tell you, I only know how you can find them. I want you to speak with them on my behalf. To convince them of your authenticity, I will supply you with documents that should provide sufficient proof. What you learn will allow me to plan our future moves. More than that, I hope whomsoever you find will return with you and bring with them the object they possess."

"I will do whatever is necessary," Orvyn said. "When do I leave?"

"Be ready to ride at first light. I've a spare horse and ample supplies. The mountain passes have been clear for a while. You must avoid contact with your fellow countrymen. There are those who, for a price, or out of misplaced loyalty, would pass details of your whereabouts to Boden and Tedrick. On the other side of the mountains, you'll be much safer. There are a few Xicaliman patrols roaming the foothills but, if you take care as you travel, you should avoid them. Once out on the plains, these hazards will be behind you."

Chapter Sixteen

Dawn. The heavens blazed with colour. Clouds streaked with red, purple, yellow and orange were interspersed with flashes of the palest of blues. Leisurely they floated towards the lone rider, rising as they approached the mountain slopes he travelled. Far below, a layer of mist undulated over the plains. Giving the appearance of islands in a calm sea, strange misshapen towers of natural rock and distant hills protruded from the miasma. It was a spectacular start to the day. One that foretold a change of weather before it ended. The sun rose above the horizon and, through a break in the cloud, its rays dazzled Orvyn. The colours faded as the sun rose higher. Its intensity overpowered the rider's eyes whenever it escaped the layers of vapour.

Orvyn guided his horse down the steep, rocky slopes. Soon he would reach the Plains of Zefreelah. His ride, through the Mogallean Mountains, would be at an end. Two weeks earlier, he had taken his leave of Hafter and Marazin. Since then, Orvyn's sole human contact had been with a Xicaliman patrol, returning to base after a period of duty at the mountains' edge.

Here, luck favoured him. The party he met consisted of men who, in the past, had served under him. They were sympathetic to his current difficulties. Rumours that Boden and Tedrick were on a mission had reached even their ears. Whether this undertaking was at the pair's own volition or at the direction of the king, no-one knew. The court had issued hasty denials of these 'scurrilous lies', which, to many, gave them even greater credence.

The patrol's commander, an arrogant spiteful individual, had gone on ahead. Because of the troops past association with Orvyn, they believed Amron had handpicked the new man to keep a watchful eye on them. The group was in no mind to capture or inform on their old leader. More helpful still, they knew the expected whereabouts, and movements, of the patrol that relieved them. This knowledge had enabled Orvyn to avoid any further contacts and, so he believed, sightings of him.

As the morning advanced, the mist lifted to reveal the hidden plains. Verdant grassland stretched as far as Orvyn could see. On the edge of a vast scree slope, a steep rock-strewn path came into view. He turned towards it. Lower down, the trail descended between a rocky outcrop on the left and a boulder, the size of a large building, to the right.

As he entered the gap, the sun reappeared. Aligned with the opening, the glare blinded him. He nudged his horse down the uneven slope. As loose stones shifted and rocked beneath the animal's weight, its hooves slipped and skidded. To shield his eyes with one hand, and control the reins with the other, demanded all of Orvyn's concentration. So much so that, when his mount bucked, the crashing blow that caught him between the shoulder blades took him by surprise.

༄ ༅

Since the early hours of the morning, Boden had been lying in wait. The previous evening, from a point high above the trail, he had watched Orvyn set up camp. To be in front of his prey, the hunter had spent half the night, riding a wide circuit so as not to be overheard. After combing the area a few days earlier, looking for tracks, the assassin was familiar with its topography.

Boden was without Tedrick's support. He disputed the idea the fugitives would try to escape over the mountains. Instead, he had decided to continue his search much closer to the Xicaliman stronghold. Boden was happier away from his fellow hunter. Tedrick had proved to be a reluctant participant, with little or no enthusiasm for the task entrusted to them.

The gap, down through which the main trail cut, was close to where Boden had tethered his horse. Several clefts and crevices made the climb from the lower end of the outcrop a simple task. A tapered vertical crevice, leading back from a narrow ledge overlooking the path, offered the ideal place for concealment. The confined space and poor angle did not allow for the use of a bow. The distance was too great for him to be certain of striking a mounted man below with a sword. A leap, onto his victim's back, was impractical. If Boden missed, or landed awkwardly against the rock walls, he could be hurt as much, if not more, than his intended target. These concerns Boden took into consideration when he selected his ambush spot.

In the tree-lined hollow where he had left his horse, a few hundred paces away across the hillside, he found a suitable branch from the dozens that littered the ground. It took little time to fashion a long-handled club with a heavy stone strapped to the business end. One solid blow against Orvyn's head would render him unconscious or, if Boden was lucky, crush the man's skull. It was a measure of the hunter's character he dismissed any thought of a fair fight. Although a highly skilled and renowned swordsman, he preferred to incapacitate his victims from ambush. If necessary, at his leisure, he could finish the job against a weakened foe.

A Xicaliman by birth, Boden had spent much of his adult life working as a mercenary. Apart from to himself, his loyalty was to the highest bidder. Had Amron's arrival with the rebels been a month or so later, it was probable Boden would be in Betlic's service already. The killer might yet change sides once the reward was his.

There would be generous recompense from Betlic, for information about the Xicaliman rebels and their defences. Knowledge Boden was more than happy to provide. A more astute person might have considered that Amron, fearful of his involvement becoming public knowledge, might solve his predicament by having his agent summarily executed. This would leave his majesty free to express outrage at the murder of Orvyn. It was well documented that Amron wanted to renew his acquaintance with his one-time aide. His majesty would not allow Boden the slightest opportunity to tell his side of the story.

The sound of hooves echoed through the gap. The sun in the rider's eyes made it difficult for him to see anything ahead. Boden steadied himself, his back wedged deep into the crevice. He was ready. A horse's head came into view. Its rider, Orvyn, followed into Boden's line of vision. On silent feet, he stepped forward onto the edge of the ledge. He swung the club, aimed at the back of Orvyn's head.

Whether it was the enemy's presence above, or the whir of the club through the air that alarmed the horse, no-one would ever know. In fright, the animal sprang upwards, taking its rider with it. The sudden change in position meant Orvyn's shoulders received the blow intended for his skull. Hurtled from the saddle, he struck his head against the rock wall to his right. The horse ran off, to leave Orvyn motionless on the ground. Blood poured from a gash in his cheek.

Boden cursed at his missed strike. As he looked down, his scowl turned to a smile. The result was better than feared; his victim was unconscious. A bloody stream trickled beneath his head. There was no sign of movement. Orvyn was down and helpless. Boden could not even be sure the man was breathing. The drop was too great to risk a leap onto the uneven rocky ground. In haste, Boden clambered over the shelf to descend by the way he had come.

With sword drawn, he ran round the outcrop to the path. Boden froze. Orvyn was missing. All that remained was a pool of blood where he had lain. A wavering trail of red droplets led up the slope towards the upper end of the boulder to his left. The splashes disappeared round the far corner of the stone face.

Careful to make no noise, Boden moved uphill. Orvyn must be aware of what had happened. If not waiting for him, he would be attempting to escape. The man must be hurt badly, so the latter was the most probable. Apart from injuries sustained in the fall, the club would have caused severe damage to Orvyn's back muscles. He would be lucky if he could lift his sword. To have the dexterity to defend himself with it was unlikely. Boden grinned in anticipation. The reward was his alone. Tedrick would miss out. The fool should have accompanied him.

The would-be assassin might have been less confident had he the ability to see round corners. Although battered and winded, his victim was without serious injury. From a ragged gash across his right cheek, blood poured down his face. A mass of grazes and bruises covered his right arm and leg. His attacker's blow had glanced across Orvyn's shoulders. The horse's sudden, violent manoeuvre had thrown him from the saddle; the club had only aided the process. Orvyn shook his head to clear it. Although unsure what had struck him, experience told him the blow could not have been accidental. Someone had attacked him. His sword was out; he was ready for whoever might come round the corner.

He did not have long to wait. The faint sound of a boot scraping across a stone gave him warning. He was already moving when a figure leapt into view. Orvyn struck savagely with his sword. Boden's reactions were quick. He threw his body sideways. The razor-sharp edge of Orvyn's blade drew a line of blood across his target's upper arm. The cut was deep. Had it struck as intended, it would have been deadly. Orvyn recognised his opponent. The man was both a swordsman and a killer. On both counts, Orvyn dared show no mercy.

Boden landed heavily on his side. Before he could retaliate, Orvyn struck again. This time his blow was more lethal. His sword sliced down Boden's chest. Using both hands and all his weight, Orvyn rammed the weapon deep into his opponent's abdomen. When he pulled it free, Boden tried to stand, but he had lost control of his lower body. It wasn't supposed to happen this way. Something was wrong with him. Liquid, hot and warm ran down his side. He attempted a slice at Orvyn's legs. The strength had gone from his arms. With ease, Orvyn sidestepped the feeble blow then plunged his own bloody sword straight through the heart of his intended assassin. Boden died at his feet, disbelief visible on his face.

Orvyn fell back against the rock. The fall had shaken him; the adrenalin pumping through his veins did not help. Now the need for it was over, he felt faint, sick and lightheaded. He ached all the way down his right side. A couple of teeth were loose. Orvyn could taste blood inside his mouth, as well as feel it trickling down his face. His knees gave way. He sat, heavily, near the body of Boden. For several minutes, Orvyn remained on the ground, head between his knees. As the feelings of nausea left him, he sat upright, wincing at the movement.

Back on his feet, Orvyn went in search of his horse. The animal had bolted. For now, he was on his own. The first thing that caught his eye was a club, lying to one side, near to where he had fallen. After striking the blow, Boden had dropped it. If that was what had hit him, Orvyn realised, it was no wonder his shoulders ached.

He retraced his steps. There was a deep hollow at the side of the rock, behind which he had waited for his attacker. Into this depression, he threw the club. Moments later, he rolled Boden's body on top of it. The killer's sword soon followed.

Orvyn scouted around the edge of the outcrop. He discovered Boden's tracks leading across the hillside. Sword in hand, Orvyn followed them towards a group of trees. It was probable Boden had been alone. He would not otherwise have risked a solo ambush; he had a reputation for never taking unnecessary risks.

After scrambling to the edge of a hollow, Orvyn found a horse tethered to a tree. Close by was Boden's saddle and supplies. Far below, beside a stream, Orvyn's horse grazed on lush grassland. He had no wish to take Boden's horse with him on his journey. Despite its rider's murderous ways, he had been a confidant of the king. If the rebels found Orvyn in possession of the animal, he would be in serious trouble. Even without proof that Orvyn had harmed its master, out of spite, Amron might hang him as a horse thief. But, before he could set the animal free, he needed it to retrieve his own.

He saddled Boden's horse. Once he had collected the dead man's belongings, Orvyn rode down to the plains. After a little hesitation, his own horse came to his call. He wasted no time in transferring the dead man's possessions to it. With a loud cry, Orvyn slapped hard the rump of the killer's mount. He turned away as it raced off.

It was the middle of the day; dark clouds were building in the east. The breeze had strengthened and chilled. Orvyn was unwell. His body ached. The wound on his cheek stung with the sweat running into it. His right arm and leg, where he had grazed them, felt to be on fire. He clambered onto his horse. Back up the trail, he threw Boden's belongings alongside his body.

Over to his left, high above the hollow containing the body, the scree slope stretched across the mountainside. A large rock perched on a ledge above it. Orvyn rode up the trail, then dismounted to lead his horse towards the object. He tried to push over the boulder. It was far too heavy for him to move. He found a log and manoeuvred it to the place. Using a smaller stone as a fulcrum, he was able to set the boulder rocking. One final time he heaved against the log. This time, the boulder tipped. The ground gave way beneath it. Both it and the log rolled down the hillside at high speed.

The boulder, as intended, set a small area of scree into movement. Rapidly it slid down the slope to fill the hollow and its surrounding area. Before the movement stopped, the vibration loosened the scree to either side of the original fall. With a roar, which became deafening, it fell away, spreading further and further out. The ground shook. Orvyn grabbed hold of his horse's reins. He held on as the animal, frightened by the noise, tried to escape. The racket stopped and the dust cleared. The horse settled, but its nostrils flared and its tail lay flat against its hind legs. It sensed there was danger still to come.

Orvyn, pre-occupied with the chaos he had caused, held tight the reins but otherwise ignored the animal. He looked over the rim. No-one was going to find Boden's body. Any evidence as to where or who had put it there was gone. A deep layer of detritus from the rockslide covered the gap between the rocks. The hollow and Boden's body were no longer visible. Lower down, the slide had triggered further, extensive falls. These had swept out onto the plains. Half the surface of the hillside had given way. The trail had disappeared. Orvyn would have to find a different, more secure route to the lower ground.

He looked towards his right where the land curved outwards. It was a few moments before he realised the ground beneath the layer of earth, on which he stood, had itself collapsed. There was little depth left to support the unstable ledge. Even as he looked, several hundred paces away, the lip began to break away. The collapse of the overhang gathered momentum as it moved towards him. The slope above was too steep for them to escape that way. His horse was pulling and jerking his arm. Orvyn, turned, grabbed tight the reins, then ran towards more solid ground.

The sounds of falling rubble grew ever louder, until no longer could he hear the pounding of his feet over the noise. Safety, beyond where the scree slope had been, was paces away from him. Beneath his feet, the lip was crumbling. With a final effort, he reached stable ground. His horse scrabbled for a foothold as the earth collapsed beneath its hind legs. Orvyn yanked hard on the reins. With one last kick, the animal gained firmer footing. Relieved, Orvyn led his trembling horse away, thankful that both of them were unharmed.

Once he found the path Boden had used, Orvyn turned his horse onto the trail, which he followed down to the plains. On the grassland, the tracks made by his horse when it had bolted, and those where he had ridden Boden's horse, were gone. Debris covered the whole area.

To a tracker, it would appear Boden had ridden to the bottom of the slope, where the rock-fall had overwhelmed him. Perhaps Boden had set up camp and been unable to reach his horse in time? The tracks left by the panicked gait of the riderless animal, as it raced away from the area, were visible. As Orvyn's tracks had come after the event, he would be seen to be blameless in regard to Boden's demise.

The wind had intensified. It was the start of summer but, despite the season, the air had a cold, cutting edge. High above, dark clouds covered the land. Lower down, pale grey ragged wisps scudded overhead. Faint drops of rain carried on the breeze. Orvyn felt no better. Riding jarred his injured muscles, many of which only now he was aware. His head ached. There was nothing more he wanted than to rest until morning. It could not be.

The main trail, which ran parallel to the mountains, lay ahead of him. From the information passed on to him by the patrol, Orvyn knew their replacements would make a sweep of this area soon. Before they did, he must be far away. If caught, his old company assured him, he would suffer no harm; but all patrols had instructions to place him into protective custody 'for his own safety'. His return to the rebel stronghold would follow soon afterwards. There, no doubt, Tedrick would be on hand to finish the job Boden had failed to complete.

Orvyn dug in his heels and continued his journey. He rode east, into the wind, away from the mountains. As the afternoon progressed, the weather became more inclement. Orvyn knew it was too dangerous to stop. By nightfall, he would be some distance from the path of the patrol. He could rest then. From his pack, he removed a thick, dark-brown leather cloak. He wrapped it round himself then pulled its hood over his head. Cold, wet, aching all over, he was utterly miserable. His mount, head and tail down, looked as wretched as its master.

Close to dark, the clouds had blown clear, the brightest stars already flickering in the heavens. The air was cooler and fresher. Orvyn reined in. When he tried to dismount, it was closer to the truth to say he fell from his horse. His muscles had tightened and stiffened. He groaned in agony as he unsaddled the animal. Picketed on a long rope, he left it within reach of a nearby stream. The trickling water ran into a gulley. In wetter times, to one side of this, the flow had worn away the slope, creating a ledge and a cut-out, which curved upwards and outwards.

There was ample room for Orvyn and his supplies. He drank from the stream. A few mouthfuls of cold meat sufficed for a meal. The moss-covered surface under the gap was soft and spongy to the touch. He spread his cloak over the ground then wrapped a blanket round himself. His wounds would have to wait until morning. For now, should he find a comfortable position, his greatest need was sleep.

Chapter Seventeen

Overnight, Orvyn slept little. Daybreak was not far away when he slipped into a brief, but much-needed, slumber. Not too long afterwards, as the sun hovered low in the early morning sky, he stirred. Birdsong filled the air. Cold and shivering, he feared a fever. He opened his eyes, to discover a sparkling white layer covered the land. A late frost. He stretched, an action he regretted straight away. A night spent on damp ground had not been beneficial for his injuries.

In a shower of white crystals, Orvyn threw off his blanket. With muscles that protested, he thrust himself to his feet. He limped towards the stream, to a place where the sun's rays had melted the bank's icy coating. He attempted to strip. The grazes to his arm and leg had started to heal. He soaked these areas and eased his garments free from them.

He was grateful that his breeches and jacket were of leather, instead of wool; otherwise, the damage to his flesh, from the ambush, would have been much more severe. Before dressing his injuries, Orvyn bathed them with care. He was thankful, too, when near the mountains' end, he had collected moss from the boggy moorland pastures. The vegetation proved effective in soothing his wounds.

His proximity to the foothills was still too close to risk a fire. Over the plains, smoke would be visible for great distances. It could attract the attention of rebel patrols, or one of the many bands of outlaws that frequented the region. After a cold breakfast, he resumed his journey. Hafter had provided him with a rough guide, a map of sorts. It contained directions, sufficient to take Orvyn to the first landmark he sought — a hill with a conical outline.

Somewhere, in its vicinity, he would find a set of coded instructions. He had no clues to their exact location. Once there, he would have to search the whole area for them. With the map came a key, to enable him to decipher what should be another set of directions. Hafter had assured Orvyn that, with this information, he would discover a different key, one that would help him decode the next set he came to, and so on until he reached his ultimate destination. Only then would he know the final number of sets. There, the person and item he sought would await him. Then, the answer as to what manner of object was the Mastig and, of more importance, its location, should become clearer. Such was Hafter's belief.

For a few days, while his flesh healed, of necessity Orvyn's progress was slow. As his discomfort lessened; the distances he covered each day extended. Soon the mountains were far behind him.

Late one evening, Orvyn, now recovered but weary after a long day's ride, eased himself from the saddle. Ahead of him, across a wide valley, was the hill he believed to be the one marked on his map. The moon's phase was the same as when Borden attacked. To Orvyn, it seemed much longer than a month since then. Moonlight, reflecting from one side of the rocky surface of the hill, set it glowing against the night sky.

A stream flowed through the area, alongside which grew isolated clumps of trees. In one such spot, Orvyn chose to spend the night. With abundant dead wood among the undergrowth to use as fuel, he lit a fire. At the edge of the blaze, he roasted the remains of a deer he had killed a few days earlier.

The past week had been scorching hot. Cloudless skies and lack of wind had made the heat unbearable. As soon as his meat was ready, Orvyn doused the flames. Away from the warmth of the ashes, the night air, for once, was cool and pleasant, freshened by a light breeze that had sprung out of the east. Tonight, he would eat and sleep well. As the sparks died, a voice from out of the darkness startled him. In an instant, he was on his guard.

"Please, may I join you?" Again, the person called out.

The accent was strange but the language familiar. The voice, was that of a child. Orvyn, his back against a tree, a hand on his sword, was wary for any sign of trickery.

"If you wish," Orvyn replied. "Make sure your hands are empty and where I can see them."

A few moments later, a rustle in the grasses on the opposite bank of the stream signalled the closeness of his visitor. Soon afterwards, visible in the moonlight, a young boy paddled across towards him. The stranger appeared to be unaccompanied. A strong odour wafted towards Orvyn, a combination of sheep mixed with sweat.

"My camp's at the other side the valley," the lad said, as he came to stand near to the embers. "I saw your fire," he added in explanation. "You're the first to visit this place since I arrived. It was late last winter when my father and I left home. For many weeks, we travelled north with a flock of sheep for summer grazing. Once I was settled, my father returned to our village. Since then, I've been on my own."

"These plains, with their plentiful supply of grass, must stretch much nearer to your people. Why bring your flock such a long distance?" There was a sharp, less than friendly edge to Orvyn's voice.

He was distrustful. It seemed strange to abandon a boy, as young as this, in such a manner. At most, he could be no older than ten. Orvyn remained uneasy. He fingered the hilt of his weapon as his eyes searched the surrounding land. Bright moonlight bathed the area, which left many parts of the terrain deep in shadow. Any number of people could be hidden by the darkness out there. The boy sensed the man's mistrust. The young one's anxiety increased as, transfixed, he watched Orvyn's fist clench and unclench around his sword hilt.

"I'm sorry, I shouldn't have disturbed you," the child said. Frightened, he stumbled over his words. "In other years, we've stayed nearer to home. There we have plenty of pasture within easy reach, enough to last us for the whole year. This season, my father became worried about events taking place in Xicalima. He said, if Betlic moves north, it would be safer here for my flock and me. I'm to stay until word comes for me to return, or my father, my brothers and sisters join me." His gaze remained fixed on the sword at Orvyn's side. "Please, please don't hurt me. I was so lonely on my own. I've had no-one to talk to since father left."

The child's plea, and unconcealed terror in his voice, penetrated Orvyn's own worries. He looked closer at his visitor. A white faced, terrified child stared back. The boy was trembling. Tears welled in the corners of his eyes. Orvyn relaxed. His expression softened. He released his grip on the sword. It took courage to walk up to a stranger's campsite in the dark. Orvyn smiled. He put out a hand in greeting. Grateful, the young lad stepped forward and accepted it.

"I'm sorry, I frightened you. Betlic's men concern me too. I'm wary of a trap. Come and join me. You're welcome to share my meal. I'm Orvyn," he added.

"My name's Sheply," the boy said, a shy smile of relief on his face.

"What of your mother? You never mentioned her. Is she not to join you?"

"No, raiders took and killed her when they entered our village late last year. My father says it was Betlic's men, returning from a mission. They rode in one night, stole food, valuables and kidnapped several of the local women. In the attack, many villagers suffered injuries and two died. The following day, those men who were able, armed themselves and tracked the raiders. They found the women several miles away. All were dead." A tear rolled down Sheply's cheek.

Orvyn wished he had left the question unasked. It was probable that a boy, so young, would be unaware of all that would have happened to them. Orvyn had little doubt. The raiders would use, abuse and then, when finished, dispose of their captives. He wondered whether the party was the same one that had attacked Amron's village and murdered everyone there. It would have been the right time of year. Far to the south of here, Sheply's home would be close to one of the most direct routes back to Xicalima. The boy's story made Orvyn more determined than ever to complete his mission. He would do everything he could to thwart Betlic's ambitions.

They talked for a while, or rather Sheply chattered without restraint. He had been on his own for so long, with only the company of his sheep, a friendly ear encouraged him to disclose much about his life, family and home. In time, his head drooped. His eyelids became heavy as tiredness overcame him. Orvyn was anxious that the boy's charges might be in danger. Without their shepherd to watch over them, would they be safe? Sheply yawned. No predator, so he said, would take advantage during his absence. His dog guarded the flock. The animal was large and well-trained. Since it was a puppy, the boy had been its master. It was fiercely loyal to its owner, and all associated with him.

Within minutes, Sheply had fallen hard asleep. Orvyn covered him with a blanket. For a while, sleep eluded the traveller. He thought long about what he had learned. The boy would suffer the loneliness even more when Orvyn left in the morning. He could do nothing to alter that. There were other, more compelling matters for him to attend.

Orvyn shared an early breakfast with his guest. In daylight, the boy's features were clearer. Fresh faced, his fair hair grew long. Half Orvyn's height, the lad was slim and wiry, his muscles hardened by his work with the flock. Sheply was sad to say goodbye. Last evening's companionship had brought home to him how solitary his existence had become.

"Where do you go now?" Sheply asked.

"I'm on a mission, but first I have to visit the hill over there. There's something on it I have to find if I am to progress."

"Do you mean the writing by the waterfall? It makes no sense to anyone, or so my father said. Although I can't read, before he left for home he showed me the marks. Some say they hide a great mystery, which no-one, scholar or otherwise, has been able to understand. Father says most people think it's a hoax, which someone chiselled on the wall for fun. Had it any importance, they believe someone would have worked-out its meaning years ago."

"It's possible that's what I'm looking for. Can you show it to me, or tell me how to find it? That would be helpful and save me a great deal of time."

"I'll take you there," Sheply replied, a wide grin across his face. "It will be a pleasure, although you'll think it a waste of time once you've seen it."

It seemed the boy would have company for a while longer. Without further delay, Orvyn packed away his possessions. After a final look round, he mounted his horse. He leaned down to scoop up the shepherd boy and place him on the saddle in front of him. They crossed the stream then cantered towards the hill. As they approached the opposite side of the valley, Orvyn saw several large grazed areas. Spread across one was Sheply's flock. A large dog kept its watchful eye over them. Whenever sheep wandered too close to the edge, the guardian darted across to bring them nearer the centre.

The dog became aware of the advancing horse. It raced towards them, its teeth bared. Sheply whistled. He called out. The animal slowed its pace and barked a welcome. Its tail wagged in greeting. The boy shouted instructions; tail down, it returned to its duty. From a distance, it watched its young master ride away with the stranger. With reluctance, the dog stayed with the flock. As the child said, he had trained it well. It was a brutish animal, with powerful muscles. With that beast to protect him, Orvyn envied no-one who threatened harm to the boy.

A faint path led the riders away from the valley. It wound its way up the steep hillside, to the ridge above. Now Orvyn was closer to the hill, it was much higher than at first sight it had appeared. For a short distance, the trail followed the line of the ridge, before it moved to one side then started to climb. As the path ascended, it took them round to the rear of the hill. They crossed a fast-flowing beck. On the other side, the way turned sharp left. It followed the torrent upstream. Soon they entered a steep-sided gully. Here they dismounted and Orvyn picketed the horse. The path ahead was too steep and narrow to risk taking the animal.

Sheply stepped out. Nimble of foot, he made easy work of the steepest slopes where they had to scramble. Less agile, Orvyn cursed when he slipped and banged his knee against a boulder. By now, Sheply was some distance in front. As soon as he realised he was on his own, he perched on a ledge and waited for his companion to catch up to him. It was hard going. Orvyn dreaded the return. After one difficult passage over loose stones, followed by a wet and greasy ascent of a pitted and cracked rock face, Orvyn pulled himself up onto a gently rising, rocky slope. They had reached the head of the gully. A few hundred paces away he could see their destination. A plume of water hurtled down a sheer rock face. The spray carried in his direction. Looking up, Orvyn could see it was the last of a series of falls, which started much higher. Sheply, who was further along, beckoned to his companion.

"This way," the lad called. "We're almost there."

Orvyn hurried after him as the boy ran over to the right of the falls. Fifty paces from where the water crashed onto the rocks, there was a vertical cleft in the cliff. It was as wide as two hay carts side by side. As Orvyn stepped into the gap, on either side of him, he could make out hundreds of marks cut into the stone. The walls were sheer and smooth, the cuts deep and sharply defined. Words covered one wall. Although the letters were familiar to him, on inspection they appeared bunched, at random, in groups of five. On the opposite wall, were several more blocks of similar symbols. These encircled a crudely executed mass of meaningless, chiselled lines and curves.

Without Hafter's explanation of how to use the key to the cypher, Orvyn would have been at a loss to determine any meaning from these inscriptions. He took out his map. On the reverse, the sage had written the key. It was a series of numbers, in blocks of three. The first number indicated the row, the second the block and, the third, the letter position within the block. Orvyn had brought a small leather-bound package with him from his pack. Sheply looked on as his companion untied the leather binding to unroll the contents. Inside were several pieces of blank vellum, a small leather ink flask and several quills.

Orvyn uncorked the flask then set it on the ground. After he had dipped a quill into the container, in small print he wrote on a sheet of vellum. With care, he entered each word as he deciphered it, letter by letter, from the writing on the wall. It was mid-morning before he had completed his task to his satisfaction.

The hardest part had been copying the relevant parts of the mass of lines to his page. His ability to read and write was much greater than his drawing skills. The script, which surrounded the lines on the wall, detailed the sequence he should use to reproduce each of the selected marks. When done, Orvyn had a rough map, to go with the directions he had written first.

What took him the longest time, was to copy the key for the set he would find when he reached his new destination. This was a series of letters. Each one represented a number, with some numbers represented by more than one letter. Without a key, this made the code more difficult to decipher. In the set, he copied, he found numbers were represented by different letters to those in Hafter's key. He checked his work with care. On arrival at his next destination, he could ill afford to discover he had made a mistake.

Being illiterate, Sheply was in awe of Orvyn. The stranger had made sense of what had been a mystery to all in the memory of the living. From the squiggles on the wall, he had created a map. Script might be beyond the boy's knowledge, but maps were not. For as long as Sheply could remember, his father had drawn basic ones, most often with a stick in the ground. He had taught his children how to follow them and had encouraged them to create their own. Orvyn folded the completed drawing before Sheply had chance to study it. It left the boy with a brief tantalising glimpse, but no clear details of its route nor destination.

Satisfied everything he had copied was correct, Orvyn placed his original map with the remaining blank sheets of vellum. He wrapped them round the recorked ink flask and quill. He secured the package inside his jacket, along with his new chart and directions. It was time to leave. Orvyn cringed at the thought of the descent to come.

Much to his surprise, the return was easier than feared. Although he slipped several times and banged his knee again, he reached his horse without major mishap. Sheply, who had the ability of a mountain goat, was waiting for him at the bottom. Orvyn's new route would take him east again. At the base of the gulley, they parted company. Sheply managed a wan smile as Orvyn waved goodbye. The boy's crestfallen look was not one he could disguise.

"Until we meet again, my young friend," Orvyn called back with a last wave.

His words were sincere — he did hope to see Sheply again. Without the boy's help, Orvyn knew he could have wasted many days, if not weeks, in exploration of the area before he discovered the right place.

"Until then." The faint sound of Sheply's voice reached Orvyn as he vanished from sight, behind the curving hillside.

Chapter Eighteen

With the aid of his latest map, and the directions transcribed, Orvyn followed an easterly route. The trail passed beyond the hill he had climbed with the shepherd boy, onto a narrow belt of rock-strewn moorland. The ground began to dip. He descended a grassy slope to rejoin the plains. For several weeks, he rode across wide open grasslands, shallow valleys and low ridges. Rivers, which flowed throughout the land, were plentiful. After a prolonged period of dry weather, their levels were low enough to make them easy to cross. Away from the watercourses, the grasses yellowed and wilted under the heat of the sun.

It was a summer hotter than any Orvyn could remember since childhood. Twice, the humidity in the air became oppressive. Columns of cloud towered high as the atmosphere became charged. The sky darkened and took on a greenish hue, a portent of the thunder, lightning and rain to follow. At the first signs, Orvyn hunted for cover.

Among the details of his route, for the most part accurate, were descriptions of various landmarks that would appear along his way. One, a rock pillar, had collapsed. The resulting mound proved adequate for his needs. Apart from wildlife, most of the land he travelled remained uninhabited. From time to time, he came across roadways, some that appeared to have seen much use. On rare occasions, he glimpsed flocks of sheep, but seldom with anyone visibly in attendance.

Certain areas he approached made him feel uneasy. Cautious that he may not be alone, he kept a wide distance between them and himself. This was a no-man's land, far away from any centre of population. There was no law, apart from the rule of the strongest and the fittest. Solitary herders, if genuine, posed little threat, but Orvyn was mindful of the risks. Betlic's agents could be anywhere, in any occupation. The traveller would prefer not to arouse the curiosity of such people.

In open country, Orvyn found tracks made by several mounted groups. These, like him, might have cause to avoid the main highways. He had to accept the possibility that some of them might be adherents of Betlic. Hafter had convinced Orvyn of the despot's intention to create a vast empire. Over the past year, numerous reports had emerged that Betlic's forces had overrun many smaller nations, to the south of Xicalima. His scouts might be anywhere, seeking to locate the best routes for incorporation into his future invasion plans.

One evening, to avoid one such group, Orvyn found it necessary to make a rapid diversion. It was providential he was between them and the setting sun. Blinded by the intense glare, they failed to detect him as, below the skyline, he rode. From a vantage point, he observed the trail through the dry and brittle branches of the scrub at the edge of the hollow where he had taken cover. In a hurry, Betlic's men galloped by, more intent on their destination than their surroundings. Despite this, Orvyn was not about to take any unnecessary risks. Almost dusk, he thought it probable the enemy would halt soon for the night, possibly within earshot. He decided to spend the night in the hollow.

The following morning, to give Betlic's men abundant time to break camp, Orvyn waited until the sun had risen high before he set off. By the time he rejoined the trail, they were nowhere to be seen or heard. He was nearing the end of his latest map. His destination could not be too far away.

On the fifth day, after a strenuous ride, Orvyn brought his horse to a halt. In front of him stood a house; its former splendour crumbled long ago. He studied the ruins with interest. They were set at the edge of an arid valley, one he had travelled since early yesterday. From the dry, deep and wide riverbed at the vale's centre, it appeared water had been plentiful once. All along the way, the remains of abandoned homes and villages dotted the landscape. Signs of ancient cultivation were plain. When the river failed, the consequences must have been disastrous for those who depended upon it for their livelihoods.

This time, the instructions on where to find his new set of directions, were more detailed. Much of what remained of the timber-framed house, with its mud and wattle walls, was in danger of collapse. Only a stone-built hearth and chimney were structurally secure. The roof had fallen in, its thatching rotted with most of it blown away. The building had been large, one in which a person of high status would have dwelt. Leading from the main hall, where most of the day-to-day living, dining and business would have taken place, were several rooms. The notes told Orvyn which one he needed to clear. It was late in the day, the atmosphere hot and oppressive. In the saddle since dawn, he was weary. The work would have to wait until morning, when both he and the air might be fresher.

By first light, Orvyn had risen and eaten. He hoped soon to be on his way again. Clear blue skies held promise of a day at least as searing as recent ones. If so, he had insufficient water in his canteen to last until evening. In this dry valley, his horse, too, needed a share of the precious liquid. Without his steed, he would be lucky to survive long enough to find another. This morning, he had a gentle breeze to cool him. Stripped to the waist, Orvyn entered the ruins.

Opposite to the main entrance was the room he wanted. He cleared a way through to it. Here, roof timbers, and accumulated debris, lay strewn haphazardly over the warped remnants of a wooden floor. This he must remove before he could hope to discover what he sought. With his energy refreshed, Orvyn set to with enthusiasm. He turned, twisted and yanked at the beams until they came free. Once he had separated and thrown out a few, he found he had more space to manoeuvre the remaining pieces of debris; his pace increased.

By mid-morning only a few floorboards, and the joists beneath, remained for him to loosen, lift and remove. The supports, similar to the main roof timbers, were large and heavy. It was hard work for one man. Sweat poured down his body. His precious supply of water was dropping rapidly. Unless he found a fresh source soon, he risked dehydration.

With a splintering crash, the final joist landed on a pile of rubble, one that had grown steadily outside the main entrance. Orvyn walked back to the emptied room, where he stepped down onto the exposed hard ground. It was nothing more than a bed of clay. Nowhere could he see any sign of writing. Outside, after rechecking his instructions, he remained confident he was searching in the correct place.

He returned and, with a length of salvaged wood, pummelled the surface. To his relief, the thin layer crumbled under the onslaught. Beneath the residue, he glimpsed smooth rock. He scraped away a layer of powder to expose a small area. Cut deep into the stone, he discovered a series of indentations, a part of his new set of instructions. All he needed to do was to uncover them all.

It was close to noon before the marks were revealed in their entirety. Orvyn moved outside for a short while. Here, before retrieving the leather-bound package, he allowed his horse a little water from his dwindling supply. Back inside the room, Orvyn opened the package. Careful to make no mistakes, he deciphered the details. This time, the de-coding came more easily. By early afternoon, he had copied everything onto a piece of vellum.

Orvyn thought about leaving the room as it was. His need to find water was becoming urgent. He hesitated. What if, sometime in the future, another sought the message? His indecision was short-lived. He knew, to protect it, he must re-cover the script. The less evidence, too, he left to point to the real motive for his journey, the better it would be for his own safety.

The mound of dirt, created when he exposed the rock, Orvyn re-spread over its surface. It took him a while longer to replace the joists and several of the wooden floorboards. He dropped a few roof timbers on top of the floor. From the adjoining rooms, Orvyn pushed hard against what remained of the partition walls. These caved-in. Dust flew everywhere. He did the same in some of the other rooms. After the dust settled, at a glance, the room in which he had been working looked little different from any other part of the ruin.

Orvyn saddled his horse, ready to leave. He studied his latest set of directions. Satisfied he knew where he was going, he urged his mount into motion. They turned southeastwards. If the information on his map was correct, a short ride away was a source of water. With his canteen now empty, it seemed a good place to be.

Late afternoon, once clear of the dry valley, Orvyn found his surroundings more agreeable. By means of a narrow winding path, he descended from a low ridge. According to the map, a spring lay at the other side of the woodland he had entered. The leafy boughs above brought welcome relief from the sun's rays. Soon, the foliage thinned. Orvyn pressed his heels into the flanks of his horse. It needed little urging. The animal could scent water ahead.

At a steady canter, they broke free of the trees to descend a gentle gradient. The path curved sharply as it cut through a gap in the hillside. Ahead, Orvyn glimpsed a pool beside the trail. To his right a small stream appeared. On the opposite side of the waters, a spring made the surface ripple.

Only when he rode clear of the opening did he notice he was no longer alone. Picketed close to the brook, lower down the slope, were three horses. Alerted by the sound of Orvyn's horse, the same number of men moved at speed to stand at one side of them. Two of the strangers had drawn their swords while the third held a bow, arrow in place, aimed towards the newcomer.

Orvyn cursed under his breath. He should have taken more care. A watering hole, so far from any other, was a place he could have expected to find fellow travellers. It was doubly unfortunate these wore the attire favoured by Betlic's men. Orvyn reined in, but kept his hands away from his own weapons. It would be unwise to give them reason to think he might be a threat.

"Good day," Orvyn greeted them, his voice sounded much calmer than he felt. "Do you mind if I join you. I wish to rest a while, and my horse is in need of water. We've come far."

His appearance gave the impression of one who had ridden all day, although his coating of dust mostly came from his toil among the ruins.

"Step down," one of the men said.

It was more an order than an invitation to join them. The speaker did lower his sword, as did his companion. Neither sheathed their weapons. The one with the bow relaxed his arm then removed the arrow. He kept hold of it. One false move by Orvyn and the bowman would have it in place, long before the rider could hope to reach him. With his options limited, Orvyn obeyed the speaker's command. He maintained a neutral expression while his mind worked at a furious pace.

"You wouldn't be some of Betlic's men, would you?" Orvyn had an idea. "I'd hoped to run into some," he added as he dismounted, not waiting for an answer to his earlier question. "I've come a long way to join him."

As if unconcerned by their presence, he turned his back to them as he led his horse to water. He must show they did not intimidate him.

"Yes, we fight for Betlic. Who are you? Where've you come from?" The bowman spoke this time. He sounded more agreeable than did his fellow.

"I'm Orvyn. I've spent the last two years fighting in the Furllands, but the rewards were meagre. A few of the lads was talking. They said Betlic was wanting experienced warriors, so I thought I'd try my luck in Xicalima. They say he pays well. Is it true, is the money good?"

"Yes, the work offers higher rewards than most. There are additional benefits for the right people, which makes fighting under Betlic's standard worthwhile," the second swordsman answered.

Both men sheathed their weapons and the archer put-down his bow. Orvyn's story was not unique. Every mercenary in the known world now seemed to gravitate towards Xicalima. This travel-stained, tough looking individual appeared to have potential as a recruit. He had plenty of confidence and looked capable of taking on all three of them. Neither did he scare easily.

Orvyn realised their horses were saddled. The bowman spoke again.

"We've somewhere to be before nightfall, so we'll leave you to your rest. It's possible we'll meet again. Betlic wants good men. You should go far."

They wasted no time in mounting their horses. With a salute, they dug in their spurs then moved out, towards the north. Their trail was different from the one Orvyn used to reach here, and on which he intended to leave. With a sigh of relief, he refilled his canteen at the water's edge. He removed his jacket then knelt beside the pool. He dipped his head deep below the surface. When he tossed it back up again, cool water fell onto his back and chest. He felt invigorated.

The ripples on the pool widened and faded. He caught sight of his reflection. A wild man stared up at him. He had difficulty in recognising himself. His hair was long; several weeks' growth of beard covered his chin. The healing scar on his cheek added a certain air of menace to his appearance. Constant exposure to the sun had tanned his face a dark-brown. Inside, he was no different, but, on the outside, he could understand what Betlic's follower meant, when he intimated Orvyn might go far in the dictator's employ. The person who gazed at him from the pool's surface, looked every part as ruthless a mercenary as he had ever seen.

After his horse had quenched its thirst, Orvyn thought it wiser to spend the night some distance from the watering hole. His presence would deter wildlife from their share of the water. Also, should anyone else arrived at the place, his absence would make discovery less likely.

At dawn, he scouted the spring, to find it unoccupied. He returned with his horse. The pair had a long day's ride ahead. Orvyn topped up his canteen. He allowed the animal a short drink. It might be a while before they found such sweet water again.

A month passed, then another. During this period, Orvyn's travels took him down many trails. He discovered a further three sets of clues and maps, which he decoded and copied. They directed him south, west and, once or twice, north. This last set brought him due south.

He had reached each location without difficulty. Orvyn now wondered whether Sheply's positioning had been as accidental as he first thought. It seemed strange the one place for which he had no concise final instructions, the young shepherd was on hand to assist. Orvyn did not believe the boy was aware of any ulterior motive as to why his father wanted to locate the flock there. But, it seemed odd that, before Sheply's parent left, he made sure his son knew how to find the secret writing beside the waterfall. It was too much of a coincidence. Yet, how had Sheply's father known someone would need a guide at that time? There were few credible explanations, unless, somehow, this mysterious Mastig had the ability to manipulate such matters.

Chapter Nineteen

Orvyn was days away from the completion of another month's travel when, hidden inside a series of low hills, he reached the cavern he sought. As instructed, he left his horse at the bottom of the rise then clambered up to the opening. His boots left no trace of his passing over the bare rock. The surrounding district, distant from any large town, showed many signs of nearby human occupation and farming. Much more of a worry to Orvyn's mind was the inside of the cave. Footprints were everywhere. On closer inspection, they belonged to two people, one much larger than the other. A man and a boy, or woman, he wondered.

Suspended from the roof, and implanted into the ground, were logs, wrapped in leather. He had used similar objects when he learned unarmed combat. At the rear of the cavern was a large wooden chest. Orvyn lifted its lid. He found it filled with swords, axes and bows, along with various other weapons of war. In secret, someone was preparing for a fight. Provided no-one returned to disturb him while he was there, its usage was none of his concern. Orvyn's interest lay in discovering his next set of instructions.

Deep within the chamber, it was gloomy. Little light penetrated so far from the tiny entrance. Near the opening, several torches hung from the walls. Orvyn stepped outside. On his return, after retrieving his tinderbox, it did not take him long to light one of the torches. His objective should be carved into the rock at the rear of the cavern — so why was the space around the cache of weapons unmarked? Orvyn returned to the box and dragged it away from the wall. There, with the aid of the torch, he found a series of chiselled inscriptions.

To his dismay, there was little to see. Where was the remainder? At all previous locations, writing had covered large expanses of stone. Here, there was nothing but a few short lines. Where was the map? Nowhere could he find any marks from which he might construct a chart. In desperation, Orvyn searched the other cavern walls. All were blank. There had to be more. What had gone wrong?

He stopped his frenzied search. With eyes closed, he made himself relax. Thoughts flowed with more clarity. He had become so used to travelling, he had forgotten his quest had to end sometime. Why not here? His ultimate goal might be only a few short clues away from discovery. In the flickering torchlight, he decoded the message.

It did not take long. He glanced down at the brief passage he had written. It gave directions to a house, a short ride away, and the person there he should contact. There was nothing else. Orvyn read it once more. He tucked the vellum inside his jacket. With the leather packet retied, he turned to leave. Taken by surprise, he stopped mid-stride.

Close to the entrance, a man leant against the cavern wall. He was old, at least compared to Orvyn. The man's head was shaved, his beard trimmed. The passage of time had lined his face. He was an inch or so shorter than Orvyn. His wiry body appeared to be in good condition. In the combined light of the torch and the opening, Orvyn could see the man was no peasant. His clothes, made from fine quality material, were rural in style. He carried with him an air of authority. His right hand rested casually near to the hilt of his sword.

Despite the man's age, there was nothing else to suggest he might struggle to defend himself. The size and shape of his boots matched well one set of footprints inside the cavern. How long he had been watching, Orvyn had no way of knowing. The fact the stranger had been able to enter without Orvyn becoming aware of his presence, was as impressive as it was unsettling.

"Now you've done eyeing me up and down, would you care to explain who you are and what you're doing here? I've followed you across country for several hours. You did not find this place, or that wall, by accident. I'm mindful of the significance of your find. Your intent, is it good, or bad?"

The man's voice was soft and cultured, the accent difficult to place. It was also firm and assured, its tone one of someone used to having his commands obeyed, instantly and without dissent.

Orvyn had commanded troops of men for too long to feel intimidated. He, too, was suspicious. Not until he was sure he was speaking to the person he sought was he prepared to divulge anything. He responded with equal politeness. "My intentions are mine to know and implement. I might ask you the same. Who are you, and what gives you the right to question me?"

The stranger maintained his stance. He neither threatened, nor evinced any sign he would back-down from his position. His face remained impassive.

"For a start, you are trespassing on my land. This chamber is a private place, one that belongs to me. In your jacket, you have a possible transcription of a cypher you found on the wall behind you. That information may, or may not be something you should know. Wrap your page round one of the stones at your feet, while I tell you what is the correct wording. When ready, toss it over. If your writing matches what I say, word for word, I shall know you have been on a long quest to find someone; at the same time, you will recognise that I'm that person you seek. I've some questions I expect you to answer. If your answers are satisfactory, we'll talk more."

"And if not?"

"You'd better hope otherwise," the stranger said. His neutral tone failed to disguise the threat carried by his words.

"Your transcription should read thus: 'From the entrance to the cavern, turn east. Take the line of the valley until you reach another vale. Follow the brook downstream. At a road that fords the waters, take the western route. After a stone-built bridge, follow a cart track that heads northwest. This will lead you to a large house with a gated entrance. Once there, ask to speak to the head of the household'. Now, if you please, throw your copy to me."

It was with relief Orvyn found the man's words matched exactly those he had recorded. It also meant this person had the knowledge to decipher the text himself, or knew someone who did. Unless, Orvyn realised, it was the stranger, or another member of his family, who had carved the original. This must be the one he sought, the one with knowledge of the Mastig and the skill to create the coded messages. Orvyn wrapped the vellum around a pebble. He threw it towards the doorway. It landed at the stranger's feet. Keeping his gaze on Orvyn, the stranger bent down to retrieve the page. He read it through, ensuring at all times Orvyn remained within his peripheral vision. When he had finished, he nodded.

"So! Someone did read the Book of Gryphrata I sent. The trail it describes, which you have followed and, later, the clues deciphered along the way, must have taken you some considerable time. Now, tell me who you are and why you seek what you do."

"My name's Orvyn. I'm aware of the book, but the reading of it was by Hafter, a rebel Xicaliman sage. Several months ago, he sent me on this mission. I followed the first set of directions, which he had copied from the book. There are documents in my baggage, which will authenticate who I am. Other than that, I shall say nothing more — not until I know who you are, and how you are able to decode the words written here."

"I'm Ryce. Hafter's reputation is known to me. Ever since confirmation reached me of Betlic's acquisition of the talisman, I realised, at some time, I would have to make contact with the rebels. As soon as I learned Betlic had discovered information that would lead him to the hiding place of the mantle, I sent the Book of Gryphrata to the sage," Ryce explained. "I was positive he would understand its significance and ensure it remained free from Betlic's hands. I was aware of Hafter's research into the Mastig and its chosen one. He's someone who I believe can be trusted to use such knowledge selflessly.

"The words here on the wall, my grandfather carved. My ancestors wrote those you found earlier. Whenever circumstances compelled them to move, they left instructions to direct anyone with the knowledge to their new location.

"Soon, more may be carved. I'm becoming too old to perform my duties. It is time for a younger person to take over. Such a one is trained in the responsibilities of the matter and is almost ready to assume the role."

"Where is he? Wouldn't it be better for me to talk to him?"

"No. That's not possible. Also, he's a she. Now is not the time to act; there's nothing we can do until the year after next. With that in mind, I would rather she remain without undue concerns. The necessary skills and knowledge, she has in abundance. The self-belief to go with them is yet to become firm. This will strengthen with time. These coming months will make a huge difference to her."

"I don't understand! How can you to do nothing for two years? Betlic strengthens his position all the time. He's already advanced Xicalima's possessions southwards. Refugees I've met tell me he has begun his expansion both eastwards and westwards. Now he has the mantle, he can declare war against any nation at any time. This thing of which you are guardian you should use now. Wouldn't it be better to prevent the misery and torment that is to come, rather than attempt to resolve it later?"

"If that was possible, your words would shame me," Ryce said. "Sadly, it cannot be. You say that Betlic has the mantle, already? That is something of which I was not aware. I had expected it to take longer for him to retrieve it. This might change many things, except the time for action. Before we discuss further, let's go to where your directions have indicated. Tonight, you will be my guest for dinner. We can talk in greater comfort then. I shall study the documents you have brought. Once they confirm what you say, I'll be more comfortable in discussing matters in depth."

It was a valid comment. In Ryce's place, Orvyn would have done the same. His invitation accepted, Ryce stepped outside and disappeared from view. Orvyn followed, still wary of an ambush. The way was clear. Ryce was already halfway down the hillside. Orvyn hurried after him.

The traveller could see another horse picketed near to his own. Again, he marvelled at how, without his being aware, someone had followed him across country and into the cavern. The man possessed formidable tracking skills. As Ryce moved down the slope, his agility belied his advancing years. If he was too old to perform his duties, how onerous could they be?

Late in the evening, they arrived at Ryce's house. Over a meal, Ryce introduced Orvyn to his daughter, Karilyn. She was young, slim and dark-haired. His host had requested Orvyn refrain from discussing the purpose of his visit in front of her and his retainers. When she asked the reason for their guest being in the area, Ryce said Orvyn was considering buying some land from him. The conversation turned to more general topics. After a short while, Karilyn excused herself and retired for the night.

With a flagon of ale each, Ryce led his guest into his private chambers. Here, behind a locked door, Orvyn took several letters and documents from his pack and passed them to his host to read. An hour went by before Ryce reached the end of the last one. He sat back for a while, in silent contemplation, before he spoke again.

"It seems our worst fears have crawled out from the darkness. This information changes nothing. Karilyn, can do nothing to help stop the tyrant, yet."

"Karilyn!" Orvyn exclaimed in surprise.

The girl had appeared shy and withdrawn. To meet the challenges ahead, he had expected it to be someone older, tougher, more dynamic, less ladylike.

133

"Yes, Karilyn is the one who'll bear the Scraufin, the object we hold. She'll accompany the chosen one to find the Mastig," Ryce said. "Her looks have deceived you. She is more than capable of defending herself. Despite that, I would rather the call had come when I was younger and able to carry out the task myself. These matters are beyond our control, as is the choice of my successor. That person is born into the position.

"I've a son, Peter. He's big, strong and not without intelligence. Much older than his sister, he's a soldier, fighting in some foreign land. To look at him, you'd expect him to be the one. But no! The person to whom the duty falls has something extra. Agility, strength beyond the normal, a way of thinking that, at times, confounds others. From the moment she started to walk and talk, it was apparent Karilyn was the one.

"For now she's beset with self-doubts. She worries when the time comes she may be found unworthy of her destiny."

"What do you think?" Orvyn asked.

"I'm convinced she'll be the finest guardian ever. It's her humility that will allow her to triumph, of that I am sure. Her brother's too impatient. He takes too many risks. These would lead to him losing both his life and the Scraufin. I have taught her everything she needs to know about her charge. Only two people have knowledge of how to locate the place where the Mastig will appear. Karilyn is one. I am the other. I have trained her to fight, with or without weapons. It would be unwise to underestimate the girl. Once she learns to trust the inner strengths, both mental and physical, with which she was born, nothing will stop her."

"As I asked earlier," Orvyn said, "now you know Betlic has possession of both talisman and mantle, why cannot Karilyn meet with the chosen one now and take him to the Mastig?"

"Because, it's revealed on only one night, once every three years. We have over half the cycle to go before Karilyn can retrieve the object."

This disclosure would upset Hafter once he found out. Now, Orvyn understood why Ryce preferred to leave his daughter in ignorance, until nearer the time when her knowledge and skills would be of use.

"You're aware Betlic's invaded several of his neighbouring territories," Orvyn said. "Your country's southern border is close to Xicalima's northern edge. People are fleeing north. Why not leave with me? It would be safer for you both to take refuge with the rebels than stay here."

"I cannot risk the Scraufin. Here, it's hidden, its location known only to Karilyn and me. If we left, anything might happen. Rumours, once started, soon spread. They obey no borders. I'm well-informed about events taking place within your stronghold. As such, I'm aware there's a potential conflict over who is the heir to the Mastig, the one to whom Karilyn must act as guide. Your king's convinced he's the chosen one, in that he's wrong. What his father, and Hafter, told him was done in good faith. I know that information was flawed, so now will the sage. Does Hafter have any idea who the chosen one might be?"

"Yes," Orvyn said, "but I cannot divulge his name. As with you and the Scraufin, it would be better for it to remain a secret for as long as possible. The king already bears ill-will towards this person. When his majesty finds out this particular individual is the chosen one, not he, the royal anger will be unpredictable in its reach. The other party involved knows he has no legitimate claim to the throne. Neither does he desire it. This is something, I suspect, the king will have difficulty in accepting. He will fear a plot to overthrow him. If so, he's certain to take action to neutralise any perceived threat."

"Then you must understand why Karilyn has to remain separate from such power struggles. Hers is a specific task. Yours and Hafter's is to protect the true chosen one, until the time is right for him and Karilyn to meet. Afterwards, the responsibility for his safety will be hers alone."

Hafter would be most unhappy. He expected his emissary to return with something tangible. The idea of a young girl chaperoning a warrior, such as Marazin, amused Orvyn. He could not avoid a wry smile to himself. From what he knew of his friend, it was doubtful he would need anyone's protection. When the time came for Karilyn to be Marazin's guide, Orvyn believed it would be the other way round.

Chapter Twenty

A few days after the winter solstice, late one evening after the streets had fallen silent, Orvyn and Marazin slipped unnoticed into the rebel capital. The pair, disguised as peasants, had wrapped well against the icy blasts that swept down the valley. Without incident, the earlier journey from Ryce's home to Hafter's mountain retreat, took Orvyn a number of weeks. Soon after his arrival, a messenger informed the sage of the traveller's return.

Hafter waited several days, until Amron and his entourage left on a planned hunting trip, before he sent word for Orvyn to travel into town. The king's absence was to last for a week or more. Hafter had learned, from his own sources, the hunt, although genuine, was also a pretext for Amron to meet with foreign emissaries in private.

After recent blizzards, deep layers of snow covered even the lower mountain reaches. Because of the conditions, it took the messenger some time to reach his destination. Marazin, frustrated by his confinement in the hills, had decided to go with his friend. A reliable informant had told Hafter that, for the winter, Tedrick had abandoned his hunt for the pair. It was too cold to waste time on what was, he felt, an unwarranted and fruitless quest.

Tedrick had heard nothing of Boden for several months. The man had ridden alone to the eastern edge of the mountains in his search for Marazin and Orvyn. Boden had either deserted, or, with fatal results, encountered the missing men. Tedrick favoured the latter. The financial incentive for a kill was too high for Boden to miss such an opportunity. Desert, afterwards? Yes, but not before claiming the reward. If Boden had perished in his attempt to assassinate the targets of Amron's spite, it was reasonable to assume they had made good their escape. For Tedrick, this provided sufficient excuse for him to spend his time hunting wild boar and dallying with a certain widow. Instead of wandering snow-packed hills in the depths of winter, looking for people he had no desire to find, he could relax in the arms of his mistress.

After Marazin and Orvyn's arrival at Hafter's house, the sage wanted first to hear the crucial parts of Orvyn's tale, not stories of his adventures on the way. The atmosphere soon became fraught. In frustration at the news, the old man slammed his fist onto the table. His goblet overturned, wine spilled everywhere. It was an indication of the level of his displeasure that he would waste such a precious vintage in this manner.

"Another year and a half before the Mastig appears again!" Hafter said, for the third time, disbelief adding fury to his tone.

Orvyn had anticipated the reaction to his news would be less than enthusiastic, so it was with some trepidation he had related it.

Hafter looked up, anger and deep disappointment evident in his expression. He glared at Orvyn as if the bad news was his entire fault.

"There's no possibility you mis-heard Ryce?" Hafter demanded. "You're positive those were the words he used when he told you about the timing of the Mastig's appearance?"

At a nod of his visitor's head, Hafter raised his eyes skywards, as if in supplication. When he spoke, his voice rose sharply from a whisper.

"This can't be true. It'll be too late. We'll all be dead!" He emphasised the last sentence by thumping the table in accompaniment to each word.

"I'm sorry, that's what Ryce said. It's the reason why, for now, he's staying where he is," Orvyn explained, keeping his voice as calm as possible.

Hafter's agitation was rising by the minute. The veins on his forehead stood out. His face was bright red. Orvyn did not want to upset him further. The sage was no longer young. As the bearer of bad news, Orvyn had no wish to be the cause of the old man's death.

"Does Ryce know who is the chosen one, or does he believe it's the king?" Hafter asked, struggling to control his temper.

"No, Ryce knows it's not Amron," Orvyn answered. "It was he who sent the Book of Gryphrata to you. From that, he was sure the line of succession would become apparent when you read it. I told him you were aware of the true one's identity. At the time, I thought it unwise to divulge Marazin's name. He agreed. That knowledge, he said, should be known to as few as possible."

Marazin and Orvyn had talked in depth about the latter's journey, and the circumstances surrounding the death of Boden. They had decided it might be better to wait until their meeting with Hafter before Orvyn revealed the details of his time with Ryce. Therefore, as these revelations were new to Marazin, he too had questions.

"I can understand why Ryce wants to keep the Scraufin safe from danger," Marazin said. "But why stay where he is, rather than move here? It must exacerbate his risk. Despite Amron's hatred of me, he has no knowledge, yet, that I'm the chosen one. I'm sure Hafter could persuade the king to arrange an escort to bring Ryce here, where he would be better protected."

"The king cannot become involved," Orvyn interrupted. "Ryce is adamant the Bearer of the Scraufin must remain above palace politics. Amron will find out the truth of the succession sometime. The bearer's duty is to protect only the Scraufin and the chosen one, no other. The king's difficulties and battles are his to fight and resolve. They are of no concern of the bearer. Ryce refuses to allow her to travel until nearer the time, or if Betlic invades."

"He's being overcautious," Hafter said, after a moment's consideration. "I'm sure we can find an acceptable compromise, so that we can bring him here."

"'Her'!" Marazin said in surprise. "Did I hear you correctly, Orvyn? I thought you said 'Her'!"

"Of course he didn't," Hafter said, his mind occupied more with the future, than the present. Orvyn's disclosure of the bearer's gender had failed to register with him. "Ryce is a man. Have you understood nothing," he added tetchily.

"Er! Yes! No!" Orvyn spluttered. "Ryce was the bearer. He feels, now, he's too old to undertake the task involved. He's trained his daughter, Karilyn, to take over from him. She's taken instruction in her duties since a child."

"A woman? Is Ryce mad? How the devil can a woman hope to cope with the rigours of the expedition ahead, or survive the dangers along the way?" Hafter was incredulous. "The bearer is there to protect the Scraufin and Marazin, not the other way round. He'll endanger himself and his mission watching out for her. This will not do. Ryce must have another child who can perform the duty."

"There's a son, Peter," Orvyn said. "He's been absent for many years. He's an experienced warrior."

"Then Ryce must send a messenger to recall him. A skilled fighting man is needed, not a woman." Hafter's tone was disparaging.

"I did suggest that to Ryce. He said it wasn't possible." Orvyn squirmed under the baleful look Hafter threw at him. "No-one chooses the bearer. His daughter was born with the special gifts, mental and physical, needed for the position. The son, although athletic and strong, is without these. Ryce has spent years training her. He states she is more than capable for the task ahead. At the moment, all she lacks is a little self-confidence."

Hafter looked as if he was going to pass comment about this last revelation. In haste, Orvyn continued.

"Ryce says her self-belief will develop with time and not compromise the outcome. Her potential is such, or so he believes, that she will be the finest upholder there has ever been. Her considered approach gives the mission much more chance of success than the bullish, over confident, risk-taking attitude of her brother."

Although surprised, Marazin, unlike Hafter, was more receptive to the idea. Across many lands, he had been a soldier for all his adult life. Women, in his experience, were no less talented than their male counterparts. He had seen them fight with, and against, the best of men. What they lacked in strength, they made up for with speed and cunning. Many a slight wisp of a girl had bested a far larger opponent, especially when he threatened her offspring. In the past, Marazin had participated in tournaments where women archers were the equal of their male challengers; and, one or two, where he would have been uncertain of the result had he gone up against female combatants with any type of weapon.

"Did you meet the girl? What's she like?" Marazin asked, curious to know more about his future travelling companion.

"Slim, dark-haired, attractive," Orvyn replied. "She seemed quiet and reserved. We talked little. After we all dined, she retired for the night. Ryce did not explain to her the real reason for my visit. For the moment, he wants Karilyn to remain in ignorance of Betlic's acquisitions. He wants her to concentrate on her training and preparations without such onerous thoughts to distract her. That was the last I saw of the girl. I left early the following morning before she was awake."

"This is a disaster," Hafter said bitterly.

He chose to ignore Orvyn's comments concerning Karilyn's competence for the task ahead. Hafter was set in his ways, used to people deferring to him. He expected others to accept his advice without question.

As with everything else, he had fixed opinions on a woman's place in society. He did not consider anyone else's point of view, unless it agreed with his own. His way was the right way. It never occurred to him the decision might not be his to make.

"We'll have to change our plans," he declared. "There's no prospect now that Marazin and the bearer can go in search of the Mastig by themselves. We'll decide later what further preparations are necessary. Of course, the pair will require an escort. With all these extra people involved, there'll be more chance of someone discovering our secret. This whole quest is turning into a disaster, a complete disaster!"

His veins were sticking out again. Sweat beaded his forehead.

"Oh! It's not that bad, Hafter." Marazin interrupted the sage before he pulled out his remaining hair, an action which looked to be in imminent danger of happening. "An escort will not be necessary. Ryce shows satisfaction with his daughter's abilities. Why should we doubt his judgement on the matter? Your own research, Hafter, has shown us the duty passes from generation to generation. The bearer, unlike the heir, is not necessarily the first-born, nor chosen at the random whim of the current holder. It's inherent at birth. Who knows how many female bearers there might have been in the past? I've fought alongside women and have no objection to doing so again. When we go, we shall do so alone."

Hafter was less than happy with this statement; but a continuation of the heated exchange was not something that was helpful now. They needed to stay united. Hafter felt confident Marazin would become more amenable as time passed. The sage would convince Marazin of the unsuitability of travelling with the girl, without an escort for her protection. It would be inappropriate, too, for the pair to travel alone and without a chaperone.

"Humph! We shall discuss these matters later," Hafter mumbled angrily.

Hafter's rapid retreat from direct confrontation did not fool Marazin. The warrior had come to know the old man well enough to understand how his mind worked. Hafter would try to persuade his young associate away from his stated position. Marazin was determined that would not happen.

He had studied in depth Hafter's collection of documents about the role of the chosen one, as well as the Book of Gryphrata. If Marazin and Karilyn were to succeed, everything he read indicated it would be by their efforts alone. There could be no escort. It would endanger them all. Two of them could travel clandestinely and, if necessary, find it easier to slip through Betlic's lines. Travelling with a group of heavily armed men would attract unwanted attention.

The rest of the evening passed in a more pleasant atmosphere. With the spilt wine cleaned away and goblets replenished, the three enjoyed a sumptuous meal. While they dined, Orvyn described his adventures in great detail. It was late when the three ceased talking. With Amron and his entourage away from the locality, Hafter invited his guests to stay for the night. They could leave before dawn and be out of the area before most of the populace was awake.

Orvyn's hair remained long, his beard untrimmed. With his scar, he was unrecognisable from the smart aide who had stood beside Amron at court. Only the hunting party that accused Marazin of the death of Amron's mother and, later, those at the palace, where Tamin proved the visitor innocent, could identify the young man by sight. Many of these courtiers and servants were either with the king on his present hunting trip, or in residence at the palace. Disguised, as the fugitives were, if seen, the chance of anyone identifying them was remote.

CB ⊗O

From that time on, until the end of spring, the pair remained hidden in the mountains. After the quarter solstice, Hafter joined them. The weather had turned mild. It was time for the elderly sage to escape the low lands before the heat became too oppressive. Marazin and Orvyn had passed the winter, training and rereading the copious manuscripts left by Hafter. Marazin increased his knowledge of the Mastig, Scraufin and talisman. Nowhere did he find anything to persuade him from his intended travel arrangements. Karilyn and he must undertake the mission alone.

From childhood, Marazin had received, as had Karilyn, instruction in a wide range of weaponry, and in the art of self-defence. Unlike Ryce with Karilyn, Marazin's father had provide no reasons for the specialised schooling he gave his son. In the fire that claimed their lives, this knowledge had perished with his parents, along with the documents they fetched with them from Xicalima. Had not circumstances led him to Hafter, Marazin's birthright would have vanished with them.

One day, when they discussed the matter, Orvyn proposed another theory. Was it possible that something other than chance brought Marazin to this place, at a time when he was needed the most. The enchantments, which imbued the objects they sought, were powerful beyond most men's comprehension. Perhaps they had drawn him here, and would have done so no matter where he had been. The more Marazin considered this premise, the more he realised how true it might be. For a long while, in Vretliana, he had been restless, with a growing urge to move away.

A part of each day, Marazin set aside to practise his skills. Orvyn, a warrior experienced with most weapons of war, was happy to assist. It provided an excellent chance for Marazin to hone his techniques. For Orvyn, it gave him an opportunity to improve his proficiency with a master. By summer, he was equal, if not superior, to most of the foes he could expect to meet. He was still unable to gain the better of his current opponent. Marazin was exceptional. In anything resembling a fair fight, Orvyn doubted many could claim a victory over that man.

With Hafter back in residence at his mountain retreat, the arrival of visitors was almost a daily occurrence. For the same reasons as the previous summer, the fugitives spent much of their time, hidden in their quarters. For months, news and rumours about Betlic's gains had been rife. Apart from to the north of Xicalima, where he was yet to advance, the consensus was that he now controlled all the lands that enclosed the country, or was close to doing so. The threat he presented to the world grew more potent by the day.

A few weeks before the summer solstice, Marazin's confinement inside the mountain retreat had started to affect his mood. The place had become a prison to him. Orvyn had 'escaped' for several months. Marazin decided it was his turn to travel.

Hafter's visitors had departed late that afternoon. For the first time in several days, the two fugitives ventured up into the main living quarters. Heardwine, who had run ahead, sprawled in front of the fireplace.

"Ryce and Karilyn must have left home," Marazin said. "I can't believe they're not on their way. I'm going to look for them. They must be aware of the number of men Betlic has amassed along his northern front. If the reports we are receiving are correct, it cannot be long before he moves in Ryce's direction. The distance between their two borders is small. Admittedly, the King of Gottenlie's army lies between the two and the fighting forces from Ryce's own country have moved closer to their southern border. Despite that, once Betlic advances, it won't matter whether two armies stand between him and Ryce or twenty-two."

"Mazarin's right, Hafter," Orvyn said in wholehearted agreement. "We know what's happened along Betlic's other fronts. He uses the talisman to demoralise his opponents, so most of their resistance crumbles before he strikes. Few, if any, are immune to his wiles, too little to lead a fight back."

"I know, I know." Hafter was unsympathetic. "Times are difficult, everywhere. Let me ask you this, Marazin. Is putting yourself in needless danger going to help? No! We know you're safe here. Amron believes you've fled the country. Thanks to Orvyn, Boden's disappearance has convinced him of this. No-one's looking for you. Ryce will bring this woman to us, here." He refused to call Karilyn by name. "Why put your life at risk? They could travel by any one of a number of routes. If you miss them, then what'll happen? Once they've found me, we'll have to go in search of you. It will create months of delay."

"Rubbish! You know as well as I do which way they'll come," Mazarin said, attempting to keep the exasperation out of his voice. "Ryce showed Orvyn the map they were to use, and their intended route. We've all the information we need. I shall ride to the other side of the mountains and keep an eye on that trail. If they are on their way, I'll find and escort them here. I expect them to be along soon. If not, the longer it takes them to reach me, the more advantageous it will be for us to meet there. It will mean that, straightaway, Karilyn and I can set off in search of the Mastig. Ryce can make his way to you and explain what has happened."

"I think not!" Hafter was furious. "You know my feelings. You and this…this woman, going away alone, it cannot be right. This whole affair is a nightmare. Apart from the impropriety, how can she be capable of watching your back? You'll be so distracted keeping her safe that both of you will end up captured or worse. I do not care what you say; to have even the remotest hope of success, an escort must ride with you to protect the woman.

"If you cannot accept that, then we have a viable alternative, persuade Ryce to continue in his role. The woman can stay here. We can find some needlework to keep her occupied until you return. And, as for you, wandering off to look for them," he shook his head in despair, "it's more than unnecessary, it's reckless," he complained, his voice rising in anger.

"We've been through this a hundred times, Hafter," Marazin warned. His voice carried a steely timbre new to the others. "This matter is no longer open to discussion. That 'woman' has a name, Karilyn. The documents you brought here for me to study are explicit. To find the Mastig, the chosen one, and the bearer of the Scraufin, must travel unaccompanied. You've read the details as many times, as have I. Why cannot you accept them?"

"Nowhere, do the manuscripts contain the eventuality of the bearer being a woman," Hafter snapped. He refused to back down.

"True," Marazin said, "neither do they indicate the bearer has to be a man. Being male, or female, historically, has no apparent influence on the choice of incumbent. I've studied the records relating to the history of the heir. Over the years, they show that on six occasions the honour has passed to a woman. One was a peasant, two were the daughters of merchants and the three others were ladies of noble birth. Similar records for the bearer are unavailable, but, without anything to the contrary, I refuse to believe Karilyn will be the first woman to hold that honour."

Marazin was in full flow now, his voice firm and authoritative. "I appreciate your concern for the future, Hafter," he said. "It must be frustrating for you to have to rely on someone else to return with the Mastig. That's not a good enough reason for you to keep up this constant pressure on me. Against my will, I'm not prepared to do your bidding. If it upsets you, I'm sorry for your distress, not my actions. No longer will I tolerate your interference. I'm the chosen one, the heir. You and I, both, have verified it from the information you've collected. I have to perform my duty, in a way I think fit. Your wisdom, on a wide range of subjects, is invaluable to me. In regard to the Mastig, you've allowed your personal prejudices to cloud your judgement. When I leave, Heardwine will keep me company. The dog has certain qualities of its own. It will warn me of any impending danger.

"Now, for the last time, I will not have you subjecting my future travelling companion to these demeaning and derogatory remarks. If Ryce possessed any doubts about his daughter's suitability, he would not have handed the responsibility to her. In future, call her by her given name and accord to her the respect she deserves.

"I suggest we bring this evening to a close," he concluded. "We're all on edge. A decent night's rest will be good for each of us. We shall meet again in the morning."

Marazin stood. He bowed, with exaggerated politeness, to Haefter then nodded to Orvyn. Heardwine, stretched, yawned then followed his master. Orvyn rose to his feet. That night, something unexpected had occurred around the table. Marazin had taken command of his destiny. Hafter sat with a bemused expression on his face. Orvyn, too, bowed to his host. In haste, he left the room.

Hafter, once he had absorbed what had taken place, was not as devastated as could be expected. To find someone who stuck to their principles, and was not afraid to disagree with him, was an uncommon experience. If his advanced years had led him to develop a narrower tolerance of other's views, Marazin's outburst had shaken him and opened his eyes to this failing.

Marriage was something Hafter had never sought. Throughout his life, his main dealings with women, though fair, were with his servants. He tolerated the wives of others, believing their petty intrigues at court a product of vacuous minds. Affairs of state concerned him more — lofty matters, which he considered of greater importance than the role of women. They were there to be mothers and homemakers, were they not?

That he wanted more evidence, to convince him that Karilyn was not a problem was irrelevant; what right did he have to question her suitability as bearer. Marazin was correct to define his position. He was the chosen one. All decisions concerning his role were his to make, his and his companion, whoever that might be. Hafter had overstepped his authority. He had spent so long researching, thinking and dreaming about what was to be, he had forgotten that, compared to others', his was a minor function.

Chapter Twenty One

Exhausted, Karilyn could go no further. On the run for several days, she feared for her life. Most of the villages and farms along her route showed signs of hasty abandonment. For years, the region had lived under the threat of invasion, its borders too close to those of Betlic. The news about his recent incursion had spread rapidly. Believing it the long-feared, full-scale offensive, most inhabitants had fled in panic. Karilyn had avoided contact with the few courageous enough to stay in their homes. How far behind, if at all, her pursuers might be, was unknown to her; but she would endanger no-one's life by leading Betlic's killers straight to them.

At the side of a stream, with a rock for a seat, Karilyn rested her back against the broad trunk of an ancient pine tree. Cold, lonely and frightened, she grieved for her family. Her body shook, uncontrollably. A tear rolled down her cheek. She wiped it away. Her eyes filled and she wept as the tribulations of the past few weeks overwhelmed her. Despite her protests, her father and brother had sacrificed themselves to allow her to escape from Betlic's men. She was the one to whom the Scraufin had passed. It was her sworn duty to protect it.

From the brow of a hill, Karilyn had watched the raiding party as it smashed down the barred gates of her childhood home. Despite how tiny the distant figures seemed, the black-clad soldiers had been easy to distinguish from her father's retainers. The end came soon. A few unfortunates had survived the onslaught. She watched as Betlic's men dragged them through the gaping gates. The horror of what followed would haunt her forever.

Although too far away to see any details, the prisoner's screams had carried on the breeze. By evening the cries had ceased, the captives were dead and the buildings aflame. An acrid smell reached Karilyn. She was unable to identify her father and brother among the victims, but was certain the pair would have died fighting. Now, apart from her, there was no-one left with knowledge of the Scraufin's whereabouts.

Only days before the attack, her brother Peter, now a battle-hardened warrior, had made a surprise return home. With him he brought disturbing news. Betlic had learned of the Scraufin, and a raiding party was advancing at speed towards the family home. How Peter knew of these events, he did not say. Karilyn suspected her brother, until recently, had been in Betlic's service. To come by such information, Peter must have been a part of the tyrant's inner circle, or an aide to someone who was. In the end, filial loyalty had proved of greater importance than his ambitions.

Ryce, the siblings' father, had brought forward his plans for the family to flee. Since news of Betlic's forays out of Xicalima first reached Ryce, the family's preparations had been ongoing. Prior to Peter's return, Ryce believed they were in no immediate danger.

When first Betlic used the talisman, after his acquisition of the mantle, the effort had weakened him. Although debilitating, these effects were temporary. Betlic had worked hard to achieve greater proficiency. Now, he was able to command near to limitless energy from his prized possessions. Faced with a potential threat to his power, he made use of the talisman to speed the progress of his men. With the object's magical powers, he filled with fear the minds of his enemies who lay between his raiding party and the Scraufin. So much so, most took flight. With no-one to resist them, the advance of Betlic's raiders was swift.

The shivers eased. Karilyn's eyes dried. She wrapped her clothes more tightly around her. Earlier in the day, she had taken scraps of fresh food from a recently abandoned cottage. At the time, she was too fearful to stop her flight. Now, two days since she had exhausted her original supplies, she was dizzy and lightheaded. Grief tightened her throat, making eating difficult. She tried smaller pieces of bread and meat, and was able to swallow some. As the meal settled, her body warmed. She felt a little better. Later, in the darkness of the night, sleep eluded her. She attempted to turn her mind to happier times. Nothing she did could prevent her thoughts from drifting back to the day she lost everything.

સ ૪૦

The day had started so well. Karilyn had woken to the bright, early morning rays of the sun, shining on her face through a stone mullioned window. She had been quick to dress, before hurrying to join her father and brother in the great hall for breakfast. Her footsteps echoed through empty wood-panelled rooms. Everything of value had gone. Their household belongings spread throughout the nearby hills, buried deep in caverns. Ryce had decided that the family, with their retainers, would leave the following day. Outside, workers filled wagons with supplies in preparation for the journey ahead.

"Where are we to go?" Peter asked.

He was curious and, until now, Ryce had been reluctant to discuss his plans. Unlike Karilyn, who suspected Peter, her father thought a small group Betlic's agents, posing as workers, had betrayed him. They had been in his employ less than a year. How they had learned of the Scraufin was a mystery to Ryce. The object was never discussed around the house. Without proof, he was unwilling to confront the suspects. Instead, he sent them on an errand that should last several days. When the group returned, the family would be a long way from here.

"We travel west, first, before we swing round to head north towards the Mogallean Mountains." Out of habit, Ryce's voice dropped to a whisper, even though there was no-one to overhear.

"We follow their line until we reach their northern end. Once there, we turn west again, still following the edge of the mountains, until we come to a gap. Through there, southwards down the centre of the peaks, for scores of miles a vast valley stretches. This is where the Xicaliman rebels base their forces. An elderly sage lives among them, a man called Hafter. He's the one we must find. Hafter possesses knowledge of the mantle and the talisman, but, of much greater importance, the identity of the chosen one is known to him. Hafter will introduce Karilyn to him, so that she can accompany him on the way to find the Mastig. Not until they reach its location can she pass to him the Scraufin."

"This talk of a Mastig is beyond me," Peter grumbled. "What is it, and what does it have to do with this Scraufin we possess? It's too fanciful, a story to entertain children. You said, years ago, there was a connection with the first-born of the last Xicaliman king, but Betlic killed every member of the royal family. There can be no chosen one.

"Even if the story were true, I should be the one to take charge of the Scraufin instead of Karilyn. I'm bigger, stronger and an experienced warrior.

With only my baby sister to care for the damned object, what will happen if someone tries to take it from her? Look at her, she'd struggle to defend herself, what chance anything that might be in her care?" he mocked.

Karilyn's face flushed with anger. She was twenty-three, no longer the child her brother remembered. Few of her childhood memories of Peter were happy ones. As did many boys with a younger sister, he regarded Karilyn as a nuisance. He knew nothing of what she had become. Even before he left, in secret, Ryce had schooled Karilyn in her role. Since Peter's return, after almost seventeen years, he had been too busy helping his father to notice her. Her brother assumed she would occupy her time with needlework, or other 'womanly' pursuits pertaining to the daughter of a wealthy landowner. Peter could not understand why she had not married. He had no concept of the rigorous training she had undergone, and maintained.

Ryce peered over his goblet. On seeing the look on his daughter's face, he turned to Peter and, in a sharp voice, told him to be quiet. Peter grinned. His father's intervention, so he thought, validated his argument.

"Little sister still needs 'Dada' to protect her," he added. His tone was patronising. He continued, more determined than ever to have his way. "She stands no chance without us. Again, I say, I should be in charge of the Scraufin."

Exasperated, Ryce spoke to Peter again, this time in a more controlled tone. "A member of the royal family does exist," he said. "but he's not the one we seek. As to the Scraufin, it's in your sister's care, where it belongs. Karilyn's more than capable of taking care of herself. I was protecting you, not her. I can't afford for you to suffer any injury. There are too many perils ahead of us."

It was Peter's turn to be angry. Karilyn, that slight thing, hurt him! Ridiculous! There was nothing he could say, without sounding childish or petulant. When his father left them, he would show her who was master. He did not have long to wait. A retainer called Ryce away. Alone with Karilyn, Peter leapt to his feet and grabbed her arm as she attempted to stand.

The wooden floor vibrated as Peter landed on his back. Stunned, he had no idea how he had reached there. His hand reached for his sword. The sheath was empty. Something cold and sharp touched his throat. He looked up into Karilyn's eyes. She stood above him. It was his sword in her hand. For a moment, her face remained expressionless.

A shiver ran down Peter's spine. Karilyn relaxed, she smiled, her face lit up. She reversed the sword and offered it by the handle. Peter took it from her and slid it into its sheath. How had she taken the weapon from him? This worried him more than the ease with which she had thrown him to the ground. He accepted the proffered hand and allowed her to help him back onto his feet.

Unwilling to consider an alternative, Peter decided what had happened must have been accidental. Luck had guided Karilyn's movements. Her actions could be due to nothing else. He kept hold of her hand and tried to twist her arm. Crash! He hit the floor again. This time he slid with force into the wall. The heavy landing knocked the air from his lungs. He gasped for breath. His sword was missing. He looked up. Again, it was in his sister's hand. How did she do that? The door swung open and Ryce peered round it, a look of frustration on his face.

"I warned you, Peter. Travelling the world hasn't changed you. You're as stubborn now as when a child. Leave your sister alone and come outside. Karilyn, give him back his sword. If he tries anything else, hit him with it."

Karilyn helped her brother up, again. He took back his weapon, careful not to make any sudden movements. He had a lump on his head and several other painful places around his body. Peter had suffered enough. He could not decide whether to be annoyed, for being so easily disarmed, or proud of his little sister. For a moment, he scowled. Karilyn giggled at his expression.

For an instant, his temper rose. Much to his surprise, his ire disappeared and he found himself grinning. He grabbed Karilyn and hugged her. She tensed and, for a second, he thought he would land on the ground again. The tension eased and she embraced him back. They parted and he limped towards the door. Peter appreciated fighting skills. He knew how much effort went into becoming proficient at them. For the first time, he had respect for his sister. There was far more to her than he had realised.

"You must show me how you do that," he called back to her as he moved outside to join their father.

CB 80

She wished with all her heart she could. Karilyn shed another tear. She could have had no better companion than Peter. They had parted on good terms, for that she was grateful. If only she had his determination. Her reactions were automatic, the result of years of training. Otherwise, lack of confidence, as now, made her fearful. By instinct, Peter knew what to do, as did her father. Now she was alone, hounded and struggling to stay alive. From a pouch, she pulled out the Scraufin. She contemplated abandoning the object where her pursuers could find it. Her father's face became clear in her mind. He was shaking his head. His voice was steady and calming. Be strong, believe in yourself. You must continue.

The vision faded but Karilyn knew the words were right. She drew strength from them. To surrender the Scraufin without a fight would be a betrayal of her father and brother. If she was to avenge them, she must pass on the object to the one who would use it best. Her mind wandered back in time again.

◌ ◌

Betlic's troops had approached the house, soon after Peter left to help his father. Many of Ryce's men were working in the open. Most died in the first few moments of the attack. The survivors put up a gallant defence but were too few to keep their enemies at bay for long. Betlic's men had brought battering rams and, with shields held above their heads, they attacked the huge oak gate.

Ryce knew the enemy would not take long to break through. After much persuasion by her father and brother, Karilyn agreed to leave. Peter led her down to an underground store, where he pulled clear from the wall a square of panelling. Behind it was a small rounded entrance into a tunnel, which opened up beyond. They embraced for one final time before Karilyn crawled through the gap. Peter passed a burning torch to her. Taking hold of it, she turned away. Her footsteps echoed as she raced along the passageway.

Peter and Ryce had to remain. Without them to lead the defence, it would crumble quickly. They had to give Karilyn the chance to distance herself as much as possible from the conflict. Their lives were of little importance compared to hers, and to the charge she carried. In the distance, she heard the panel slam back into place. The sounds of battle disappeared. She was on her own.

Chapter Twenty Two

Once again, nightmares haunted Karilyn's sleep. She awoke with a start, soaked with perspiration and gasping for air. For a moment, she was afraid to move. Her nerves steadied as the dream faded. The land was silent, the stars fading with the first hint of dawn. She shivered in the cool air. Despite the rude awakening, the food last night, followed by the rest, had improved her mood. Somewhat less dispirited, she felt more able to persevere.

She was stiff from lying on the hard ground. Her head rested on a pack, pushed against the base of a tree. She had acquired her 'pillow' from the cottage where she found the food. The only items that she could say, with honesty, belonged to her were the clothes she wore, the Scraufin and her sword. Her dress was filthy. Early on, she had ripped the sides of both it and her shift, to allow her legs freedom of movement. Garments inside her pack were 'borrowed', too. These were clean, but much different from her usual attire. She hoped they would allow her to travel in greater comfort.

The sky brightened. Karilyn stood and stretched, wincing as her muscles protested. For the first time, since fleeing, she felt hungry. Nearby was the ridge she crossed the previous night. She ate while she climbed back to the summit. From there she studied her back-trail with care. There was no visible movement, no smoke from campfires nor any sudden panicked flight of birds. Where were her pursuers?

Karilyn was certain they would be hunting for her, although nothing she had seen supported this assumption. The men, whom her father sent on a spurious errand, had returned to the house during the defenders' final hours. Even at the distance she had been, she recognised the group. The traitors had studied each prisoner, living or dead, as well as those cut down in the fields. Afterwards, members of the group entered the house. Several times they carried out bodies, which they tossed into a nearby ditch. She was too far away to identify the remains. Her father and brother, she knew, must be among them. The family's treacherous retainers would discover soon that Karilyn was missing.

After lengthy questioning of the survivors, a large group of Betlic's men entered the house. She assumed the men's commanders thought she was hiding somewhere inside the building. It was some time before they came out. A short while later, several others entered. They carried flaming torches. Smoke billowed behind the soldiers as they ran outside. Troops encircled the outer walls where they kept watch. They must have believed that Karilyn, if still inside, would be driven from her place of concealment by the flames.

The building collapsed. It was apparent she had fled, before the assault, or had chosen to die in the blaze. While soldiers searched the area, Karilyn gave thanks the tunnel, down which she had escaped, led to a natural cave-system. Her eventual scramble, from a pothole, was at a considerable distance from the house. Her feet had left no marks on the dry, rocky streambed. Karilyn had seen enough. She returned to the dry valley then followed it into the hills.

A few days later, Karilyn was in unfamiliar territory. Her father had given her a map, drawn in great detail on a piece of vellum. The map was ancient, although the directions she followed were a recent addition. Without it, she would have been lost.

If Ryce had been correct in his belief, Betlic must know, by now, she was alive. Without prove of a body, he would use the Eye of the talisman to ascertain whether she lived. The tyrant would be able to see both her and her immediate surroundings. Whether he, or anyone else, recognised the area was irrelevant, the Eye would indicate in which direction his men should travel.

There was another possibility, which did not occur to Karilyn until much later. Betlic's men could have been too afraid to admit the possibility that someone might have escaped. Failure, and the reasons for it, would be subject to intense scrutiny. Any hint of incompetence seldom went unpunished.

For a while, after Karilyn's escape, Betlic's men had widened their search. Their diligence went unrewarded. Her tracks remained hidden from them. The flames from the house had been intense. Little remained, other than ashes and stone. The tunnel entrance had collapsed under a pile of rubble. The raiders found nothing that, with any certainty, they could identify as human remains. A lump of silver, its origins made unrecognisable by the inferno, they took to their master.

Betlic had been in a meeting with his commanders, his mind concentrated on running his campaign. When told the item was all that remained of the Scraufin, and everyone from the bearer's family was dead, he barely looked up. The threat was over.

☙ ❧

The stream, beside which Karilyn had slept, looked inviting. She was dirty and dishevelled. In her pack was a block of lye and animal-fat soap, taken from a farm. After a final survey of the countryside from the ridge, she returned to the stream. She stripped then washed her clothes. After she had hung them to dry on a tree, she took the soap and stepped into the icy waters. Her legs were sore, covered in scratches. She cleaned the dirt from the wounds. To her relief, none appeared infected.

The cold water made her skin tingle. For the first time in many days she felt alive. She caught sight of her reflection in a nearby pool. Her hair, wet and recently trimmed to shoulder-length, lay flat against her head. Nipples, pointed in the cold air, stood proud from her pert breasts. Naturally slim, her body was in danger of emaciation after days of running and lack of food. Apart from the marks on her legs, her skin was flawless, the palest of brown. The local men had considered her a beauty, but, because she spurned their many advances, they dismissed her as cold and aloof. Karilyn was neither. There was no-one among them whose life she wanted to share.

Without warning, the sound of galloping horses interrupted Karilyn's reverie. Before she could move, three horsemen had ridden down from the ridge. They reined in at the water's edge. She knew who they were. Their black uniforms were the same as those worn by the men who had attacked her home.

Betlic's men leered at her. She should have been terrified. Their eyes told her the men's intensions. One of them licked his lips while another urged his horse across the stream to cut off any escape. In a slow, deliberate manner, they dismounted. No-one spoke. Karilyn, her nakedness forgotten, remained motionless. She was poised to respond to the situation as her training had prepared her, in the same way it had done with her brother.

Her senses heightened, Karilyn focussed on the two men in front. Behind her came a splash. The one who had crossed the stream had stepped into the water. She remained motionless. The soldier to her left also entered the stream. The third one, who remained on the bank, unfastened his belt. He loosened his trousers. She could smell the foul odour of the men who approached her. It was their intention to pin her down on the bank, then take turns with her body. Certain of their superiority, her lack of movement convinced them she was too frightened to react.

A rush of water sounded behind Karilyn. A huge pair of hands took hold of her arms and pulled them backwards. As the man to her left sprang forward, her trained reflexes took over. She had not rinsed the soap from her body so, with ease, she pulled free her slippery arms. She turned then took hold of the startled soldier's arm. Using his weight and forward momentum, she spun him round to crash heavily into his companion. Karilyn was already holding her first attacker's sword, when the men hit the water. The soldier on the bank, his breaches around his ankles, struggled to draw his sword. He raised the weapon, too late. Karilyn was out of the water. She struck once. The soldier collapsed, head first into the stream, taking her borrowed weapon with him.

The other two men had untangled themselves. One was climbing onto the bank, his sword drawn. His companion sought his weapon in the water, unaware that Karilyn had taken it from him. She stepped back. Her sword was beside her pack. Seeing she was unarmed, the soldier on the bank moved forward, head down, ready to rush her. He charged. Karilyn was ready. She threw herself to one side then rolled over on the ground. Her sword was beside her. She grasped hold of it and flung the sheath away in one flowing movement. As her assailant turned, she deflected his weapon, twisted and cut a huge gash in his side. Bloodied, his mind filled with rage, he ignored the pain as he tried to overpower his opponent. With heavy blows, he forced Karilyn towards the stream.

The man in the water had abandoned the search for his sword. He splashed his way towards his fallen comrade. It was with surprise he pulled his own weapon from the body. Out of the corner of her eye, Karilyn saw him. Her opponents were about to box her in. The bank to her side was steep. Behind her, over a waterfall, the stream descended to her level. With both soldiers in pursuit, she turned and ran. Within seconds, she reached the cascade. She leapt high and, as both feet hit the rock face beside the flow, her knees bent to absorb the impact. She kicked hard then somersaulted over the leading soldier. He looked up as his intended victim flew overhead. Karilyn slashed downwards, the blade of her sword slicing across his throat. Her lithe body twisted in mid-air. She landed on both feet, perfectly balanced. There was a thud behind her.

Furious at the death of both his companions, the remaining soldier faced Karilyn. Despite his anger, he cast an admiring glance at the naked woman in front of him. Confident in his own abilities, he would disarm her, then take his revenge. She stood her ground, holding the sword with both hands, the blade pointed downwards. Blood dripped from its tip. Droplets of red spattered her face and body.

The man slowed his pace. He stopped. The woman's expression, or lack of one, unsettled him. Her eyes followed his every move. His mouth was dry. He feinted to his right. She stood motionless. He lunged. His sword swept down, in an attempt to smash hers out of her grasp. The weapon was no longer there. His body, prepared for the impact, overbalanced. Karilyn's blade sliced upwards and sideways, between his outstretched arms and body. He sank to his knees as she stepped away. She watched him, wary of a last response. There was no need. He slid sideways. After a few moments, he breathed no more.

Karilyn started to shake. The sword fell from her hand. She was violently ill. Ryce's training might have given her the skills to defeat her foes, but nothing could have prepared her for the realisation she had killed a human being. Not one, but three. She sat on the grass banking. For the first time, since the men's arrival, she was aware of her nakedness. The blood glistened on her skin. She was ill once more. Moments later, she staggered to the waterfall. Under its waters, she scrubbed her body over and over again, until she felt cleansed.

The icy coldness of the water drove Karilyn from the torrent. The flow had numbed her body. She shivered as she walked towards her belongings. The two bodies on the bank were in her way. Karilyn averted her eyes from the bloodstained ground and stepped round the remains. Her nerve-endings were on fire as feeling returned to them. The pain concentrated her mind. It brought her out of her trance. She wasted no time in drying herself.

From her pack, Karilyn brought out a pair of short linen trousers. She put these on. A pair of soft woollen breeches, she pulled over the top. To stop the loose fabric from flapping, she tied leather leggings over the breeches, above the ankles. The bottom of her shift had worn beyond repair so she trimmed it to fall a little below her hips. The sides, already torn up to her waist, allowed for easier movement. She pulled on her dress and clasped it at the shoulders with brooches. Again, she had to trim the bottom, but this time to mid-calf. The slits up the side would leave her free to defend herself, or ride in comfort. The breeches, beneath, would preserve her modesty if she met company.

Dressed, Karilyn paused for a moment while she deliberated what she should do now. The altercation had left her better equipped than before the arrival of her attackers. Although the horse, left on the opposite side of the stream, had bolted, the two that remained grazed on the banking nearby. They allowed her to gather their reins and tether them to a sapling. Both animals carried sacks tied to their saddles that contained several days' supply of dried food. She found little else of use, apart from a small dagger, which she hid in the leggings on her right leg.

To ride off and leave the bodies where they lay would risk drawing attention to them. Scavengers, already gathering in the sky, would be visible for miles. Karilyn was positive these men were not from the raiding party. Those members would have attempted to take her prisoner. They would have feared incurring Betlic's wrath by ravishing her. He would want her fit enough for interrogation, to find out what she knew about the Scraufin.

Karilyn blushed when she remembered how they had found her. A woman alone, bathing in a stream. It must have seemed an ideal opportunity for them to satisfy their lust. They had arrived out of nowhere. She had seen no sign of them from the ridge. Was it possible there could be more of Betlic's men in the region, as well as those who hunted for her? The risk posed by discovery of the bodies was too great. She had to find somewhere to hide them.

The stream had not always taken its current path. On the opposite side, a dry channel ended in a pothole. This was limestone country where such features were commonplace. The body in the water had floated face down, towards the other side of the pool. She took a shallower route and paddled across the stream. It was a difficult task to pull the man out the water, he was heavy and his clothes waterlogged. Once clear, she dragged him to the pothole. The opening was large and the drop deep. She rolled him over the edge. He fell from view, although she could hear his body, as it caught the sides for several seconds. Karilyn shuddered as the faint sound of a splash reached her. Now she must fetch the other bodies.

Later, as Karilyn rode away, her legs and back ached. She had wrapped the other two soldiers in their cloaks. It had taken some effort to manoeuvre them up the bank into a position where she could lift them onto her shoulders, to carry them across the stream. Once she had disposed of the last body, she threw any surplus belongings into the abyss. The bloodstains, she covered with fresh soil, which she brushed with branches in an attempt to make it blend with the surrounding area. Satisfied, Karilyn had collected her belongings, then ridden off.

Chapter Twenty Three

Karilyn kept to a steady pace as she rode away from the stream, her spare horse on a lead rope. To the best of her ability, she had removed the traces of her fight with Betlic's men. As days turned to weeks, she progressed westwards across a low range of dusty hills. In time, she left behind the higher ground, as an undulating landscape of grass and woodland opened up in front of her.

She followed the instructions on the map, changed course and headed northwest. Within days, the tips of a distant mountain range came into view. The Mogallean Mountains was their name on the chart. Making regular switches between horses meant her progress was rapid. As she drew near to the towering peaks, as directed, Karilyn followed their line northwards, keeping to the lower ground, away from any of the major routes. She was confident the chosen one awaited her arrival, somewhere beyond the snow-capped mountains.

The young woman had matured much over this period. For most of her life, it had been unusual for Karilyn to be alone for more than a few hours. Now, out of necessity, her self-reliance and confidence in her abilities had grown. At first, in shock at the death of her family, panic rather than reasoned thought had dictated her actions. As the days and weeks passed, the survival lessons she learned many years ago, while travelling with her father, came to her aid.

Karilyn grieved for her loved ones. It was rare for them to be long out of her thoughts. Their fate, she had come to accept. That she possessed the means to contribute to the downfall of those who had killed her family, was a comfort to her. She would succeed.

At first, revenge had been uppermost in Karilyn's mind. Her father had always argued against vengeance for its own sake. Such negative emotions were too powerful. They devastated people, leaving them embittered and empty. When first these thoughts threatened to overwhelm her, Karilyn had recalled his words. Her efforts were rewarded, she conquered the hatred that earlier clouded her reasoning. Ryce had taught her well. She would carry out her duty as a tribute to all whose lives Betlic had destroyed.

On occasion, Karilyn stayed overnight with parties of travellers she met on the trail. Many, fearful of Betlic's intentions, had fled their homes, while others were refugees from lands conquered already. Sometimes she accompanied them for several days. It made a pleasant change from her solitary existence. Tales of attacks by marauding bands on poorly armed groups were common. More than once, she defended herself against outlaws who thought her easy prey.

By the time Karilyn reached the northernmost part of the mountain range, autumn was upon her. In all their multi-coloured splendour, trees carpeted the ground with falling leaves.

She was uneasy. Over recent weeks, on occasion, she had the sensation someone was watching her? This was different to how she felt when bandits tracked her, or wary travellers watched as she rode close to them. After a sudden shiver down her spine, Karilyn would experience the uncomfortable impression that something evil was looking over her shoulder. Whenever she turned there was nothing to see. It made her flesh crawl.

Since the fight in the stream, there had been no indication that anyone followed her. Some time ago she reached the conclusion, Betlic thought her dead. Therefore, it was with some disquiet, she had to accept something had happened to change his mind. He must be using the Eye to track her. There could be no other explanation for her foreboding. Her one hope was to find sanctuary with the rebels before Betlic caught her.

A day or so earlier, Karilyn crossed the main trails to enter an area of broken ground at the edges of the foothills. The path she followed wound through narrow gorges, beside roaring streams and fast flowing rivers. Whenever she found a high point from which she could study her back-trail, she looked for signs that someone might be following her. She feared a whole army could lie hidden among the jumble of canyons. Not until they attacked would she know.

The feelings of impending danger grew stronger and increased in frequency. Despite the lack of sightings, Karilyn was positive Betlic and his men must be close. Camped that night, beside a stream, she resisted the temptation to light a fire. During the early hours of the morning she awoke, startled by the howl of a wolf on the nearby slopes. Her horses stirred, unsettled by the haunting call. In a soft and gentle tone, she talked to the animals. Her voice calmed them. They returned to grazing.

As Karilyn wrapped her blankets round her, a sound made her freeze. Carried on the wind, she caught the faint murmur of voices. It lasted for a few, brief seconds before the breeze died. Now she was fully awake. Wasting no time, she packed away her bed. She saddled a horse. For the moment, it was too dark to ride. She led the animals along the path. As soon as the sky began to brighten, she mounted and increased her pace.

To Karilyn's right, a rugged cliff wall towered. It overhung the path in many places. A few paces to her left, the ground dropped sheer to a distant raging torrent. Beyond the waters, the land rose steeply, rising high to a rocky ridge that dominated the narrow valley. In time, hidden from sight, the sun cleared the horizon in the east. Its rays caught the tip of the ridge opposite. Beneath the summit, as the band of light broadened, the hillside revealed its secrets.

Karilyn had come some distance from her campsite. The sensation something was close behind persisted. She dug in her heels. Her horse responded to the pressure. Horses and rider followed the path up the meandering valley. Her enemies were drawing near. She felt powerless to escape the threat they posed. This feeling of hopelessness, she was sure, Betlic transmitted to her through his use of the talisman. This knowledge was of little comfort. It made it no easier to counter its effect.

A figure launched itself from a fissure in the cliff face. The attack was so swift, Karilyn was unable to take avoiding action. Dragged from her horse, she landed flat on the stony ground, her assailant partly on top. Although winded, her reaction was instant. She kicked out, rolled clear and drew her sword from its sheath. Her attacker tried to speak, but she gave him no time. Obliged to defend himself, he drew his own weapon.

There was a look of desperation on his face. It was not, Karilyn soon realised, from fear for his life. He was easily her equal with the sword. The man blocked a beautifully timed blow, then before she could strike again, he grabbed hold of her sword-arm. She performed the same move as she had on Peter, her brother. This time, as well as her opponent, she found herself on the ground. Wary now, she gained her feet. Her attacker was no novice; he was a match for her in many of the techniques in which she had herself trained. To her surprise, he lowered his weapon.

"Stop, will you," he said, a note of desperation in his voice. "Betlic and his men are closing in on you. Another group of his soldiers has circled round and is lying in wait up ahead. You're riding into a trap."

"Who are you and why should I trust you? Why didn't you step out to speak to me?"

"Would you have stopped for a stranger on a lonely-path? No! I thought so," he said, as she shook her head. "We can talk later. If you want to remain free, you must come with me. We have little time. Give me your cloak, and bring some of your possessions to the edge of the cliff."

"Why?" she answered after a moment's hesitation.

Wary as she was, Karilyn found herself drawn to the stranger. She accepted, he posed her no immediate threat. If she was about to ride into a trap, and her instincts were in accord with this assumption, it was sensible to listen to this man's suggestions. For the moment, she would follow his lead, but keep her weapons to hand in case he proved treacherous.

"If Betlic reaches the others without a sighting, he'll search the area in an attempt to find your hiding place. If we can make him think you've fallen down the cliff, he'll believe you dead and call-off the hunt."

There were numerous scuff marks on the ground where they had fought. The stranger made several more, leading towards the edge. Karilyn followed his example. He took her cloak and slashed it several times. When he pulled out a dagger, she stepped away, wary of his intentions. It was on himself he used it. He drew it across his arm. The blood from the cut, he smeared and dripped around some of the slices in the cloak. He left it beside the drop then tossed the bloodied dagger further back.

A strip of cloth, torn from his own tunic, he also bloodied. Near the edge, he ripped up a bush, which he tossed into the waters, before snagging the rag on the remaining stump. Despite her protestations, he opened one of her bags, then threw many of her belongings over the edge. Some came to rest on the rocks, the remainder landed in the torrent. Her other possessions he tossed onto the ground. A bungled robbery had taken place. In the ensuing fight, both parties had fallen to their deaths in the river below, or so it would appear.

"This way," he said, beckoning to her. "Leave the horses. We cannot take them with us. If you've anything small you value, bring it with you, if you're quick."

Apart from her map, there was nothing else. The Scraufin was beneath her tunic, her sword in her hand. Careful to make no further tracks, they moved over the hard, rock-strewn ground to return to the path. The stranger began to climb the rock face. Within moments, he reached the fissure from which earlier he had leapt. He moved beyond Karilyn's line of sight. She sheathed her sword then followed his lead. Once above the height of a mounted person, she found a slit in the stone. Karilyn squeezed through the narrow opening to step into a gap hidden from the pathway. To her right it ascended steeply, concealed from below by a wall of rock strata. She could see the feet of her attacker as he sprinted away from her. After one last look at her horses, she took a deep breath and hurried after him.

The climb was strenuous. Her legs felt leaden. When she caught up with the stranger, Karilyn was out of breath. She found him stretched-out on a ledge, high above the pathway. With a finger to his lips to indicate she remain silent, he motioned her to his side. For a while they remained unmoving, their gazes focused on an area lower down the gorge, where the trail came into sight. Their ears strained to pick up the sound of any movement or voices. A cold icy chill crept over Karilyn's body. Betlic, she knew, was close.

A lone horseman rode into sight. As he cantered up the valley, the rider turned and beckoned to someone hidden from the watchers' view. Within minutes, the path filled with dozens of mounted men. All carried weapons, some swords, others bows. Many had both. The group parted. Through the centre, a huge man rode, accompanied by numerous bodyguards. Karilyn needed no telling. This was Betlic. The icy chill struck deeper. Now she was frightened. If he brought out the Eye, he would locate her in an instant. She pressed her body down onto the rocks and tried to whisper a warning to her companion. Again, he put a finger to his lips. He shook his head.

Ahead of the riders, Karilyn's horses grazed on the sparse grass. With the approach of the soldiers, the animals stirred. The troops surrounded them. Several men leapt to the ground. A couple took hold of the horses' reins. Others checked the opened packs and their former contents, which lay strewn around. Two scouts studied the bloodied cloak and the signs of struggle. The pair followed them to the cliff top. Their voices carried to the ledge high above them.

"It looks as though someone's done our job for us Master," one of the men called out to Betlic.

"What of the Scraufin? Is it here?"

"No, your highness, it must have gone over the edge with the woman and her attacker."

Betlic was sceptical. It was too convenient. He knew a way by which he could determine the truth. If she still lived, the Eye would find her. She must be nearby. Betlic took hold of a leather bag, suspended by a gold chain hung around his neck. With practised ease, he removed the contents. Even though the distance was too great for Karilyn to make out the object, she knew beyond doubt what Betlic held, and what he would do with it next. She ignored her companion's warning look, to whisper in his ear.

"Run, save yourself. Betlic has the Eye of the talisman. He'll find me the instant he uses it. Now, go, or you, too, will become a target."

"Never, it's taken me months to find you. I cannot leave now."

"You must. Don't you understand, once he puts on the cloak, he'll be able to see me here? If you stay, he'll see you, too, and hunt you down."

"Don't worry, you'll be safe with me."

Before Karilyn could speak further, something brushed against her legs. For a moment, the thought of snakes entered her mind. She stifled a cry and looked behind, straight into the eyes of the largest dog she had ever seen. Unnerved, she grabbed hold of the stranger's arm. He stared at where she pointed and smiled.

"Here Heardwine, quickly, come, lie down beside us," he kept his voice low as he patted the ground at his side.

Karilyn looked in astonishment as the dog stretched-out between them.

"It's all right," the stranger whispered. "The animal won't hurt you. It'll protect you from the Eye. Keep quiet. I'll explain later," he said, forestalling the questions she was anxious to ask.

Below, Betlic wrapped the mantle around his shoulders. He cupped the Eye in his hands and raised it aloft. He chanted. Strands of mist materialised a short distance in front of him. For a moment or two, the vapour wreathed. It became darker, denser and started to spin. With each revolution, its speed increased, until it took the form of a large, slim vertical disc. Ever louder Betlic chanted. Ghostly shapes flickered and raced across the manifestation. After several minutes he fell silent, the imagery faded. He returned the Eye to its leather bag. The disc collapsed in on itself, to explode with a sharp crack, its strands soon dispersed into the atmosphere.

"So, it's true. She's gone over the cliff," Betlic exclaimed with satisfaction.

He turned towards his commanders.

"For a moment I glimpsed her, with someone else. A vague impression that faded to nothing, as did her likeness. This only happens when people die while the Eye is focused on them. The torrent must have swept both her, and her attacker, away. There was no time for me to see where their bodies lie. Lower some men to the river bank," he commanded one of his aides. "Let them work their way downstream, it's possible they might come across the remains. It's a damned pity this river flows underground lower down. If the waters have taken them below, no-one will ever find the woman and her assailant. The Scraufin, if it's not recovered before then, is lost to everyone. Nothing can stop me now.

"If those fools had told me earlier about the woman, we could have caught her weeks ago and saved ourselves much of this journey. Now, we must return. I've been away too long; there's much that requires my attention."

The latest news, received from the commanders in the field, had spoken of setbacks. To undermine his opponents' resolve, the talisman needed to be much closer to their positions. Since its absence, the enemy had rallied.

"You," Betlic shouted to one of his followers. "Ride on. Bring back the ambush party. Rejoin me as soon as possible."

On the rocks, high above, Karilyn and the stranger remained silent. Neither of them dared move. The dog appeared to be sleeping, its heavy head resting against Karilyn's arm. As they watched, Betlic's men lowered several of their fellows into the gorge. A small group tracked them from above, leading the search party's horses and their own. Betlic turned away and, with the rest of his followers, rode off. With them, they took Karilyn's horses and possessions. Soon, no-one remained on the ledge. Silence returned to the gorge.

The watchers maintained their position. Without speaking, they awaited the arrival of the ambush party. The delay was short. Karilyn now understood how close she had been to falling into Betlic's trap. She was grateful for the stranger's intervention. Without it she would be dead or a prisoner, the tyrant would possess the Scraufin and any hope of justice for her family would be at an end. The last of the riders disappeared from sight.

After several minutes the dog moved away, along the cliff top, in the direction taken by Betlic's men.

"We can move and talk now," the stranger said. He stood and stretched, lazily, to ease his cramped muscles. "If they turn back, Heardwine will warn us in plenty of time," he added.

He offered his hand. Karilyn allowed him to help her to her feet. She too was stiff from lying on the hard rock. His arm was strong, his grip firm but not brutal. She brushed her fingers against her sword, to confirm it was still in place. Karilyn felt a degree of guilt. She blushed when she realised he had noticed her actions. This man had saved her from certain capture, torture and death. It seemed churlish to behave towards him in this way.

"I understand," he said. "You do well to trust no-one. Your safety is paramount, especially with the charge you carry."

"What charge?" Karilyn's voice and face expressed innocent surprise.

Who was this man? What did he know? Earlier, he said he had spent months searching for her. Why? She had been travelling only since early summer. Her hand drifted towards her sword. Could his attempt to save her from Betlic be a trick? How could a dog shield her from the Eye? She stepped back a pace and gripped tight the handle of her sword. Her movement took her too close to the cliff's edge. The rock crumbled beneath her foot and she slipped backwards. Alert to the danger, the stranger leapt forward and pulled her to safety.

"Please, you're in no danger from me," he said as Karilyn, once clear of the drop, again grasped the hilt of her weapon. "I'm a Xicaliman, one of the rebels and an ally of Hafter. Once we confirmed Betlic was making use of the talisman and moving men towards his northern border, I came to look for you. We expected to find both you and your father travelling this way. I'm here to act as your guide. Where is your father?"

Karilyn relaxed her grip. Hafter was the person her father had mentioned, the one she sought. She studied this man in greater detail. He was a little taller than was she. His face was rugged, burnt by sun and wind. He carried several days' growth of beard. She stared straight into his deep blue eyes. Something inside her stirred, a feeling never before experienced. The stranger smiled. She smiled back, only to blush and avert her gaze in confusion. She felt drawn to him in a way not experienced with any other. He offered his hand to her.

"I'm Marazin. You must be Karilyn."

"How do you know my name, and all these other things?" Karilyn asked in astonishment. Was he a magician?

"Hafter told me. Early last year, he learned much from a set of ancient scrolls and a book, given to him by a stranger. This included information about the Mastig and a Scraufin, which, if true, confirmed and expanded details he already knew. Seeking confirmation, he sent someone to follow the clues laid out in the writings. After several months, the trail led that person to your father, whose hospitality he enjoyed one evening, around autumn last year."

"A wild looking man, with a fresh scar across his cheek?" she recalled without difficulty.

"Yes, that's him," Marazin said with a chuckle. "Please remember, he'd been travelling for some time. Usually he looks far more civilised."

"I remember him, Orvyn was his name. He arrived with my father one evening. We shared a meal. When I asked my father about him, he said they were to discuss some land the man wanted to buy. Afterwards, they talked in private, late into the night. When I awoke the following morning, Orvyn had left. My father said they'd failed to reach an agreement. I'd no reason to give it any further thought. Why did he keep it from me that Orvyn was an emissary of Hafter? I'd knowledge of everything else."

"Your father knew unrest was stirring abroad, but, not until Orvyn's arrival, did he become aware Betlic had obtained the mantle. Even with the tyrant's newfound ability to control the talisman, unless Betlic became a direct threat, your father said he would not make a move. He suspected some recent additions to his workforce might be spies, sent to watch over the land. He was wary that someone might overhear mention of Hafter and the Xicaliman rebels, then relate this to Betlic. That would have put you all in danger. For the moment your home was little different to any other place from which his agents operated. It held no special interest for him.

"We expected you sooner. When you failed to arrive, I came in search of you. Why did you delay so long? At the time, Orvyn said your father told him he believed you were in no imminent danger. Later, you must have learned Betlic's army was massing to the south."

"Yes, father heard the stories, and about Betlic's use of the talisman. He said we were safe for the moment. We had ample time to prepare before we needed to leave. You are aware the Mastig appears only at certain times? To show our hand too soon could have put us in grave danger. He was fond of our home. He knew once he left, it would be doubtful if he would see it, or my mother's grave, again. It wasn't until my brother, Peter, arrived that my father understood he'd delayed too long.

"Peter brought bad news. Betlic had learned of the threat to his power posed by the Mastig, and my family's involvement with it through the Scraufin. He had despatched a company of troops to find us. The warning came too late. Betlic's men were only days behind my brother. Before our preparations were complete, the enemy arrived. My father insisted I go alone, my charge was too important to risk capture. Both he and Peter died, defending our home, giving me the chance to escape. I've been running ever since."

"How did Betlic learn about the Scraufin and its association with the Mastig, was it the men your father suspected?"

"I cannot know for certain. In front of the workers, newcomers or old, my father never discussed the objects. Any matters relating to the Mastig we dealt with when the house was empty, or when we were alone out in the countryside. We'd a cave, in the hills, where I received instruction in combat skills; it contained nothing directly related to our secret. All my knowledge of the Mastig, I have memorised for years.

"It rankled with Peter that the guardianship of the Scraufin passed to me. My personal belief is that one night, when drunk, he let the story slip, or the part he knew. He was a soldier of fortune. For the past few years, I believe it probable he was in Betlic's service, working for someone of high rank. The amount of information he knew, how he managed to evade Betlic's men on his way home, and the way he avoided any questions when he arrived convinces me of this. Once he realised what he'd done, family loyalty over-rode any allegiance he had to Betlic. Peter deserted, then tried to make amends by alerting us."

"I see, but Betlic cannot have been following you all this time. Using the talisman as he did today, he would soon have caught you."

"I imagine he thought I'd perished in the flames of my home, along with the object I bear. It's in these past few weeks I've become aware of someone watching from afar. Something has alerted him to my escape. Over recent weeks, he's been using the Eye to track me. For him to catch me so quickly, it must have taken him across country. What I can't understand is why he couldn't find me when he was standing so close?"

"Heardwine, the dog, possesses some strange powers," Marazin explained. "When close by, the animal shields you from the Eye. Hafter knows more detail. The dog's main role seems to be to protect the chosen one and those who aid him or her. I can tell you more while we ride. We must travel fast and far."

"Ah! Heardwine must be the Guardian, I should have realised," Karilyn said. Ryce had told her about the beast. "But you're forgetting Betlic's men took my horses and supplies," she reminded him. "I'm without a mount."

"I've a spare horse and rations sufficient for two. My camp is over the ridge. Shall we go?"

Karilyn nodded. In truth, her choices were limited. She was on foot, without provisions, in a strange land. Marazin whistled twice in a high-pitched tone. The dog bounded back into sight. It flopped down in front of Karilyn and, as she bent down to pat it, she gazed into its eyes. For several seconds she was unable to move. The beast appeared to look deep inside her, stripping away her defences until it exposed her soul. Heardwine blinked and the moment passed. It held out its paw. Karilyn shook it.

"It's taken to you," Marazin said. "It does that only to people it trusts."

With the dog alongside, the couple climbed the hillside and over the ridge to the valley beyond. It was a steep and none too pleasant descent from the heights. Loose shale covered the slope. Several times the walkers' feet slid from beneath them. Neither was sorry to reach firmer ground at the base. Curious as to what type of man Marazin was, Karilyn studied his campsite. Nestled in a hollow, it was neatly set out. It showed evidence of several days' use. The initial impression she gained of her companion was favourable. This was not the campsite of a ruffian. Before breaking camp, the couple shared a quick meal. After a last look around, they turned their horses northwards then rode away.

Chapter Twenty Four

Deep in thought, Betlic reviewed the many reports that had reached him earlier in the day. Clean-shaven, square-jawed and dark-eyed, he exuded power, which many women found more attractive than his evident good looks. Over six foot in height and broad in shoulder, Betlic's body was muscular, his waist narrow. His short-cropped hair was black, streaked with silver at the temples. A thin scar ran across his forehead. His clothes, cut from the finest cloth, were practical in design rather than for show.

Was he an evil person? Had such a notion occurred to him, Betlic would not have thought of himself in that way. Power was his interest, power and order. His order. He considered everything else subservient to that overriding passion. To Betlic's mind, two types of people populated the world, those who agreed with him and those who were insignificant. It was a simple philosophy.

To be fair, those who followed him and did his bidding without question, he treated well. They received food, clothing and money. Those more senior, Betlic recompensed with the pick of the land; property confiscated from those who opposed him. Men with aptitude progressed through the ranks, with little to hinder them. Those, who believed they had a right by birth to a certain position in life, were unpopular and, unless capable, seldom tolerated. His commanders attained their status by worth. Every man knew that. As a result, each had the utmost confidence in the other.

Those whose nations Betlic over-ran faced similar options. Any who embraced the life offered, without reservation, he made welcome. Once they proved their worth, they became a part of his force, treated with scant difference from his original followers. Of course, there were those who objected or resisted. For those taken prisoner, it depended much on their circumstances whether they faced execution or enslavement until their spirits withered and died. Those who could, fled, or perished in the attempt.

Men, whose loyalties were untested or suspect, found themselves in special companies of Betlic's army, their behaviour under constant scrutiny.

Sent into battle ahead of regular troops, to weaken the enemy in readiness for the main onslaught, huge numbers died in action. If they survived long enough to prove their allegiance, they earned a transfer to a regular unit.

For those sympathisers who were willing, but too old to fight, the most able joined supply units. Others, incapable of heavy work, returned to their earlier lives. Those whose loyalty remained in doubt, worked the land, or performed menial work as slaves. Any woman, whose husband or father refused to serve under Betlic, could find herself auctioned as a slave, or used for soldiers' recreational purposes.

For the ordinary peasant, it was arguable that Betlic offered many a better way of life. Under his rule, there was little in the way of social barriers to hold them back. Those with ability could succeed, no matter how lowly their beginning. It was regrettable he was so intolerant of transgressions. Even the smallest deviation from his rules incurred the severest of penalties.

The more expertise Betlic gained in the use of the talisman, the more its power over him increased. What empathy he possessed, and understanding of the suffering he caused, eroded under the object's influence. It became his way or death; a far from comfortable regime under which to live. Yet many, whose acceptance was without reservation, prospered.

Betlic believed the choices he offered the vanquished were generous. The concept of individual freedom was foreign to him. Not that such a thought process differed to any great extent from those of the rulers he overthrew. Whoever won, those unfortunates without drive or ambition who remained at the bottom of the social and military hierarchy, would find their bleak and miserable existences little changed. It was the barbarity, with which Betlic enforced his rule, that made the difference. Kingdoms, although autocratic, had monarchs whose authority depended on the support of powerful families. These nobles often commanded sufficient leverage to keep a check on some royal excesses.

Betlic had dispensed with this layer of support, and any subsequent need to appease. From peasant stock, early in his youth he escaped the drudgery of serfdom. After a period of travelling, learning to survive by his own wits, he came to join a group of mercenary soldiers. His fighting techniques, knowledge and proficiency with weapons improved, as did his leadership skills. Many times on the field of battle, where he showed a keen strategic grasp, he proved his courage.

At a young age, he became their leader. His reputation grew, as did the number of his followers. His thirst for power intensified. He first heard of the talisman, and its location, from an old man he had taken prisoner. In disguise, Betlic paid Xicalima a visit. He discovered its leaders were ill prepared for conflict. The strength of Betlic's private army, as it had become, enabled him to seize power. It did not take long for him to establish a reputation for ruthlessness, against any who opposed or plotted against him.

Such an attitude ensured his generals followed him with utmost loyalty, not that they were afraid to speak their minds, or offer suggestions. They had gained their rank on merit. Betlic had great respect for his battle-hardened commanders. He was shrewd enough to listen to their wise council. In particular, during campaign planning, he encouraged open discussion. Well thought-out suggestions Betlic never discounted, but the final decisions he made alone. Once he had decided upon a strategy, without fail or complaint, implementation was by everyone.

Despite his callous behaviour, Betlic could be highly charismatic. He was a fine orator when necessary. Wherever he went, he inspired his followers, the talisman made certain of that. His generals were aware that the loyalty of the men they oversaw was foremost to their leader.

There was much among the reports, on the table beside Betlic, for him to reap satisfaction. The war was progressing well. Since returning from seeking out the Scraufin bearer, Betlic was overseeing matters again. Campaign oversight was much easier and more efficient when he was back at its centre of operations.

It was unfortunate he had needed to find the girl. As he refused to allow the talisman and the mantle to leave his side, he had little choice than to go in search of her himself. Without the repeated use of the Eye, the girl's location would have been difficult to find. To use messengers to relay the information would have been impractical and taken too long. That would have allowed her to escape. Even so, he had been too late. She was dead, along with the thief who tried to rob her.

It irked him that his men had not recovered their bodies. The mountain torrent had swept their remains deep underground, taking with them the object he sought. His sources said it was a silver cylinder, its dimensions unknown. What did it do? Did it contain something, a potion, a piece of manuscript covered in ancient script that, when read aloud, counteracted his power? It must be something that worked against the talisman. Whatever this wretched item was, it was lost forever.

The whole affair had been unsatisfactory. This was the second time Betlic had missed-out on the object, and the girl declared dead. Why had those fools kept silent about the possibility the woman had escaped death in the fire? This omission had infuriated Betlic. If they had told him the blaze was too intense for them to identify her remains in the ashes, he could have been on her trail within weeks. Under such circumstances, he would have attached no blame to the men. She could have been in his hands weeks, months ago, along with the Scraufin. The men had lied about that, too. They had passed off a lump of silver as the remains of the object.

In the wrong place at the right time, he had overheard the story being discussed. The fools concerned had paid the price for their stupidity. He had ensured as many of their fellows as possible witnessed their execution. Being sparing with the truth to their leader was a habit he discouraged. It did no harm to re-enforce the principle.

Betlic had used the Eye on a number of occasions during, and since, his return journey. Each attempt failed to locate the girl; no images appeared to suggest she still lived. She must be dead. There could be no other conclusion. Otherwise, the Eye would have reacted. There was nothing to gain in making further attempts. He needed to conserve his energies, to concentrate on the talisman's powers to help him progress the war; but his mind refused to let his concerns rest.

He was missing something, something important, some knowledge that might explain his unease. At night, he would leave his bed and the charms of his current mistress. By the light of a tallow lamp, he reread his scrolls and ancient manuscripts. He was yet to find anything to cause him concern. The girl, and the object she carried, were in a place where no-one could find them. Whatever the Mastig was, or could have done to thwart his plans, without the Scraufin, it was no longer a threat. He was safe — so why was he worried?

CB ED

When Betlic reached his base after his search for Karilyn, the winter solstice was less than a week away. So far, there had been no snowfall in this region. The winds, when they blew, were icy cold. Frost covered the land. Soon the ground would freeze hard beneath the crystal coating. The mountains, through whose foothills he had followed Karilyn, would carry a deep blanket of snow. It would be foolhardy to advance far in that direction until spring. Planning his offensive would help make the time pass.

He knew the Xicaliman rebels operated from somewhere inside that vast mountain range. Their exact location remained unknown. To enhance his knowledge of the area, his men had undertaken numerous missions. None had returned. To be able to conceal their centre of operations from him, the passes around their base must be well-guarded and patrolled.

Betlic assumed the rebels operated from a high mountain stronghold. The sierra had proved an obstacle to his use of the Eye. For some reason it could not penetrate them. Had he knowledge of the central lowlands and their access from the far north, his preparations would have been vastly different, his chances of a successful and speedier campaign much greater.

While he drew up his plans for the coming offensive, Betlic did not forget about his earlier conquests. Since breaking out from their home territory of Xicalima, his forces had spread far. To fight on too many fronts would stretch his resources until they became unsustainable (the main reason he had halted his advance north last summer). Had not someone related Peter's drunken story about the Scraufin to Betlic, Ryce and his family would still be living, untroubled in their home.

Betlic's armies had reached the coasts to the south, east and west of Xicalima. In-between, he controlled the whole peninsula. His territories and their resources were vast. Vanquished populations either changed allegiance or were enslaved. At Betlic's command, the construction of temporary garrisons in strategic places had taken place. Once he had established and consolidated his empire, he would build structures of a more permanent nature. Maintaining control did not require huge concentrations of men. Betlic recalled and rested large numbers of his occupying troops. New recruits received training in the ways of Betlic before integration into his forces.

He anticipated his future expansion plans would come at a greater cost than his earlier invasions. The kingdoms overrun already had fought alone. Countries had abandoned their alliances, to watch their neighbours crumble under the onslaught of Betlic's armies. He had conquered them, one-by-one.

Had they stood together, they might have been able to resist, for a while at least. Each had lived in the vain hope that, if they ignored the calls for help from their former allies, Betlic might leave them alone. This idea was one he did his best to foster.

By now, the world knew his ways. His future targets would be more inclined to unite against him. To Betlic's fury, King Grogant, from Vretliana, was ready to sign a pact with someone whose name was familiar. A person who Betlic had believed was dead. Talon, the man who had recovered the mantle for him, had sworn he killed the last member of the Xicaliman royal family. So, if the boy king was dead, how had Grogant managed to agree a pact with him? King Amron of Xicalima! Betlic flew into a wild rage when he first learned of this. He was the supreme ruler of Xicalima. There could be no other.

This had provided the motivation, behind Betlic's recent decision, to launch his next offensive against the mountain stronghold. His original intent had been to subjugate the lowland countries, to leave the sierra isolated, cut off from any support. After then, he would have the luxury of being able to crush the rebels in his own time.

Now, with the upstart Amron claiming the throne of Xicalima, the rebel threat was too great to ignore. Even with the talisman to demoralise the spirits of his enemies, and boost his own men's morale, Betlic was not indomitable. With the overthrow of the old Xicaliman king, tens of thousands of refugees had fled the new regime. These fugitives had spread far and wide. With the rallying call of a new and legitimate heir, how many of these might flock to the rebel standard? They could attract others, too, who had escaped Betlic's rule elsewhere.

What Betlic thought of as being a small, hotchpotch of disaffected Xicalimans, could burgeon into a major fighting force. This would exacerbate if Amron kept forging alliances with other kingdoms. With the Mastig lost to him, against the talisman, Amron had no other support than his band of rebels, for now. On their own, they were too weak to stand up to a massed assault. If Betlic left Amron alone for too long, this freedom would allow other territories time to forge alliances with him and each other. Betlic had a suspicion it was Amron alone, the man of whom the legends spoke, who could unite them all. If this union came about, the despot's forces would meet far stronger resistance than they had ever faced. He must defeat Amron before this happened. Once the snows cleared from the mountain passes, Betlic would strike.

To that end, over the following months, Betlic moved his armies northeastwards. By early spring, his men were on the plains, to the south of the Mogallean Mountains. They were ready to strike, but against whom? Determined to promote confusion, he sent scouts out in many directions. He gave them conflicting stories as to where and against which lowland country his spring offensive was to take place. Enemy forces captured many of his men. It would have surprised him had events been otherwise. Knowingly, he had sent them to areas where he knew his enemies had concentrated forces in large numbers. Because of this misdirection, when the high passes cleared, his sudden move towards the mountains would take most of his potential victims by surprise.

Of what Betlic was unaware, was the length of time Amron had been in power. Before his arrival, rebel numbers had been considerable, that of a small country. Now refugees from all nations seeking sanctuary had swelled them. Since early in the year, despite the mis-information received, Amron's forces had prepared for an assault. In the narrow passes and among the peaks, they were ready for Betlic's men. Although not immune to the demoralising effects of the talisman, Amron's men knew the reasons behind the thoughts they would experience. Hafter had explained, in detail, to the rebel commanders what could be the effects of Betlic's manipulation of the talisman. In turn, they relayed his words among their men.

Chapter Twenty Five

The sun, masked by the high peaks of the western mountains, cast the land deep into shadow. Nightfall was imminent. Marazin and Karilyn had spent most of the day in the saddle. Apart from an occasional brief respite to rest their horses, they had ridden long across the rugged foothills. Their close encounter with Betlic had left them wanting to widen the distance between themselves and him as much as possible.

Soon after leaving Marazin's campsite, Karilyn, who tended to be shy with strangers, was in animated conversation with her riding companion. As a soldier, Marazin had spent most of his adult life in male-dominated surroundings. It was to his great surprise, he, too, found little difficulty in expressing himself. So relaxed were they in each other's company, it was difficult to believe that morning they had met for the first time. Each learned about the other's life, family and upbringing. They laughed at each other's tales of youthful escapades. Later, neither of them could recall a happier day.

Before darkness was complete, they tethered and rubbed down their horses. Over a blazing fire, they prepared a meal. They shared the chores and, before too long, had eaten their fill. In a cloudless sky, the heavens were alight with stars. This late in the year, once the sun went down, the temperature dipped sharply. Marazin, ever attentive, retrieved a spare blanket from his supplies. Karilyn wrapped it round her shoulders. She was curious how he had learned his fighting skills. When they had fought, his prowess in countering her every move intrigued her.

"From my earliest years, my father taught me combat skills," Marazin said. "He'd trained under some of the best teachers. After Betlic overthrew the king, my grandparents organised my parents' escape from Xicalima. Apart from my mother and father, the rest of the family became involved in resisting the invaders. My relatives dissuaded my parents from joining the struggle. Apart from them, I've no knowledge of my kinsmen's fate.

"A few years ago, I went in search of them. I found nothing. In Xicalima, so I discovered, Betlic's spies are everywhere. Someone risked their life to warn me I'd come under suspicion. With luck and a few helping hands, I evaded the authorities long enough to escape across the border. My relatives are either dead, or scattered throughout the nations. I keep hoping, if any have survived, they might be drawn to the rebel stronghold." Marazin added more fuel to the fire before continuing.

"My parents fled before I was born, so I never met any of my extended family. Because of that, I can't identify them by their looks. My uncles', aunts' and some of my cousins' names are known to me. Over the years, I suppose, they'll have changed these to conceal their identities. Once we defeat Betlic, with Hafter's aid, it might be possible to trace some of my kin, if any survive."

"It seems strange your relatives joined the rebels, yet did not expect your parents to stay and fight alongside them," Karilyn said. "Do you have any idea why they were chosen to leave?"

"I can't say I attached much importance to it, until I met Hafter. It was part of my parents' past. I accepted it, without query. I'd been too busy living my own life to worry about theirs. For hours, Hafter questioned me about them and my childhood. I can remember my father, once, telling me it was their obligation to survive and produce an heir. He'd a huge wooden chest, filled with documents. Most of these papers related to their life, and lands, in Xicalima. Hafter has convinced me they would have contained information relating to another matter as well. We'll come to that in a moment, and the answer to your question."

"What happened to your parents, and the chest?"

"I was a soldier, fighting in lands overseas. On the day I left home, my father said there was something I needed to know. He would await my homecoming before burdening me with it. Once abroad, I moved from one campaign to another. Later, to my great sorrow, I learned I'd left it too late. I received word my parents had perished in a fire. Hafter believes the blaze was set deliberately and Betlic's men murdered them.

"My father kept the box hidden beneath the roof. When I reached my home, only its ashes remained. The blaze had been extreme and destroyed everything. I realise now that it had been far too fierce for an ordinary house fire. Neighbours had sifted through the ruins. They buried what they could find of my parent's bodies. Apart from a few twisted pieces of metal, nothing else recovered was recognisable.

"What I do know is, since gaining power, Betlic has engaged in hunting down and destroying his enemies. According to Hafter, both my father and mother were of noble birth. Their families had taken-up arms against Betlic. Combined, those two factors meant it was possible that the rebels, to rally support against Betlic's rule, could have made use of my parents. If he discovered their existence, I have little doubt he would want them dead."

"What of this other matter you spoke of? The one Hafter thinks was detailed among the papers inside the chest?" Karilyn was curious.

"How much do you know about the heir and the Mastig?" Marazin asked. "Did your father discover the heir's identity?"

"Father said it's not Amron, although he is the rightful king of Xicalima. Father insisted that, if possible, I avoid all contact with the man. Led to believe he's the heir, Amron, if allowed to interfere, could delay my journey. That would place everyone in danger. Beyond that, father told me something of the history of the heir and their duties. As to their identity, he did not know. He said Hafter would introduce me. My knowledge centres on the Mastig and the Scraufin. That's the reason for my being here, to bring them and the heir together."

"Hafter suspected this might be the extent of your knowledge," Marazin paused a moment. He resumed in a far gentler tone. "I've a letter for you, from your father. He sent it with Orvyn for Hafter to pass to you, should circumstances compel you to travel alone. Your father's intention was to accompany you, but he was aware of his own mortality. If anything happened to him, he wanted you to be sure the person you met was the true heir."

Karilyn was speechless. She waited while Marazin fetched the letter from his pack. The tightly rolled parchment showed numerous signs of staining and creasing from its storage. Ryce's wax seal, which had remained intact, secured its outer edge. The contents were unread. In large letters, close to the seal, he had written 'For K'. Karilyn's heart missed a beat. Her father's writing was unmistakable. Marazin pulled a brand from the fire and held the flames close so she could see to read. She took a deep breath, broke the seal and unrolled the sheet of yellowing manuscript. Her vision blurred in the flickering light. A tear trickled down her cheek. She wiped her eyes and tried to concentrate on her father's words.

My dearest Karilyn,

I fear if you are reading this, I am no longer alive. It pains me to think of you on your own, yet I know you will find the strength to carry on, to fulfil the promise you made when first you understood your duty to the Scraufin.

With the arrival, today, of Orvyn, Hafter's emissary, I have taken the opportunity to send this letter. If, for whatever reason, Hafter is unable to bring you and the heir together, for safekeeping he will pass this note to the one whom you seek. Therefore, Karilyn, the bearer of this epistle, with my seal unbroken, is the Chosen One.

He, or she, will have a travelling companion, a dog that goes by the name of Heardwine. This is the Guardian of which I have spoken. The animal has many unusual qualities. Do not ignore them. They will help to protect you both. If necessary, you must trust your lives to the beast.

Do not be sad for my passing. I have had a good life, made complete by the gift of you and your brother. My blessings, as always, go with you. Dada

Tears fell freely. He had signed the letter with the name Karilyn had used for him throughout her childhood and, later, whenever she wanted something she thought he might not allow. His resolve, she knew, would weaken when she called him dada. She felt Marazin's hand on her shoulder. He squeezed it gently in support. Karilyn turned. She buried her head against his chest and wept. He held her close until, sometime later, she could weep no more.

Chapter Twenty Six

The crackle of nearby flames woke Karilyn. Disorientated, she tensed her muscles. Used to being on her own, her immediate reaction was that she was under attack. Ready to strike out at whatever might threaten, she opened her eyes a mere slit. Across a newly lit fire, Marazin crouched, warming his hands. Reassured, she sat up. Heardwine, who had slept at her feet, moved away. The early morning air was chill. She lifted the blanket, which covered her, and wrapped it round her shoulders.

Yesterday, once Karilyn recovered from the shock of receiving the letter from her father, she and Marazin talked long into the night. Even after her tears dried, she had remained at his side, content to sit with her head resting against his chest, his arm round her. The feelings this close contact aroused had strengthened. Her heart beat faster as she remembered. It both frightened and excited her.

"Good morning," he said, beaming.

"Good morning to you, too," she responded with a smile, her face lighting up at the sound of his voice.

Their fingers brushed as Marazin passed her a goblet of water. A spark of energy flashed between them, an ember that threatened to ignite her whole being. Karilyn looked into his eyes. She realised the sensations she experienced were mutual. They both blushed and averted their gazes. Embarrassed, Marazin turned away and went to find some provisions from his supplies. Karilyn quickly ran her fingers through her hair. By the time Marazin returned, with something for their breakfast, both had their emotions under control.

Karilyn hoped this mutual attraction would not complicate further the task ahead of them. She was the bearer of the Scraufin. Marazin was the heir to the Mastig. The letter from her father had made her companion's position clear. Her role was to guide and protect him, even if it cost her life.

Marazin, too, was unsure what the future held. His duty, as was Karilyn's, was predetermined. If there came a time when he must sacrifice something, or someone, to fulfil his destiny, he would have no alternative but to do so. It had never occurred to him until now. Marazin looked across, towards Karilyn. He realised it was a decision he would rather not have to make.

For the first time in his life, he had found a woman he wanted to know better. Never would he have believed it possible for someone to stir such feelings in him. They had known each other a single day, but, in those few short hours, the direction of both their lives had changed forever.

For a while they ate in silence, suddenly shy in each other's company. When they did begin to talk, it was simultaneous. Within moments, they were laughing and chattering, much as on the previous day. Whatever problems or hardships lay ahead, they would tackle them together. Both had spent their lives in preparation for this moment — Karilyn with her father, Marazin as a warrior. No-one was invincible, each of them knew that. They had to survive.

Later, Heardwine padded alongside them for much of the time as they rode northwards. On occasion, it would race ahead, to check the land in front, then wait at the side of the path until they caught up to it. The riders kept to the lower foothills. The easier trails, on the plains to the east, they shunned. Once Karilyn learned the full extent of Amron's hatred for Marazin, she agreed it would be better to avoid areas where they could expect contact with rebel patrols.

The pair's most direct route, to Hafter's mountain retreat, lay across the mountains to the west. Here in the foothills, the weather had turned bitter. Over the past week, early snowstorms had hit the higher parts of the region. The central mountains were unfamiliar territory to Marazin, their passes guarded. To avoid them would mean climbing the inhospitable snow-capped peaks, which would be foolhardy. Neither traveller had the experience to undertake such a treacherous enterprise. They went north instead, along the route shown by Karilyn's original map.

Days turned to weeks. The couple, as they now thought of themselves, became closer. A touch, a smile, a word was sufficient to excite their senses. Soon, their nights were as passionate as were their feelings for each other. Marazin wondered what Hafter would think? Probably, that his worst fears had come to pass and the world would end tomorrow. Marazin had no such worries.

Each evening, the couple sparred. They took time, too, to hone each other's combat skills. It was soon apparent that they had no need to concern themselves about either one's ability to protect the other. Both, physically and mentally, Marazin and Karilyn were well-matched. What advantage he gained over her in strength, she made up for in agility.

One morning, for once pre-occupied with their thoughts, they lapsed into an extended period of silence. It would soon be four weeks since their first meeting. The northernmost reaches of the Mogallean Mountains were within a few days ride.

"I think we're being followed," Marazin said, although there was little concern in his tone.

"So do I," Karilyn agreed. "I've thought so since we joined this path, but I've not caught sight of anyone, have you?"

"No, not yet. Whoever is coming up behind can't be a threat. Heardwine would have let us know. The problem is that if they reach us and recognise me, matters may become troublesome."

"That would be awkward," Karilyn acknowledged. "There's a gorge ahead that the trail passes through. Let's see, at the other end, if there's somewhere we can hide and watch to see who's following us."

"It's unlikely they'll be friends of mine, but, I doubt they're actively seeking me. It probable they'll ride on. Let's keep going, as if we suspect nothing. Once inside the gap, we should be able to increase the distance between us."

The path twisted and turned as the gorge closed in. The riders dug in their heels. Their horses responded. Heardwine raced ahead to disappear from sight. The ravine was longer than expected. It was some time before the gap widened and they reached open ground. They raced towards it. No sooner had they cleared the gorge when, round the next bend, they came to a side-path. It led up into a wooded area. Heardwine, who had waited for them, started up the slope.

"This way," Marazin called.

He turned his horse and headed after the dog. Karilyn followed. Marazin pulled up then dismounted. He spent a little time, covering up the tracks leading away from the trail. Soon afterwards, the couple wound their way through the woodland. The higher they rode the more densely packed became the trees, which concealed the riders from the main trail.

After several minutes, the path took a sharp turn to the left. It brought the pair onto a heading, parallel to the track beneath, back towards the top of the gorge. The woods opened out. They entered a glade. A little distance ahead, a gap in the foliage gave the couple an uninterrupted view of the trail below. They dismounted and looped their horse's reins round a large fallen branch.

For a long while, they waited in vain for someone to appear. They remained patient. Heardwine slept. They were certain their assumptions were correct. More time passed. The sun journeyed overhead. Shadows lengthened down the hillside. Yet, no-one ventured into sight. Marazin trusted his instincts implicitly, as did Karilyn hers. Whoever it was, they were drawing close.

Heardwine's eyes opened and his ears pricked-up. The faint sound of distant hooves, ringing out on stony ground, reached the watchers. Below, the slope and path were deep in shade. They tensed in expectation. From the noise, it was a single rider. This meant nothing. The pair had observed the way Betlic travelled. Whoever approached could be a forward scout, a target sent ahead to draw fire and alert those behind to danger. Louder, the noise echoed, before it faded as the horse reached softer ground beyond. Round a bend in the trail, a lone horseman came into view. Karilyn did not recognise him. Marazin had no such problem.

"Up here!" he shouted as, on his feet, he waved his arms.

The rider looked upwards. Heardwine barked, its tail wagging. Karilyn saw a scar running across the horseman's cheek. It took several moments before she recognised him. With his hair cut short and beard trimmed, it was difficult to associate the man below with the wild traveller who had visited her father.

"Take the first path to your left," Marazin shouted, "we've found somewhere to make camp."

He smiled with pleasure. Since his departure from Hafter's home, several months earlier, the two friends had not met.

"I hardly recognised him," Karilyn said in disbelief.

Marazin laughed. "I did warn you that Orvyn would look different when you saw him again. When he visited your home, he'd been on the trail for many months. I wonder why he's here? I hope Amron's not causing more trouble."

While they awaited Orvyn's arrival, Marazin unsaddled the horses. Karilyn built a fire. By the time their visitor reached them, flames had taken hold. It was a welcoming sight. Now the sun was setting, the air had turned much cooler, with the hint of a frost to come. As the weary rider tethered his horse, Heardwine bounded over to greet him. Orvyn made a huge fuss of the beast.

"I have fresh meat," Orvyn said, when at last he removed his saddle and supplies. He came closer to the fire. "So, you two did meet. It's good to see you again Karilyn," he took hold of her hand and shook it warmly.

She looked different, Orvyn noted with satisfaction. Although she always carried herself in the manner of a lady, Karilyn was no longer dressed as one. She was still wearing the clothes gathered together months ago, with the addition of a cloak borrowed from Marazin. It was not so much her outfit, although that was unusual, as her demeanour that struck him most. Ryce had been correct when he said time would mature her. She looked, and sounded, confident and self-assured. However, something was wrong, Ryce was missing.

"Where's your father?" Orvyn asked. "I thought you were to journey together."

Marazin interrupted. He explained, briefly, what had happened. The memories were still too raw for Karilyn to speak about them. Orvyn listened in silence, an angry expression on his face. Although he had met Ryce the once, he had taken to the old man. The account of his and Peter's passing was sad to hear. He offered his condolences to Karilyn. Hafter would have to accept Karilyn now, Orvyn thought. There was no-one left who could take her place.

After a moment's silence, he fetched a sack from his belongings. He took out a fresh haunch and various cuts of venison. He had killed the deer that morning. Karilyn took the meat and tossed a large bone to Heardwine. As she prepared a meal, she listened while the two men caught up on news. There was nothing of great importance to relate. Hafter, worried by Marazin's long absence, had sent Orvyn in search of him, to make sure the heir was safe.

"What news of Amron? Is he looking for us again?" Marazin asked.

"No!" Orvyn said. "He still holds the belief we fled the area. Otherwise, on the surface, the king remains much the same. As usual, he gives the appearance of being more interested in hunting and feasting than anything else. Behind the scenes, so Hafter tells me, he is acting more statesmanlike. He has initiated contacts with the rulers of several other countries, many of which are not yet a target for Betlic. Their leaders are no fools. They know, once he has subdued the lands in-between them, they will be directly in his path."

"It's good to know he can do something right." Marazin's admission was grudging. Praise was not worth wasting on the man who had tried to have him killed. He doubted the king would ever make a great ruler. "I presume Hafter has yet to tell his majesty that he is not the heir? That's one conversation I would prefer to be absent from."

"When I left, he was still wondering how to announce it. It'll be pretty explosive when he does. The best place to be will be far, far away."

"But why should it be so dire?" Karilyn asked. "If somebody else is heir, I would have thought it would please Amron. Why wouldn't he be grateful for someone else to do the dirty work? It would allow him more time to be all kingly. Once victory has been achieved, he can take credit for arranging everything."

"Oh! He's a king all right, in attitude at least," Orvyn replied. "As such, he believes he has a divine right to everything. Ever since his father told him about his birthright, he's understood the role of heir to be his. In part, it's because he wants to be a hero. Of greater importance, he deludes himself that, as heir, he could become master of both mantle and talisman."

"Orvyn's right," Marazin said. "Amron's convinced he has the strength to command the objects to enhance his own power. It's an illusion. Once used, the talisman begins to take possession of the one who wields it. A person, such as Amron, who is to some extent weak willed, will offer little resistance to its malevolence. In no time, the objects would dominate his every move. Betlic's will is much stronger and, for now, he's able to resist its more dangerous effects."

"Now I see," Karilyn said.

"As for Amron," Orvyn interrupted, "once he discovers it's Marazin who has displaced him as chosen one, the king will waste no time in hunting him down."

Karilyn cast a worried glance towards Marazin. She grabbed hold of his hand and held it tight, up against her chest. Orvyn observed the look and gesture. Marazin moved closer to Karilyn. He put his arm round her and pulled her close. Orvyn's eyebrow rose. This was a development that would upset Hafter.

"There are other reasons, too, why Amron might come to fear Marazin. They will enrage his majesty when he discovers the truth," Orvyn said.

"What else can there be?" Karilyn demanded, although she feared the answer would not be to her liking.

"For one, if anything should happen to Amron before he produces an heir, the young man beside you could challenge for the title," Orvyn paused a moment as Marazin snorted in disgust at the idea. "I know Marazin does not have a legitimate claim to the throne, nor does he want it. That will make no difference to Amron. Once he discovers their shared ancestry, he will believe otherwise. He might expect, too, once Marazin retrieves the objects, he will behave in the same manner as would Amron — that Marazin will use them against the throne to gain power."

"This is not good," Karilyn said, gazing into Marazin's eyes.

"And," Orvyn was relentless, "there's something else to consider. If, as I said, Amron died, Marazin could claim the crown. Likewise, as Marazin is also childless, if anything happened to him, it's possible the role of heir would pass to Amron."

"Damn, I hadn't thought about that," Marazin said, "and find out I am the heir, he must. Hafter will have to tell him, sooner rather than later. Despite his failings, Amron is king. He has the task of rallying his men and those of other nations. As long as he believes his destiny lies in retrieving whatever the Mastig represents, his efforts into fulfilling his true role will be much reduced."

"What a mess," Karilyn commented. "However, there's nothing we can do to change things, except try to keep out of his way. It's unfortunate we have so long to wait until we can carry out our part of the enterprise. Whatever happens, my love, you must evade Amron's clutches."

"I'll do my best," he said dryly.

"Which, I am afraid, brings me to one last thing that Hafter insisted I tell you," Orvyn again interrupted.

"And what might that be?" Marazin asked with a feeling of dread.

"He said, if both of you appear to be in imminent danger of capture by Amron's men, you, Marazin, must attempt to escape, alone. Under pain of death, the leaders of the king's patrols have to keep safe any who claim knowledge of a strange object and demand to see Hafter. Because Amron still believes he is the heir, he has decreed such a person must travel under escort to him at the palace, not to Hafter as intended. As for you, Marazin, you know your fate if you're taken. However hard it is for you to contemplate such an action, you must run. Once Karilyn makes herself known to a patrol, they won't chase after you. They would be flayed alive if anything happened to her in their absence."

Marazin flared at the suggestion. It spoke of cowardice. Before he could speak, Karilyn gripped his arm.

"Think about it, my love," she implored. "Orvyn makes sense. If I'm under royal protection, I shall be safe. The king knows that, whatever happens, I'm the only one with the knowledge to find the Mastig. Even if, to his mind, the worst was to happen and I accompanied you, he's unlikely to cause me harm. He knows his future depends on my involvement in stopping Betlic.

"You can make your way to the house in the mountains you told me about, you'll be safe there. Hafter may persuade the king to let me live at his home. If not, when the time is right, Hafter will have to find a means to reunite us. We have reached this far without trouble, we must remain positive."

Marazin muttered to himself in a half-hearted way. There was logic in the idea. Although he suspected one of Hafter's main aims was to keep him away from Karilyn. If this was his intention, any efforts the sage made to bring them together under the same roof would be few. Damn the man. Why did he always have to have his own way? One thing was certain. He would miss Karilyn desperately if they had to separate. She could read his thoughts by his expression. Separation was not something she desired either. She squeezed his hand to reassure him.

Chapter Twenty Seven

Orvyn's first posting, on joining the rebel forces, had been to the region north of the Mogallean Mountains. His knowledge of the area, although not recent, was something of which Marazin and Karilyn could take advantage. As a result, they decided it would be better to let Orvyn accompany them. If they came under attack, his sword would be a welcome addition. There were other risks, too, besides those of rebel patrols. Bands of outlaws, displaced by warring factions, had moved north in search of easier prey. Anarchic by nature, Betlic considered such groups a threat to his authority. Whenever possible, his men hunted them down.

Orvyn was quick to notice how attached Marazin had become to Karilyn, and she to he. At first Orvyn feared, as did Hafter, a close relationship between the couple might be problematic to the successful completion of their mission. Over time, he dismissed these qualms. The pair complemented each other to perfection. It looked to be a partnership of both equal standing and mutual understanding.

During the evenings, while they practised their martial skills, at first Orvyn joined in. After several dismal and embarrassing displays on his part, he excused himself from further involvement. He needed no telling that he fell short of being the equal of his companions.

With Heardwine's head resting on his knees, he would sit and watch in awe as Marazin and Karilyn each tried to gain the upper hand. Skill, dexterity, agility, all combined in two remarkable people. Heaven help Amron if he challenged either one to a fair fight — although that was an unlikely prospect. In such a situation, he would choose a champion in his stead.

The idea of a contest with Amron was not of real concern to the trio. What caused them greater anxiety was how to react to an encounter with a rebel patrol. Allegedly, they were on the same side, so for them to resist capture by force was not an option. To injure, or kill, a rebel would make them outlaws. Such an outcome would delight Amron, as it would legitimise his hunt for them. A royal decree, ordering the execution of either Marazin, or Orvyn for such crimes would find little resistance. As Hafter had suggested, if a confrontation with the rebels looked inevitable, it would be better for them to separate. It was unlikely all three would face pursuit. If a patrol captured one of them, it would be up to the others to decide on their best course of action.

When it was Orvyn's turn to keep watch, he preferred to do so away from camp, or so he said. Neither Marazin, nor Karilyn, offered much resistance to this idea. A week passed. With Heardwine ranging far ahead, the trio were close to the most northerly point of their journey.

Soon after turning west, the terrain became too rugged in the hills for them to remain on horseback. They had little choice but to descend. Out on the plains, rebel patrols were numerous. Every few hours they cantered over the landscape on their designated routes. Apart from providing protection for those who used the roads, the patrols looked for signs that Betlic might have discovered the rebel stronghold's weakest point.

Orvyn, despite worries over their own safety, was happy with the improvements in security. Along the roadways, at regular intervals, the rebels had set up checkpoints. Attached to these were stockades, inside which billets, large enough to house several dozen men, were recent additions. With patrols roaming in-between the stations and surrounding areas, it would be difficult for the trio to travel unnoticed.

From a vantage point, they studied the land. The roads were not devoid of movement. Alone, or in small groups, people made their way westwards. Most were on foot. A few pulled handcarts, piled high with possessions. It was a pitiful trickle of refugees, whose only hope of sanctuary lay with the rebel forces. Of those who rode, most were astride heavy horses, more used to the plough than the open road. Once Betlic moved north, this movement of people would become a flood.

"With these extra patrols and checkpoints," Orvyn declared, "someone will recognise me before long. It might better if we separate."

"What do you have in mind?" Marazin asked.

"Apart from your clothes, as a couple, you two stand a good chance of being able to pass as refugees. Do you have anything else you can wear?"

"No," Karilyn said. "I'm wearing all I possess, most of which I collected while on the run. When I fled my home, my wardrobe was not a concern."

"There, at the bottom of the slope," Marazin pointed. "There's an abandoned cart. Can you see it?"

"Yes," Karilyn said after a moment. "It looks well-laden. There may be something there we can use."

"Let's take a look," Orvyn said, already moving towards his horse.

They reached the cart, without revealing themselves to a patrol that moved across the land. The reason for the carriage's abandonment was soon evident, its axle had snapped, breaking a wheel. From the state of the load, it looked as if the owners had salvaged what they could carry. The accident appeared recent. A few days earlier it had rained heavily for several hours, yet none of the contents of the opened boxes showed signs of water damage.

Orvyn did not seek items for himself. No matter what he wore, his face was too well known. Marazin's apparel, though travel-stained, was of high quality, which would mark him out. Karilyn's strange mix of garments was unusual; she would attract a great deal of attention. A quick search of the wagon revealed a bundle of clothing. Although in good condition, none of the items were new. The travellers counted themselves lucky to find even these. Clothes were a valuable asset, often left to relatives as an inheritance.

The fresh garments transformed the couple. The pair would blend in with other travellers on the road. Karilyn had chosen a dark coloured, tubular dress, which she fastened at the shoulders with a pair of brooches. Beneath it, she wore a long sleeved white linen shift. Marazin had uncovered a pair of woollen breeches, and a thick, sleeved tunic. On his feet, he wore his own boots; there were none on the cart to fit him. Before he could fasten his belt and scabbard round his waist, Orvyn stopped him.

"You can't wear a sword," he said.

"Why not?"

"Because you're dressed as a peasant and such people rarely carry such weapons, if at all. The one you have would not be out of place on a nobleman, or a warrior of high standing. Look at the trouble it caused when you and Amron first met. I know he thought it was his mother's sword, but, that aside, it's an exceptionally good and valuable weapon. In those clothes, if anyone sees you with it, they'll think you stole it."

"You might be right," Marazin said, "but you could say the same about our horses. They're better than anything people in our position would ride. We can't abandon them, and neither can I lose my sword. It stays with me."

"Then hide it, with mine, in our baggage," Karilyn suggested. "No-one will expect to see me wearing one. We can keep our daggers in view. They should not excite much interest. These days, I doubt if anyone is travelling without some means to defend themselves. As to our horses, we'll have to risk those. It would take too long to reach our destination on foot."

"What will you do, Orvyn?" Marazin turned his attention to his friend; he was concerned for his welfare.

"I know the layout of the land between here and the start of the rebel's main territory. It'll be safer for me if I travel alone. If I fall behind, I'll catch up after dark. When I've been on watch, I've heard little sound of movement between dusk and dawn. As we discussed, if anything should go wrong for you, I'll ride ahead to warn Hafter or, if practicable, come to your aid."

"Don't take any unnecessary risks," Karilyn warned. "If the rebels take Marazin prisoner, it would be better for his sake if you go for help. Both your lives would be in peril if they catch you, too."

Orvyn nodded. He watched as the pair hid their weapons, not an easy task, considering their bulk. Because of the risk that the couple might have to part, they concealed their swords separately, among their own supplies. Marazin helped Karilyn onto her horse. As was the custom, now she was wearing a dress, she would have to ride side-saddle. Most people would consider it indecent for her to travel any other way. It was a surprise to find such a saddle on board the broken cart. Stranger still, there had been more than one, along with many other valuable items hidden among the goods. These the travellers ignored.

With the loose folds of a borrowed heavy winter cloak pulled up to form a hood, only her face was visible. She was indistinguishable from most other women on the road. Marazin wrapped a cloak round his shoulders and pulled up the back, too, to make a hood for himself. Without haste, he mounted.

For a little way, Orvyn climbed the slope they had descended earlier. Heardwine went with him. The dog, which had accompanied the king to the rebel stronghold, was at least as recognisable as Orvyn.

Losing the protection of the beast was of concern to Marazin. Without Heardwine nearby, Betlic could locate Karilyn with the Eye. The warrior reassured himself with the belief that, as the despot believed she was dead, he was unlikely to continue to seek her. It was fortunate, for Marazin's peace of mind, he was unaware that Betlic, on occasion, used the Eye to dispel his fears about Karilyn — her missing body still troubled him.

Since Marazin's first meeting with Karilyn, Heardwine had sheltered her from the Eye's all-seeing gaze. Now, in the absence of the dog, something else had taken its place. The mountains, as Betlic was later to discover, possessed their own natural ability to cloud the Eye. With the range between the despot and her, she remained obscured from his view.

As soon as the land ahead was clear, Orvyn called down to the others. With a farewell wave, Marazin and Karilyn rode towards the nearest roadway. They joined the track in-between checkpoints, at a place hidden from both and devoid of fellow travellers. Gossip about their sudden appearance was something the couple wanted to avoid. With a sigh of relief, they turned their horses westwards towards the first barrier, a short ride away, where they queued to pass through.

The glance the soldiers on duty gave the travellers was perfunctory. These were two more miserable, shapeless bundles sitting upon their horses. Neither rider appeared to pose a threat. One soldier lifted a wooden pole clear while another waved them through. With relief, and careful not to rush, the pair rode on. They rode as if weary beyond belief, beaten down by travel, loss of home, land and family. At the checkpoint, they had watched how those in front carried themselves. If the couple expected to pass unnoticed, they knew the way they behaved must be no different.

For several days, Marazin and Karilyn rode westwards. The pair continued to mimic their fellow travellers as best they could. The couple took a keen interest in how others behaved when shouted at, or manhandled by sentries. The refugees cowered, their faces downcast, too frightened to resist. They would accept any humiliation, provided it allowed them to progress towards safety. Only a minority of soldiers were cruel or insensitive. The majority sympathised with the people they ushered through — most of the rebels, too, were exiles.

The first time Karilyn received adverse treatment, it was a severe test of Marazin's self-control. A sentry had mumbled some instructions to her. Unable to understand him, she asked him to repeat them. Angered, the oaf shouted them at her, then slapped her horse. The animal reared and, sitting sideways, Karilyn struggled to stay in her saddle. The sentry would never know how close he came to a learning a lesson in manners.

With difficulty, Karilyn brought the animal back under control. Keeping her expression neutral, she offered a grovelling apology, as if it had been her fault. Impatient, the sentry moved her on without further trouble. Seething, Marazin kept his back hunched and his head down. He passed through without delay; the guard much too occupied in complaining to his fellows, about fools unable to understand even the simplest of instructions.

When Marazin caught up with Karilyn, his face reflected the anger he felt. During their time in the foothills, whenever Marazin had been on watch, she had conversed long with Orvyn. He had been happy to discuss his friend. From these conversations, she learned much about the heir. One thing about him, she knew impressed Orvyn. It was the way Marazin treated others, always with courtesy and respect, no matter what their status. He detested rudeness. The sentry's treatment, of both her and the others who waited in line, she knew, would infuriate him.

"Please, don't let men like that rile you," she said gently. "Remember, we have to behave as others and accept such behaviour. The poor man; no doubt he's been on duty since dawn. He must be tired, bored and frustrated at having to give out the same instructions, over and over again."

"Poor man! I hope, for his sake, if ever we cross paths again, his manners have improved."

Karilyn caught sight of his expression. She giggled. Marazin attempted to keep a straight face. Moments later he, too, laughed.

"You could be right," he conceded. "I suppose if I'd been standing in the same place for weeks on end, I would be a little short-tempered."

She leant across and, for a moment, they shared a kiss. Both smiled. They were content. Out of sight of both checkpoint and, for the moment, other travellers, they chattered happily.

A long dreary week passed. Nobody was in a hurry, so the couple kept their pace to a minimum. It was noticeable, the closer they came to the valley they sought, the more alert did the sentries become. They paid greater attention to the stream of people on the trail. On several occasions, sentries led anxious travellers away for questioning. Marazin and Karilyn had perfected their roles as refugees. They were convincing in the stories of their fictional origins and family histories. Of Orvyn, they saw no sign.

It was late afternoon. The day, which promised much at dawn, had turned cold and dismal. When they reached the final checkpoint of the day, the sky was dark and overcast. A steady fall of drizzle contributed to a general air of despondency among the travellers. The couple were wet and exhausted. Once past the sentries, they would find somewhere to rest for the night. After a few perfunctory questions, to which Marazin answered to the guards' satisfaction, they allowed the pair to pass. As the wooden barrier dropped into place behind them, a small group of travellers, earlier taken for questioning, rejoined those waiting to cross the barrier. At the centre of the group, a large, red-faced, stout, balding man stood. Furiously, he waved a finger at Marazin and Karilyn. At the top of his voice, he began to shout.

"Hey, you! Stop, thieves! Guards, those two on the horses, stop them. Those are our clothes they're wearing!" he spluttered in anger.

Beside him stood a woman of equal stoutness, her double-chinned face wrinkled and her hair grey.

"That's my cloak from our cart," she screamed. "We had to leave our belongings behind when it's wheel broke. Those two have been through them and taken everything they fancied. Quick, before they escape."

Marazin looked at Karilyn in despair. Sentries were moving towards them. Others, on hearing the commotion were coming out of their billets. They, too, headed in the couple's direction.

"Let's make a run for it," Marazin urged. "We can outrun them if we're quick."

"It's too late," Karilyn cried. "Look over there."

A patrol had ridden into view. It halted, a few hundred paces behind the barrier. When the riders noticed the tumult, they urged their horses into motion.

"Run, my love. Save yourself," Karilyn pleaded. "Once I tell them who I am, they'll not pursue you. Go! Now, before it's too late."

Marazin was torn. It went against his instincts to desert Karilyn. She could see the quandary in his face. She leant over and slapped hard the rump of Marazin's horse. Startled, it shot forward. Marazin grabbed hold of the reins and clung on as it galloped away at full speed. He glanced back. Karilyn had turned to face her accusers. The mob had closed in around her. His horse took him down a steep slope to the banks of a river. Karilyn disappeared from sight. With a heavy heart, Marazin crossed the flowing waters to follow a dim trail into the growing darkness. It was only now he realised how much Karilyn meant to him.

Not too far ahead, a shadowy figure stood, hidden from sight in a thicket on top of a small rounded hill. Gauging his move, the man mounted his horse and set it on a course that would intercept the racing rider. Unaware of the watcher, Marazin continued in abject misery, his mind too occupied with thoughts of Karilyn to concentrate on anything else. He approached a bend where, to his left, in time of flood, the torrent had cut-out a large section of the hillside. The gap, between its steep, unstable slope and the river, narrowed to little more than a horse's width.

He rounded the bend. Ahead of him, a horse and hooded rider blocked his path. Marazin pulled hard on the reins. His horse skidded to a halt. He grabbed for his sword. It was not there. He cursed. The weapon was where he had stored it, inside his supplies. Marazin drew his dagger. He waited for the man in front to make clear his intentions.

Chapter Twenty Eight

For a moment, the stranger remained motionless. Marazin was quick to notice the rider held his horse's reins only, no weapon was in view. The silent figure lifted an arm. He drew back his hood. Marazin relaxed. He returned his dagger to its sheath. Despite the dim light, the face now revealed was one he knew well.

"I'm glad to see it's you, Orvyn," Marazin said with relief. "But we'd better be quick. A patrol can't be far behind me."

"No-one's following. I watched from above as you headed this way. Until you drew nearer, I couldn't be sure it was you. What went wrong?"

"What did you see?" Marazin ignored Orvyn's question, so desperate was he for news. "Is Karilyn all right?"

"I don't know. The checkpoint was too far away. It was misty and people were milling around. I couldn't see what the problem was, nor recognise anyone. Soon after you left, the place caught the edge of a shower. After that, I saw nothing more."

The downpour had caught up with them. With increasing intensity, rain was falling. Orvyn had a suggestion.

"I know somewhere where we can rest and stay dry for the night. While we ride, why not tell me everything that's happened?"

Marazin's distress was noticeable. Whatever had taken place, Orvyn hoped that Karilyn was safe. Bit by bit, as they rode, Marazin explained what had befallen them.

"Once my horse was back under control, I should have gone back to help her," Marazin insisted as he ended his narrative.

"No, you shouldn't. We all agreed what to do in such a situation. Karilyn did the right thing. Of the three of us, she's the only one welcome at the palace. No-one dare harm her, including Amron."

"We can't be sure! What if no-one believes her? They accused us of stealing those wretched clothes we borrowed. She could hang. I'm sorry Orvyn. I have to go back," Marazin said, reining in.

"My friend, you can't," Orvyn said, as he manoeuvred his horse to block Marazin's way. "I know you're upset, but you have to exercise caution. Don't let your heart rule your mind. If you'd tried to escape together, they'd have hunted you down. Karilyn won't have wasted a moment before telling them her true identity. She knows it would be your only chance to make good your escape. With the Scraufin as evidence, they must have accepted her word. Otherwise, they'd be close behind us now."

"Not necessarily. Anything might have happened."

"Damn it, Marazin, Karilyn's in no danger." Orvyn's voice had become more forceful. "You know the rebels are on the look out for her. Her safety is paramount to them. Had they caught you, then I would fear for your future. Karilyn's treatment will be different. They'll take her to the palace with all speed. Imagine how she'll feel if, because of a needless rescue attempt, you suffered harm. You have to exercise restraint."

Marazin knew he was being irrational. It changed nothing. His guilt at leaving Karilyn threatened to overwhelm him. The pain he felt at their separation was unbearable. He had loved no other as he did her. Orvyn, however, spoke sense. With evident reluctance, Marazin turned his horse.

The path narrowed further. A steep slope led them away from the river's side. Orvyn took the lead. As night fell, he guided them to shelter. Darkness was complete as they dismounted beside an old hut. It was located at the edge of a valley that led into the mountains. Below, from a stream they had crossed lower down the slope, came the sound of rushing water. They unsaddled then rubbed down their horses. Inside the hut, with difficulty, Marazin found a tallow lamp. He lit it. Whoever had made use last of the long-abandoned building had left a stack of logs, piled against one of the walls. A fire soon crackled inside a stone hearth. Nearby, their sodden cloaks steamed as the air warmed.

"Where's Heardwine?" Marazin had only now realised the dog was absent.

"He could be anywhere. The dog comes and goes at will. Sometimes he's away all day. When he does return, he never stays for long. No doubt, he's been keeping an eye on you. I'm sure he'll reappear soon now you're here."

Earlier that day, Orvyn had caught a large trout. Marazin was not hungry. The thought of food made him feel ill. After much persuasion,

Orvyn coaxed his friend into accepting a little roasted fish. While Orvyn ate his fill, Marazin played with his food, although he ate some baked apple he was given later. He remained morose. Orvyn gave up his attempts to make conversation; he wrapped himself in his blanket. He was asleep within moments. For Marazin, the night was long and lonely. Accustomed to Karilyn sharing his bed these past few weeks, he struggled to sleep. Her scent lingered on his blanket, a constant reminder. He gazed into the glowing embers, his mind far away.

In the morning, Marazin seemed more his old self, although his concern for Karilyn remained undiminished. Despite that, his companion's words the previous evening had given him much to consider. Orvyn was right. Karilyn was safer with a rebel escort, more than at any other time since losing her family. But, until he could confirm she was safe at the palace, nothing would allay Marazin's fears.

By sunrise, the pair was already on the move. Marazin had changed into his original clothes, which Orvyn had stored among his own supplies. With his sword retrieved and belted to his waist, Marazin was more at ease. Once across the stream, they made their way down the valley. As Orvyn had thought, Heardwine joined them. From then onwards the dog, apart from an occasional brief absence, remained at Marazin's side. For several days they skirted the mountains. On constant alert for patrols, their progress was slow. Despite the presence of several large, well-armed rebel units travelling the main routes, Marazin saw no sign of Karilyn. In time, the pair reached the mouth of the central valley.

Near the centre of the gap, between the mountain peaks, a river hurtled violently through a gorge, no wider than a pair of hay wagons. Towering, on either side, the land formed a ridge, which inclined slightly upwards towards both east and west. Behind it, millennia ago, the valley had once formed a vast lake, until escaping waters cut-out the ravine. The gap here, between the mountains, was narrow. A man on foot could gain either edge, from the gorge, within a few thousand paces.

In a line, beneath the top of the ridge, deep into the ground, the rebels had embedded a defensive barrier of massive tree trunks. Angled outwards, their tops had savage points. Back-filled with earth and stone, the fortifications provided a firm footing for defending soldiers. Above the ramparts, the heads of those on duty were visible.

Near to the eastern edge of the gorge, a massive pair of timbered gates stood open. This seemed to be the only way through the defences. On the plains, roads came together to form a single track that climbed steeply towards the fortified opening.

"This is new," Orvyn said, in surprise, when first he saw the fortifications.

"How are we going to cross?" Marazin asked, dismayed. "Are there any routes through the mountains that can take us round it?"

"I doubt it. The high passes are no longer open. Lower down, those that remain clear will have guards to watch over them. Not every footpath will be under surveillance, so it might be possible to travel on foot. The problem is, without horses on the other side, it will take us much too long to reach Hafter."

This was not a viable option. Marazin needed to be close to Karilyn. Her welfare was more than important. Apart from his own personal involvement with her, the Mastig's appearance drew ever nearer. Karilyn was the only one who knew to where, and for how long, they both were to travel.

For two days Orvyn and Marazin kept watch, in the vain hope they could find a weakness in the defences. The pair had hidden in a small area of woodland, nestled beneath the high ground to the east. It was soon apparent the guards at the gateway were alert and suspicious. Several times, they escorted travellers away under duress. By the third morning, lack of progress had frustrated both men. Orvyn decided to reconnoitre the land nearer to the roadway. He had found a route that, for most of the way, would keep him out of sight of the defences. Providing he took care, when visible, the expedition should allow him chance to study the fortifications to the west of the river. To view, from a different angle, those at this side of the gorge might be beneficial too.

For some time, Marazin kept an eye on Orvyn's progress, until the lie of the land cut him off from sight. Noon passed. Marazin was not overly worried. By late afternoon, his concern was palpable. As dusk turned to darkness, Marazin's unease deepened. As there had been no commotion, it was probable Orvyn remained free. Could he have injured himself? The waiting warrior paced backwards and forwards, unable to settle.

Marazin froze. The sound of a hoof, clicking on stone carried to him. Within minutes, there came another, from much closer this time. Orvyn had been on foot. Their horses were tethered nearby in the undergrowth. Marazin stepped back, deeper into the woods. His sword was in his hand. There was no moonlight, only the light from the stars. Vague shapes flickered near the edge of the woodland. He was patient. Whoever it was, he was ready for them. Heardwine, he realised, had shown no signs of alarm. Marazin relaxed a little.

"Marazin," Orvyn's low call came from nearby, "it's me, and I've brought someone with me."

For a moment, Marazin's heart leapt. Could Orvyn have found Karilyn? His hope was short-lived.

"It's one of Hafter's men," Orvyn added.

"I'm over here." Marazin's attempt to keep the bitter disappointed out of his tone was unsuccessful.

The sound of movement came closer. Through the trees, someone led a horse to join those of the travellers, tethered nearby. Soon afterwards, Orvyn and the stranger appeared at Marazin's side. Although too dark to make out the man's face, as soon as he spoke, Marazin recognised his voice. It belonged to one of the messengers used by Hafter last winter.

"Greetings Daegmund," Marazin said as he shook the man's hand. "What brings you this far north?"

"Looking for us," Orvyn said. "Once I saw him on the road, I realised who it was and made myself known to him. To avoid being seen, we waited until after dark before coming here."

"That's right," Daegmund said. "Hafter sent me to search for you. With heavy snowfall in the mountains this early, he suspected you might travel this way. Once he heard the northern defences were operational, he realised you'd be cut off."

"What's the solution? Do you know of a place where we can cross without being seen?" Marazin asked.

"There's none that I know, in fact I hope none exist, otherwise Betlic's men might be able to exploit them."

"So, how do we enter? Fly?"

"Nothing so fanciful," Daegmund laughed. "I have a letter from Hafter, authorising me to bring emissaries from Vernalaka, the marshlands, to meet with him. I have cloaks and hoods for you to wear, similar to those used by them. When we reach the gates, with your hoods pulled forward, no-one will recognise you. It's the Marshlanders' custom to travel in this manner. With the passes I have for you, the gatemen will not want to risk Hafter's wrath, nor dare offend you by demanding you reveal yourselves."

"Are you sure?" Marazin was unconvinced. It seemed a risky strategy.

"Of course," Orvyn said. "Marshlanders have many strange customs, one of which is to conceal their faces from strangers, except in battle or to guests within their homes. They have a reputation for violent reaction against any who offend them. The men on duty will be aware of this."

Marazin conceded. He could think of no realistic alternative to the plan. Although it was a strange custom, during his years as a mercenary he had come across others equally bizarre.

Despite the coldness of the night, they endured another one without a fire. As close as they were to the fortifications, any sighting of a blaze would come under investigation at first light. Huddled in their blankets, they shared cold fare, while Orvyn described the events of his day. Daegmund, when asked about Karilyn, could not provide any information. He had heard no rumours about her, either by name or as Bearer of the Scraufin. This might be because he had been on the road for a number of weeks. During that period, at no time had he seen any prisoners being escorted towards the rebel stronghold. To Marazin this added further worries. Karilyn should be a long way ahead of them. What had happened to her?

Without endangering himself and Orvyn, his best hope of tracing her was to reach Hafter as soon as possible. He was one of only two people with sufficient power, influence and a valid reason to find out her whereabouts. Amron was the other. Marazin had no reason to believe the king would be as amenable.

Before dawn, the three men were on the road, leading to the gateway above. Earlier, Marazin had ordered Heardwine to enter the hills, to find its way round the defences. The dog could travel, undetected, where no human could. It was a constant source of amazement, to Marazin, the animal's ability to both understand and interpret his words.

The hooded cloaks, provided by Daegmund, although light-weight, were warm to wear. Their hoods, pulled forward, left the faces of Marazin and Orvyn deep in shadow. Stitched into each hood was a piece of fine black gossamer fabric. Without hampering the vision of the wearer, it prevented anyone from seeing the features of the person behind. The hoods were spacious at the opening, which allowed for a wide field of vision. It was apparent Hafter had given some thought to how he was to bring the two men safely through the border-crossing.

Daegmund took the lead. Marazin and Orvyn stayed a horse's length behind him. The pair sat upright, their gazes straight ahead, their swords in full view. Their body language spoke of their absolute right to be there. Marshlanders bowed-down to no-one. At the gate, Daegmund presented his papers to the sentries on duty. The 'Marshlanders' remained in their saddles, neither moving nor speaking. Unsure how to proceed, one of the sentries fetched his commander. The men had authorisation to search anybody who passed through the gates, and to check their descriptions against a list of those sought after. That said, Marshlanders had a fearsome reputation. Unless it proved necessary, the men on duty would prefer not to find out how fierce the new arrivals could be.

A captain arrived at the run, followed by the original sentry and several others. For a moment, Marazin thought the three of them were to become prisoners. It transpired that curiosity was the uppermost reason for the additional forces. Marshlanders were seldom seen this far south. The captain read the letter from Hafter, several times. He studied the two strangers. At no time did he try to speak to them. The man was quick to reach a decision. Daegmund, he knew by sight. The captain had been at rebel headquarters a number of times when Hafter and his aide had been present. The soldier returned the letter to Daegmund and bowed to his companions. They nodded their heads in acknowledgement. Without further delay, they passed through the gateway.

They continued for several miles before stopping. The border-crossing had long-since passed from sight. In the shelter of a small copse, Marazin and Orvyn removed their disguises. They had served their purpose. To remain dressed in that fashion would attract too much attention. A more senior officer, if met on the road, might take it upon himself to escort them to Amron. He would believe the king, rather than Hafter, a person more appropriate for discussions with emissaries from another country.

Heardwine rejoined them later that day. Apart from a slight limp, the dog had suffered no serious harm from its more strenuous travels. The remainder of the journey proved uneventful. Their guide knew of many, seldom-used paths, which took them either beside, or among, the lower mountain reaches. The party stayed at several houses along the route, their occupants, every one, fiercely loyal to Hafter. This was a network set up by the sage, long before Amron's arrival. Whenever Hafter had need of privacy in his travels, this chain of houses, enabled him, or his visitors, to come and go in complete secrecy.

ೞ ಐ

Two days after the winter solstice, Marazin and Orvyn dismounted at their destination. They were to stay at a farm, belonging to some of Hafter's most loyal associates. These people had prospered well from the sage's patronage. To repay his belief in them, they were willing to risk everything. Situated several hours ride from Amron's palace, in a secluded valley, the farmhouse nestled in the midst of open farmland. Concealed beneath the buildings, several underground chambers and passageways provided the fugitives with somewhere to hide, or, if necessary, a means of escape.

Daegmund, whose parent's farm this was, stayed with them. On the party's arrival, his nephew set off to inform Hafter of their whereabouts. To Marazin's frustration, it was five days before the sage came to the farm. When he did arrive, Hafter was in disguise. He dismounted in some discomfort, to walk stiff-legged toward the cottage. On long journeys, he was more used to a carriage than a horse. A fact he had counted on when he had ridden out. No-one would expect to see him leave town astride a horse. After removing his cloak and hood, he eased himself into a chair, placed close to a roaring fire. He warmed his hands while Marazin poured him a goblet of mulled mead. Hafter took a long swallow of the liquid. The colour returned to his cheeks. He leaned down and patted Heardwine on the head. The dog curled up and went to sleep in front of the hearth.

"Damn his majesty," Hafter said. "I cannot leave my home without one or more of his agents following me. Today, I had to sneak out, dressed as one of my own servants. For some reason, the king believes you two might have returned. He suspects I know where you are and thinks I will lead him to you."

"Never mind Amron, how's Karilyn? When did she arrive? Is she with you, or still at the palace?" Marazin was frantic for news. This was of far more importance to him than the king's paranoia.

"Karilyn? The Scraufin bearer?" Hafter looked bemused. "What makes you think she's at the palace? If I recall, you were to find and return with her. Why would I have dragged myself all this way, if not to meet with her?"

"Karilyn's not at the palace yet?" Marazin said in disbelief. "She should have arrived days ago. Something's gone wrong. I told you, Orvyn, I should have gone back for her."

"Sit down and take a deep breath, Marazin. Tell me everything that's befallen you both," Hafter interrupted, shocked by the vehemence in Marazin's voice.

Slowly, between the pair of them, the story unfolded. Hafter, as expected, was unhappy about the relationship that had developed between Marazin and Karilyn. The look Marazin gave Hafter, when he presumed to comment upon it, silenced him. He knew when he was beaten.

"It's strange I've heard no rumours of her being at the palace," Hafter said. "I'm in agreement with Orvyn. Once she said who she was, there's no-one in the land who would dare harm her. Amron's instructions are explicit on that."

"Damn Amron and his instructions, something's gone wrong," Marazin insisted. "In the morning, I'm going back to look for her."

"No you're not," Hafter flared. "You're too valuable. Let me look into the matter first. That's my expertise. Although I no longer enjoy his full confidence in some matters, the king still listens to my advice on others. As a result, I'm welcome to visit the palace, at any time, without an invitation. However implausible it seems, if Amron's willed it, it's possible for news of Karilyn's arrival to have stayed within the palace walls. It's time I paid Tamin a visit. He, more than anyone, might know. As you're aware, he sees through his son's guile and observes with distaste his antics. He does what he can to curb his majesty's excesses."

"You've three days, Hafter," Marazin said, in a tone that tolerated no opposition. "Either come back with something positive, or I'll find her myself."

Hafter nodded. He had met his match for stubbornness. Without delay, he drained his goblet. With his horse laden with vegetables from the farm's storerooms, he took his leave. To those who kept watch over his home, his appearance was that of a servant, returning from an errand.

Chapter Twenty Nine

The crowd's hostility was increasing. Karilyn sat upright in the saddle. It would be foolish to wait for the mob to reach her. She took the initiative. With her hood thrown back, she turned her horse to face them head on. In a sharp, penetrating voice, she addressed the sentry at the front of the muddle.

"You! Go, fetch your commander, now," she ordered. "I am the Bearer of the Scraufin. I need an escort, immediately, to take me to your sage, Hafter."

The sentry stumbled to a halt, several paces short of her. A chill ran through him. The Scraufin, and its bearer, was not something he had heard about by name. Carriers of strange objects, seeking Hafter, were. He had received numerous warnings about their importance. All the men had. They had strict instructions relating to the treatment of any such person. He dreaded to think of the consequences, should anything happen to the object's carrier. Would the authorities hold him responsible? The crowd bumped and jostled as they tried to force him forward.

"Hold back!" he shouted.

He drew his sword as he turned to face the mass.

"Don't listen to her," bellowed the man who had started the trouble. "She's a thief. Arrest her."

The complainant's face was becoming redder by the moment. His companion, the woman at his side, yelled in agreement, further trying to inflame the crowd. The mob chanted their support. This was the first taste of excitement most had experienced in several months of travel. At a time when the measure of a person's wealth lay in the possessions they carried or wore, the theft of even the smallest item was a hanging matter. Before the crowd could take matters further, troops from the billet arrived. Members of the patrol followed. They placed themselves and their horses between Karilyn and the enraged throng.

The patrol leader, a figure of some seniority, at once took control of the situation.

"What's going on?" he barked at the sentry who had attempted to hold back the rabble.

Before he could answer, the owner of the cloak shouted out about thieves, as did the red-faced man at her side. The crowd joined in the cries. A dozen or more voices talked at once. Exasperated, the patrol leader snatched a whip from his saddle. There was loud crack as he struck out with the weapon. It flicked, a light touch, against the hand of one of the people at the front of the mob. He howled, more in surprise than in pain, and leapt backwards. The crowd fell back, muttering.

"Now, what's the problem here?"

"That man, Commander, the one over there with that female," the soldier pointed towards the complainants. "They say this woman here, and the man who rode off, stole the clothes they're wearing from a broken-down cart that belongs to the pair."

"You, woman, is this true?" the patrol leader demanded to know from Karilyn.

"I am the Bearer of the Scraufin," she repeated, in a clear and sharp tone, showing no signs of the stress she felt. "We needed something to wear and found the cart, abandoned. Now I know who the owners are, I'll recompense them for their loss. The king, I'm sure, will be similarly generous. Now," she dismissed the complaint as if it was irrelevant, "you have instructions concerning me?"

The man nodded.

"Good, then you must be aware I have important business with Hafter. I must meet with him at the earliest opportunity. Don't sit there with your mouth open, staring at me. Do something and disperse this crowd, without delay."

The patrol leader, as did the troops, knew his orders, and that they came from the king. Mindful of these, he was suspicious of this young woman's claim. He had expected a man, a battled hardened warrior, to be the carrier. He was quick to recover his wits.

"Prove you are who you say you are," he demanded of Karilyn. To his men, he said. "You, the three at the end, go bring him back," he pointed in the direction in which Marazin had ridden.

The commander eased his horse towards Karilyn. From under her cloak, she took out an object. She held it up, high in the air.

"Hold your men, Commander. This is what I bear," she cried.

The man moved his horse closer to her. He demanded she give it to him, so he could examine it. She shook her head.

"It's not for the likes of you to touch," she said.

He ignored her and tried to snatch it. For an instant, his fingers brushed against the Scraufin. He yelped in pain and snatched his hand away. Burn marks, deep and angry, spread across his fingertips.

"I did warn you," Karilyn said with little sympathy. "It allows no-one but me to hold it."

This was true, in part. After she had read the letter from her father, she had allowed Marazin to handle the object. As heir to the Mastig, he suffered no ill-effects. That had provided proof beyond doubt of his true calling.

The patrol leader, angered by the pain, with his other hand grabbed hold of Karilyn's cloak. He yanked hard. Sitting side-saddle, she slid from her horse. Agile as always, she landed on her feet. As she twisted round, she returned the Scraufin to its place of keeping. She was at the patrol leader's side. His foot cleared his stirrup. He aimed a kick at her. As she sidestepped to avoid the blow, she placed her cupped hands beneath his boot. As he pushed down hard against her, Karilyn, in one swift movement, tipped him out of the saddle. He hit the ground in a heap. Furious, he staggered to his feet. His horse trotted a few paces away, to leave its master facing his opponent. He drew his sword. Nobody made a fool of him.

Karilyn stood her ground. She showed no signs of fear. With a deft movement of her hand, she threw off her cloak and waited for him to make his move. The patrol leader raised his weapon and aimed a blow at her body. To his credit, he attempted to use the flat of the blade instead of its edge. Karilyn, though hampered by the dress, was too quick for him. One moment he was bearing down on her, the next she was dodging under the blade and using his momentum to throw him to the ground.

He lay on his back, neither injured nor able to move. His sword was in the hands of the young woman, its razor-sharp edge resting against his throat. He looked into her eyes, then regretted it. There was an intensity in her expression that frightened him, a rare experience in his life. She blinked, her expression softened a little.

"Shall we start again, Commander," Karilyn said. Her measured tone was calm. "No, keep quiet," she added as the man attempted to speak. "I

THE MASTIG

would prefer you to listen to me first... Whoever's behind me — another step and you'll need a new leader. Turn around. Go back and stand with your fellows."

In his haste to move away, the soldier who had crept close stumbled backwards. The crowd had fallen silent. Was the woman a witch? How did she know someone was behind her? The man had made no noise. Moreover, how had she gained the upper hand over the one at her feet; he was twice her size? Those standing at the front, edged backwards. If she uttered a curse, they had no desire to find themselves in direct line of her.

"Commander, I weary of repeating myself. For what I hope is the final time, I warn you I am the Bearer of the Scraufin. With all urgency, I have to consult with the sage, Hafter. He possesses information vital for me to complete my undertaking. Any further attempt to harm, or hinder me, will bring down your king's displeasure upon you.

"I've spent the past few months on the road, where, not long ago, I avoided capture by Betlic and his men. You doubt me?" she said, at the man's look of astonished disbelief. "I'm sorry, but that's the truth. The enemy himself was at the eastern edge of your mountains, little more than a few weeks ago.

"I had hoped to reach Hafter without trouble. Now, because of you, everyone knows my business. I suggest we go somewhere else, out of this rain and more private, to discuss matters. I shall step back now. When you stand, I'll return your sword. Be warned, if you attempt to attack me, or take my charge again, I'll deal with you much less gently."

"When do I get my property back?" demanded the red-faced man from the crowd.

"Your property?" Karilyn's voice was filled with contempt. "I suspect little on that cart belongs to you. Because my own clothes were in tatters, I looked to see if there was something I might wear. I borrowed nothing more. I left a note, stating, at the house of Hafter, the owner would receive generous recompense from me. What I did find strange among your so-called possessions, were the dozens of valuable items, crafted from gold, silver and precious stones, hidden among them. An explanation of how you came to acquire them might be worth hearing. I think it no coincidence I discovered it at the edge of the hills, away from the road and out of sight of the patrols. Had I been you, I might have remained silent."

A look of hatred crossed the man's face. He started to bluster. With some urgency, his companion whispered to him. The man grabbed her arm. The crowd parted as the pair ran off. Several soldiers gave chase. Within minutes, the accusers were in custody.

The patrol leader gained his feet. Karilyn, as promised, reversed the sword and presented it to him, hilt first. His anger had cooled. With the recent revelation about the original accusers, the facts were more apparent. He recalled the woman's words about the king's displeasure. His majesty's instructions were clear. After the claims she had made, and the evidence of his burnt hand, he must offer her immediate protection.

Until now, the name of the object concerned had remained a mystery to him. Amron had no wish for knowledge of the Scraufin's existence to become common. Person and object had to come, in secret, under escort to him at his palace. Under no circumstances were they to go to Hafter as the woman demanded. After considering her reactions when challenged, the commander, unaware Karilyn already knew the details of his orders, decided he might save this information until later.

Whoever this woman was, he had no desire to rile her again. She had taken his weapon with ease. What other tricks might she possess? Whatever they were, he did not want to suffer the consequences of their use. To return to him his sword, was a sign of great courage. It also showed supreme confidence in her ability. If he tried to restrain her again, he had few doubts that she would disarm him.

"My apologies, young lady," the commander said. "It seems I might have been a little hasty. I am Eadgard, captain of the guard. Shall we go to my quarters where, in private, we can discuss matters further?"

"Apology accepted, I'm Karilyn," she said, shaking his proffered hand.

The mist closed in as the rainfall became heavier. The invitation to talk undercover was welcome.

"Your companion, shall we find him and fetch him back? Although, it surprises me that he deserted you. It was that, more than anything else, which convinced me of your guilt."

"No, Commander, leave him be. The man is no coward. He has proven himself many times. He agreed to accompany me until I reached safety. Once I revealed my identity to members of the rebel forces, he knew I would be safe with them. It was always understood he would leave me then."

"But who is he? How could you know you'd be safe with us?"

"My companion wishes to remain anonymous. I shall not break his trust. As to my safekeeping, even though I come from a distant land, I have excellent sources of information. Again, I see no reason to disclose anything further."

Eadgard had his suspicions about the departing rider. The bearer of this so-called Scraufin was not the only person whom, if found, he had orders to escort back to the palace. Orvyn, he knew well. They had met on several occasions after the man came to prominence as an aide to the king. The rider was not he, so, Eadgard wondered, could it have been Marazin?

He had a brief description of the rider. From what he had seen, he bore a vague resemblance to the facts given. So did a thousand others. Eadgard's orders worried him, too. He had heard talk that, contrary to the official position, if found, the two men's lives would be in grave danger. Orvyn, he liked. The man was a fine soldier. His loyalty was without question. If Marazin, as rumoured, was a friend of Orvyn, then he, too, was unlikely to be an enemy of the rebel forces.

For now, Eadgard decided, he would keep his thoughts private. His arrival at the palace would be soon enough for him to voice his suspicions. No-one could accuse him of dereliction of duty. His instructions were explicit; the bearer and the object she carried took priority over everything. Someone else could take responsibility for the other rider, later. By then, traces of the man would have disappeared. Eadgard would have fulfilled his obligations. His conscience would be clear.

Over a meal, after a short discussion, Karilyn convinced Eadgard of her authenticity. The Scraufin she possessed had magical properties, as his burnt fingers could attest. Papers she produced, which included a letter from Hafter to her father, confirmed her story. Eadgard surrendered his quarters to her. While she slept, the captain of the guard had much to organise. Unlike their men, higher ranked officers had orders of a more specific nature.

A few days ride from here, inside the rebel valley, a special stockade lay empty. When war came, it was Amron's intention to house high-ranking captives there. Such people might have value as hostages. Although, not linked to the anticipated arrival of the bearer, it was at the disposal of all field commanders, if needed.

Nobody knew how many agents of the enemy might live, unsuspected, among the rebels. If any of Betlic's supporters learned that the bearer was alive and nearby, they would attempt to kill her. Therefore, until she left the rebel lands, to go in search of the Mastig, all knowledge of her must remain secret. The crowd, along with the two suspected thieves, would stay interned until the king decreed their knowledge no longer posed a threat. It was unfortunate for so many people to have been close enough to hear a part of Karilyn's story. Before Eadgard made his arrangements, he dispatched a rider to the palace. His majesty would want to prepare for the bearer's arrival.

An empty covered wagon, which had dropped supplies at the post that afternoon, was commandeered. Several soldiers worked through the night, to make it comfortable for Karilyn. Unseen, she would travel to her destination in the back. Stacked at the rear of the wagon were several barrels, placed there to add weight. If anyone were to enquire why the cart required such a large armed guard, they would say it carried fine wines for the king's table. Such wagons were a familiar sight on the roads.

Soon after dawn, alerted by a messenger, another patrol arrived at the post. They would take over duties here. Half the guards from the post would escort the detainees, then integrate with the existing garrison at the stockade. The others would travel with Eadgard and Karilyn.

Over breakfast, Eadgard informed Karilyn of his preparations. She understood his concerns regarding her safety and, although unhappy with the arrangement, accepted his advice to travel in the wagon. Within the hour, they were away. Seated behind the wagon-driver, Karilyn had a curtain, which she could draw across to hide her from view, whenever they came across others on the road. At checkpoints, she would remain hidden. To protect her identity, they would camp away from such places. Because of this, they carried supplies enough to last for several weeks.

The wagon-driver, an elderly man, possessed a vast repertoire of stories. During the long days, Karilyn was grateful for his idle chatter; it occupied her mind. At night, when alone, thoughts of Marazin were never far from her. The memories of their days and nights together made the pain of their separation intense. She longed for him to be beside her, yet prayed he would do nothing to endanger himself by trying to free her. They would meet again, before too long, or so she tried to convince herself.

Chapter Thirty

A bridge spanned the evil smelling waters of the moat. Over wooden planks, a horse's hooves clattered. With care, Hafter guided the animal as it threaded its way, in-between a wandering line of people. They filled the track, all the way to the gateway ahead. They waited in hope, eager for an audience with the king; if not today, possibly tomorrow, or the day after that.

From outside Hafter's home, his watchers had followed him, at a discreet distance. Once confident of his destination, they halted to await his return. Hafter was well-known to the guards on duty. They waved him through into the palace grounds. Other visitors gazed in envy at his swift progress. Oblivious of their resentful stares, Hafter moved on. He rode along a well-worn track round the seat of power, towards a large single-storey outbuilding. Within minutes, the animal was in the care of a young stable-boy. Stiff from the saddle, Hafter hobbled towards an annex, built onto the rear of the palace.

As he approached, a heavy wooden door swung open. A buxom woman ushered him inside, out of the cold. Tamin's housekeeper was fiercely protective of him. Her waspish tongue, in defence of her master's privacy, was well known and feared. Many men would have gone into battle, rather than confront her. Hafter, unlike others, was a favoured visitor.

"Good morning, Mildthryth," Hafter greeted her with warmth, as she took his cloak. Once she had laid it on a nearby table, he passed to her a large bag, taken from his belt. "Here you are," he said, "I've brought you some feferfuge leaves I picked this morning. They should help with the pain in your joints."

"Thank you," she said with a beaming smile, giving him a warm embrace. This was something many others would have refused to believe. "This damp, cold weather is a trial for me. I was down to the last of my supplies."

She had a soft spot for the sage. They had known each other for many years. Mildthryth's husband had assisted Hafter with his studies of historic scripts. When her spouse died, Hafter recommended her to Tamin for the position of housekeeper. A renowned scholar of ancient languages, her husband had earned great respect from his peers, but had amassed little wealth. Pride had prevented her from accepting the allowance Hafter wanted to settle on her. It was a small price to pay for the help her husband had given him over the years. The position at the palace had been a mutually acceptable compromise.

Without further delay, she ushered Hafter into a large, comfortable room. Brightly coloured wall-hangings partly covered two sides. Spread across most of a third, a large wooden-framed mullioned window gave a blurred outlook onto the world beyond. Glass was a rare and valuable commodity. Amron used it much throughout his palace, a sign of his power and status. Beneath the mullions stood a large oak table, upon which the remains of a meal were evident. To the right of the window, a stone hearth and surround filled much of the remaining wall. Above the mantle, a stag's head stood proud. Inside the alcoves, a selection of weapons adorned the plaster and timber-framed walls.

In front of the fire, Tamin, settled in a large chair, warmed himself before the flames. Documents littered his lap and the surrounding floor. The door creaked as it opened. He looked up. As soon as he saw Hafter, a broad smile lit Tamin's face. He stood. Papers cascaded everywhere. In haste, he retrieved those most in danger from the flames.

"Welcome, my friend," Tamin said, limping over to greet his guest. His broken legs had long-since healed, but had left one limb a fraction shorter than the other. "I was only saying, earlier, that it's some time since last we enjoyed your company. Come, pull up a chair and warm yourself. Please, Mildthryth, fetch us some wine."

The housekeeper, who had already collected the dirty plates, nodded as she left the room. A few minutes later, she returned, bearing a large flagon of mulberry wine and two goblets. Tamin pulled up a small table between himself and Hafter. Mildthryth filled each goblet before setting down the flagon. She bowed, left the men to talk, then closed the door behind her.

"I would be lost without her," Tamin admitted. "Nobody, unless I wish to meet them, is allowed in, no matter how hard they threaten or bluster. She's indomitable. Can she cook? Her meals and baking are beyond compare. She keeps everything in its rightful place, too, exactly how I prefer it."

"You ought to be careful," Hafter laughed. "She may have marriage in mind."

Tamin laughed too, though such thoughts had crossed his mind. He had been a widower for a while and had become fond of Mildthryth. How Amron would take to the idea, was not something on which Tamin cared to dwell. He doubted it would meet with his son's approval. The thought of a parent remarrying was one thing. For the king's father to marry his housekeeper, unless of noble birth, would be problematic for the boy.

A few minutes of pleasant idle chatter passed, while Hafter and Tamin sampled the wine. Once more Mildthryth wandered in with a tray, on which stood a plate stacked high with slices of Gesufel bread. Alongside the spiced loaf was a dish filled with clotted cream. Hafter's eyes lit up at the sight of the offering. Tamin's description of Mildthryth's culinary expertise was no exaggeration. The mix of spices and herbs she used in her baking and cooking, without fail, produced results of a high order.

"You spoil me Mildthryth," Hafter said, taking a slice then spreading a generous layer of cream over it.

She laughed and left the room, which fell silent, as the two men savoured the delights of the tray. Hafter picked the crumbs from the plate. He washed them down with a drink from his goblet. Sitting back in his chair, he was a happy man. This state of affairs soon ended. Tamin broke the silence.

"Now Hafter, what's the real reason for your visit today?" Tamin asked. "I'm sure it was for more than to fill your stomach."

Tamin was aware Hafter's relationship with Amron had been better. The same was true about many other people, with whom the king came into regular contact. Tamin trod with care between them all. Openly, he showed absolute support for the king at all times. In secret, Tamin worked hard to undo as much of the damage, caused by his son's failings, as he could. Hafter decided to be straightforward about why he had come. He respected Tamin too much to be deceitful.

Hafter said, "I've learned that the bearer of the Scraufin is alive. As you know, I must speak with her. It's my understanding she's here, already, but, so far, there's been neither news, nor rumour, of her arrival. I thought I should come, in person, to see if I could establish the truth of the matter. If my information is correct, I want to know why no-one's informed me."

"Nobody dare speak of it. We're sworn to secrecy by the king," Tamin said, his tone apologetic. "Even I can't discuss anything, unless with someone already privy to the information. As you're aware already of many aspects, I see no reason to keep anything else from you. Your knowledge that the bearer is a woman, not a warrior, is correct. She arrived, in secret, almost two weeks ago. For any member of the palace staff who has contact with her, communication with the outside has been cut off."

"I've known the bearer's gender for a while," Hafter admitted, a little shamefaced. "As a warrior, I believe she's formidable with any weapon."

"Why didn't *you* say anything?"

"I kept it to myself, I suppose, because, at first, I hoped my information was wrong. I was certain the woman was a temporary aberration. As such, I expected a man to arrive from somewhere, to take on the role, but I was wrong. The woman, so I'm told, is more than capable of fulfilling the assignment asked of her. I'm sorry, Tamin. I should have spoken sooner."

"There is no need to apologise, dear friend. I must admit some surprise at the turn of events myself. Her name's Karilyn. I presume you're aware of that, too?"

"Yes, her name is known to me. Is she well?"

"In her physical being she is fine. As to her detention, that's another matter, she's most unhappy. She demands a meeting with you; in fact, she wants transferring to your custody. Amron, of course, refuses to allow it."

"Why? I know Betlic believes her dead, so I accept the reasons behind why her presence must remain secret. We all know her life would be in grave danger if news reached him, or any of his agents among us. What does confuse me is why Amron is behaving this way towards me. Despite our differences, the importance of the bearer is something upon which we do agree."

"Amron considers any further involvement by you unnecessary. It's the king's opinion that your earlier research provides him with everything he needs to succeed. He feels you should concentrate on other ways to defeat Betlic's army. When the time is right, both he and the bearer will go in search of the Mastig.

"The problem is, Karilyn refuses to discuss it with him. She says she must speak to you, first. Nothing will persuade her otherwise. She insists there are matters you alone can make clear. Amron is stubborn, he won't back down while, at the same time, she is a most determined young lady. We have reached deadlock." He threw his hands in the air in despair.

"Hmm!" Hafter said. He knew the reason behind Karilyn's obduracy. It was not her job to speak the truth to Amron about his role. Hafter was the one to advise the king as to the change in his situation, and to reveal to him the identity of the Mastig's true heir. First, Hafter wanted to know more about Karilyn. He needed to assess her state of mind. If she was unable to reside with the sage, under his protection, would she be content to stay here a while longer — at least until Amron learned the truth?

If only a part of what Marazin and Orvyn had told him about Karilyn was true, Amron had no idea with what type of person he was dealing. She was a very dangerous young woman. Once she decided to leave, unless held in chains, there would be little Amron could do to stop her. She could hurt him if he tried. If she did escape, Amron would create havoc in an attempt to uncover her whereabouts. Hafter wanted no trouble. The king should know about his altered position, but Hafter struggled to find a way to make the news more acceptable to his majesty.

Then Tamin said something unexpected. Something that made everything much more complicated and dangerous than Hafter could have anticipated.

"Amron's fallen in love with her," Tamin confessed. "He's offered her his hand in marriage but, though she declines, he refuses to take 'No' for an answer."

"Oh! No!" Hafter cried out in shock. "Please, please tell me you're jesting."

"No, it's true, every bit of it," Tamin answered, startled at the look of horror on Hafter's face. "What's wrong?"

So stunned was Hafter, he answered without thinking.

"She cannot marry Amron, she's already in love with the heir, and he with her."

"But Amron's the heir. What are you talking about?" Tamin was bewildered.

Hafter fell silent. He realised the enormity of his outburst. It was too late to retract his words. He became aware of a draught of air, blowing against the back of his neck. Hafter shuddered. He eased himself out of his chair. In dread, he turned round. The drape, hanging across the centre of the wall behind his chair, was moving. It fluttered in a breeze that had been absent when he entered the room. Hafter had forgotten about the king's private entrance to his father's quarters.

Before Hafter could react further, the drape was thrown back to reveal an open doorway. At its centre stood the king, an expression on his face as bewildered as that of his father's. How long had he been listening? Hafter feared the worst. The door slammed behind, as Amron strode into the room. His boots resounded on the wooden floor. Hafter bowed low.

An aide had interrupted his majesty, during an audience with one of his subjects. As standing orders dictated, Amron wanted to know whenever the sage visited the palace. The king had excused himself to return to his chambers. The hinges on the door, which led into his father's room, had a good layer of grease on them. In secret, Amron had listened to his father's conversations a number of times. This was the first occasion he had revealed his presence.

"Well, come on Hafter. I want an answer to my father's question, now?" Amron demanded.

Flustered, Hafter's face turned red. This promised to be one of the most uncomfortable encounters of his life. His mind raced as he tried to find a suitable way to relate the news to the king.

"I tire of waiting, Hafter," Amron snapped.

Hafter decided to speak the truth. It would be his best option, or would it? If he was lucky, an edited version might spare him serious trouble.

"I've, er, recently discovered something of interest," Hafter said. "But, until I'd confirmed my facts, I thought it better to say nothing. I'm here, today, to tell you the results of my labours."

"Stop dithering. Tell me what you've found out. It can't be anything good, or you'd have come to see me first, instead of my father. What were you hoping? That Tamin would break the bad news to me, instead of you?"

"No! Of course not, your Majesty, I intended to inform you myself. I thought Tamin might…"

"… know a way to tell me the news more gently, whatever that might be? Now," Amron commanded, "before I have you flogged, speak."

Hafter flinched. He took a deep breath.

"Your Majesty, I know now the role of heir (to the Mastig) belongs to another."

Hafter paused. He waited for Amron to react.

"Go on," was the king's muted response.

Fact by fact, Hafter related the lineage of the heir. To his surprise, Amron seemed to accept his change of status without rancour. Probably, because Hafter was clear to reaffirm Amron's rightful claim to the throne. The sage was quick to assert that the heir was a descendant of an illegitimate son. As such, under Xicaliman laws governing succession, he had no sovereign rights. Hafter prayed the king would not ask the one question that would create mayhem. It was a forlorn hope, and Hafter knew it. He tried to change the direction of the conversation, by asking after Karilyn.

"Never mind her," Amron said. "You've yet to tell me about my long-lost cousin, the new heir. It will be a pleasure to meet a relative. We were led to believe none existed, weren't we Father?"

Although Tamin nodded in agreement, he had been studying Hafter's expression. The impression he gained was that the revelation, when it came, would not be welcome. The sage appeared to have shrunk inside himself. No longer red, his face had turned white. His attempt to speak ended in a croak. His throat was too dry. Tamin handed him a goblet of wine. Hafter took a swallow.

"It's Marazin," he whispered.

His words were too quiet for Amron to hear. Tamin, who was sitting beside his friend, heard them though. He, too, paled a little. He was aware of Amron's feelings towards Marazin. Hafter's reluctance to tell the king the heir's true identity was understandable.

"Speak up," the king demanded, "I can't hear if you mumble."

"It's Marazin, your Majesty," Hafter said, his face paler than ever.

There was a moment's silence.

"MAR-A-ZIN! Bloody MAR-A-ZIN!" Amron screamed in fury.

He raised a fist and took a step towards Hafter. Tamin, despite his bad leg, leapt out of his chair and moved over to block his son's path.

"Calm yourself, Amron. Can't you see what effect you have on people? No wonder Hafter delayed telling you. Your reaction is becoming far too predictable. How can you expect anyone to advise you of anything important, if they think you're going to turn on them in this way? How is it Hafter's fault if the news he brings is disagreeable? He must have spent weeks examining his conclusions to make sure they're correct."

Amron stopped. He lowered his fist. His father was correct. Had it been any other, the king would have been less concerned. Marazin appeared to be mocking him. After months of being the target of a manhunt, the warrior had evaded all attempts to find him, as had Amron's former aide, Orvyn. Now, it seemed Marazin was a relative. Worse still, somehow, the man had formed a relationship with Karilyn.

The leader of the patrol that escorted her to the palace, had spoken of his suspicions about the man who had abandoned her. At the time, unaware of anything to link the pair, Amron's inclination had been to dismiss the escort's claims. Although a slight, niggling doubt had persuaded the king, as a precaution, to put an extra watch on Hafter's home.

"If you were wrong about me being the heir, how can you be certain this man, Marazin, is who you think he is?" Amron asked

Sensing he might survive a while longer, Hafter replied immediately.

"Some time ago, I received a copy of the Book of Gryphrata, which contains a history of the lineage of the heir. Ryce, the late father of the current bearer of the Scraufin, sent it. The book provides proof that the descendants of the first-born are the heirs to the Mastig. You descend from the first legitimate son. Therefore, your claim to the throne is absolute. Marazin, who comes from the illegitimate line, inherits the role of heir to nothing more than the Mastig."

Amron was silent for a moment. His mind was working at speed.

"If anything happens to Marazin, what would be the result? If he were to die without child, surely the role would pass to me, his nearest living blood relative?"

"It's possible, if you're the only one," Hafter said after a moment's reflection.

"What do you mean, if I'm the only one? How many more distant relatives have you discovered?" Amron was becoming agitated again.

"None, your Majesty," Hafter answered in haste, "but, after the fall of Xicalima, Marazin has no knowledge of the fate of his mother's family. She was the one from whom he inherited his position. I'm unable to discover if any survived or to where they may have fled. We cannot discount there may be cousins, extant, to whom the role might fall. If there are, it could take months or years to find the person we need. We do not have this time. Betlic is unlikely to delay much longer, before he begins his offensive."

Amron nodded, as if in recognition of the inevitable. Hafter was not deceived. He had feared long what might be the result of these revelations. Amron, so the sage believed, would not give up easily his dream, as the Mastig's heir, of saving the nation. Marazin must stay at the farm, where he would be safe, until the moment came for him and Karilyn to leave. Hafter realised his own house, and visitors, would come under greater scrutiny than ever. It would make communication between him and the fugitives even more difficult.

"May I speak with Karilyn?" Hafter asked.

To his surprise, Amron agreed. The king made it clear that, under no circumstances, would he allow her to leave the palace. Hafter suspected Amron would risk much, to find and eliminate his rival for Karilyn's favours. It was this, as much as Marazin's claim to the Mastig that would spur the king's endeavours. He must hope that, if she was to remain a prisoner, Marazin might be tempted to risk a rescue bid. Hafter anticipated that, within hours, the palace would become lethal to any who tried to enter without due authority.

Amron returned to his quarters. Once there, he set about reorganising security, in particular around Karilyn's rooms. The guilt he had once felt about sending Tedrick and Boden to hunt Marazin down, he had buried deep. Boden was dead, or rumoured to be, and Tedrick was away from the rebel capital. He had found a wealthy widow, with whom he expected to pass the winter in comfort. Amron took great pleasure in sending a messenger to recall the man he believed to be an unscrupulous assassin. Marazin was back and almost certain to be hiding within easy reach of the palace. The awaiting charms of Tedrick's mistress might well be the incentive needed for the man to locate his target this time.

Once Marazin was dead, Amron had no doubts he would become the new heir. When he defeated Betlic, Amron would become master over all. He would possess both talisman and mantle. With the Scraufin and Mastig under his control, too, there would be no-one capable of challenging him. Karilyn would soon come to appreciate the advantages of what a relationship with an all-powerful king could bring her.

As usual, thoughts of the young woman inflamed Amron's desire for her. How long he would be able to control his urges was uncertain. Until now, only the fear of what harm he might inflict, if he forced himself upon her, restrained him. Unlike the heir, she was irreplaceable. Without Karilyn, no-one knew when and where to go to retrieve the Mastig and, afterwards, how he could use it to defeat Betlic. Her knowledge was beyond price.

Despite all his bluster, Amron remained uncomfortable with his rise to power. He believed possession of the talisman would give him the stature he struggled to achieve on his own. His infatuation with Karilyn, and her constant rejections of his advances, fuelled his insecurity. He had yet to believe in himself. His nobles were self-assured, confident in their position in society. In many ways, Amron had not escaped the shackles of his early life working the fields. All of which contributed to his frequent lapses of judgement and extremes of petty, childish behaviour.

Chapter Thirty One

Tamin led Hafter outside, to a part of the palace that was new to him. The wind had strengthened. Hafter shivered; he had left his cloak in Tamin's quarters. The sage was quick to notice that, unlike much of the king's residence, the single-storey building ahead was stone-built. On hearing the bearer was a woman, travelling under escort towards the palace, Amron had extended and converted a wine store, at the rear of the palace, into living quarters.

Several small windows, behind heavy metal bars, allowed light to enter. Doorways were absent from the outer walls. Tamin and Hafter walked on, to where the stonework met the timber-framed palace walls. Here, a short passageway took them towards a doorway. Beside the entrance, at head-height, set into the wall was a slit. Through the gap, a pair of eyes studied the arrivals.

A heavy, wooden door swung inwards. Hinges groaned under the weight. A guard ushered the pair inside. Before they could enter further, both Hafter and Tamin underwent a brief search for weapons. Being the king's father did not spare Tamin from this.

This way," Tamin said, as they entered a narrow corridor.

Blazing torches lit the way. Twice more the visitors passed guards, stationed beside entrances to the main areas of the palace. Soon, the pair entered a small room. Three walls had panelled linings. Ahead, a closed door, so Tamin said, led into Amron's private chambers. To the right was a wall of bare stonework, at its centre, a solid oak door. A stout wooden batten, slotted securely into position, barred the entrance. On each side of the doorway, a member of Amron's personal guard stood on duty.

At Tamin's command, one of the men lifted the batten clear. Tamin gave a double knock as he lifted the latch. He pulled open the door and stepped over the threshold. Hafter followed him. Once they were inside, the door closed behind them. The sound of the bar dropping into place was loud.

To Hafter's surprise, the room they entered was large and airy. Pale oak panels lined the walls. Colourful drapes, similar to those in Tamin's rooms, covered large parts of the woodwork. Blazing on a central stone hearth, logs added warmth and a touch of comfort, the smoke drawn through a small hole, high in the roof. In one corner, in a tangled heap, lay a pile of coloured threads and fabrics. They were untouched. It seemed the traditional pursuits of a lady held no interest for Karilyn. Instead, she had combined various objects to create an area that, Hafter could tell, had seen much use both for exercise and weapon-practice.

A door, to an inner room, was ajar. Through the opening walked a young woman. An air of confidence surrounded her. She carried herself with dignity. Her self-control was absolute.

"Good morning, Tamin," Karilyn said with warmth. Her voice was pleasant, firm and assured. She seemed pleased to see him.

"Good morning to you, too, Karilyn," Tamin replied, with a smile. "I've brought someone with me, someone with whom you've asked to meet."

As Karilyn stepped over, Tamin made the introductions. She shook Hafter's hand. The implied strength in her grip surprised him. He looked into her brown eyes and, for a moment, was lost for words. Hafter could see why Marazin had lost his heart to her, Amron too.

Against convention, although she had braided her shoulder-length dark hair, it remained uncovered. The plain gold band of her circlet, she wore without benefit of a veil beneath. On her feet was a pair of black craftsman made, soft leather shoes, tied with yellow laces. Her dress was a deep purple, woollen cyrtel, an overgown that reached below her knees. Its sleeves ended part-way down her forearms. Intricate embroidery circled the neck and hem. Beneath this outer garment, the embroidered cuffs of a longer sleeved, cream-coloured smock showed. The hem of this finely woven woollen garment reached to her ankles. Most women's garments hung straight to the hem. The skirt of Karilyn's cyrtel had pleats from the waist down. It was only when Hafter saw her walking, he realised how much freedom of movement they allowed her. If necessary, should anyone threatened her, the garments would allow her to spin and kick with ease. As he had thought earlier — she was a dangerous woman.

Hafter tore away his gaze. He had gained no meaningful insight from her expression but, somehow, he feared she had learnt everything she needed to know about him. It was an uncomfortable sensation. The events of the past year had shaped and moulded her character. Her father had told Orvyn his daughter needed time to mature. Had Ryce been here to see her now, Hafter was sure the man would have taken immense pride in his daughter's progress.

"It's an honour to meet, at last, the man who thinks I should spend my time sewing and producing embroidered panels," Karilyn said dryly.

She and Hafter were sitting at a small circular table beneath one of the barred windows. Hafter coloured. He mumbled apologies. Embarrassed, he looked into her eyes. There was a twinkle there. A smile lit her face. The laugh that followed was mischievous. If only he was a half-century younger.

Tamin declined to join them. Instead, he found a comfortable chair at the opposite side of the room. Whatever the two had to discuss, he doubted it would be anything to which he should be a party. Before Hafter could speak, Karilyn placed a finger to her lips, to indicate he remain silent.

"Swanhild," she called out, summoning an elderly maidservant from another room.

"I'm sure Tamin would enjoy some entertainment," Karilyn said, as the woman entered. "Please, bring out your lyre and sing to him."

"Yes mistress," Swanhild said, with pleasure, as she left the room.

Within minutes, she returned. The honeyed tones and skilful fingering, with which she entertained, provided a pleasant background. Hafter had remained silent, content to nod as Karilyn made small talk until the music started.

"My apologies for keeping you waiting," she said in a quiet voice. "Hidden behind the panelling, in the corner to the right of the doorway, is a gap in the stonework. Amron's chambers are beyond that. When I have visitors, sometimes he listens in. Unless I have something I want the king to overhear, Swanhild's music will cover our conversation."

Hafter understood her meaning, so, as the first melody ended, he was ready when Karilyn changed the subject and, instead, questioned him about Marazin and his whereabouts.

"Marazin?" he said, sounding surprised, "I've not seen him. The last news I heard, he was in hiding, somewhere beyond the mountains."

Karilyn indicated that Swanhild should restart her repertoire. Music filled the air again. Karilyn and Hafter returned to their conversation. As

Marazin had been most concerned about Karilyn's safety, so was she to learn of his welfare. Only when Hafter could tell her no more would she speak of other matters.

It was regrettable her relationship with Marazin had become known to Amron. She thought it less problematic for him to find out he was no longer heir to the Mastig. That, the king needed to know. For him to discover it was his enemy who had inherited his role and was also his rival in love, was less than ideal. Amron might take out his ire on Karilyn, or redouble his attempts to court her. She suspected it would be the second option. He would be more determined than ever to win her affection, or attempt to take her to spite his rival.

"How soon before I can rejoin Marazin," Karilyn demanded to know. "I become more and more wary of the king. He wishes to make me his queen. I detest him. Is there no way he can be persuaded to let me live under your roof?"

"I'm sorry, that's impossible. As you know, he fixates on you. I tried to talk to him earlier. He refuses to discuss any thought of your departure. For a while, it would be safer for Marazin if you stayed away from him. Amron has the idea that, on the death of the heir, the role will pass to him. With that thought in mind, he'll be desperate to discover Marazin's whereabouts. If Amron did release you now, it would be to use you as bait. Until the time comes for both you and Marazin to leave, I'm better able to protect Marazin if he's alone. Tell me, please, how long do you have to wait, before you begin your journey?"

She lowered her voice.

"From now! The second complete cycle of the moon, a few days after that. This will leave time for us to reach our destination before the Mastig appears."

She glanced towards Tamin. With her voice now a whisper, she said.

"So far, the king has gone no further in his attempts to seduce me, than the use of words and gifts of great value. For how long this might continue I don't know. I see his eyes; they undress me whenever he visits. I keep a dagger close at all times, but to use it would outlaw me. I've no wish to find myself in that position. To avoid that, I may need to leave here earlier than you want. Despite his loathsome personality, Amron is the true King of Xicalima, the one who will unite the nations against the evil of the talisman.

Until Marazin and I return from our mission, it falls to Amron to keep the enemy at bay. To do serious injury, or worse, to his majesty would be harmful to that cause."

"It seems strange that Amron lets you keep your weapons," Hafter exclaimed.

"Oh! At first, they did try to take them," she said, smiling. "After several attempts, the king decided that, as a 'guest', I might be allowed to retain them. Only a few his men knew of my arrival. Their injuries, though slight, placed a strain on his ability to keep me safe, as he phrased it."

Hafter laughed. Karilyn looked so sweet and demur, as she sipped from her goblet filled with rose water. It was difficult to imagine she could lift a sword, and impossible to consider she would have the strength and courage to use one.

"So, what will you do, if he tries to force himself on you?" Hafter said.

He needed to know. Although, he doubted Amron would be so foolish. Or would he? In his heart, Hafter already knew the answer. The king had become accustomed to the fulfilment of his desires. He had developed a low tolerance to opposition. Hafter was more amazed to find the man's patience enduring. Lamentable as it was, Hafter agreed with Karilyn. There may come a point when Amron's loins overruled his brains. Hafter doubted the king would gain the advantage but, as Karilyn acknowledged, he, too, was in a unique position. The problem appeared to be of little concern to her.

"I hope it won't come to that," she said. "Now he knows of Marazin's involvement, it's possible his attitude towards me might change. Once I sense he becomes a danger, I shall leave at the first opportunity."

"But how will you escape? Where will you go?"

"How I break out is my business. Although, it would be of great assistance if you told me where best I should go, once I'm free."

It occurred to Hafter that Karilyn would have started to plan her escape, the moment she arrived in her prison. First, he described to her the layout of the palace grounds. Once she had memorised these, he gave her detailed instruction on how to find the farm, where Marazin and Orvyn were in hiding. Karilyn kept glancing at the door. It was clear she expected their meeting to end soon. For a moment, she excused herself and left the room. When she returned, a few minutes later, she carried a letter. Karilyn passed it to Hafter. The wax of the seal was warm to the touch. He placed it deep within his tunic. No sooner had he concealed the packet when, from the far side of the door, came the scraping of the bar.

"Please, whenever you're able, pass my note to Marazin," she whispered.

Hafter nodded as the door swung open and the guards entered. They bowed low to Karilyn.

"It's time for your guests to leave. His majesty has no wish for them to tire you."

"How considerate of him," Karilyn said, with more than a hint of sarcasm.

As Swanhild left the room, Tamin thanked her for her music. It had been a pleasure to hear her sing and play.

"Let's hope we meet again before too long," Hafter said to Karilyn.

"Indeed so. Please, excuse me for not escorting you outside, it's a courtesy denied me," Karilyn replied, as she walked across to Tamin.

She kissed him on the cheek. Tamin was a regular visitor to Karilyn. Until now, apart from the king's unwelcome attentions, he and Swanhild had been the only people allowed to see her. It was clear to Hafter she both liked and trusted Amron's father. If only the son could have taken after his parent for temperament.

Chapter Thirty Two

The passing of the winter solstice was a memory. Spring was still too far away to be anything but a distant hope. Despite Karilyn's earlier reservations, deterioration in her relationship with the king had not been as rapid as at first feared. On a number of occasions, for several days at a time, Amron had absented himself from the palace on hunting trips. From Tamin, she learned that, in secret, his majesty met with emissaries from other nations, ones most at threat from Betlic's forces. Or so Tamin believed. Amron no longer told his father everything. Karilyn hoped such undertakings would bear fruit. As they took up so much of Amron's time, she wished they would happen with greater frequency, at least until after she had fled. His infrequent visits to her rooms, late into the evening, had become tedious.

The continued failure to find Marazin was causing Amron intense irritation. For months, Tedrick had hunted the man, without a single sighting. Wherever Marazin had taken refuge, it was proving impossible to trace. The secrecy, created by his reasons for the search, prevented Amron from enlarging the size of his force, or posting a reward for information. Again, unknown to Amron, Tedrick's limited enthusiasm for his assignment meant much of his supposed chasing took place at the home of his friendly widow.

The thought that abhorred Amron the most about Marazin was that, if he did undertake his quest and it succeeded, he would be lauded a hero. For his majesty's enemy to receive such an accolade was something the king could not tolerate. He wanted it. He deserved it. It was his. From the day he learned of his royal heritage, it had been a role promised to him. Did his father, and the doddery old sage, expect him to accept this change of circumstances without a fight?

He dreamed of a triumphant entry into Xicalima, as the saviour of the land. Karilyn would be at his side. She would turn to gaze at him, the adoration of his people unashamedly reflected in her eyes. At that point, he would awake to realise that, while his rival still breathed, his vision was unattainable. What would happen if the people decided to depose their king, would they place Marazin on the throne in his stead? Despite Hafter's repeated affirmations that Amron's rival had neither claim nor desire for the throne, the king could not persuade himself otherwise.

Karilyn remained immune to his charms. Damn it, there were few other women in the land who, if he so desired, would refuse an invitation to his bed. This was the only one he had offered to make queen, yet she continued to decline his proposals. Why? It was beyond his comprehension. He showered her with rare and expensive gifts, to no avail. Without fail, she was polite in her rejections. Somehow, she managed to divert the conversation to other matters, in such a way he bore no resentment at the time. That would come later, in his chambers, where, late into the night, he would brood over his failed attempts.

Amron knew the time approached when he would have to set free Karilyn. No matter how much he desired her, if he could not eliminate Marazin by then, Amron would have no alternative. The quest for the Mastig was paramount. Even he dared not prevent that. Without the Mastig to challenge him, Betlic was proving invincible.

Alone in his chambers, smarting from his latest rebuff from Karilyn, a morose Amron pondered over his options. An idea came to him. Was it feasible, he wondered? He shouted for more candles. From out of a side room, he brought several volumes of manuscript. Late into the night, he studied them. He ignored the flagon of wine by his table, instead he called for spring-water. A clear head was necessary for him to study the tomes in depth.

Dawn was approaching before he sat back. He rubbed his eyes. His neck was stiff, while his back and legs ached. He stretched to ease the tightness in his muscles. With satisfaction, he assessed the results of his studies. Only the heir, with the help of the bearer, could find the Mastig — of this fact he was aware. What he had failed to find, anywhere, was a reference to the exclusivity of the heir over its function. To Amron, it appeared that whoever possessed the object could make use of it. Once found, the role of heir was irrelevant. Had he access to Hafter's tomes, the king would have known this supposition to be false. In his ignorance, he began to work on a plan.

Tedrick might prove his worth after all. When the time came, once Tedrick was in place, Amron would allow Karilyn to leave. With a contingent of men, the killer would track her every move. Without interference, Marazin could join forces with her. Tedrick would bide his time. Once Marazin had retrieved the Mastig, Tedrick would attack; although, Amron decided, it might be better to wait a while longer. He had seen the injuries inflicted on the men who had tried to search Karilyn's room. He doubted anyone more capable of the object's safekeeping than she, Tedrick included.

Let Karilyn and Marazin return with their prize. Once they were within sight of the Mogallean Mountains, Tedrick would ambush them. Amron would ensure his lackey had overwhelming force at his disposal. Karilyn would face a stark choice — return to the palace of her own free will, or in chains. With Marazin dead, Amron felt sure she would ally herself with the person best placed to provide for her. That would be the king. Once he defeated Betlic, Amron would be supreme.

On several occasions, Hafter visited Karilyn. As usual, Amron's benevolence had an ulterior motive. He hoped the two might take advantage of these visits to pass notes between his rival and Karilyn. So far, Hafter's watchers had found nothing to link the sage with anyone suspicious. He was too clever for that. As a result, Karilyn treasured the notes he smuggled in from Marazin, rereading them numerous times, as did Marazin those he received from her.

Despite his intentions, Amron's obsession with Karilyn intensified. Seldom was she out of his thoughts. Whenever in residence, in vain he visited her. He could do nothing, it seemed, to win her affection. His patience was close to breaking.

03 80

It was towards the middle of the second month of the new year, when a large party of horsemen left the palace. For once, the hunt Amron had arranged was genuine. On this occasion, no emissary from a foreign land awaited a clandestine meeting with the king. It was to be a few days of relaxation, where, away from matters of state, his majesty could enjoy the thrills of the chase.

They had been riding for less than an hour when Amron's horse, his favourite, caught its right foreleg in a rabbit hole. The animal had gone down, throwing the king to the ground. His majesty escaped injury more serious than bruises. His horse was not so fortunate. Its leg was broken. They could do nothing for it. Amron turned away as one of his attendant's put-down the animal.

The king was no longer in the mood for the chase. On a borrowed horse, he left the hunting party. With only his personal guards to accompany him, he returned to the palace. Alone in his chambers, to console himself, he had one drink followed by another. By evening, although not drunk, he was close to that state. When sober, Amron could be unpleasant; when intoxicated, his moods, at best, were unpredictable. As usual, his thoughts turned to Karilyn. In his alcoholic haze, she became the person to blame for the death of his horse. Had she not spurned his advances, he would not have gone hunting. He would have been dallying with her.

She needed to learn her place. What right had she to deny the king his due? He would take her tonight. That would teach her damned lover, Marazin, a lesson. His majesty imagined the traitor's face, when Karilyn confessed the king had possessed her. He chuckled to himself. The wretch would spurn her then. So pleased was Amron with himself, he roared for his servant to refill his goblet. The thought his actions might injure Karilyn, so keep her from her duty, no longer concerned him. Drink had robbed him of any ability to apply moral judgements to his actions.

No sooner had his servant done his bidding, than Amron dismissed all his servants until the morning. When the last one departed, Amron opened the door to the adjoining room, between his and Karilyn's. Again, he commanded the men on duty to abandon their posts for the night, along with their fellows down the corridor. He was the king, he could do what he wanted, or so he told himself. Despite his inebriated state, he retained sufficient awareness that there should be no witnesses to what was about to follow.

He had forgotten Swanhild, Karilyn's maidservant. Had he remembered, he would have given her little consideration. Swanhild was his spy. She reported everything that occurred inside Karilyn's rooms to him — or so he thought. Swanhild had soon come to realise her mistress was different from those she had served in the past. Karilyn was someone for whom the maidservant was proud to work. The woman soon confessed her role. From then, they had decided between them what information Amron should, or should not receive. Swanhild would give her life for her mistress.

Karilyn had overheard Amron's slurred dismissal of the guards outside her door. At once, she was on the alert. The entrance to her room had never gone unguarded. Swanhild, who was free to come and go, had reported what had taken place on the hunt. Amron, Karilyn suspected, was about to take out his frustrations on her.

"Swanhild," she called out, keeping her voice low.

"Yes, mistress," the maidservant said as she came into the room.

"Before long," Karilyn said, "I fear the king will pay me another visit."

"Shall I prepare something for him as usual?" Swanhild interrupted.

"Quiet, Swanhild, listen to me." There was a sharpness to Karilyn's tone.

The servant looked up, startled. Her mistress's voice held an edge not used before on Swanhild. Something was amiss. A worried frown crossed her forehead.

"There's no-one on duty outside the door. Amron has dismissed the guards, including the men down the corridor."

"Are you sure, mistress?"

"Yes! A few moments ago, I heard him telling them to leave. By the sound of his voice, the little sot is drunker than usual."

Swanhild was a simple woman, but not a simpleton. The daughter of a servant, she grew up in the halls of nobles, and was wise in the ways of powerful men. The significance of Karilyn's words was not lost on her.

"What do you want me to do?"

"Sit over there in the corner. With the candles out, the screen and darkness will hide you from the door. If Amron enters, slip out behind him and fetch Tamin. There's no-one else who can control his son."

"But mistress, I can't leave you alone with that monster. You'll be in grave danger. Before I can raise Tamin, it might be too late." There were tears in Swanhild's eyes. "When I was young, one of my master's guests attacked me. I could not live with myself if you were to suffer what I went through. Please, let me stay to help you," she pleaded.

"I'll be all right. The king's the one who's in danger. If possible, I don't want to hurt him, more than I have to. The best thing you can do is to go find Tamin with all speed."

Swanhild was unhappy. She cared for Karilyn as she would a child of her own. As Swanhild would have cared, had her masters' allowed, for the daughter who had resulted from her assault all those years ago. Although brutalised by her attacker, Swanhild survived, only to have the infant taken from her at birth. Months later, word reached her the child had taken sick and died. Swanhild had never recovered from this experience.

Distressed, the maidservant moved a chair into the corner, near to the doorway. She blew out the candles. In silence, she waited while her mistress went to her room. Karilyn left a candle burning, so she was visible as she lay in the bed. She covered herself with a blanket. When Amron entered, he would see her, through the open doorway into her bedchamber. Once he reached there, Swanhild would escape, along the corridor through which Hafter gained access.

In his rooms, Amron paced backwards and forwards. No longer was he tempered by feelings of restraint. His destiny was at the mercy of his alcohol-fuelled desires. Months of lusting had brought him to this state. He dismissed thoughts of more wine. It would impair his capabilities. His mind raced with the possibilities of what he could do to Karilyn. Tonight, she would learn how unwise it was to make a fool out of a king.

Amron waited, until he was confident she would be asleep. He removed some strong cord, used in his furnishings. He cut it into several lengths, which he looped ready for use. Although dampened by drink, his survival instincts retained some of their ability. He was aware he needed to restrain her before she became fully awake.

Amron opened his door and tiptoed from his room. Within moments, he lifted the bar away from the one leading into Karilyn's quarters. He cringed as it scraped against the wood behind. Swaying, he managed to place the bar against the wall, without making any further noise. The latch clicked as he opened it. He paused for a second, then pulled open the door. Once inside, he listened for sounds of movement. There were none.

His eyes adjusted to the dim light. He could see across the room, into Karilyn's bedchamber. The candle, beside her bed, flickered in the draught blowing from the outer door. Her dark hair lay across the pillow. His eyes followed the outline of her body, its curves revealed by the fall of the blankets. Amron lips were dry. He licked them. His body trembled with anticipation. With only one thought in mind, he moved forward.

Chapter Thirty Three

With his generals and aides attending to their duties, Betlic sat alone at his table. He sought a few moments of peace, for solitary contemplation of his plans. The start of his new offensive was weeks away. His agents had confirmed that his enemies believed the disinformation he had supplied, given to them by the captured scouts, was true. Similar to many other nations, Vretlianan forces were preparing to repel an invasion they expected to take place, early the following spring.

Vretliana was the only country, so far, known to have signed a pact with the rebels; an act Betlic perceived as being his main threat. To reinforce the idea of an invasion, Betlic had stationed several brigades of troops, on the plains to the south of the Mogallean Mountains. Over the next few weeks, to maintain this subterfuge, these forces would advance closer to the Vretlianan border.

As Betlic had anticipated, King Grogant, with an offensive imminent, failed to honour his agreement with the rebels. Instead of joining with them, his men were gathering along his southeast border. Several weeks had passed since last Betlic had heard from his agents. The winter had been hard and travel difficult. It came as no surprise to him that communications had faltered. Only in spring, after his troops approached Vretliana, did he expect contact to resume. By the time Grogant realised he was not the immediate target, Betlic's main armies would be in the mountains. With the talisman undermining their will and without Vretlianan support, the rebel forces would soon crumble. Once he had crushed Amron, it would be the turn of King Grogant to face his nemesis.

Betlic occupied a large room attached to the side of a former mead-hall. It was spacious, with a hearth at its centre. Smoke rose lazily to an opening in the thatched roof. A dozen candles contributed further to the grey haze created by the smoke. Windows, shuttered against a cold north wind, allowed none of the brightness of the day to enter. A few weeks earlier, in a small abandoned village, Betlic had discovered the building. Ideal for his needs, he set up his headquarters there. The hall he used as a place of meeting with his commanders.

A knock on the door disturbed his thoughts. Betlic scowled. His instructions had been clear. The sound came again. He hoped there was a good reason for the intrusion. In response to his call, one of his aides made a tentative entrance. He hurried to Betlic's side, to whisper something in his ear. His eyebrows rose for a moment. He frowned, then nodded.

"Send him in. No, I don't require a bodyguard," Betlic added in reply to another question. "He may be many things, but a threat to me is not one of them."

Betlic was more than capable of defending himself. His bodyguards, ever vigilant, would wait outside. The aide bowed low. He left. A moment later, the visitor stepped into the room. The door shut with a firm click as the latch dropped into place. Betlic looked up from his papers to study his guest.

The man in front was close to forty. His tanned face showed much exposure to the outside air. Premature silver hair and beard, where splashes of the original black remained, surrounded a lean and determined looking face. His eyes, an intense blue, gazed back without fear at Betlic. A few inches short of six foot, the man's body was muscular. His black leather uniform, dusty from riding, was smart and cared for.

Betlic's thoughts were ambivalent about the man who waited, in silence, before him. For many years, this person had played a useful part in Betlic's plans. Beyond question, the man was loyal. He had proved himself, many times, on the diverse missions his master had chosen for him. The victor of countless combats, he killed with neither thought, nor conscience. Yet, on his last major mission, even he had failed to carry out all his instructions. Betlic's verbal lashing of the man had sent him reeling. Only his many years of faithful service had spared him from suffering the same fate as his lieutenant, Egesa. He had undergone a public flogging, then execution by a thousand cuts. Betlic noticed his visitor still wore the sword, taken from Amron's mother. It was a constant irritation to Betlic that both father and son had survived. More so now, as their reappearance was proving detrimental to the despot's plans.

Betlic was curious, too. Why would his guest tempt fate by paying an uninvited visit to his master? The man's recent command, of a group of field workers, was punishment for his failure to kill Amron. Unless he was careful, he risked much greater penalties. Betlic had never intended to let the man rot forever. Whether the leader had forgiven him, enough to permit an early return, would depend on what the man was about to say.

"Well, Talon, this is a surprise. I can't recall sending for you, or am I mistaken?" Betlic's tone was cold and inhospitable.

"Your Highness, as always, is correct," Talon answered without hesitation.

Fear was something he had conquered early in his career. For the moment, he had his feelings under control, but he was wary. He was right to be so. Betlic had been ever unpredictable. This had become more noticeable since the arrival of the mantle. By arriving uninvited and requesting a meeting, Talon knew the risk he was taking. What he had to offer Betlic, Talon hoped, would restore his fortunes. He had relished his previous wide-ranging roles, undertaken on his master's behalf. Talon missed the excitement and the thrill from the secret knowledge he gained on such ventures.

"Then the reason for your visit must lie with you. Would you care to explain?" Betlic's voice remained cold.

For a moment, Talon had the uncomfortable feeling his explanation might lack credence. It was too late to reconsider. The tedium of forcing a mixed group of unwilling peasants and nobles to toil in the fields, was destroying his mind. That, to him, was worse than death. He took a deep breath.

"As you're aware, master, I spend my time supervising some of your field workers," he began.

"Yes, yes, I know. I assigned you to the task. I presume you are unhappy and have come to beg for reinstatement?"

"Er, no, yes, well, in part," was Talon's hesitant reply.

A trickle of sweat ran down his back. He was unsure. There were pitfalls to whatever he said. To say no, meant he was happy where he was. The alternative also was unacceptable. He never begged. With the information he had, he hoped to bargain.

"I cannot deny that my work for you, elsewhere, has been more to my satisfaction," Talon acknowledged. "However, your Highness, if you would permit me to start, I hope my words might be of interest to you."

"I can't wait. Please, share with me this enthralling account."

As he started his narrative, Talon decided Betlic's manners had improved little.

"A few days ago, a recent recruit stopped by the fields. It seems his cousin was one of my workers. I accompanied them while they met. It transpired the man had come to gloat over his cousin's predicament. As he told her, had she accepted your leadership, your Highness, she would have had a better life."

"Fascinating," Betlic said with heavy sarcasm. "And what did this young woman do, prostrate herself on the ground and plead for forgiveness?"

"She pulled her young son to her side," Talon persevered, "and called the man a traitor. Matters became somewhat heated. It seems that, to prove his worth to his new masters, the man betrayed the woman and her family. Her husband was killed when he went to their defence."

"And this is relevant to me, how? It's a common enough tale. What makes these people so special?" Betlic had thought better of Talon. The warrior was astute enough to have found something of greater interest to attract his master's attention.

"That I'm coming to, your Highness," Talon said. "The man was stopping the woman from working. I intervened and sent him on his way. The following morning, the woman and her child had gone. They'd broken through the wattle wall at the back of her quarters, slipped past the perimeter guards and disappeared.

"After several days, with no sign of her, I went in search of the man. At first, I suspected his visit might have been a ploy, and that he'd helped her escape. Please bear with me," he implored Betlic, who was displaying signs of ending the meeting. "I caught up with him and his unit. It was soon clear he'd done nothing to help the woman. There's bad blood between them. Thinking she might head back to where she came from, I asked him the region where they originated. What he said surprised me."

"This is your last chance, Talon. I promise you, if this revelation is not worth the wait, it will be you working the fields, not supervising them."

"He said," Talon persisted, desperate to reach the end of his tale, "that they lived near to the place your Highness's men burned down last year. I questioned him further. He said yes, it was the home of Karilyn, the lady who escaped with the object you sought. Throughout childhood, his cousin, the woman from the fields, had been this Karilyn's best friend."

"Well, a little long in the telling, but your news does hold some interest after all. What a pity you're too late. Your ability to keep up-to-date amazes me, apart from the one detail that matters the most. The bearer of the Scraufin is dead. This woman and child can be of no further use to me. Find and kill them."

"Your Highness, can you be certain that the bearer is no longer alive?" Talon dared to disagree. He braved Betlic's icy glare to continue. "To my own cost, I know that to believe someone is dead, without proof of a body, can be unreliable. It's not the first time this woman has 'died'. Can you be positive she perished in the mountains?"

"Many, many times I've sought her with the Eye. She does not appear. The bearer must be dead," Betlic said, more as reassurance to himself than to refute Talon.

For weeks, Betlic had suffered nightmares. Night after night he awoke from foul dreams, Karilyn's name pounding in his head. Logic and the Eye told him she was dead. The horrors of the night contradicted such beliefs.

What if, by some miracle, she survived the fall, and the caverns down which the torrent took her? Although he had extensive knowledge of the talisman and mantle, he knew little about the Scraufin and the Mastig. That they posed a threat was indisputable. What was also beyond doubt was that, without the bearer's assistance, the Mastig was lost forever. What other properties they might possess was unclear. Was it feasible for the Scraufin to hide the bearer from his gaze? Yet, if so, why had it failed to do so, when he followed her to the mountains?

Betlic looked at Talon. The man was intelligent and resourceful. Minding prisoners was a waste of his talents. It was time he had a chance to redeem himself.

"Congratulations, Talon," Betlic addressed him. "Consider yourself released from your current duties. Instead, I want you to manage a small task for me. Do you think you're capable?"

Talon struggled to stop himself from smiling. He contented himself with a nod of acceptance.

"Please be aware, should you fail, it would be better for you to have died in the act, rather than to return to me with your mission incomplete. Do you understand?"

"Your meaning is clear, your Highness."

"The woman, Karilyn, I meant what I said. I have no evidence to suggest she's alive. My instincts, though, tell me something is wrong. I survive today only because, throughout my life, I have trusted them. This man, the cousin to the escapee, is he still where you can find him?"

"Of course, your Highness, he stands outside with the horses."

"I should have known you would not risk losing him. Take him with you, go find the woman and child. Bring them back to me. If you have to choose between them, save the child. It might prove more useful as leverage against the bearer, should she spring back into life. Otherwise, if at all possible, bring the mother, too, you'll need someone to care for the brat."

"I won't let you down again, your Highness." Talon bowed low before he turned to leave.

"I know you won't," Betlic said. It was more a threat than words of encouragement.

The meaning was clear to Talon. He hurried outside. Within minutes, he was in the saddle. He turned to his new travelling companion.

"Well, Halwende, we have a job to do. Betlic commands we find your cousin Willa, and her child. He wants them brought to him, with all speed."

Halwende was ecstatic. He believed his fortune was secure. His decision to join forces with the invaders had been the right one. In the few short months, since he betrayed his family, he had risen from raw recruit, to involvement in a mission for Betlic. His star was in the ascendant. He was impatient to confront his cousin. The manner of the rejection to his marriage proposal to her friend was an embarrassment he would never forget, nor forgive. Karilyn was dead and beyond his revenge. Willa was not. She was the one who had played matchmaker. He would pay her back in full.

Chapter Thirty Four

Amron's mind was so focused on his victim, he missed the slight swish of Swanhild's skirts as she fled the room. Her stockinged feet moved ghostlike over the corridor's stone floor. She reached the external doorway where she put on her shoes. The heavy beam, which barred the door, was difficult for her to lift. Panic gave her added strength. A huge pair of bolts was all that remained to release. These were stiff. Fearful of the noise, she worked them clear. With a cry of relief, she pulled open the heavy wooden door and ran outside, into the freezing air.

The ground was treacherous underfoot. Swanhild fell twice on the ice, banging her arm against a wall the second time. Crying with pain, she picked herself up and limped on. On reaching the entrance to Tamin's quarters, she was gasping for breath. Swanhild's pounding was feeble. Her injured arm lacked the strength to make sufficient noise to raise anyone. She cast around and, nearby, saw a stone. With it in her other hand, her banging on the wooden panels quickly gained results. With a protesting creak, the door opened. Mildthryth, holding a candle and dressed only in a thin gown, looked in bewilderment at the wide-eyed, breathless woman in the doorway. Before she could speak, Swanhild pushed past her.

"Where…is…Tamin?" she gasped.

From a doorway, he appeared, pulling on his breeches. As soon as he saw who the visitor was, and the look on her face, he guessed what had happened.

"Quick…Karilyn…Amron…Drunk!" Swanhild spat out the words as she struggled for breath.

The quick dash and cold air had seized her lungs. She collapsed into Mildthryth's arms. Tamin picked-up a stout walking stick. He tried the door into Amron's chambers. Bolts were in place on the other side. At a pace that defied the disability in his leg, Tamin turned and ran from the house. The outer door to the palace gaped wide, as Swanhild had left it. Tamin noted the absence of guards. The meaning was clear to him, as it was to Karilyn earlier.

His son was a bloody fool. Tamin prayed he was not too late. At speed, he moved towards her rooms.

Had it not been for his father, Amron was sure he would have died that night. He had crept into Karilyn's bedchamber. To avoid disturbing her, he had inched back her sheets. In haste, he grabbed for her wrists, his looped rope ready to bind them tight. She had been on her side, with her knees drawn up, almost to her chin. Karilyn had feigned sleep, her body coiled and muscles prepared for action. Afterwards, the only thing Amron remembered, with any clarity, was lying on his back, on the floor. Karilyn, who had remained dressed, straddled his semi-naked body. The point of her sword pricked against his throat. By the pale light of the candle, Karilyn's eyes seemed dead, her face devoid of expression.

Amron remained frozen to the spot. He feared she might misinterpret any move he made. Karilyn retained her position, her gaze inscrutable. Minutes passed. Amron was conscious of the coldness of the floor. He had removed his breeches before leaving his rooms and his flimsy tunic had ridden up. The prominence of his earlier passion lay flaccidly in view. His brain, fogged by alcohol, could think of nothing to say that might not be his final undoing. The sound of footsteps, rushing into the outer room, brought relief to Amron's mind.

As Tamin entered the bedchamber, he was quick to assess the situation. His respect for his son was at a new low. Keeping his voice calm, Tamin spoke to Karilyn. She stepped back, a move that allowed Tamin to help Amron to his feet. At all times, she maintained her guard. The old man whispered to her, to await his return. Karilyn nodded. As Tamin had something she needed, she was unable to leave yet.

Outside Karilyn's rooms, in relative safety, Amron's slurred and incoherent angry words echoed down the corridor. With his father's assistance, he staggered into his chambers. All the while, Amron continued to curse and threaten vengeance. He was limping. The floor, on which he had landed, was hard. The back of his head, where a large lump had formed, was painful. His chest was sore, already starting to bruise. Karilyn's booted feet had hit with considerable force, to propel him away from her bed. Tamin managed to calm the king, sufficient to guide him to a chair. Amron snatched a flagon of strong wine from nearby. He poured the contents straight into his mouth. Some of the liquid spilled down his chin and over his tunic. The additional drink soon took effect. Within moments Amron passed out. He started to snore. In disgust, his father left him.

Tamin unbolted the door to his rooms and entered his bedchamber. In the kitchen, he could hear Mildthryth as she tried to comfort a weeping Swanhild. For the moment, he ignored them. From beneath a loose floorboard beside his bed, he retrieved a well-wrapped package. With extreme caution, he walked through Amron's chambers. Only the sound of snoring broke the silence.

Shamed by what had taken place, it was with reluctance Tamin returned to Karilyn's room. He had grown fond of the girl. In many ways, she reminded him of his late wife. He could not stand by and let Amron harm her. Neither could he allow her to hurt his son, no matter how deserving he was of retribution. Both had a job to do. Of the two, he had no doubt Amron would be the one who would suffer most from another encounter.

It was time the girl moved on, to somewhere safe from molestation. When first Tamin learned of his son's infatuation with her, he should have insisted he house her elsewhere, out of harm's way. Instead, he had listened to Hafter's advice and been persuaded it would be safer for everyone if she remained.

Tamin was wise enough to give Karilyn's door a sharp knock, then announce who it was. Only when he heard her invitation to enter did he step inside. Karilyn stopped him at once when he tried to apologise for Amron's assault.

"Your son's no longer a boy, Tamin. Amron's actions are his own responsibility. These past few months I've come to know you both. The king's behaviour is no fault of yours. The choice is his alone. His ways are reprehensible. He knows that, yet continues with them as if they were normal. No matter. It's almost time for Marazin and I to leave. Even without this incident, I would have been away before long."

"Are you aware, when Amron allowed you to go, he would have had you followed?" Tamin asked, as he handed her the package taken from his room.

Karilyn, who had started to un-wrap the object, seemed amused.

"Whatever makes you think that?" she said. There was no doubt in her voice as she added, "I could have left whenever I wanted; permission has never been an issue. I only stayed because Hafter insisted, otherwise I would have gone before the solstice."

Despite his curiosity, Tamin decided it would be better to remain in ignorance as to how she would have accomplished this feat. It was of no importance now. There were no guards on the door. Even if he wanted to, Tamin doubted he could have stopped her.

"Thank you, for keeping this safe for me," she said.

The package contained a leather bag. From the moment of Karilyn's arrival, Amron had wanted to take possession of the Scraufin. Without it, he knew she could not start her journey to collect the Mastig. With only instinct to guide her, Karilyn had passed the object to Tamin, in the hope he would keep it safe. Her trust had been well-placed.

During Tamin's absence, Karilyn had changed her clothes. Beneath a dark, shorter cyrtel, slit at the sides, she wore a pair of leather breeches. A heavy cloak lay on a chair nearby. An outfit that Swanhild had made for her. On her feet, Karilyn wore a pair of fine, fur-lined leather boots. From a leather belt, she had fastened round her waist, hung a scabbard and sword. As he gazed at Karilyn, Tamin gave thanks she had spared Amron.

Something about the way she looked made him recall Hafter's words from a while ago. She was not someone you would want as an enemy. In an instant, her expression changed, in a most unexpected way. Her self-assurance faltered, she looked lost and vulnerable, almost childlike. Karilyn's eyes were moist as she came over to him. She threw her arms around his neck and, for a moment, hugged him.

"Look after yourself," she said as she broke away. "Your company and friendship have made my stay here bearable. Whatever you do, be wary of Amron. I know he's your son, but, if he suspects you played any part in my escape, your relationship will count for nought."

"Have no concerns over me, I shall be fine," Tamin said, with a confidence he hoped was not overstated.

"Please, keep Swanhild safe. Her companionship has been invaluable. Amron must never know it was she who warned you, or that she's aware of the events here tonight."

"Have no worries, I'll tell him she slept through everything. When she awoke, she found you gone, the guards absent and the door open. Once convinced no-one knows what happened, he'll not bother about a servant. Swanhild can stay at my house. Mildthryth would welcome some help."

"Please tell Swanhild, when I return, there'll be a place for her with me."

They said their farewells. Once Tamin had gone, Karilyn felt a twinge of guilt as she studied the Scraufin. He might have risked much to hide it for her, but he was the king's father. It would have been foolhardy to set off without the original, and fatal to her and Marazin, had they tried to use a copy when the time came. Satisfied, she returned it to the bag, which she attached to the belt on her breeches. Moments later, the carrier lay concealed beneath her overgown. Her few belongings she had packed while she awaited Tamin's return.

Without a backward glance, she made her way along the corridor, then out into the darkness beyond. With her cloak wrapped round her, she walked towards the stables. She called softly. From the far end came a whinny. Her horse remembered her. Careful not to waken the stable-boy, who was sound asleep on a bale of hay, she saddled the animal and led it outside. With her possessions tied in place, she hooked the reins over a nearby fence post.

Light-footed, she moved towards the gates that barred the way out of the palace grounds. A single guard was on duty. Standing to one side of the gateway, he warmed himself beside a glowing brazier. He was unaware of Karilyn's presence, until the point of her sword pricked against his back. At her whispered command, he dropped to his knees. With the rope Amron had brought, she bound her prisoner's hands and feet, then gagged him.

Satisfied the man would be unable to free himself for some time, Karilyn turned her attention towards the gates. The huge wooden bar, which secured them in place, ran smoothly on greased mountings. After a struggle, she pulled open one of the heavy barriers. Wasting no time, Karilyn returned for her horse, which she led through the grounds towards the entrance. An icy mist floated in through the open gateway. Once across the moat, she mounted. Within minutes, they were lost to sight. In the stable, she had tied leather shoes over her horse's hooves. Because of these, and the frozen ground, the animal left no tracks.

Karilyn rode throughout the night. The mist remained confined to the lower levels that surrounded the palace and its sprawling township. On higher ground, once clear of the silent streets, the vapour cleared. The stars were bright. By their light, she navigated the route, memorised from Hafter's instructions. As the sky lightened in the east, a weary rider approached a farm. She prayed Marazin still waited for her there.

Chapter Thirty Five

When Amron awoke, or came round as was nearer to the truth, it was close to noon. He had a blinding headache. Hungover, and with a lump the size of his thumb on the back of his head, he felt nauseous. His chest and back showed heavy bruising, as did his leg. Hazy memories of the night before, and his intentions, came back to him. Whether the injuries resulted from what had happened then, or the earlier fall from his horse, Amron was unsure. He was shivering with cold. He had spent the night in the chair, without benefit of blanket nor fire in the hearth.

As he staggered to his feet, his head spun and his stomach heaved. Afterwards, although he felt better inside, the pounding in his head had become worse. He was shaking now, his body colder than ever. A cloak lay strewn across a nearby table. He snatched the garment and wrapped it round his shoulders.

Several times, without answer, he called for his servants. Only as his anger rose, did he remembered ordering them to leave the night before. His breeches were lying on the floor where he dropped them. With eyes half-closed, he caught his foot on the untidy heap. He was lucky to keep his balance. Groaning and swaying, he bent down to pull on the garment.

Flashes of disjointed memory returned to him. He had drunk too much. The vague parts of what he did remember made his mood deteriorate further. Karilyn had gone too far. In a blind rage, he hobbled out of his chambers, towards her rooms. It was time she understood the truth about her position. He would no longer tolerate her high and mighty attitude. She was his property now. Whenever he visited, she would accept his attentions, willingly or, if necessary, tied to her bed, whatever — he cared not. If she threatened him again, he would have her chained. When the time came for her to find the Mastig, he would drag her to its hiding place bound and gagged. She would be…!

Amron stopped. His mouth fell open. Stunned, he stared at the gaping doorway at the entrance to her chambers. He stumbled inside. She was gone, her possessions too. His valuable gifts, she had tossed aside. Furious, Amron retraced his steps. He moved towards the doorway that led into his father's rooms.

Startled, Tamin looked up from his dinner table as Amron's door flew open. With its hooks ripped from the panelling, the wall-hanging, that covered the opening to his son's chambers, dropped onto the figure beneath. Amron hurled the fabric out of his way. The room shook as the door slammed behind him. Even without shoes, he stomped loudly across the wooden floor, towards his father.

"What have you done with her? Where's she gone?" he yelled, spittle flying from his lips.

"Who? Karilyn?" Tamin stuttered. The calmness of his tone belied the anxiety he felt. Throughout the morning, he had been dreading this confrontation. Will power alone prevented his hands from shaking. "The last time I saw her was when we left her rooms last night," he lied.

"Didn't you lock her door?" Amron was incredulous.

"No! You were my main concern. I was too busy looking after you. By the time I finished, it was late, and I was weary. I came straight to my rooms. Can't you remember? You told me to unbolt my door, in case you needed me in the night. I was falling asleep on my feet. I'd been so concerned with your welfare, I'd forgotten about Karilyn."

Amron's mind filled with suspicion. "You don't seem surprised to learn she's gone."

"Why should I? I found out earlier today."

"You knew, yet did nothing?" Livid, Amron banged his hand on the table. "If you've been in your rooms all day, how did you find out? Who else knows what happened last night?"

"I know because Swanhild told me. When she left her room this morning, the first thing she saw was the outer door standing open. There were no guards outside and Karilyn was missing. Straight away, Swanhild ran to tell me. Mildthryth, who'd gone to the market, returned at the same time. She reported a commotion at the palace gates. The relief watch found them unbarred this morning, and the night guard tied up. I, of course, came in to see you as soon as I heard. When I did manage to rouse you from your sleep, you swore and waved me away. You said you'd deal with it. Don't you remember?"

Tamin had observed Amron much over the years. From the son, the father had learned the art of a convincing lie. Amron hesitated. As Tamin thought, his son's recollections were incomplete and confused. Within a short time, the false memories Tamin had seeded in Amron's mind, would blend with the meagre details he remembered. He would convince himself they were real. Again, Amron began to feel unwell. He swayed as he tried to remember but his thoughts were muddled.

"The servant, Swanhild, what does she know about last night?"

"Nothing! The woman had a toothache. Karilyn gave her some strong mead to help ease the pain. Afterwards, the maid retired to her room where she slept through the night. She knows Karilyn has gone, nothing more. The maid was aware her mistress would soon be going on an important journey. I told Swanhild the time had come for Karilyn to leave and that you'd agreed to release her. Without question, the maid has accepted the explanation. I'll keep my eye on her. She can stay here and be of some help to Mildthryth."

Amron grunted. He dismissed the servant from his mind; she was no threat to him. Again, doubts clouded his thoughts.

"So, if Swanhild was asleep, she couldn't have been the one to rouse you. How was it you arrived last night when you did? Did someone else wake you?" Amron had moved closer to Tamin.

His son's bloodshot eyes were inches from his own. The foul stench of Amron's breath pervaded the air. Tamin's mind raced.

"I'd used the last of my spiced apple wine," he said as an idea came to him. "I wanted some more. Mildthryth had retired for the night. I thought I'd fetch some myself. Once in the main hall, I found the doorway, to the passage outside your chambers, ajar. I thought it strange that no-one was on watch. I went to investigate and found you."

As Amron had dismissed his servants, and guards, for the night, Tamin knew no-one could contradict him. The king accepted the explanation, his thoughts, once more focusing on the woman who had spurned him. How dare she walk out? It was his decision to make. She had no say in the matter.

"Damn it!" he yelled. "I won't allow her to run away from me. Call my guards now."

"Forget Karilyn. Let her go," Tamin's own anger was rising. "You know she has to find Marazin. The Mastig's their concern, not yours. Let them carry out their mission. Once they've found the object, they have to return to confront Betlic, wherever he might be. You'll have a close involvement with any hostilities, so, the paths of you, Marazin and Karilyn are bound to cross again. Sort out your differences then. Whatever happens, it's at your peril if you distract them from their task.

"We know details of your pact, with Vretliana, have reached the ears of Betlic. It's time for you to concentrate, with a single-mind, on your duties. You've plans to make. There are conflicting opinions as to when, or where, Betlic will start his attack. Your decisions, as to where you position your army, will define whether we win or lose the battles ahead. Personal feuds are a dangerous distraction.

"Have you learned nothing in your time as king? In peacetime, you can afford the luxury to indulge your passions and whims. Now is not that time. And, unless you do something to organise our defences, such times have gone forever. This is not a game; it's time you stopped acting the part of a Monarch and started being one."

Tamin had lost patience. What the consequences of his outburst might be, he no longer cared. Angrily, he continued.

"Gather your Generals. Listen to them. They think Betlic will attack us first. From legend, he must know you're a rallying point. Your own thoughts are not at variance with this, or so you have told me a number of times. Work out a strategy. From the prisoners he's taken, Grogant believes he is Betlic's intended target. The enemy gathers to the south of the mountains. Vretliana is unwilling to commit any men to you until they know, for certain, which way Betlic advances.

"It could take months before Grogant's forces join us. You must be ready, to sacrifice everything, if necessary, to delay Betlic's advance. Other countries are in the same predicament as Grogant. No-one will dare to move their armies, not until they have confirmation of Betlic's intentions. For once, show some leadership, instead of behaving like a petty, spoilt child, running around as if scared of its own shadow. It's time for you to grow up."

In shock, Amron stared at his father. How dare he? No-one spoke to the king in this manner. Yet, despite a rush of blood to his head and a raging desire to strike out, his father's words rang true. If only for a while, it was time to put revengeful thoughts to one side. Tamin was correct, Amron should be concentrating his mind on keeping himself and his followers alive and free from Betlic's tyranny. Certain matters could be set in motion, in regard to Marazin and Karilyn, ones that might proceed without the king's direct involvement.

Although well-informed, Tamin was not privy to all his son's actions. Amron had been less indolent than his father believed. There was much the king had discussed, agreed and set in motion with many of the emissaries he had met, matters that, in time, would have great impact on the conflict to come. The intervention of the Mastig was crucial. Despite his fixation on Karilyn and his desire to be the heir, Amron had not allowed its ownership to cloud his entire strategy. When the time was right, it was irrelevant who commanded the object, it was only necessary for that person to be there. For once, Amron found some definition for his role. It was not as the heir, it was as a king.

"You're right, Father. Excuse me, I have duties to attend to," Amron said.

His angry and flushed face belied the cold and controlled tone of his voice. Amron turned on his heel and stalked out of his father's room. The old man let out a sigh of relief as he heard the bolts on the other side of the door slam home. Tamin knew he had gone too far. He had been too enraged to stop himself. His son's attitude and recent behaviour disgusted him. The boy had to accept the realities of his position. His murderous expression, before he stormed out, had chilled Tamin. With some justification, for the first time in his life, he was afraid of his son. Tamin started to tremble. He tried to pick up his goblet. His hands shook so much, he spilt the contents over the remains of his meal. He hurled the vessel against the wall. Shaken, he leant forward to rest his head in his hands.

The door to the kitchen opened. Mildthryth entered. Through the flimsy wood, she had overheard everything. Although she never presumed to speak it aloud, Mildthryth had her own opinion of Amron — it was a pity he had survived his infancy. She walked over to Tamin and put her arms around him. He turned, placed his head against her amble bosom and wept.

Chapter Thirty Six

For several weeks, Willa, along with her young son Scard, had been a fugitive. Before her escape, she had listened to the talk among her fellow slaves. They had discussed in great depth any scraps of information that came their way about the rebels. From these snippets, Willa believed, if she moved north for long enough, she would find sanctuary with Betlic's opponents. In truth, she was too far east. She would miss the mountains, and the many other refugees, by a considerable margin. One advantage her direction of travel did have over a more westerly approach, it would take her away from the intended path of Betlic's armies.

By circumstance, her route had not been straightforward, but Willa had succeeded in avoiding her pursuers. To do so, she had made random and, sometimes, substantial diversions, before returning to her northerly path. Even though Scard's stamina improved, by the afternoon his legs ached and he became weary. Most days, Willa had to wait an hour or more while he rested. At five years of age, Scard was too big and heavy for her to carry for any distance. These concerns and difficulties conspired to slow her progress.

Late one evening, she entered a ruined village. Ashes were all that was left of its thatched huts. By the light of the setting sun, she could see the remains of some of the inhabitants. Only the remnants of their clothes allowed her to recognise them as either men or women. With their children and infants, they lay sprawled where they had fallen. Some had died alone, others in grotesque family groups. The massacre was not recent, little remained but scraps of blackened skin and bone. Scavengers had disarranged many of the corpses. Willa covered her child's eyes, and averted her own, as she rushed through the scene of horror to reach the other side.

With the village behind her, Willa cast around for somewhere to set up camp. Although close to spring, the day had been cold. Both she and Scard had clothing sufficient to keep warm. As had her old friend, Karilyn, Willa had taken what they needed from deserted houses. Over the past few nights, a gentle wind had prevented a frost from forming. Hand-in-hand, mother and son walked along a narrow lane. An ancient and dense beech hedge, at head-height, was to their right. Willa paused as the sound of movement reached her. In panic, she grabbed Scard and threw herself down, into the base of the hedgerow.

The noise came from the other side of the barrier. The thickly layered branches had retained many of last years' dried leaves, making it difficult for her to see what lay beyond. On her knees, Willa crawled until she found a spot through which she could see. In the dim light, she made out the figure of a boy. Beside him was a large hole, which he had dug out of the cold ground. To his other side were several bodies wrapped in cloth. As she watched, the boy dragged the smallest one to the hole. With reverence, he eased it into its final resting place. The other bodies were larger and unwieldy. It was clear he wanted to lay them out, instead of throwing the bones into a heap. Willa could see the exhaustion in his movements. After digging the grave, he must have dragged the remains all the way from the village. Taking a risk, she stood and walked towards a gap in the hedge.

"Please, let me help you," she called out, as Scard ran to her side.

The stranger froze. Although frightened, the youngster stood his ground. To him, his task was important. He would flee only if there was no other choice.

"Who's there?" he asked, his voice faltering.

"My name's Willa. I have my little boy with me. I mean you no harm, but I do think you need some help. Please, let me assist."

With Scard at her side, Willa stepped into the field. She held out her hands, to show she bore no weapons. The lad was suspicious. He was also weary beyond measure. It had taken him most of the day, first to dig the grave out of the heavy clay soil and then fetch the remains of his family. Drained of both energy and emotion, he nodded in acceptance. If it was a trap, so be it. He would die with his loved ones.

Willa spoke to Scard, as she sat him down beside the hedge, and told him to stay. The child was wise now in the ways of running and hiding. When told to sit, he did so without question. Willa produced something for him to eat from her pack. She left it, and a water bottle, with him. At a slow pace, so as not to appear a threat, she approached the graveside.

Without speaking, Willa bent down and took hold of the shroud at the opposite end to the one held by the boy. She shuddered as she felt bone move inside. Steeling herself, she looked up and nodded to the boy to indicate her readiness. Between them, they laid whatever remained of the body inside the grave. Five more times, they repeated the process, each body larger than the previous one. Only one bundle was left. This was the largest of them all. Tears appeared in the boy's eyes as they laid it to rest on top of the others.

He picked-up a spade. Earth rained down over the bodies. Willa cast around. Another spade, with a broken tip, lay on the ground nearby. Of no use for digging, the tool was adequate for moving the loose soil. Willa worked alongside the boy, until the hole was no more. For a moment, they prayed over the grave. The lad was shivering in the cold. Willa wondered when last he ate. Without warning, he fainted. She dragged him, out of the wind, to the shelter provided by the hedge. There, she wrapped a blanket round his ice-cold body.

Without warmth, Willa was certain, the boy would take ill by morning. Although it was a while since last she sighted her pursuers, it was with trepidation she gathered a pile of wood. The fire was slow to start. She persevered until the flames took hold. The damp wood spit and crackled. Thick smoke spiralled skywards. As the blaze strengthened, the chill, which surrounded the travellers, diminished.

Willa heated some food. Scard, his hunger satisfied, fell asleep. As the heat from the blaze increased, the newcomer stirred. His eyes opened and, for a moment, he stared wild-eyed around him. His gaze focused on Willa. Recognition dawned. He glanced toward the mound of earth. Beyond the reach of the flickering light from the flames, the grave was no longer visible.

"Thank you," he said at last.

Willa handed him a goblet of water, warmed in the embers, and a plate of hot food. After several mouthfuls of water, he devoured the food. Again, she wondered how long it had been since he had eaten.

"That was good," he said, with a shy smile, as he passed back the empty plate to Willa. "My name's Sheply," he added.

"I'm so happy to meet you. What happened in the village?" Willa asked.

Sheply explained he had been away from home for almost a year, tending his sheep. He had expected his father, either to send for him or, if Betlic invaded, to bring his brothers and sisters to join him. Summer came and went, autumn, too, had passed without news.

Alone, Sheply spent the winter solstice with still no word from home. Over time, his concern for his family overcame his sense of duty. He decided to return. His dog, he left to guard the flock. He had walked for weeks before he reached his village. Used to living off the land, even when the ground was frozen, he had foraged sufficient food to survive.

Only since his arrival home had he forgotten to eat. For two, or three days, in a state of shock, he had wandered the surrounding area, hoping to find someone who had survived. Few outlying homes had suffered damage. Those untouched were empty, their owners fled. They had left nothing that might have been useful to him.

Sheply's father had been a man of some means, the owner of several flocks of sheep and a trader in meat and wool. His sheep and horses were missing, his house and belongings burnt to the ground. Elsewhere in the village, everything of value was gone, either stolen, or incinerated in the conflagration. There was nothing to keep Sheply here. He would return to his flock and move them on. Before he left, there had been one last thing he could do for his family. He would bury them. It was not decent to leave their bones exposed to the elements.

Willa's heart went out to the boy. His story was not unique. Wherever Betlic's men went, she feared, they left a trail of destruction and broken lives. She was curious. Betlic's armies were yet to come this way. Earlier in her travels, other villages she had passed had not suffered the same fate as this one.

"Why do you think Betlic's men did this to your village, but left others untouched?" she asked.

"I doubt Betlic's men did this," Sheply said after a moment's hesitation. "Several years ago, some of his followers raided our village. My mother died at that time. They use differing ways. Women, they take for their pleasure. In a raid, they kill or injure, only those who stand in their way. If it had been their intention to murder everyone, they would have rounded-up the people, then executed them together, as an example to others. There's another settlement some miles to the north. It looks similar to this one. If I had to choose, I would say these were attacked by bandits."

For a while longer they talked. Sheply was happy to accept Willa's suggestion they travel north, together. The boy would have company, and, if necessary, he would be there to help Willa with Scard. It would be advantageous to have someone with her, with the skills to survive off the land. Of equal importance, the boy's father, wary he might be unable to return for his son, had given the boy detailed instructions on how to reach the rebel base. If Willa was fortunate enough to avoid capture before they reached Sheply's flock, her pursuers might not think to look for her in her new role as shepherdess.

Early next morning, Willa left the boys asleep. She returned to the village. The task she had in mind, though unpleasant, was one she hoped might aid their survival. With care, she scoured the areas surrounding the burnt-out shells of the buildings. The raiders must have struck, either late evening, or first thing in the morning. In among the undergrowth, in various stages of undress, were a number of bodies. Some had picked-up their boots and fled. These lay abandoned, where their owners died. (Nothing could have persuaded Willa to remove footwear from the dead.)

She returned to the boys, two pairs of fresh boots in her hands. There had been no rain for several days. Although cold and damp, the footwear was wearable. Willa wiped the dirt and mould from them as best she could. Each pair she had chosen was larger than the one she intended to replace, and of a different design. She pulled on extra stockings, until her boots fitted. When he awoke, she did the same for Scard. Their footprints would show substantial differences from those her pursuers knew. This, Willa hoped, along with the tracks of Sheply, would throw Betlic's men off her trail. For a while, this proved to be true.

CB ED

Close to the farm where she had slaved in the fields, Talon, Halwende and their band of men picked-up Willa's trail. In the panic to escape, she had done little to conceal her tracks. This omission lasted only a short while. It was soon apparent she had made an effort to hide traces of her movements. After that, there had been nothing. She had disappeared! In an attempt to pick up their quarry's trail, the pursuers spent several frustrating weeks criss-crossing the land. Talon feared the fugitives might have doubled back.

The group moved south. Apart from a few tracks, seen earlier, their search proved fruitless. How Willa had managed it, Talon did not know, but she had eluded him, where few had before. Halwende was in a permanent rage, unlike Talon who was intrigued more than angered. The woman was proving far more resourceful than expected. This was someone worthy of respect. He had no doubts he would find her. The challenge, presented by her ghostlike ability to move across the land, stimulated his mind.

It had been almost six weeks since they had found any trace of the fugitives. Word reached them that Betlic had begun his advance on the Xicaliman rebels. The same messenger warned Talon of his master's displeasure. How difficult could it be to track a woman with a small child? In principle, Talon agreed. He spent most of the following night pondering on the problem. By daybreak, he had made a decision.

"We head north again," he instructed his party. "We've no tracks, no sightings, nothing to show in what direction Willa's moving. My instincts tell me she's fleeing north. At some time, she may turn west, towards the rebels. That'll come later. For now, she'll try to distance herself as much as possible from where she escaped."

"But what if you're wrong, again? We'll have wasted more of our time," Halwende's mood was deteriorating.

"Then we're all in trouble," Talon snapped back.

His subordinate's constant complaints irritated him.

"You don't want to ride with us? Fine, stay here! Look for her on your own. We've searched everywhere, yet found nothing. Over the years, I've hunted down dozens of people. My experience tells me to go north. That's where we'll find her."

Halwende backed-down. He lacked the courage to argue further. In silent anger, he threw together his belongings. His handling was rough as he saddled his horse. The animal reacted to his rider's mood, by snorting and pulling away. The others had already moved on before Halwende managed to mount. He dug in his heels with excessive force. His horse bucked. He was fortunate to stay in the saddle. Talon had cautioned him earlier about the treatment of his mount. Under his leader's distant watchful eye, Halwende resisted the temptation to use his whip.

ಞ ಜ

Spring worked its magic over the land. The grasses grew deep and lush. Despite the occasional late frost catching the travellers by surprise, the lengthening days and strengthening sun lifted Willa's spirits. In the weeks since Sheply joined her, she had seen no sign of her followers. Was it possible, she wondered, that she had outrun them? Could they have given up? Of one thing, Willa was certain — until she reached the safety of the rebel stronghold, it would be reckless of her to drop her guard.

Sheply was invaluable. His ability to find food, vegetable or animal was uncanny. Armed only with a homemade bow, and a knife, it was rare for him to return without something for Willa to turn into a meal. With someone to provide for them, Willa could concentrate on moving forward. The distance they travelled, daily, far exceeded her earlier attempts. Scard, too, had taken to Sheply and he to Scard. On an afternoon, when the child could travel no more, Sheply carried him on his shoulders.

For now, Sheply was eager to keep moving. A little farther along the valley, his flock was waiting for him. Ahead of him was the cone-shaped hill Orvyn had sought the year before. Sheply raced in front; no longer able to contain his excitement. He called aloud for his dog. Willa listened. It was much too quiet. She could hear neither barking nor the bleating of sheep. Gathering her skirt, she clambered onto a rock to look around. Nothing seemed untoward. Ahead, in the distance, she could see a scattering of white rocks lying in the long grass.

There was a scream of anguish. Sheply dropped to his knees, head bowed. Willa told Scard to wait. She ran to reach her young companion. As she came up behind Sheply, she saw the cause of his distress. The body of a large dog lay on its side, an arrow embedded in its heart. After a while, she helped him cover the animal with stones.

Willa looked at the young shepherd. The boy remained dry eyed; mixed with the grief, there was a great deal of anger in his face. He was a little older than Orvyn had believed him to be. Since their meeting, Sheply had grown several inches. His chest had broadened, his voice deepened. As tall as Willa, he was strong beyond his years. For a moment, something in his expression sent a shiver down her spine. Whoever these people were who had destroyed everything he had, this boy would grow up to hunt them down. Of that she had little doubt.

The 'white rocks' Willa had seen earlier, she soon discovered, were the remains of some of his flock. Elsewhere, others lay butchered, the choice cuts removed from the carcasses. Over half of the animals were missing. For several hours, Sheply scoured the area. There were no fresh droppings. His flock was gone. Much more than did Sheply, Willa understood what this loss meant to him. The sheep represented a future for the boy. With these to breed from, he would have had meat and wool to sell. The young shepherd could have prospered.

In the morning, as they moved on, the party was in low spirits. It would not be long, according to Sheply's instructions from his father, before the three turned westwards. Unbeknown to them, this new bearing would take them towards the streams of refugees, now fleeing Betlic's advance.

Willa was wary. This latest incident had unnerved her. The tracks, around the area of Sheply's slaughtered flock, were similar to those in his village. It seemed the travellers were following a similar route to the outlaws. No matter what her treatment might be, should her pursuers catch her, she had an uneasy feeling it would be preferable to that which she would endure at the hands of these killers.

☙ ❧

Talon had gained on Willa, but not by as much as he would have hoped. By necessity, he had to cover a wide swath of land, something that neutralised his advantage of being able to travel faster on horseback than the fugitives. On the same day that Willa's party discovered the destroyed flock, the group's hunters reached Sheply's village.

Talon recognised the area. On his return from Vretliana with the mantle, he had passed it by. That night, some of his troop had slipped back into the hamlet. Before taking flight with several women, the men had killed a number of villagers who tried to intervene. Talon had been furious when he found out. The mantle was too valuable to risk the hue and cry such a raid would create. His party had escaped, but those who had placed the enterprise in jeopardy had paid the price for their stupidity.

Like the boy before him, Talon believed the carnage to be the result of an outlaw attack. Had he not enough problems? Now they would have to keep a watch out for an ambush. If the renegades were of sufficient number to wipe-out a whole village, Talon's small band would be more a target than a deterrent to them. What if they found Willa before he did? That was something he would rather not have to explain to Betlic.

Close to the ruins of the village, Talon discovered a large grave of recent origin. In the earth, beside it, much to his surprise, were several footprints he recognised. Willa! To his relief, when his men re-opened the grave, the remains appeared to be old ones from the village. As Willa's child was not among them, it was doubtful she was involved with the burial. Talon's men kicked the soil back into the hole, then searched throughout the area. Nowhere could they find further signs of the fugitives.

Over the coming weeks, as the searchers moved north, they discovered various other tracks. Talon ignored them. Although, three distinct sets were common, none matched in size nor shape the ones he sought. It was not until the band reached the remains of Sheply's flock that, for once, Halwende proved the value of his inclusion in the party.

Near to the area a stream flowed. Before they moved on, the group watered their horses. Whoever the three makers of the oft-seen footprints were, they had visited the watercourse. The tracks led to the water's edge. Afterwards, for a considerable distance, the travellers had walked in the soft earth that followed the path of the channel upstream.

Idly, Halwende looked at the line of tracks. One of them reminded him of something, someone in his past. Willa! She had broken a leg when a child. It had healed well; she had escaped a permanent limp, but, when tired, she sometimes favoured the leg. Since childhood, Halwende had been familiar with her walk. There was something odd about the gait, too, and about one of the other sets of footprints. The imprints were large, but the steps did not match. The strides were too short.

At first, Talon gave little credence to Halwende's words. The man was a fool. Later, when the leader did wander along the path to take a look, he realised what his companion meant about the stride. The sets of footprints did have a distinctive gait to them. Halwende was onto something.

Talon remounted his horse and smiled. Good girl! His admiration for Willa increased. Somehow, she had acquired new boots. A size too large, she must have packed them so she could walk without difficulty, and done the same for her son. To whom the third set belonged, although a mystery, was of less importance. Talon had her now. All would be explained when he caught up with her, unless she blundered into the outlaws first. He hoped not. It was a matter of pride to him that he found her first.

Chapter Thirty Seven

Amron paced. The enormity of what he was about to do made him restless. Early in the evening, apart from his movements, nothing broke the silence inside his chambers. His servants had gone, their services dispensed with until morning. On his way out, the last to leave had brought a flagon of wine for his master. The guards, who kept watch outside his chambers, had instructions to admit no-one except his summoned guest. For what the king hoped to instigate, there could be no witnesses.

Several days earlier, a chain of beacons, which crossed the Mogallean Mountains from the east, had signalled their warning. Betlic's armies had entered the foothills. Amron had curbed his impatience and waited, unable yet to call this meeting. Now, the delay was over. Yesterday, the last of his expected messengers had arrived, their identities known to him alone. The couriers had gone, to return to their masters; the replies they carried for the eyes of the recipients only.

These visits had aroused the curiosity of the High Council. Amron refused to discuss the matter with them. His intentions, he felt sure, would not receive universal sanction from his strategists. Although most were trustworthy, he was finding that issues discussed behind closed doors, especially matters that failed to gain full approval, were reaching a wider audience. The king did not intend to allow this leakage of information to disrupt his plans.

A sharp knock sounded. Without pause for acknowledgement, a doorway opened. Amron's visitor stepped into view. He closed the heavy door, shutting out the empty great-hall behind. Tedrick strode forward with confidence. He bowed to the king, who indicated a chair, placed opposite to the one towards which his majesty moved. Once seated, Tedrick accepted the offer of wine.

With disregard to his original intentions, Amron had decided against the use of Tedrick's talents to track Marazin and Karilyn. In the days that followed her escape, the king reflected much on Tamin's harsh words. The weeks since then had seen a thaw in the relationship between father and son; although a noticeable tension persisted.

Amron had admitted to himself that his actions had been reckless. The ardour of his feelings towards Karilyn had cooled. At first, love had turned to hate. In an emotional state, he convinced himself that, once she had served her purpose, he would see she suffered the same fate as her lover. As time passed, the more he pondered over Tamin's comments, the more foolish Amron realised were his intentions. What he had felt for Karilyn had been infatuation, nothing deeper.

Several times he reread the documents relating to the heir, the throne and what limited information was known about the Bearer of the Scraufin. Looking at them afresh, Amron acknowledged everyone involved had their own role to play. It was not a competition. It was ironic to realise his whole strategy was based now on the success of the two people he had tried to separate and bring to harm. Unlike him, they had put duty before personal consideration. Instead of hindering Marazin and Karilyn, he should have been helping them. Of one thing he was certain, without them, everything was lost.

Amron and Hafter reconciled their differences. Again, the king came to value the sage's advice. Hafter, with knowledge gained from his conversations with Karilyn, had calculated how long it would take before she and Marazin reappeared. This timing was crucial for Amron's plans. These he kept to himself, not even the sage could be party to them.

For Amron, his task was clear. His duty was to keep Betlic at bay until salvation arrived. The king worked hard to convince everyone he was committed fully to this role, which he was. In truth, and in secret, what he intended went far beyond that and involved greater risk. As to how much of his plans were possible, it depended on the response of his guest.

Would his visitor agree to the mission, which Amron was about to invite him to undertake? The king was desperate to know. This was not something he could order the man to accept. It was fortunate that Tedrick, unlike his late comrade Boden, was loyal to his king and country.

Tedrick tasted a sip of wine from his silver goblet. He was wary. Whenever he met the king, in circumstances such as these, his majesty wanted some underhand scheme carried out. Tedrick did not suffer the burden of a heavy moral conscience. What did concern him was if these enterprises became common knowledge. The king, he knew, would disown him and deny any involvement. From such a predicament, it might prove difficult for him to extricate himself.

Neither were these assignments always to his liking — Orvyn and Marazin, for instance. Orvyn was a fool. He had been a special aide to the king, fêted everywhere. With a fortune there for him to take, he had thrown it away because of a sense of honour. Tedrick had little sympathy for Orvyn, but he did not deserve to die for his high moral stance. Marazin, too, had suffered an injustice at Amron's hands. The stranger was tough and had character. Despite his qualms, had Tedrick caught either Marazin or Orvyn, in a fair fight, as ordered, he would have attempted to kill them. Although, if Tedrick was honest, he had never looked for them with any enthusiasm and neither would he.

He waited. The king, for some reason, struggled to speak. His explanation for the meeting was slow to come. The longer the silence, the more apprehensive did his visitor become. Tedrick wished himself back with the widow with whom he had settled. She had land, property, money, was fun to be with and, of greater importance, she wanted him to settle down and marry her. It had surprised Tedrick to realise this was not something to which he was adverse.

As a warrior, Tedrick had survived longer than most. This, in part, contributed to his desire for a new life. Of late, he had been compelled to accept his reactions had slowed. Nor were his movements as fluid as they used to be. His muscles ached more and for much longer. His lady's wealth was sufficient to keep him in comfort for the rest of his days. She would not wait forever. Already, his absences were a source of discord between them.

Amron cleared his throat, unsure of how to start. It was more usual for him to be in a rage, demanding retribution on whatever luckless person had incurred his wrath. A scarcity of words was something new. Amron could stall no longer. He broke the silence.

"Tedrick," he said, "my most loyal and trusted servant."

His guest cringed. This promised to be an assignment much worse than anything asked of him previously. His majesty had called him by many names in the past, sometimes of a derogatory nature, but never 'most loyal and trusted'. A description more suited to that of a good hunting dog, rather than a person.

"As doubtless you've heard, Betlic's armies are moving in our direction," the king continued.

Tedrick nodded. He had seen the smoke rising from the beacons and was aware of its significance. Amron took a sip of wine. He spoke again.

"Since late autumn, I've had workers labouring in the mountains. These men are fortifying the passes, to obstruct Betlic's access. My forces, once driven back by the enemy, will take up position behind these. No," Amron said, in response to a questioning look from Tedrick, "I'm not being defeatist, but I have to be realistic. With Betlic's use of the talisman to demoralise our warriors, they will fall back."

"How have we been able to escape its powers here?" Tedrick was curious.

People in the valley were apprehensive, even fearful, for the future. Nowhere had he sensed an overwhelming spirit of despair among his fellows.

"As usual, Hafter has a theory. He believes, somehow, the mountains shelter us. When driven out of Xicalima, this, he thinks, is the reason why the exiles felt drawn to this place. A base nearer to our homeland would have been more logical, a base where operations against Betlic could have been much easier to mount.

"Whatever we do, Betlic will drive back my men. He has overwhelming forces at his disposal. Once safe behind the defences, my troops will seal the gaps. Armourers and fletchers have worked hard to supply these fortresses. The men have ample provisions and materials. Arrangements are in hand to relieve them on a regular basis, to enable them to return to our side of the mountains to recover their spirits.

"My commanders chose the narrowest, most easily defendable places to build our defences. Here, a small number of men can keep an army at bay for months. If the enemy breaks through, we have a series of similar fortifications behind the initial ones. My forces will fall back to these, as necessary. We have placed observers, high in the mountains, with troops in reserve should the enemy try to make use of the peaks to circumvent our positions."

As he refilled his goblet, Amron cast a surreptitious glance towards his visitor. Did he believe the information presented to him? The details, concerning the construction and positioning of his mountain defences were accurate. From early the year before, from far and wide, Amron's agents had procured the services of every mason, and those skilled in the design and construction of fortifications, they could find.

For their services, at times in atrocious conditions, these workers received generous reward. As to how long the results of their industry would stand against Betlic's weapons of war was speculative. Until these defences were put to the test, no-one could know. This aspect was something Amron wanted to avoid discussing with his guest. All that Tedrick needed to understand was that the rebels had the capacity to defend their mountain territory.

Without query, Tedrick accepted the king's words. He had no reason to do otherwise. What remained a mystery to him, was why Amron would want to share this information with him. This briefing was unlike any other he had received from his majesty. It was more usual for Amron, in a fury, to demand someone be frightened, coerced or given a severe beating. Defence strategy was not an area in which Tedrick felt qualified to comment.

"That is welcome news," Tedrick said. "But, once he breaks through, he'll be in a position to reach our valley within weeks. Without the mountains in-between, there'll be nothing to shield our people against the talisman."

"That's true," Amron conceded, "but, we'll have delayed Betlic's armies long enough for our allies to come to our aid. We have to hold out until the new year. By then, King Grogant will acknowledge the forces sent against him are a diversion. The kingdoms to the east will realise the same. Even with the talisman to aid him, Betlic will be unable to overcome our combined numbers."

"What of this Mastig? I've heard so many tales about it. Does it exist? They say it can counter the effects of the talisman. If so, when will you be able to make use of it?" Tedrick's mind was full of questions.

"Forget the Mastig," Amron was dismissive. "If ever it was possible for it to perform such magic, it's now beyond us. The one who would lead me to it is dead, killed by the forces of Betlic."

Amron had succeeded in his attempt to maintain the secrecy that surrounded Karilyn's time at the palace, and subsequent escape. Apart from Amron, Tamin and their personal servants, those with knowledge had left the palace. The stockades that held those who witnessed Karilyn's arrival in the rebel lands, now housed them all.

"So, no mystical solution," Tedrick said, unable to keep the disappointment out of his voice. "In which case, if Betlic learns of the northern route into our valley, before winter's end, we'll be in trouble."

Somehow, Tedrick had stumbled on the reason for his meeting with the king. It was almost time for Amron to reveal the truth to his guest about his visit.

"We have a traitor in our midst," Amron stated, changing track.

Tedrick leapt to his feet.

"Your Majesty," he said, outraged at the perceived accusation, "I've always been loyal to you."

"Sit down," the king said, unperturbed. "If I'd thought it was you, we wouldn't be having this talk."

Relieved, Tedrick returned to his seat.

"What do you know of my advisor, Raulf?" Amron asked.

"He was sent as an emissary, by King Grogant. The man was a replacement for Sherwyn, after his recall to Vretliana."

"Correct! But, it's also true he's an agent of Betlic."

"Are you sure? Has Grogant tried to undermine us?"

"No, before he sent his envoy, Grogant advised me of the man's loyalties. The king believed Raulf might be of value to us, as someone I could use to feed false information to the enemy. For a while, Grogant has used this tactic with others at his court, with some success."

Tedrick did not understand what this had to do with him. Perhaps the king wanted the spy killed! Tedrick had no scruples regarding traitors. Without giving his guest a chance to interrupt, Amron continued.

"Since his arrival, I've limited Raulf's opportunities to learn anything useful. A little while ago, I changed my mind. In confidence, I spoke to him. We discussed certain matters I thought might be of interest to Betlic. That night, a messenger left his house. I had him intercepted and interrogated."

"But, if you wanted Betlic to receive the information you passed to Raulf, why stop his man from leaving?" Tedrick asked, bemused.

"Because there was another reason I gave Raulf the information. I wanted to know what it was his messenger carried, or knew what to say, to prove his authenticity. A note, written by Raulf, along with a spoken phrase, will gain you an audience with Betlic. The first, I obtained with the messenger's capture, the second has taken a while longer to acquire."

"Raulf's agent?"

"He awaits my disposal." Amron's meaning was clear.

"Your Majesty, fascinating as this talk is, what has any of it to do with me?"

"I want you to impersonate the messenger."

Dumbfounded, Tedrick stared in disbelief. This request was beyond his darkest nightmare. Never could he have anticipated something to the extent of this enterprise.

"There are certain matters I want Betlic made aware of, those and nothing more. I can think of no-one else who I can trust to carry out a mission of such magnitude. You're courageous and resourceful. I believe you'd give up your life for your country and your king. If you're convincing, Betlic will send you back with instructions for Raulf; not that he'll be in any position to receive them."

Tedrick remained silent. He recognised flattery, but, there was truth behind Amron's words. The king's assessment of the man's character was accurate.

For once, Amron was patient. He knew the extent of what he was asking of Tedrick. Despite the king's air of confidence, the chances of survival were low. By the time he reached Betlic, the mountain passes would be under attack. Tedrick would find himself trapped behind enemy lines, forced to live a lie, under constant fear of exposure.

Tedrick took his time as he deliberated over the matter. The idea appealed to his latent sense of adventure, and to his ego. He had carried out many deeds over his lifetime, some which others would have found reprehensible, even repulsive. The grounding in subterfuge these actions gave him was something not easy replicated. Rather than his ability to deceive, as important as that might be, it was the nerve to carry it through to the end that set him apart.

"If I was to agree to your Majesty's request," Tedrick said, "I have some matters of my own I wish to discuss."

"Go ahead," Amron said with relief. He was confident now that Tedrick would accept his mission.

"First, success or failure, if I survive this undertaking, it's my last one for you. After this, you leave me in peace."

"Agreed; and your second condition?"

"As you're aware, I've been living with a widow. Before I go, I wish to make her my wife. She's wealthy, far beyond my meagre means. I, myself, though honoured by your patronage, am a man of few possessions. I want to assure her my circumstances have changed; that I'll be her equal in both wealth here, and, once we return to Xicalima, in land."

Tedrick hoped the king would not judge his request too avaricious. In the end, it was Tedrick's life that was at risk.

"Also, acceptable," Amron agreed without hesitation. "You've a week to arrange your affairs. I'll instruct Hafter to arrange for you to receive gold, sufficient to prove your suitability for marriage, and the deeds to an estate in Xicalima. When we take back our country, the land is yours. Remember, no-one, including your wife-to-be, must learn anything about your mission. If they ask, you must only say that your king requires your services."

"What is this matter you wish Betlic to know?"

"I want you to tell him about our stronghold, and the way to reach it from the north."

In disbelief, Tedrick stared at Amron. At first, he thought he'd misheard. How could his king want him to betray his kinsmen? Tedrick might be a rogue, but he was no traitor. Anger replaced his shock.

He stood, his eyes fiery. "You can kill me now," he snarled, "but I'll never betray my people?"

"Sit!" Amron's voice was steel.

Tedrick sank back into his chair.

"It's only a matter of time before Betlic learns of the route." Amron spoke in a whisper. "His patrols already range north of his current position. For now, so my scouts tell me, his men are there to warn of a surprise assault from that direction. With the aid of Grogant, and others, we've fed much disinformation to Betlic through his spies. This should have led him to believe that we, the rebels, are a small force. His understanding is our refuge is a high mountain stronghold, towards the southern end of the range. As such, he concentrates his efforts in this direction.

"Betlic has moved companies of his men to the borders of nearby kingdoms, such as Vretliana. Betlic knows that, while these countries fear an invasion, they cannot join with us. He is counting on that. With a small number of troops, he keeps vast armies tied down. His priority is to eliminate the rebels, and, as a rallying point, myself in particular."

"If this is true, why do you suggest we give him the key to our back door?" Tedrick was puzzled.

The king was making little sense. His words were full of apparent contradictions.

"Because I want Betlic to know, now, rather than by chance at a time that is less advantageous to me," Amron said. "It's too good an opportunity for him, one he'll seize upon without delay."

By now, Tedrick feared his master's powers of reasoning were failing. His doubts were clearly visible in his expression.

"Tedrick," Amron said, "I've told you the strength of our mountain defences, and the forces that control them. You know when we can expect our allies to re-enforce us. Along with this information, you'll be able to tell Betlic that, instead of in the hills, our base is here in this valley. You're capable of estimating how many men are here and those held in reserve elsewhere. It's vital Betlic knows this and, most of all, how much easier it will be for him to enter our lands from the north. He must appreciate how important it is for him to complete his operation before winter comes.

"I know you don't understand why. For that, I'm sorry, but I can reveal nothing more. If interrogated, you can disclose only what you know. I beg that you trust me. I am the rightful King of Xicalima. The risks I take, I do so after great consideration. If any of this becomes public knowledge, before the proper time, the loss of life will be huge, myself included. The same will apply if you fail."

Tedrick hesitated. Did he believe the king? One thing, in the end, swayed his decision. In the past, in his dealings with Amron, his master had been arrogant, pompous, vindictive or in some other vile mood, always demanding. Never before had the king made a plea. There was no coercion. Tedrick realised the choice was his to make. He studied Amron. For the first time, his sincerity rang true.

"I'm at your command, your Majesty. I will deliver your message to Betlic."

Although Tedrick's reservations about the validity of the mission still troubled him, he would not let down his master.

Amron sighed with relief. There was much to organise, most of which needed doing in secret. Dare he involve anyone else? No! He needed to exercise extreme caution in his arrangements. If, before everything was in place, the High Council became aware of this escapade, his reign would come to a premature and bloody end.

Amron had little appetite to engage in a prolonged war with Betlic. Even if the Mastig countered the effects of the talisman, the enemy would still have huge resources of manpower at his disposal. Amron needed to crush Betlic in one decisive action. He believed he knew how best to do that.

Chapter Thirty Eight

It was late in the day. Since mid-morning, Marazin and Karilyn had been riding towards a column of rock. No sooner had it come into view than their pace quickened. At first, its tip had been an insignificant dot on the horizon. Now, the giant pillar towered ahead of them. The worried expression, which Marazin had observed on Karilyn's face this last week, had turned to one of relief. He understood the urgency. Tonight, the Mastig would appear.

On a number of occasions, during the weeks spent riding, the travellers had paused in their journey to study their back-trail, once for a whole day. They had assumed that Amron, if nothing else, would attempt to have them followed. To their surprise, the trail behind remained empty. Although it was possible that his men might lie in wait somewhere, ready to ensnare the couple on their return.

Untroubled by Amron, the same was not true of Betlic. Earlier in the couple's travels, his scouts had been a problem. His men roamed the countryside in small groups, which the travellers did their best to avoid. Heardwine had been invaluable. Many times, the dog's speedy return had been sufficient warning for them to take cover. There had been instances when conflict was unavoidable. The couple, along with Orvyn at the start of their journey, had been troubled little by these encounters. None had borne injuries more serious than minor cuts and slight bruising. As the weeks passed, they had fewer sightings of Betlic's men, until they ceased altogether.

☙ ❧

Time had moved on rapidly for Marazin and Karilyn. She found it hard to believe that months had gone by since, one frosty morning, she had arrived at the farm. It had been eerily quiet. No-one was in sight, neither among the buildings, nor in the surrounding fields. Not that Karilyn needed anything visible to warn her. Her period of detention at the palace had done nothing to dull her senses. She was aware she was under observation. She felt neither threatened, nor welcome. It was a neutral — someone waiting to see what she did — feeling.

Ahead, through a gap in a dense thorn hedge, the trail entered a farmyard. From behind the growth, a large dog leapt onto the path. The animal bounded towards her. Karilyn's horse reared. For an instant, she thought it would bolt before it settled, snorted, then trotted forward. Karilyn, too, recognised the beast. She reined in, slipped out of the saddle and ran towards the barking dog. Its tail wagged in excitement. Her hood fell back. She knelt and hugged the beast as if it were a long-lost friend.

In the farmyard, from an outbuilding, a door flew open. Someone was running towards her. Karilyn leapt to her feet. A tall figure swept her off the ground, to hold her in a vice-like grip. Without risk of serious injury, there was only one person who could do that to her. As their lips met, Karilyn flung her arms round Marazin's neck and clung to him.

Separation had strengthened, rather than diminished their feelings. They remained locked in a passionate embrace until the door to the farmhouse opened. A figure stepped out. Flushed, the pair separated. With their arms linked, Marazin and Karilyn walked on to meet Orvyn. In its mouth, Heardwine took hold of the horse's reins and led it into the yard.

The rest of the day passed in a bewilderment of activity, throughout which the reunited pair stayed close to each other's side. The tale, about Amron's attack on Karilyn, incensed Marazin and Orvyn. It was with some reluctance, Marazin accepted her plea to do nothing to harm the king. He had to be in a condition to rally his people. By evening, with the help of the farmer and his family, the couple had supplies enough to last them for a considerable part of the ride to come.

As dusk fell, a group of armed horsemen approached the farm. The trio went underground, into one of the hidden passageways created beneath the buildings. Several anxious minutes passed before the stone slab, which concealed the steps to the chamber, was wrenched open again. Blinking in the sudden light, the fugitives took up defensive positions, swords in hands. To their relief, it was the farmer. He called them up into the warmth.

Hafter had sent the band of men. They carried a letter from him. Orvyn recognised several of the newcomers, who, by now, were inside the farmhouse. They had been members of his former units. He greeted, then introduced them to Marazin and Karilyn.

In his letter, Hafter issued a warning. If Amron went on the rampage over Karilyn's disappearance, the sage could no longer guarantee Orvyn's safety. Marazin and Karilyn accepted the sage's suggestion that, for the first part of their mission, their friend accompany them. No-one but the couple could know their final destination.

The reason why it was necessary for so many people to deliver one message, too, was forthcoming. Hafter believed it advisable, for the trio's safekeeping, they be escorted out of rebel lands. The following morning, in the half-light before dawn, the combined party took its leave of the farmer and his family. The riders headed north. Use of the eastern passes was out of the question. Those not blocked by snow housed thousands of workers, involved in the construction of fortifications, many of whom would know Orvyn by sight.

Hafter had sent a messenger on before them. The officer, who now commanded the entrance to the valley, was an ally of the sage. He would ensure the party had a smooth, unhindered passage through the defences. The travellers' escort would stay, until they had passed beyond the checkpoints and patrols to the north of the mountains. After that, the trio's survival rested with them.

With both escort and mountains behind them, the three rode east, on the northern edge of the Plains of Zefreelah. The landscape they travelled was a mixture of rolling hills and shallow valleys. As the weeks passed, the air warmed. The frosty nights became fewer. A month after the spring equinox, Marazin and Karilyn took their leave of Orvyn. In a secluded valley, cut deep into high moorland, they had found an abandoned mine. Outside was a hut that, with a little work, could become habitable. This would be Orvyn's home until the return of his companions.

Almost two cycles of the moon would pass before Orvyn could expect to see them again. As he waved farewell to the couple, he wondered whether it might have been better for him to stay at the farm.

ೞ ಐ

With their horses tethered a little distance below them, Marazin studied the pillar. He estimated its height would be twenty times his own, three times higher than the width at its base. Oval in shape, its sheer, jagged sides towered to an irregular top, where dark green foliage hung from the edges. Though its many facets were smooth to the touch, the rock face showed no signs of any intervention by human hand. The column jutted out from the surface of a large, flat-topped natural knoll that rose to a similar height above the surrounding land. The remains of a petrified forest covered the slopes of the mound. In the glow of the setting sun, the area carried a strange haunting beauty.

Movement caught Marazin's eye. On the plains below, riding towards them, six abreast, was a group of horsemen. He grabbed hold of Karilyn's arm and pointed towards the intruders.

"Quick," he said, "let's find somewhere to take cover."

"There's no need to worry." Karilyn seemed unconcerned. "They can't see us."

To Marazin's astonishment, as the riders reached the base of the knoll, they vanished from sight. Karilyn turned. She indicated the opposite side, where the group reappeared. The men rode on, unaware that anything strange had happened. Marazin was speechless.

"The magic of the Mastig keeps this place of ceremonies from the world. From ancient times, its only visitors have been those forebears of ours, who carried the burden we now share. It's the obligation of each bearer to take the next generation on a pilgrimage, to this rock, before they take responsibility for the Scraufin. In comparison, it's rare for your ancestors to enter these grounds. Only those unfortunate ones, such as you, who are called upon to fight against the talisman may enter."

What he had witnessed, moments ago, was something Marazin had difficulty in believing. Of more concern to him were some of the other gaps in his knowledge.

"What are the origins of these events that now involve us?" he asked. "Who created the objects over which we fight, and why?"

Karilyn paused to collect her thoughts. On this same spot, she had asked similar questions of her father. Although it had been a long time ago, his words were clear in her mind, as if he were standing beside her.

"The countries we know today," she began, "have not always existed. Over time, boundaries have been redrawn. Empires rise and fall, then new nations form to take their place. Long before even these events happened, there were only two realms. Between them, they controlled everything. For centuries they co-existed peaceably, until one country, unaware of the consequences their actions might bring, diverted the course of a river. Within their borders it brought life to a desert region, but had the opposite effect in the lands of the other nation.

"War broke out, after which an uneasy truce was followed by more hostilities. For decades, the two sides fought for supremacy. During one extended period of heavy rain the river flooded. It reverted to its original course. By then it was too late. Conflict had become entrenched. Each nation had its faults, but neither was truly evil at the start. Over time, one side's reliance on ever-darker enchantments to aid them in their struggle grew greater. The other side, in turn, became skilled in countering the effects of these. Over the generations, they fought each other to a standstill."

"What happened then?"

"A truce came into effect. With their enchanters, leaders from both sides came together. It took several months, but, in the end, they negotiated a peace treaty. Those whose powers were beyond that of normal man agreed to renounce them for all time. In blood, they signed an agreement — all except one man, a dark enchanter of immense power. Enraged by attempts to curtail his practise of the mystical arts, he fled. In hiding, he created both talisman and mantle. Only the combined powers of his peers, from both sides, were able to find him and his creations. However, the magic, with which he brought the objects into being, proved too strong. The other enchanters were unable to destroy his work."

"What happened to the enchanter?"

"He faced trial before his equals. In front of his accusers, he cast a spell upon himself. In flames, his body turned to dust. They spread his ashes throughout the lands, in the hope they might never mingle again."

"How did the Mastig come into existence?"

"The dark enchanter had destroyed everything that related to his last creations. Although some believe his powers died with him, he did leave a promise. To the one who reunited the talisman and mantle, the world was theirs to conquer. Once they ruled over all, to them the darkest secrets of the enchanter's magic would pass.

"Those enchanters, who remained, laboured long as they made use of their powers for the final time. To counter the deadly objects, the wizards brought into being the Scraufin, the Mastig and the magic which surrounds them. To serve them, two people, one from each nation, were bestowed with certain abilities. We have inherited those special faculties. Separated from each other by a great distance, the enchanters hoped the talisman and mantle would never be brought together. It was an ambitious dream. Over the centuries, the presence of evil within the objects has seduced many. Once corrupted, they bring the items back together. Whenever the talisman and mantle have been reunited, our ancestors have fought to restore order.

"I understand now," Marazin said. "Saving Xicalima, or any other nation, is incidental. Our fight is to prevent Betlic from gaining absolute power and thus, mastery of the dark master's enchantments."

"Should he succeed, Betlic may not be the one to fear," Karilyn said. "There's a suspicion the dark enchanter's intent, when he spoke of his powers being revealed, was that he would return. That's why our ancestors spread his ashes so widely. Because his knowledge was so deep, no-one knows how powerful was the spell he cast upon himself at the end."

"How much of this is Hafter aware?"

"Nothing more than what he's told you. Only you and I know the whole truth. Certain matters are best kept secret, even from him."

"How did Heardwine, and his strange aptitudes, become a part of the story?" Marazin thought to ask as the dog came to sit at his side.

"No-one knows for certain. There is a story that, when the enchanters cast their spells on our original ancestors, a large hunting dog lay asleep across the feet of one. Because man and beast were in contact, some of the magic spilled onto it. Who knows whether this is true? But, since that time, whenever needed, an animal has appeared."

Karilyn fell silent. Light was fading. It was time to prepare for what was to come. She led Marazin from the pillar, nearer to the northern edge of the knoll. Here, they came to a place covered with paving. Lying in twelve rows of twelve, each slab was of smooth-dressed stone a good stride square. They slotted together, leaving no gaps. Over the four slabs at the centre, a large pair of firedogs stood. These faced away from the pillar, each one sculpted from a stone trunk, taken from the petrified forest.

Twice as tall as they were wide, each firedog had at its front, a carving in the shape of a mythical beast. Cut into the edges of the rock were symbols of a type unknown to Marazin. The firedogs had clawed feet, while their tops were flat. As high again as the base, on the tip of the left-hand one, a thin vertical column of stone stood. A similar item was missing from the right-hand base. In its place, bored into the surface, was a small cylindrical hole.

To one side of the paved area, a pile of petrified logs had been stacked. Karilyn seemed to know what to do. Between them, Marazin and she carried the heavy stone branches and placed them across the andirons, behind the firedogs. Before long, they built a substantial setting for what would have been a large blaze, had the branches been real. Marazin wanted to ask many more questions, but time was short. Soon they must be ready. Although it was strange the work they had done, he presumed, before the night was over, everything would become clear.

Heardwine, who had been absent during the building of the 'fire', returned. Between his jaws, he carried a pair of torches. Where they came from was a mystery. So was most everything else that was taking place. Only a faint glow now lit the sky. Marazin took the torches and lit them. Why was he not surprised when Karilyn showed him two slots, cut into nearby stone trunks, into which the flaming brands fitted with ease?

As dusk turned to night, a full moon shone over the horizon in the east. Its glow spread over the land as the orb rose and began to arc across the sky. The shadow, cast by the pillar, inched towards the square.

The couple were sitting cross-legged, facing each other, in front of the firedogs. With their arms outstretched and crossed, Marazin held Karilyn's hands in his. She closed her eyes, to enter a trancelike state. She chanted words in a language long-lost to the world. Afterwards, she would remember nothing of this. These were not mantras she had learned by rote. The enchanted stones on which they rested channelled the verse through her.

At first, apart from discomfort caused by sitting in an unnatural position, Marazin felt little different. As time passed, tension grew inside him. Karilyn was aglow with an inner energy. With increasing strength, it flowed through her hands into his. He became lightheaded, his senses afire. It seemed as though the countless spirits of those who had borne his burden in the past now joined with him. He was empowered. There seemed no limit to what he was capable of doing.

The moon passed behind the pillar; the couple now were in partial shadow. Karilyn's eyes opened. She released Marazin's hands then pulled the Scraufin from its place of concealment. She turned, to place it in the hole on top of the right-hand firedog. It fitted precisely, to stand upright, a match to the column on the left.

When instructed by Karilyn, Marazin knelt before the firedogs. With his right hand clenched round the Scraufin, his other round the stone column to his left, he leaned forward. The moon was no longer in sight. High in the pillar, angled downward, was a circular hole, through which a beam of moonlight streamed. A small patch of light formed in the shadows to Marazin's left. It crept closer, growing larger as it did.

Involuntarily, Marazin's head lowered. The stone logs on top of the 'fire', chilled his forehead as it rested upon them. The beam reached the edge of the hearth. It spread across it. A brilliant white glow bathed Marazin, and the area in front of him. Vivid flashes of light flickered from his forehead. They twisted and spiralled over the layers of stone logs. The energy, he had absorbed from Karilyn, discharged in a flash. Marazin found himself floating. His hands sprang open as he drifted backwards, to land, gently, on the paving, a pace or two behind.

Ethereal flames of blue and green sprang from the petrified branches. The beam of light moved eastwards then faded. The flames turned to silver. They rose ever higher into the night sky. Unlike the hot, fiery fingers of a campfire blaze, these were ice-cold flickering slivers of light. As they spread to the edges of the hearth, the logs began to spin, casting out silver threads. These rose above the icy flames, to float skywards.

The creatures, carved into the stone dogs, came alive. They stepped out of their rock prisons. Their bodies moved in a slow and sinuous manner as they took up position, on opposite sides of the blaze. Wings sprouted from their backs. At speed they flew, round and round the flames. The movement of air created by the wings formed a vortex above the flames. The threads intertwined to become a fine cord. A line to the stars, Marazin thought, as he gazed in wonder. Karilyn took his hand and squeezed. She crept closer. He put his arm round her and held her close.

The moon traversed further across the sky. Heardwine moved to lie down, behind the blaze. Dark-brown hair, from its coat, floated into the vortex, to mix with the final layers of silver thread. Minutes later, through another opening, a second beam of moonlight settled on the flames. They faded and died, as did the silver glow they created. As the logs ceased to spin, the column of cord broke free. The strange creatures returned to their resting places, to become one again with their hosts. Heardwine, his coat trimmed short, moved away from the fire. Exhausted, he stretched-out and slept.

Without the creatures to support it, the vortex collapsed, the cord with it. A flap opened, at the tip of the Scraufin, to reveal a cylindrical hollow at its centre. From out of the middle of the opening, a needle-thin spike appeared. It reached almost to the height of its host. Its tip parted where, inside the gap, it snagged the base of the rotating thread. As the Scraufin began to spin, the tip snapped together again, securing the line. The cord coiled around the central spike as its base retracted back into its holder.

The line was so fine, it seemed impossible, but, as it descended, it split into a thousand separate threads. At its centre, it spun a nucleus of fine silver thread, before the outer threads, a mix of brown and silver, plaited into several strands. These, too, came together, to form plaits over the central core. A braided rope, a little wider than the width of Marazin's thumb, formed from the end of the Scraufin. It tapered away to half the width of Karilyn's little finger at the tip.

The rope was as long as Marazin was tall, then half again. At its base, it wrapped and sealed itself around the Scraufin as it rose up. Its rotation slowed. It came to a halt as, from behind the pillar to the west, the moon came into sight. The Scraufin, in its new guise, shot skywards. Marazin's eyes followed its movement. He thrust out his free hand and caught the object as it descended. He glanced downwards. The hearth, the firedogs, the logs, everything, all trace had vanished. So it would remain, for three more years.

Chapter Thirty Nine

Brambles pulled and tugged at Willa as she hurtled downhill. Blood oozed from the many scratches that covered her legs. The shepherd boy was close behind, with Scard clinging to his back. Thorn-covered shoots wrapped themselves round her ankles. Willa fell again. Entangled in the prickly growth, her hands and arms were soon a mass of tiny cuts and scrapes. Tears streamed down her face. With dogged determination, she picked herself off the ground. The boys were in front now. How Sheply negotiated the slope, without falling, was beyond her comprehension. He seemed to a have an innate ability to avoid the pitfalls.

At the valley bottom, a watercourse flowed. An ancient watermill stood beside the running brook. In places, its thatched roof gaped to expose skeletal rafters to the elements. The planks of the mill's timber walls had warped and twisted. Several boards lay in a heap at the side of the building, lost in shoots of grass that grew round and in-between them. Upstream, the silted pond and millrace, whose waters once powered the wheel's vanes, were dry. The sluice-gates had long crumbled to dust. Further up the valley, water cascaded over a series of steep falls before it passed by the mill.

Sheply gained the bank of the stream where, at the side the building, he waited for Willa. Unable to move further, she collapsed, gasping for air. He was little better. For a thirteen-year-old, the child was a heavy load to carry. Sheply eased the younger boy down, beside his mother. The shepherd's own legs gave way. He sank to the ground, his back against the mill wall.

For several minutes they stayed, neither able to move nor think with any cohesion. Willa's breathing returned to normal. She took in her surroundings. On the opposite side of the stream, the hillside rose high above her position. Unlike the slope they had descended, bracken more than bramble covered this one. Not that it would aid the group. The growth was as tall as Willa. In the party's present condition, it would be impossible to hack a way through. Any attempt would leave a trail even the most inept tracker would follow with ease.

An overgrown track, which kept to the side of the stream, meandered down the valley. It led, in the distance, to vast expanses of open land. This area, which once fed the mill wheel, appeared deserted. Her pursuers would reconnoitre the route leading to the mill as soon as they finished searching it.

With her hand clutching one of the exposed uprights of the structure, Willa pulled herself to her feet. Her head spun. She closed her eyes and waited until the sensation abated. The sun was overhead and, in the confines of the valley, the trio sweltered. Far away, high on the moors, came the faint sound of shouting. Her pursuers had found their trail. Willa knew she should start running again, but her legs refused to move. Her body had nothing left to give. Tears burned her cheeks. Why follow her for such an extended period? They had more than enough slaves at their beck and call. Why should the retrieval of two escapees be so important to Betlic's overseers, so vital they spent weeks in search of them?

Since that picnic with Karilyn, her cousin Halwende's rancour had festered within him. Had he been in command, she would have understood the reasons behind the pursuit. What drove Talon to hunt her was a mystery? This lack of knowledge puzzled and frightened her the most. Earlier in her escape, in hiding, Willa had observed her pursuers several times. Talon, the man from the farm, was their leader. Compared to that one, Halwende was a vindictive child. Talon did scare Willa. Something about him screamed danger.

Although the riders were still out of sight, their voices were clearer. Once they reached the edge of the moor, the mill, from that height a tiny toy building, would be in their view. On horseback, they would be quick to cover the distance. She tried to gather the courage to face them, and her probable death. Would they kill her now, or take her back for execution — in front of her old work fellows, as a warning to them? Such a fate had befallen others.

Willa's thoughts drifted again. She remembered how angry she had been with Karilyn at the picnic. The girl had been so dismissive about Halwende and his prospects. The years since then had proved her instincts to be correct. If only Willa had swallowed her pride, ridden over and made friends again. She had missed Karilyn's company. It was too late now. Halwende had taken pleasure in relating the details of her demise. To learn of Karilyn's association with the strange object, the Scraufin, explained much about her attitude to life. It looked as though death would reunite them both soon.

A tugging at her sleeve brought Willa out of her reverie. Sheply had recovered enough energy to explore the outside of the mill.

"Come with me, Willa," he said, unable to keep the excitement out of his voice. "I've found somewhere to hide."

Not daring to hope, Willa followed Sheply. She looked inside the ruins, but could see nowhere they could conceal themselves. The floorboards appeared rotten. One false step, and someone would crash through into the dry channel of the race. The building was small, the boards covered with debris from the roof. Because the wooden shaft connecting the millstones to the vanes beneath had weakened, the heavy stones had sunk deep into the floor

"No, not inside," Sheply said, to Willa's questioning glance. "Down there," he pointed, towards the empty race.

Sheply had lost none of the agility he displayed when guiding Orvyn through the hills. The boy leapt down, then put up his hands to help Willa negotiate the drop. Following the path of the former watercourse, on bended knees, Sheply led her under the mill. Deep inside, the passage opened out beneath the millstones. Here, the crumbling remnants of the upright vanes still protruded from the shaft of the side-shot mill wheel. Willa realised the chamber was large enough for the three of them to hide.

"Stay here," Sheply said. "I'll bring Scard."

After a moment's hesitation, Willa agreed. She had no strength left to fetch her son. The ground was damp, the air musty. Fungal growths spread across the decaying timber-lined walls, onto the joists and boarding overhead. Many boards had shrunk, to leave large gaps between them. Seconds later, Sheply returned with Scard. The youngster struggled to keep awake.

Willa took her child into her arms. Sheply disappeared again. When he rejoined them, their belongings were in his hands. From her pack, Willa removed an old sack they had used many times on which to sleep. Filthy, it looked little different from the ground beneath them. She spread out the sacking, then pulled it over them as they lay down in the darkest corner. They huddled together for comfort. Willa prayed. She could think of nothing else that might save them.

Soon afterwards, the sound of horses reached the chamber. The noise stopped. The riders were outside the mill. Willa shuddered when she heard Talon speak.

"They've been here," someone else shouted. The voice was unfamiliar to Willa.

Floorboards groaned.

"There's no-one here now."

She recognised the last speaker as Halwende. He sounded close. Boards creaked again. He was in the room above the fugitives. Footsteps moved overhead. Dislodged by the intruder's movements, a fine shower of debris landed on the sack. Willa held her breath. For a moment, everything fell silent. Halwende stepped away. She relaxed. For an instant, she thought they might escape detection. Someone, with a much heavier tread, entered the building. He, too, walked towards the area above the trio's hiding place.

The vibrations created by his movements disturbed the mill stones. With an awful ripping sound, they crashed through the floorboards, to smash into the vanes in the lower chamber. The thunderous noise made Scard start. Willa clasped her hand over his mouth. Fragments of wood and dust showered the sacking. The fresh layer of rubble camouflaged their position. Had the remaining boarding been stronger, the trio might have been safe.

Moments later, another heavy object landed nearby. The second person, whose additional weight instigated the collapse, had dropped through the opening when its edge gave way. He staggered, fell forwards, then rolled over as he hit the ground. His grasping hand caught hold of something soft that lay on the damp earth.

Light poured through the hole from gaps in the roof. The bright beam caused Willa to blink as the sack slipped from her grasp. The newcomer, pulled himself to his feet. He looked up from the cloth, clenched in his fist, to stare at three pairs of frightened eyes. He drew his sword and pointed it towards them.

"Talon," he shouted. "I've found them, they're down here."

Along the path of the race, others arrived. Rough hands grabbed Willa. they hauled her outside, then tossed her onto the ground behind the mill. She could hear Scard crying for her. Willa tried to stand. Halwende's booted foot kicked her hard in the stomach. Doubled in agony, she rolled backwards and forwards. Encouraged by the result, he attempted to strike her again. Talon's fingers dug deep as he dragged away her attacker.

"Betlic said, if possible, he wanted her alive. If you hurt her so much she can't ride, she dies and you nursemaid the boy," Talon growled.

Furious, Halwende wrenched himself free. The temptation to lash out at his leader was high. Self-preservation proved greater. He stayed his arm. Halwende, no different to Willa in this respect, found Talon intimidating.

Willa straightened her body. Hands yanked her to her feet, her arms held rigid in vice-like grips. Talon stepped towards her. His fingers pinched hard against her chin. He forced her head upwards. In pain, she was powerless to stop him. He turned her face towards his. So intense had Willa's agony been, she had missed Talon's words to her cousin. Without hope, she prepared herself for her execution.

Nothing happened. Talon kept staring at her. "You're good," he said at last. "No-one's ever evaded me for as long as you." There was open admiration in his voice.

"What happens now? Are you going to kill us?" Willa asked, frightened for Scard.

"No, I've to take you to Betlic, it's he who wants you. He thinks you and your son might be useful if your old friend, Karilyn, comes back from the grave again."

"But she's dead. Betlic killed her. Halwende told me."

"In truth, the lack of a body means he can't be sure. You have a choice. Travel with me, without trouble, and I promise that you and the child will come to no harm, at least until Betlic feels satisfied your old friend no longer poses a threat. Even then, if you agree to follow him, I expect he'll allow you to prove yourself. The alternative? Your dear cousin's greatest wish is to end your life. If that's what you choose, I shall let him do it, here and now, then hand custody of your son over to him. Is that what you want?"

Willa looked into Talon's face. His eyes betrayed no emotion at all. He was a professional. Nothing was personal. For some strange reason, though more frightened than ever of the man, Willa realised she could trust him. Relief flooded through her. She would live, at least for now.

"I'll come," she whispered. "I won't be any trouble."

Talon nodded. "Find her a horse," he told the men holding her. He turned to the person, in whose arms Scard struggled. "When she's ready, pass the child to her."

"What shall I do with this one?" asked the man with Sheply.

"Kill him," Talon ordered as, without a backward glance, he walked away.

"NO!" Willa screamed. "The lad's nothing to do with this! He's someone we found on the trail. Please, please let him go, or bring him with us. I'll take care of him," she pleaded in desperation.

"My orders are to fetch the child and, if possible, you," Talon said. "It's unfortunate for the boy, but you're the one who involved him. I can no more free him than return with him. These past few months, I've endured enough trouble from Betlic. I refuse to risk more by incurring his wrath by sparing this young man."

Before Willa had chance to speak further, from behind came the sound of a blow. An unnatural groan preceded a thud as a body hit the ground. Willa's knees buckled. The guards, deaf to her hysterical screams, dragged her towards a horse.

Chapter Forty

For the briefest of moments, the ground shuddered. Marazin swayed, he felt faint. He shook his head as he attempted to clear it. The nauseous sensation eased. He blinked, then stared in disbelief. Some things had stayed the same. The object, created in the fire, was still clasped in his hand. His left arm remained around Karilyn's waist. Relative to them, neither Heardwine nor their horses had changed position. Careful not to poke himself with the Scraufin, he rubbed his eyes.

He looked round again. The surrounding countryside looked no different, but, instead of stone-paving, grass grew beneath his feet. The place of ceremonies had disappeared. Nowhere was there a knoll or pillar of rock in sight. Marazin turned to look at Karilyn. After experiencing the events earlier in the night, strange happenings were becoming normal for him.

"What's happened?" he asked.

Karilyn would know. She must have an explanation for this final stage of the evening's ceremonies.

"We're at the foot of the mound," she said, pointing straight ahead. "The column is over there."

"If it's visible to you, why can't I see it?"

"No-one can. The magic of the knoll transported us, as it did the riders we saw earlier. Until it's time to restore the Scraufin to its former self, the place of ceremonies will stay veiled from sight. For now, its purpose is complete."

Now the early hours of the morning, the couple were weary. Too exhausted to ask further questions, Marazin linked arms with Karilyn. Together, they walked towards their horses to retrieved their blankets. No sooner did they lay down, wrap themselves in their covers, than they were asleep. A chill was in the night air. In her slumber, Karilyn snuggled closer to Marazin. He pulled her to him, to hold her in a tight embrace.

They awoke to find the morning sun high in the sky. A little while later, her hair tousled, cheeks flushed and laughing aloud, Karilyn leapt to her feet and adjusted her clothes. Marazin, a contented smile on his face, watched for a moment as she searched for kindling.

With Heardwine at his side, Marazin, bow in hand, headed towards the lush meadows, out of sight of the campsite. Within minutes, he brought down several large rabbits, which the dog fetched to his feet. With fresh meat, they walked back to where Karilyn tended a blazing fire.

While Marazin skinned the game, Karilyn found a bed of nettles and garlic beside the stream close to their camp. She took extra care as she picked the nettles. While they blanched in a small pot, she returned to uproot several cloves of garlic. Although part formed, they added flavour to the meal. Within the hour, they had eaten their fill.

Heardwine left them, to go catch his own dinner. Overnight, the animal's hair had grown at a remarkable rate. The dog's proximity to the enchanted knoll had affected its metabolism. Heardwine was now more similar in look to his former self.

While they ate, Marazin studied the Scraufin, or rather the object made from it. What it appeared to be, it seemed absurd — so preposterous, he hesitated to voice his thoughts. It was difficult to believe they had come so far and risked everything for a whip! But, if true, did it mean this was the Mastig, or was that the name for those strange creatures that helped create it?

He looked again at the whip. Could it be anything else? No! Of a length similar to those used by wagon drivers or cattle drovers, it lay at his side. The thong had coiled itself with no effort from him. Karilyn's Scraufin provided an ideal base for the handle. The material now wrapped around it formed a solid heel-knot. It fitted his hand as if made for him. He supposed, it had.

The resemblance between this, and any other whip, ended with the handle. Although the braiding on the thong was unremarkable, the silver and brown material of its manufacture was beyond anything he had seen. Yet even this was ordinary, compared to what happened whenever he disturbed the coil. Along the whole of its length, it emitted a silvery green light, which pulsed and shimmered with a vibrancy that was startling. At its tip, the fall, as long as his arm, was a continuation of the core. On a normal whip, the fall consisted of a strip of replaceable leather. As Marazin grasped hold of it, he realised this substance was something that would wear forever.

"Yes, it's a whip," Karilyn said, on seeing the questioning expression on his face. "Only you can bring from it the spark needed to end the dominance of the talisman. My Scraufin was needed to make the firedog whole. Once the rod was in place, the light of the moon, combined with the energy provided by you, transformed it into the object you hold. The whip is the Mastig. It is your destiny to wield it. Why not try a throw?"

Marazin was skilled in handling many weapons, but, whips were something with which he had little experience. He preferred to trust his life to the sword, axe or bow. Not that he belittled the whip, it had its uses, but he did not consider it a weapon of war. He wondered, too, whether his use of the object might pose a greater danger to himself, than a threat to anyone else.

On his feet, Marazin stood with them shoulder-width apart. In his right hand, thumb on top, he held the whip's handle, by the heel-knot. He moved his arm backwards. The thong stretched-out behind him. In one quick movement, he swept his arm forward. Moments later, hopping around on one foot, he swore. He had done something wrong. At high speed, the tip of the thong had wrapped itself round his right leg. The pain was intense.

To one side, Karilyn doubled up, tears of laughter running down her face. Marazin glared at her. It set her off again. Determined, he struggled to remember a lesson taught to him in his youth. This time, with his feet together, he placed the thong behind and further out from his leg. With a smoother action, he moved his arm forward. As he followed through, he flicked his wrist. Partial success. Instead of a satisfying crack, a slight pop was the result. The whip glowed for a few seconds. Karilyn paused from wiping her eyes to applaud this attempt.

"I expected something more impressive," Marazin said, disappointed.

"It needs a cracker yet."

"A what?" Marazin stared at her.

"The strip you attach to the end of the whip. It's that which makes the crack sound louder. Tonight, at camp, I'll make one out of hair from our horses' tails. You can practise throwing while we ride. Try not to hit your horse, as you did your leg," she added, mischief in her voice. "It'll be a long day if I have to keep picking you up from the trail."

True to her word, by late that evening, she had plaited the horsehair into a thin flexible length with an eye at one end. She slipped this over the tip of the fall then attached it with a half-hitch knot. Marazin pulled it tight. The small length of fall above the knot defied all his efforts to trim it with his knife. When he stopped trying, the excess disappeared by itself. At the end of the cracker, strands of hair hung loose.

Marazin took a deep breath. He stood back. Karilyn stopped him before he began his throw.

"Wait," she said, "let me make sure the horses are secure."

Afterwards, as she settled herself beside the fire, Heardwine cocked open an eye. He looked at the whip in Marazin's hand. The dog moved over and buried its head in Karilyn's skirts. Now what was the problem? After his earlier attempts, what could he do with the object to cause this much consternation? He took another deep breath. Karilyn put her hands over her ears. Marazin scowled in mock anger. He thought she was making fun of him again. With great concentration, as he had practised during the day, he swept his arm forwards and upwards to finish with a flick of his wrist. What followed explained everything.

The sound of the thunderous crack rolled across the plains. Brilliant green lights lit up the night sky. Along the length of the whip, the thong crackled and sparked for a few moments, before its light faded to a steady pulse. Marazin stepped back in astonishment. He watched as the whip recoiled itself. In an instant, he recovered his wits. In triumph, he turned towards Karilyn. She had uncovered her ears. Although she knew the user of the whip never suffered from the deafening noise it created, Karilyn had been unsure how it would affect her. She had taken precautions this first time. The sound, to her relief, had been bearable.

"Now, that was a whip-crack," he said, a broad grin across his face.

Karilyn smiled as she joined him. She placed her arms around his waist, then gazed into his eyes.

"Now you know how effective it can be, you must remove the cracker until it's time for you to wield the Mastig against Betlic," she warned.

"This can't be right. I have to practise to improve."

"No, my love, I'm sorry but you can't," Karilyn went on to explain. "After tonight, you may use the Mastig as much as you want. It will progress your throw; but to create the crucial crack is too dangerous. That single one you made will have affected Betlic. From this distance, it should cast little more than a temporary shadow over his power. For a few hours, his control, over the minds of both followers and enemies alike, may weaken. At best, it'll be too slight for him to notice. Although unlikely, at worst he might suspect what's to come. If you persist with the cracker, he'll know the Mastig is at work. The nearer to him, the greater its influence. Forewarned, and before we are close enough to defeat him, he'll take steps to find and stop us. If you do nothing further to disturb his powers, they will regenerate within hours. Once his strength returns to normal, he'll dismiss the incident."

"How can you be sure he'll ignore what's happened?"

"Because tiredness, over-exertion, sickness, causes his authority over the talisman to weaken. This won't be the first time this problem has affected him. Similar setbacks will happen again, but, as long as he recovers when it does, he'll have few concerns. You needed to see for yourself what happens when you throw the whip the correct way. Now you know, you'll never forget."

Marazin mulled over Karilyn's words. The dangers inherent in overuse of the object, he accepted. To protect himself, Betlic might send an army against them. That was a prospect that boded ill for the success of his mission. Marazin's trust in Karilyn's judgement was absolute. It would be foolish to reject her advice. With regret, he removed the cracker and placed it inside his pack. There, the temptation to use it should be much reduced.

The hour was late. Tomorrow, and the days that followed would be long ones, most of their time spent in the saddle. Several months must pass before the couple reached rebel territory. They hoped Amron could keep control of his realm during this period. Karilyn rolled out their blankets. In the darkness, Heardwine disappeared to find a high point to keep watch. His master was on the final stages of his quest. It was the dog's purpose to make sure Marazin completed it.

Chapter Forty One

With a start, Betlic came out of a deep sleep. Disorientated, he clawed his blanket from his face. He dragged himself upright. Though it seemed moments ago, he knew it must have been much earlier when he returned to his room. Then, his mistress, at the sound of his approaching footsteps, had wiped the look of boredom and resignation from her otherwise attractive countenance. Stretched-out on his bed, she tried making herself as alluring as possible. Too exhausted to notice, he sent her away. He wanted to rest, for once, alone.

Moonlight cast shadows through his windows. The beam's angle told him it was the middle of the night. Sweat poured from him. His arms and legs felt weak, his thoughts muddled. Something had happened, but what? His dream! He remembered little — only a blinding flash of green light, followed by a crash of thunder. Betlic staggered from his bed.

Despite it being mid-spring, the temperature of the mountain air hovered around freezing point. With his blankets wrapped round his shoulders, he lurched towards the remains of his fire. He shivered as he gazed into the embers. Outside, in the distance, someone laughed. Others joined in the merriment. Betlic swore. Jollity was an unwelcome distraction, something he discouraged. Another shiver ran through his body. The talisman controlled the thoughts of his followers, with those who travelled closest to him the most under its spell. Either they should be asleep, or have their minds concentrated on their work. He had no memory of when last that dreadful sound assailed his ears.

His mind raced. With the Scraufin lost forever, it could not be the Mastig affecting his control — or could it. Again, doubts surrounding the death of the bearer surfaced. Betlic experienced a stab of fear. This weakness in his limbs — was he losing his power? He sneezed several times. It was nothing, he had caught a chill. That was what ailed him. Many of his men had suffered a similar fate during the past month. He called for fresh water. Once his servant departed, Betlic hunted for a potion he kept among his belongings. He swallowed it, a grimace on his face. His goblet was nearby. He emptied it as he washed away the foul taste of the mixture.

By morning, he would feel better, his strength back to normal. Laughter would no longer disturb his peace. To set his mind at rest, he would use the Eye of the Talisman once more, to try to find the bearer. If, as expected, the Eye did not locate her; it was time to dismiss his fears about the Mastig.

His thoughts active now, Betlic stirred the embers. A tiny red glow grew brighter. He added slivers of wood. As the fire took hold, flames flickered around the logs he piled on top. Betlic remained feverish. He pulled the blanket tighter. There was a chair nearby. He dragged it closer to the blaze. The cushioned seat was comfortable. He thrust out his hands to warm them. The flagon of cold water, fetched by his servant, helped slake his thirst and refresh his body.

Flames danced before his eyes. His attention settled on the mountain campaign against the rebels. This operation was proving more difficult than expected. His belief that the enemy forces were weak and ineffective had proved incorrect. As expected, Betlic's initial advance through the foothills into the higher mountains had been rapid. The small groups of rebels his armies encountered had fallen back in disarray. With inadequate weaponry, they had no stomach for the conflict.

Within weeks, so Betlic believed, their puny fortress kingdom, among the peaks, would fall under his control. To these enemies, he could show no mercy. Since his overthrow of the Xicaliman king, the rebels had vowed to end Betlic's rule. Instead, he would crush these traitors as an example to others. No matter how much they repented their ways, any integration into his forces was an abomination to him. Word would spread. Betlic's spies would make sure this happened. Any who opposed him would receive similar treatment. Death to dissenters was a just reward.

After their earlier successes, his troops were swift to reach higher ground. Here, their advance came to an abrupt halt. In every pass, at its narrowest point, huge defensive walls blocked his generals' progress. Once behind their fortification, set between towering peaks, the rebels sealed any gaps.

Betlic sent scouts into the mountains, to seek ways by which his men might bypass these obstructions. Not many pathfinders returned. The few trails they located, were well-guarded. Small numbers of rebel warriors could defend them with ease. To circumvent these routes, he required skilled climbers. Such men did exist among his battalions, although, too few so far to make viable an assault.

For now, his commanders concentrated their efforts on the fortifications. To hasten this, among the lower mountain slopes, engineers felled trees for use in constructing the components for mangonels. Once assembled in the passes, these large catapults would pound the defences with boulders. Wooden shelters, penthouses, were under construction. Covered with toughened hide, these protected the men who swung heavy, metal-tipped rams against the stonework, or those who tried to undermine it by tunnelling beneath the foundations. Although, wherever his followers attempted this last method, they failed. The builders had constructed their walls on solid rock.

No longer shivering, Betlic added another log to the fire. His mind was still active. In the morning, with the Eye, he decided to search for the bearer first. Afterwards, he would use the talisman to exhort his troops to greater effort. His earlier attempts to demoralise the enemy had not produced the expected results. With the Eye, he had studied the rebels' defences. When he tried to see further, he found the land beyond impenetrable to his magic. What he did notice was a steady stream of combatants, coming and going. The Xicalimans, he discovered, relieved their defenders on a regular basis. For reasons unknown to him, the mountains protected his opponents and allowed them to recover their spirits. Each day, as Betlic attempted to influence these refreshed minds, the talisman drained him of strength.

His body warmed. Feeling the benefit of his potion, Betlic returned to his bed. In the moonlight, his eyes caught sight of a square of parchment on a nearby table. If the stranger who carried that message was what he claimed, tomorrow might bring better news. Yesterday, several days after he gave himself up to a passing patrol, the captive had undergone interrogation. His story had enough credence to delay further, more intensive, questioning. First, Betlic wanted to meet him.

At first glance, Betlic recognised the writing. Raulf had been his most reliable spy at the court of King Grogant. Raulf's last message indicated he was to become Grogant's emissary to the rebels. Since then, nothing, from either Raulf, or any other source within the rebel lands. Other than stating the messenger was Raulf's agent, the note contained no additional information Once he met the go-between, Betlic expected to learn more. The messenger's words would determine whether he was genuine, or marked for death.

Betlic rose at dawn, fever gone and strength returned. A fruitless search for the Scraufin bearer, reassured him she was dead. With the mantle settled in a more comfortable position, he reattached the Eye to the talisman. Throughout the rest of the morning, he devoted his energies into rallying his men.

As noon approached, the sound of horses disturbed Betlic's concentration. He frowned in irritation at the distraction. Not for long; he remembered the captive he had arranged to question that day. Betlic removed the mantle. He hung the talisman round his neck. Out of habit, he concealed the object beneath his tunic.

Soon after the start of the campaign, Betlic had moved his headquarters to an old abandoned hunting lodge at the mountains' edge. With private quarters added for him, it became the hub of activity. Before the escort and their charge dismounted, Betlic entered a large hall connected to his rooms. It was empty, except for two guards. Tomorrow, when his generals returned from the front-lines, the chamber would fill with noise. Every third week, his commanders came together to discuss their progress, or lack of such, and to consider new strategies, if required.

At one end of the hall, opposite to the main entrance, he seated himself behind a heavy oaken table. On this, within easy reach of his master, a servant placed a goblet and a flagon of water. During a campaign, Betlic avoided wine. He preferred to keep a clear head. On either side of him, his bodyguards stationed themselves, each with his back to a corner of the room. The parchment Betlic had studied earlier, he placed on the tabletop.

The outer door swung inwards. Two burly soldiers entered. In-between them, a dishevelled prisoner shuffled, his face swollen and bruised. The shackles on his legs allowed sparse movement. Ropes bound his hands behind him. Although he had spent little time with his interrogators, the effects were visible. Despite his injuries, he thought himself lucky to be alive. Betlic looked at the escorts.

"Go now," he commanded. "You, too," he said to his bodyguards.

Unhappy at leaving Betlic with a stranger, they adjusted the captive's bindings before, with reluctance, they stepped outside.

"Come, stand over here." Betlic pointed to a spot, a pace in front of the table. In pain, the prisoner hobbled forwards.

"This letter," Betlic indicated the note by his fingertips, "you say it's yours?"

"Yes, your Highness."

"So, Raulf has a new man. What happened to his last one?"

"Earlier in the year, the rebels caught him trying to leave their stronghold."

"I see. They captured the messenger, yet your master remains free and able to send a replacement. Remarkable! I met your predecessor, several times. His ingenuity and cunning were beyond question, unlike his courage. Any competent inquisitor could have made him talk within hours. So, tell me, why did he not scream everything he knew to his torturers? Everyone who lives long enough to talk, does, even the tough ones."

"The messenger carried a small phial of poison, your Highness," the prisoner explained. "It was hidden in his clothing. His captors locked him in a room to await his inquisitors. When they came for him they found him dead."

"A phial of poison, you say. Do you carry such an item?"

"Yes, your Highness, stitched inside the hem of my tunic."

Betlic called out. In an instant, a bodyguard entered. He followed his master's instructions to search the prisoner's tunic. From an opened seam, he removed a small object. The guard placed it, beside the piece of paper, on the table. Betlic picked-up the tiny phial and held it up to the light. The clear liquid inside was unidentifiable. He lifted the stopper to sniff the contents. They were odourless. Betlic poured them into his goblet of water.

"Have you executed the fool who tried to steal from me?" Betlic demanded from the guard.

"No, your Highness, we await your order."

"Good! Bring him here, now."

The man hurried out. Several minutes later, with his fellow bodyguard, he returned. Between them, they dragged another, less fortunate prisoner into the hall. After seeing the condition of this captive, the messenger prayed fate would spare him the same treatment. His own sufferings were insignificant compared to this man's. The guards yanked him by his chains across the floor. The newcomer's face was unrecognisable as that of a human being, his body burned, bones broken. Through swollen eyes, he stared at Betlic and tried to speak. No recognisable words came out; his voice was hoarse and cracked.

"I can't hear him," Betlic said to one of the guards, "here, give him this water to drink. It will clear his throat."

The guard took the goblet. The messenger remained silent. He looked straight ahead. To interfere would not change the result. The other prisoner would die, anyway. At least this way, his death would be quick and much less painful than with his tormentors. The guards raised the head of the prisoner, then poured a quarter of the liquid into his mouth. He swallowed, then drank more. The vessel soon emptied. For a minute or two, nothing happened. Betlic tapped his fingers. The messenger's gaze did not waiver. Sweat beaded on his forehead.

On the floor, the prisoner grasped for his throat. A spasm passed through his torso. For a second, his limbs stiffened, his whole body arched. As his muscles relaxed, he crumpled, little more than a collection of rags in the dust. A guard knelt beside him. Unable to find a pulse, the guard shook his head at Betlic. The prisoner was dead. At Betlic's command, the guards dragged away the remains. The door closed behind them.

Betlic looked his visitor in the eye. "It seems you're telling the truth. By what name are you known?"

"Tedrick, your Highness."

"Well, Tedrick, if you are the person you purport to be, let me hear something that proves it. A short message, perhaps, meant for me, alone," Betlic raised his eyebrows to indicate Tedrick should start talking.

These words, he memorised the night Amron relayed them. Tedrick prayed the phrase, obtained from the original messenger, was correct. His fail-safe, the phial of poison, was no longer available to him. He took a deep breath. With care, he spoke in a firm voice. If his host mis-heard a single word, Tedrick doubted the offer of a second chance would be forthcoming.

During his lifetime, few people had worried Tedrick, as did Betlic. Something was not quite right about him. His eyes were dead and fishlike. An icy chill spread throughout Tedrick's body. Betlic listened to each word. Once the messenger had finished, Betlic waited a moment before he spoke.

"You said 'message' five times. Your predecessor only made four mentions of this word. Why does your count differ?"

"Because, your Highness, he was Raulf's fourth messenger, I have the honour to be his fifth."

Betlic sat back, satisfied. Raulf's choice of intermediary had improved. This one showed potential. The man reminded him of Talon. As he was finding it a struggle to capture a single woman and child, a little rivalry might inspire and return him to his best.

Betlic bellowed for his bodyguards, who released Tedrick from his bindings. The guards resumed their earlier positions, in corners of the room. It was only confirmation of Tedrick's authenticity that Betlic wished to stay confidential.

For an hour or two, Betlic quizzed his visitor. He replied with the information given to him by Amron. As the king had instructed, Tedrick emphasised the strength of the mountain defences. He explained how hard it would be to breach them. Once through, the invaders faced a series of similar fortifications, against which they would have to repeat the whole process. Winter would be upon them before they could hope to complete their task. Before then, snow would have blocked the mountain passes.

Amron had paid a high price for these measures. He had exhausted many of his available hoards of gold, those his father had mentioned before the pair had fled Vretliana. Although Amron's lifestyle might have been extravagant, one of his greatest successes had been to persuade others to fund it. Against expectations, he had shown greater wisdom when spending his own reserves.

"Then we shall dig in and wait until spring," Betlic said, surprised by the depth of the enemy preparations.

"That may be too late your Highness. By then reinforcements will have strengthened the rebel forces. Their king has made pacts with several nations. Over winter, their intention is to combine forces to present a united front. At a huge cost in men, only with the talisman's help will you prevail.

"The mountains shield the rebels from much of its power. They had hoped for salvation in the form of a Mastig. Raulf could not discover what manner of object it was, but no longer is it relevant. Only one person knew where it was hidden. That person was killed by your men."

This last piece of information was welcome to Betlic. It confirmed his findings. But, talk of the rebels becoming stronger was not what he wanted to hear.

"Is this all Raulf has to offer? Warnings. What solutions does he propose? He's been with the rebels long enough to have discovered some weaknesses."

"He advises that you keep up your assault in the mountains. By doing so, the rebels will remain confident you intend to enter their lands by that route."

"What lands? Is there another route? Explain yourself!"

"Your Highness, the sierra's shaped like a horseshoe. The rebel base is deep inside a valley that lies at their centre. Far to the north, a narrow entrance gives access. Through that you can lead your armies. With your engines of war, you'll breach their puny defences without difficulty. They're insignificant compared to those in the mountains. With ease, your forces will push through the lowlands. You'll trap the rebels between your battalions there, and those on this side of the peaks. Long before reinforcements can arrive, their battles will be at an end."

Although Tedrick expanded on this information in ever-greater detail, still he had his doubts. Unless Amron's plans were secure, events might follow a course similar to that his agent had outlined.

After he had finished his 'message from Raulf', the grilling Tedrick endured, was something he hoped to experience never again. Betlic's questioning was relentless. To stay alive, Tedrick revealed more than he wanted. He was right to be wary. For him to prevaricate about anything Betlic might already be aware, could prove fatal. If Tedrick's inquisitor suspected even a minor untruth, it would throw suspicion on everything the captive said.

In took a long time before he satisfied Betlic he was genuine. Tedrick fell silent. Soon afterwards, an escort showed him to new quarters. He was free to move about the camp, although, it was soon plain his every movement was under scrutiny. Later that afternoon, Tedrick watched as a large party of horsemen rode away, northwards. A spare horse trailed behind each rider. If they changed mounts at regular intervals, they should be able to confirm his story and be back within the month. Tedrick had advised Betlic to follow the refugee trail. The rebels had planted false stories, about their wide dispersal across the north. This route, Tedrick assured Betlic, would lead them to the rebel stronghold.

Chapter Forty Two

Betlic lay back. His day had gone well; so too his evening. Exhausted, his mistress slept at his side. She rolled over, muttering. With his elbow, he jabbed her in her ribs. Again, she changed position, swearing in her sleep. When awake, it was doubtful she would have dared use such words towards her lover. It was fortunate for her, his mind was elsewhere. She fell silent. His thoughts became clearer. Again, he concentrated on the day's events.

That morning, Betlic's generals had paid close attention while he imparted the details provided by Tedrick. At their request, an aide brought him before them. Betlic had to admit, with fresh clothes and his injuries tended to, the man presented himself well. The messenger confirmed everything Betlic had shared with his commanders. Tedrick's responses to other concerns were precise and delivered with confidence. After his dismissal, the generals discussed this newfound knowledge. Hours passed. Their ideas and suggestions formulated into definite plans.

Betlic had reached his conclusions earlier. But, before he committed himself, as usual, he paid close attention to the advice of those who commanded his armies. It took most of the day. By the end of the afternoon, the consensus, overall, corresponded with his initial thoughts. Mountain based troops, with sufficient men in reserve, would maintain pressure on the rebels. Two of his commanders would co-ordinate this activity. Until these men breached the defences, Betlic saw no necessity for additional forces. Insufficient space in the high passes made it difficult to accommodate the battalions already in place.

The bulk of his men at arms remained on standby. Arrangements and planning for these would follow in more detail. In units of a thousand, they had set up camp in holding areas, spread out across the plains. This arrangement provided each group with local resources enough to be self-sufficient for most of their needs. Over the following weeks, while Betlic awaited the return of his scouts, these groups would reunite, in readiness for their advance north.

THE MASTIG

Until the campaign ended, his army of procurers would have little rest while they toiled to supply the vast numbers of troops on the move. Over recent years, these ruthless gatherers had become expert in these matters. Across the many diverse territories over which Betlic now ruled, they had kept busy over the winter months. From these regions, large quantities of meat, living or salted, moved-up the supply-chain. Wagons, piled high with most other items an army might need, travelled alongside. As supplies kept pace with the troops as they advanced, so did the camp followers who provided night-time entertainment.

Betlic intended his move north to be rapid. The later the rebels learned of his advance, the less time they would have to rearrange their defences. Amron and his commanders would face a dilemma. To withdraw too many defenders from the mountains would leave the passes open to being overrun. If they recalled insufficient numbers, the lowland forces faced annihilation. Survivors would find themselves trapped in the hills. It mattered little which course of action the rebels took, so Betlic believed, the outcome was inevitable. His combined forces outnumbered the enemy by a huge margin. By autumn, the rebel challenge would be a memory, one not soon forgotten by those who thought to challenge him.

Then would be the time to turn his attention towards those nations who had signed treaties with the upstart Amron. Once he had vanquished them, other countries, ones that lacked the courage to commit to either side, would sue for peace. Betlic's belief in his own destiny was solid. When he ruled the world, the ultimate secrets of the talisman would be his. Once it yielded its dark magic to him, his influence would be absolute.

Power was a great aphrodisiac. He rolled closer to his mistress and, with practised expertise, caressed her awake.

ൟ ಖ

Much to Betlic's satisfaction, progress was swift. His scouts, riding in relays, returned in less than four weeks, to confirm Tedrick's story. The valley, its entrance in the north, did exist. Betlic had not wasted this period of waiting. Already, his men were on the move. His army increased daily as units came together to join the main thrust. Patrols ranged far ahead. These were substantial groups, tasked with hunting down those seeking refuge. Refugee or rebel — it was of no concern to the hunters, they killed whosoever they found. This ensured no word of the advance reached the enemy.

A month after the summer solstice, Betlic's men rounded the northern end of the mountains. The army veered west. At speed, they advanced, overwhelming any rebels in their way. A week later, the invaders gathered at the entrance to Amron's stronghold. Betlic surveyed the fortifications that stretched across the valley. Since Marazin and Karilyn had passed through, much work had gone into improving their defensive capacity. Behind the wooden ramparts on the low ridge, stonework created a stronger barrier. It was unfortunate that a length of wall, near to the centre of the high ground, remained half built.

With siege engines only days' away, Betlic could afford to wait their arrival before beginning his full assault. Until then, with those units whose loyalty was unproven, he would test the defences. He had his men charge in waves against the areas under the walls. His generals watched and learned much from the enemy's response. Weaknesses in the ramparts, the attacking forces earmarked for later pounding by the mangonels.

Penthouses provided cover as Betlic's men filled ditches and uneven ground beneath the enemy positions, in readiness for siege towers. Once assembled, it would not take long to wheel them to those parts of the ridge that rose sheer to the fortifications. Betlic's men would force their way forward, along walkways extended, or lowered, from the tops of the towers. He did not expect rebel opposition to delay his plans for long. Elsewhere, ladders would be more effective where slopes were too steep for fully-armed warriors to climb unaided.

With the rebels in clear sight, Betlic redirected his energies towards the talisman. His sworn intention was to destroy their morale. For two days, hunched over his possession, his concentrated his mental efforts on trying to influence the minds of Amron's men. On the third morning, he left his temporary quarters, to move closer to the defences. He wished to see for himself the results of his work. On this occasion, all the knowledge, garnered over the years, he had applied to his task. The power he unleashed against this enemy was unparalleled.

Without the mountain range between him and the rebels, Betlic believed the talisman's influence would devastate them. This, so he soon discovered, was a serious miscalculation. The distant warriors looked far from disheartened. It was true they swaggered less. Their response to his forces' advances lacked some of its initial vigour, but, to Betlic's fury, the defenders were not the spent force they should have been. He cursed the mountains. The strange power that resided deep within them, maintained its ability to counter the effects of the talisman.

The same was true with the Eye. Several times, Betlic tried to use it to observe the valley and to locate Amron. All he could conjure were wavering, misty visions, in which vague shadowy shapes flashed in front of him.

Disgruntled, Betlic returned to his tent, to study again his manuscripts. Perhaps he had missed something that might allow him to increase the talisman's power. He picked-up the oldest set of texts he possessed. Contained within the yellowed, musty leaves was an enchantment he knew would give him limitless energy. To voice aloud the invocation would involve great personal risk; as a result, he had avoided its use. The spell was long, complex and accompanied with the direst of warnings. Once committed, a single mistake, one word out of place or mis-pronounced, and the charm would destroy him. He studied the manuscript for a while. Again, he rejected it. If ever his situation should become hopeless, he might have to reconsider. He dismissed the idea. Such thoughts were ridiculous

Later in the day, his engines of war would arrive. Once in operation, they would bolster his attempts to lower the defenders' morale. Their resolve would crumble, along with their wall. Betlic decided to wait until then before he redoubled his efforts with the talisman.

Overnight, and into the morning, his engineers assembled their mangonels. By noon, they were in position. Late that summer's evening, as darkness fell, large areas of rebel defences lay in ruins. Other parts appeared in imminent danger of collapse, as rocks and boulders slammed into the walls and earthworks. Countless defenders lay dead or injured. Siege towers were in the final stages of construction. Tomorrow, the assault would intensify. It was plain these fortifications were inferior to those in the mountains. Betlic did not realise this was intentional. Although Amron wanted his forces to show stiff, determined resistance, he did not want a protracted engagement. He could lose too many men in that process, ones he needed for later.

Once the pounding of the rebel line started, Betlic withdrew to his quarters. He spent his time huddled over the talisman. The effort appeared to be worthwhile. News from the front-line was encouraging. The enemy showed signs of weakness. Betlic increased his incantations. By the end of the second day, his exhaustion was visible, but the results of his labours were satisfactory. Once his men had broken through, and consolidated their position on the other side of the ridge, he could allow himself to sleep. It was inconceivable the defenders could resist for much longer. Betlic was certain he would spend the following night in former rebel territory.

Morning broke. The skies were clear. A mild breeze refreshed the air. Later, when the sun rose above the tips of the mountains, the day would be hot. Siege towers, moved into position under cover of darkness, were ready for action. Stretched-out behind them were lines of penthouses. Lying end-to-end, they provided shelter for the columns of expectant warriors, who waited their turn in the imminent assault. Betlic left his tent to join his generals for a short while. Everything was in place, their reports positive. Betlic nodded his agreement and, at his signal, a horn bellowed out. All along the front, others copied its call. Today, the rebels would experience their first taste of defeat. Betlic hoped they enjoyed it. In future, it would be a daily experience.

A roar spread across the valley as the assault began. Soldiers scrambled up the protected ladders, inside the wooden structures. As the walkways bridged the gap between the towers and the ruined walls, Betlic's men ran onto them. Fighting was hand-to-hand, vicious, bloody, and without mercy. Shouts, battle cries, screams of the dying, filled the air. Despite the pounding in their heads and the feelings of dread inspired by the talisman, the defenders fought with tenacity. Their bodies and blood mixed with those of Betlic's men.

For most of the invading force, it was the first time they had met determined opposition. The inferior fighting skills exhibited by the attackers would not affect the result. They had the advantage of numbers. In the confined spaces in which they fought, it was quantity, not quality, which counted. By noon, the defenders were without reserves to fill the gaps left by the dead. Betlic's men kept coming, a flow that had no end. As mid-afternoon approached, the battle for the walls reached its violent conclusion. With assaults from too many locations, it proved impossible to contain the invaders. Through the initial breaches, the attackers spread out, joined forces, then conquered.

Prisoners were rare. Only those rebels, whose injuries prevented their escape at the battle's end, remained — not that they survived for long. Betlic's men, as instructed, executed them without mercy. A few, unlucky ones, endured questioning first. Betlic gained little knowledge of rebel strategy, and what might lay ahead as he moved along the valley. As Amron refused to discuss details of his plans with anyone, these captives could reveal nothing of use. If the defences failed, rebels had instructions to escape, then join with their comrades stationed down the eastern edge of the mountains. It would appear Betlic had taken the rebels unawares. Amron, it appeared, had no comprehensive battle plan for the defence of his lowland territory.

This information did not surprise Betlic. It was in line with his expectations. Unprepared, the rebels would try to fight a rear-guard action, while they waited in vain for their allies to arrive. It was clear the enemy had failed to grasp how large was the force they opposed. He would overwhelm them. If any allied armies were on the way, once they heard news of the rebel's collapse, they would turn tail and run for home.

For the rest of that day and the whole of the next, Betlic consolidated his position. The roadway up to the fortifications, which the rebels had tried to destroy, his engineers soon repaired. Men flowed across the ridge as they would for several more days. Scouts, sent ahead, down the centre of the valley, reported it deserted for as far as they could see. The opposite end, and the mountains that enclosed it to the south, remained beyond their sight. His advance party had ridden through numerous settlements, all abandoned and burnt to the ground. To the east, his scouts came under attack. Westwards, the land was empty and secure.

Betlic and his generals came together. They agreed to move a significant part of their forces down the centre of the valley, to command the middle ground. Units would patrol the valley's western side, to warn of any attempt by the rebels to circle the advancing army. The rest of his men would sweep down the edge of the mountains. The troops in the centre would move to secure the lands behind, and kill any who tried to escape into the hills. As a rallying point, the boy king, Amron had met with limited success. But, as a strategist, history would record him as a failure. Instructions regarding him were clear. Betlic wanted Amron taken alive. The despot had some ingenious ideas on how to give the young upstart a long and painful demise.

For almost a week, Betlic's forces pushed forward. Progress was slow. The rebel army was tenacious. It fought for every step of earth it relinquished. They knew the lie of the land. They had prepared better than expected. Each knoll, hill and piece of broken ground, they used to hinder the invaders. Betlic's frustration was rising. Using the talisman to demoralise the enemy and empower his own men, was draining him of strength. He could not believe how difficult it was to wipe-out the rebels. Where did they find all their men? Although his units outnumbered them dozens to one, the rebels seemed able to bring fresh fighters to the front at will.

Tedrick had assured him rebel numbers were small. It was conceivable Raulf had few details of their troop deployments. The shortness of his time at Amron's court would have limited his intelligence gathering. Since Tedrick's arrival, there had been no further messages from Raulf. In the mean-time, Betlic had sent Tedrick with a party to recall Talon. His talents were needed here. It was appropriate, too, that Talon and the new man became acquainted. If compatible, they might excel as a team. The woman and child no longer mattered. Had Amron possessed the Mastig, by now he would have used it.

Two more days passed. The invaders' progress slowed as the rebels intensified their resistance. In the distance, a large flat-topped promontory protruded from a steep mountainside. The edges of this outcrop consisted of rocky scars. At the front, facing onto the valley, a road wound up the sheer slope. As the advancing army drew nearer, the troops could see that fortifications surrounded the top and protected the roadway beneath the cliffs. Amron had taken more care with this stronghold. Betlic sent men into the hills, to attempt an incursion from the sides. The terrain was difficult. The rebels defended it with ease. A frontal assault seemed a more viable option.

The sound of a rider coming to a halt outside disturbed Betlic's concentration. He stopped work on the talisman. Through bleary eyes, he looked up as the intruder entered the tent. It was an aide to one of the field commanders.

"What do you want? Can't you see I'm busy?" Betlic snapped at him.

"Your general, Ragenald, asks that you join him with some urgency."

"Why, what's so important he cannot come himself?"

"He has something to show you."

Betlic stood, his back ached from too long spent hunched over the talisman. His eyes were red and sore from concentrating in the gloomy light. His anger faded as he relaxed his muscles. A short break from his efforts would be good for him. A ride in the sunshine might boost his energy. He hung the talisman round his neck, removed the mantle then strapped on his sword. An hour later, accompanied by the aide and a large party of bodyguards, Betlic approached the frenzied activity along the front-line.

He joined with a group of men, including Ragenald. They were on a mound, in clear sight of the rebel hilltop stronghold. In front of them, riders charged towards the defenders on the valley floor. They replied, first, with arrows then, once the horses drew close, with axes, spears and swords. Elsewhere, warriors surged forward to engage in hand-to-hand combat, before falling back.

Cries of the antagonists, combined with the sound of steel against steel, were deafening. Rebel forces were putting up a determined defence. The smell of the battlefield was everywhere. From both sides the pungent odours of sweat, fear, leather and horses mingled, to combine with the stench of the dead. Under the blazing sun, bloated bodies lay strewn across the landscape. This was an aroma that excited Betlic. It made him feel alive. Since he left home, he had become accustomed to this life.

"Well Ragenald, what's so important you've brought me all this way?"

"Up there, your Highness, on the battlements," Ragenald pointed to a place high above on the rebel hilltop. "As soon as I caught sight of it, I thought you'd want to see it yourself."

Betlic squinted against the glare. A solitary pennant flew from a pole near to the entrance gates. At first, it meant nothing to him. He rubbed his eyes, then looked again. A distant memory came back to him. He had seen that design before, on a flag flying from the top of a tower. Where? Of course, *his* palace, the day he wrested it from the king of Xicalima. It was the king's standard, flown only in his presence. Betlic sat upright in his saddle, satisfied. He had no need to chase Amron. The man was waiting for him, trapped within his stronghold.

Within hours, Betlic received confirmation that the majority of his forces were inside the confines of the valley. That night Betlic met with his generals. He issued orders to bring his armies together. With cliffs behind and an army on every other sides, the king, in exile, had ensnared himself.

The elevation of the promontory was problematic. A redesign of Betlic's siege engines was necessary, so they could project their loads so high above, onto the defences and defenders. His engineers would have to construct towers too, to a height greater than in the past. Betlic had no doubts they would achieve this feat. There would be huge rewards for success, and death for failure. He found this combination produced most favourable results. The end was in sight. Once the king was dead, the rebels would lose heart. Betlic knew victory was his.

Chapter Forty Three

Almost two months had passed since the Mastig's creation. Marazin and Karilyn had retraced their outward movements from the Place of Ceremonies, back to where Orvyn greeted them with relief. To stay on his own for much longer, so he said, would have driven him to despair. To occupy his time, he had done impressive work on the hut, but, he acknowledged, there had been little else to occupy his time. The following morning, the trio cantered away, towards an uncertain future.

Over the next two weeks, the party rode westwards, on a route that Heardwine followed by instinct. The travellers had a greater sense of urgency. All three suspected that, after their departure from the mountains, events could have developed at speed. The rebels might be in desperate need of the riders' services, Marazin's in particular.

The land was quiet. Since the trio's outward journey, they found no signs that others had travelled this way. High on the moors they pounded over heather. It was too early for blossom. The windblown moorland was a carpet of green and brown. To the riders, it was a landscape filled with beauty. Beneath the horses' hooves, the peaty soil deadened their impact, making for an almost silent passing. As usual, Heardwine disappeared at regular intervals, although, his absences were short. For the rest of the time, he stayed near to his master's side.

One day, mid-morning, at the head of a shallow valley, the group stopped beside the waters of a stream. Through its centre trickled a stream. After refilling their canteens, they allowed their horses to drink a little. Heardwine, who had been absent for longer than usual, returned. Although the dog lapped the water, the animal was restless. When the trio remounted, Heardwine turned south, to follow the watercourse. The riders resumed their original path. Agitated, the dog barked to attract their attention, then ran off down the valley. Marazin reined in, as did his companions.

"Heardwine wants us to follow the stream. Shall we?" he asked.

Orvyn murmured his approval. Without hesitation, Karilyn agreed.

"My father's letter said we were to put our trust in him."

"I can't remember the dog acting this way before," Marazin warned, "but he's yet to let us down. Come, let's ride."

Eager not to lose sight of Heardwine, who raced ahead, they altered course then gave chase. The valley sides became steeper as it wound southwards. Rivulets, from the moors above, joined the stream. These channels varied; a few were dry while others bore a steady flow of water. As morning drew on, the vale continued to deepen. Under the summer sun, the air warmed and humidity levels rose. Bracken covered the slopes on either side. The lower they descended, the more brambles flourished along the eastern flanks. At the water's edge, the group followed the route of an ancient track.

By noon, the heat was stifling. The edges of the moor stretched high above the riders. Without warning, Heardwine crouched low. He began to stalk. Marazin whispered to the others. They slid from their saddles, making as little noise as possible. With the horses tethered to the branches of a nearby bush, the three dropped to the ground. With care, they crawled towards where Heardwine had come to rest.

At the top of a steep slope, the dog stretched-out. It peered through the long grasses. Beneath, the path meandered round a series of falls, which carried the stream to a natural rock-pool. From its rippling waters, the flow continued downstream, past the ruins of a small building. There, the dried-out pond and channel that connected it to the structure, led the observers to believe it was the remains of an old water mill. Marazin parted the grass to study the land below. The mill and surrounding area looked deserted. What had alerted Heardwine? Karilyn grabbed Marazin's arm. She pointed upwards, towards his left.

"Look," she whispered. "Two people, running down the hill."

Marazin and Orvyn stared at the slope. At first, neither of them could see anything, then Marazin caught sight of the distant figures. He studied them as best he could.

"I believe the one in front's a woman," he said.

"I count three," Orvyn said, squinting against the sunlight as he located them. "The person behind is carrying a child on their back."

As Orvyn spoke, the woman caught her foot and tumbled. Those behind took the lead. She gained her feet then stumbled after the others.

Once at the bottom of the slope, the mill blocked the runners from sight. Marazin made as if to stand. He eased back when Heardwine growled at him. Whatever was taking place must be ongoing. The watchers concentrated their attention on the slopes, to each side. They could see nothing untoward. The group at the mill remained out of sight.

"There," Orvyn said, "in the bracken, part-way up the hillside beyond the stream."

As they watched, they could detect movement in the growth. With the greenery at head-height, it made it difficult to pick-out details. If they concentrated, it was possible to make out a line of people, moving down the slope towards the mill. Back, along the hillside, the watchers could see the heads of several horses, their bodies hidden in a dip. As the line crossed a gully, for a moment, its members were visible.

"Oh! No!" Orvyn said

"Why, what is it?" Karilyn asked.

"Outlaws," Orvyn answered. "I've seen them before, not long after you and Marazin left to find the Mastig. From the top of a cliff, while out hunting, I saw them ambush a party of travellers. What they did to them was beyond evil. We have to warn those people below before they're taken."

Before he could move, another low, fierce growl rumbled from Heardwine's mouth.

"Keep down," Marazin said. "We can't afford to become involved. We have a job to do. Against so many, even if we defeat them, our chances of coming through unscathed are remote. We can't take that risk. Nations depend on our safe return."

It was patent from Marazin's expression that this was neither a course of action, nor inaction, with which he was comfortable. Without his responsibility towards the Mastig's safekeeping, nothing would have stopped him from going to the aid of the strangers at the mill. Saddened, Karilyn nodded in agreement. Had circumstances been different, she, too, would have been quick to go to their assistance. Orvyn relaxed. His companions were correct. Marazin's charge was too important for them to take any unnecessary risks that might jeopardise his mission.

From round the corner of the mill, one of the three runners came into sight. It was a youth. Orvyn felt there was something familiar about his looks. The lad jumped into the channel then disappeared beneath the building. Moments later, he clambered out to move behind the walls again. He reappeared with the woman. With her head bent forwards, her face was hidden. The youth helped her into the conduit where he led her under the structure. He came out twice more, once to fetch the child, then to collect their packs. After this, he, too, remained concealed under the mill.

"They're hiding from someone," Karilyn said. "If it's outlaws, I'm afraid it's too late. Those killers have watched their every move."

"Shush," Orvyn said. "I can hear something."

They fell silent. The sound of voices carried to them. At the top of the hill, near to where the runners had appeared, a bunch of riders came into view. They milled around before starting their horses onto the slope. Marazin counted seven. As they drew nearer, their black leather outfits identified them. Betlic's warriors! On their approach to the mill, they disappeared from sight behind it.

One man walked into sight. He stepped inside the building through the gaping doorway at the back. It was Karilyn's turn to stare. Had it not been for the uniform he wore, she could have believed it was someone she once knew. The idea had merit. Was it so unfeasible that, to save his own skin, such a bully would join with Betlic?

A larger man, entered the building. Moments later, as the first person moved outside, a cloud of dust billowed out from the doorway. More rose through the ruined roof while beneath, a funnel of fine powder spewed from the channel. The sounds of splintering timber and crashing noises reached those at the falls. Over this chaos, shouts of alarm sounded.

Men rushed round the mill. They leapt into the conduit. Minutes later they reappeared, dragging with them the three from hiding. When the men threw the woman onto the walkway, the one Karilyn thought she recognised lashed out with his boot. The woman rolled over in agony. For a moment, her face was visible to the watchers.

Karilyn gasped. Her hand went to her mouth. She knew that face. Willa! Another man appeared. He wrenched the attacker away from his victim. Now, Karilyn was sure her old friend's assailant was Halwende. The new arrival took command. He shouted instructions. Two men lifted Willa by her arms, then dragged her from sight.

To his surprise, Orvyn identified the youth. Older, taller, and broader in the shoulder, Sheply, the young shepherd boy, was in serious trouble.

The outlaws drew closer to their targets. Soon they would be in a position to launch an assault. Beyond the mill, another, smaller group of riders was coming up the valley towards the scene of action. Whoever they were, they rode below the watchers' line of sight.

What was going on, Marazin wondered? For weeks, his party had seen no-one. Now, it seemed, the busiest crossroads in the land lay in front them. How many more people would appear? Anxious, he looked around at the landscape. To his relief, elsewhere, it was empty. Their decision to avoid involvement had been wise. No sooner had he congratulated himself on that when Heardwine moved towards the path and started down the hill.

Before Marazin could call the dog back, both Karilyn and Orvyn rushed after it. Stunned, for an instant, Marazin remained where he was. Damn the consequences he thought as he leapt to his feet. It had not felt right to sit and watch a woman and child fall captive to brigands, nor Betlic's men. With sword in hand, he charged after his companions.

With their focus concentrated on the the mill, the outlaws never glanced back towards the upper valley. Concentrating on making the least noise possible, the group was directing its efforts on reaching the bottom of the slope. For several days, the men had camped on the hillside where their horses remained tethered. Their man on watch had caught sight of the woman, earlier, on the opposite hilltop. For a short while, before her companions joined her, her silhouetted figure had stood out against the skyline.

Unknown to Willa, her treatment at the hands of the outlaw band would have differed from that which she feared. They intended no physical harm. Once out of their custody, her conditions might have shown a significant deterioration. Among the northern slave markets, where the band planned to travel next, a strong nubile woman would fetch a high price. The child and youth were valuable commodities too.

The warriors' arrival was unwelcome, but a fair fight was not a consideration for the bandits. They would deplete the new arrivals with an initial flurry of arrows. Those who survived would die under the swords of their attackers.

Nine outlaws reached the low ground, where, near to the mill, they remained hidden from their targets. Away from the bracken, the men spread out, taking up positions of concealment from which they could mount their attack. Under cover of the scrub, four more of their fellows, with bows, moved towards the front of the mill, to where the warriors had relocated.

The outlaws prepared to attack as the warriors' leader walked towards his horse. The woman's guards frogmarched her in the same direction. Someone readied a horse for her while another carried the child towards her. The man, who had kicked the woman, was already on his horse. At the rear, close to the building, was the captured youth. The warrior, who kept him under restraint, called out a question to the leader. He shouted back, 'kill him'.

The outlaws' chief took immediate action. A third of his profit faced imminent execution. He signalled to his archers. An arrow flashed through the air. The man holding the knife to the boy's throat collapsed on top of his prisoner. At the sound of a body hitting the ground, the woman's knees buckled. Her guards forced her, screaming, to the horses. Two more missiles struck, felling their targets in an instant. The warrior's leader was no fool. The thud of arrows striking flesh had alerted him. He shouted for his men to take cover.

Arrows rained overhead. The woman, still crying, crawled back towards the mill. Her child was on the grass, the warrior who had held him, now reached for his sword. The youngster sprinted after his mother. With her son cradled in her arms, she curled up into as little space as possible, against the wall of the mill. The youth struggled free. Bent double, he ran over to join the pair where he attempted to shield them with his body.

The archers dropped their bows as they sprang clear of the bracken. They drew their swords as they headed towards the rocks where the warriors had taken cover. The rest of the outlaw band came out of hiding, too. With odds now of thirteen against four, their chief expected a quick resolution to the fight. For him, it was over in seconds. A dagger, hurled with force and accuracy buried itself into his throat. He fell to the ground, a gurgling noise issuing from his mouth.

In anger, his followers launched themselves at the defenders. Two more suffered a similar fate. As swords clashed, the area became a muddle of moving figures. The outlaws had great fighting skills, and many dirty tricks. So too did the soldier's leader. It was clear to his attackers he was much more adept at such tactics than were they, as were the men at his side — except for one.

Halwende was wise enough to leave the bulk of the action to the others. He used his limited skills to engage and kill the enemy injured. Several outlaws went down, along with two more warriors. Only the man in command, and his weakest follower, remained. The odds had become six against two. The bandits renewed their assault. They drove the defendants back against the rocks.

Without warning, a flight of arrows caught the attackers by surprise. From lower down the valley, the final group had arrived. The two outlaws, who remained, fought hard. They were no match for the enemy leader and the newcomers. The pair died fighting, but not before slaying one of the new arrivals.

Chapter Forty Four

It took moments for Talon to study the three remaining newcomers, two of whom, like him, wore the uniform of Betlic. Their leader's clothes were those of a wealthy traveller. He stepped forward, hand outstretched.

"From the way you fight, I presume you're Talon? I'm Tedrick. Betlic sent me to find you."

Talon was wary as he returned a firm, but not overpowering grip. Tedrick exuded an air of confidence. His self-assurance was unsettling. Although dissimilar in looks, they could have been mirror images in the way they carried themselves. Talon decided, this one would be worth watching. In his absence, Tedrick had appeared from nowhere. Already, he had ingratiated himself so far into Betlic's favour, he was acting under the master's direct orders. It was rare for Talon to meet anyone who posed this much of a threat to him.

"Betlic, you say," Talon said. "What does his highness want now?"

"You're to return with me, Forget the woman and child; they're no longer of importance. Betlic has confirmed the loss of the Scraufin, and the death of its keeper."

Talon turned to look at Willa. She was sitting with her back against the mill wall, clutching her son to her bosom.

"I'm sorry." His regret was sincere. "Betlic has no more use for you. It was a pleasure to pit my wits against yours. Make peace with your gods, for yourself and the young one."

Talon nodded to Halwende. He grinned with delight as he lifted his bloodied sword. Willa had reached the end, and she knew it, but she refused to plead for her life. The young mother would die with dignity, not on her knees begging for mercy. She stood, with Scard in her arms. Sheply leapt-up and, with immense courage, placed himself between his friends and their executioner. Halwende lashed out with his weapon. Sheply ducked but was too slow. The flat of the blade caught him a glancing blow. He careered head first into the mill wall. Dazed, he collapsed in a heap.

There was no fear in his cousin's eyes now, only resignation. Halwende felt cheated. He hesitated. His ego demanded Willa beg for mercy.

"Stop wasting time," Talon yelled at him. "We have to leave."

"Wait," Tedrick interjected. He had killed many times, but women and children? Never! He turned to Talon. "Betlic said to forget them, not kill them."

"This isn't your affair," Talon snarled. "Keep out of it. The matter between them is personal. If it were otherwise, I'd do it myself. Nobody escapes from Talon. It's the way of things. Accept it."

Talon indicated Halwende should continue with the execution. Tedrick shrugged his shoulders. Outnumbered four to one, although unhappy with the situation, he decided not to make an issue of it. Talon's reputation, alone, was fearsome. Besides, Tedrick's mission was at an end. His aim was to rejoin the rebels unharmed, and return to the charms of his new wife. Had he found it possible to slip away from his companions on the way here, he could have avoided this predicament.

Unless a miracle happened, soon he would have to ride back to Betlic's campaign headquarters, a prospect for which Tedrick had no appetite. It was clear that Talon took an uncompromising view of his duties. Any attempt to flee would incur dangerous consequences. The man had spent months tracking his prey. Tedrick could expect nothing less for himself if, without good cause, he disappeared.

Everyone's eyes were on Halwende, who revelled in the attention. Playing to his audience, two-handed, he raised his sword higher above his head. From round the side of the mill, a figure moved into view. It took several quick steps, then inserted itself between Halwende and his intended victims. Startled, he fell back a pace. Mixed emotions crossed his face. Shock, incredulity, then hatred, before satisfaction triumphed. In front of him was the person he loathed most, even more than his simpering cousin and her dreadful child.

"Well, Karilyn, I see you fooled everyone and cheated death a second time. You won't escape again," he said with relish. "Betlic will be most grateful when I present him with the Scraufin, and the head of its bearer."

The stranger's sudden manifestation had taken Talon by surprise. Boots, leather trousers, knee length tunic — she was a woman like no other in his experience. He was quick to note the scabbard hanging from her belt, and

315

the hand, resting on the handle of her sword. Only when Halwende's words registered with Talon did he launch into action. If this was *the* Karilyn, the Bearer of the Scraufin, to bring her back to Betlic, alive, would wipe-out all of Talon's past mistakes.

"No, Halwende, stop!" Talon ordered.

Willa, too, stared in astonishment. From behind, she had not recognised the person who came to stand between her and her cousin. The Karilyn, she knew, dressed in the manner of a lady. Neither did her old friend ever carry a sword, or weapon of any kind. But, when the figure spoke, its voice was one Willa remembered well.

"Go now, Willa, take Scard, with you!"

Karilyn kept her gaze fixed on the man in front as she addressed him.

"You disgust me, Halwende," she said, her tone cold and deliberate. "How could you contemplate the murder of your own cousin and her child? Lay down your sword then leave — or die. The choice is yours."

Halwende dismissed Karilyn's words and ignored Talon's shouted order. She was a mere woman; one so stupid, she threatened without a weapon in her hand. No-one would deny Halwende his satisfaction. He had lived with the memory of his humiliation for too long. It was time to take his revenge. Karilyn would die first, then the others.

He lunged forward. With all his might, he brought down his sword. It was a vicious strike, intended to cleave Karilyn's skull. She drew her own weapon as, with ease, she sidestepped the blow. Off balance, Halwende tried to move out of range. He was not adept enough. Karilyn never hesitated. Her sword swept across, almost slicing Halwende in two. His body crashed to the ground, coming to rest where, moments before, Willa and Scard had stood.

Tedrick realised the significance of Halwende's words, much more so than did Talon. In an instant, he understood the reason behind his mission. Somehow, Amron had known the bearer was alive. Whatever Karilyn was to initiate, this must be why the king had betrayed the rebels. No wonder his majesty had kept the whole truth from his agent. Had Betlic extracted it from him, it would have led to the despot making fundamental alterations to his plans.

Moments after Halwende's demise, two others came to stand beside Karilyn. Tedrick recognised them straight away. Orvyn, he had known for years. Marazin, Tedrick knew from that fateful hunting trip. Talon drew his sword, then moved forward. Tedrick stuck out his foot as he grabbed for his own weapon. Talon tripped and fell. Tedrick swung round, to inflict a fatal blow to one of the men with whom he had ridden. He took a step forward, then collapsed as something heavy smashed into the back of his skull. His attacker dropped his club, then pulled Talon to his feet.

"We'll take care of these two," Marazin told Karilyn when he and Orvyn reached her side. "You tend to the others."

"Care for the lad," Orvyn said, "he helped me the other year when I went in search of your father."

Karilyn nodded. Sheply had regained his senses. She put out a hand to help him to stand. With her arm as a support, she led him round the corner, away from the scene of battle. From his tunic, Karilyn ripped a length of cloth. She folded it several times. Still dazed, Sheply pressed it against the cut along the side of his head. Karilyn turned towards her old friend. Willa had set down Scard. Terrified, the child clung to her. There were tears running down both their faces. After a moment's hesitation, the two women embraced — their past troubles forgotten.

To find Tedrick was a willing member of Betlic's forces had outraged Orvyn. Yet, before a blow from a club sent the traitor to the ground, Tedrick had killed one of his comrades and tripped the group's head. This man was back on his feet while Tedrick's assailant had exchanged his club for a sword. As the adversaries faced each other, Marazin's instincts cautioned him against the leader. This was no ordinary foot soldier. He was too confident. The way he held his weapon, as though a part of his arm, was a warning any challenger would be a fool to ignore. Marazin had the most experience, this was his fight.

As they circled, Marazin took notice of his opponent's sword. It was similar to his own, and that used by Amron. Was this the third weapon from the original set? If so, it once belonged to the king's mother. Therefore, the person he faced could be her killer.

"What's it feel like, Talon, to face a man, instead of a couple too crippled to fight back?" Marazin taunted.

The remark, as intended, unsettled his opponent. Talon wondered how this stranger knew his name. He, too, carried an air of confidence, but to a much greater degree than had Tedrick.

"Are we known to each other?" Talon felt compelled to ask. His eyes remained fixed on Marazin.

"No! But the sword you hold belonged to the king's mother. It's part of a set of three. You killed her for it. The king has the second one and I the third. Amron will be grateful for its return."

"That snivelling little wretch." Talon was derisive. "His mother might have been old and crippled, but, in the defence of her husband, she showed more courage than most of my men. We had no choice but to kill her. Her man, that coward's father, was one of the bravest I've met. My only regret is that I didn't confirm their worthless brat was dead."

The sound of clashing swords rang out. For an instant, the noise distracted Talon. Marazin took advantage of this to strike with his sword. Talon moved to counter. Despite his delayed reaction, he blocked the blow, but staggered under the ferocity of the impact. Marazin raised his weapon, ready to take another slice. Talon kept low, spinning round and swinging his sword, intending to slash behind his opponent's knees.

Marazin leapt upwards as the razor-sharp blade swept beneath, missing his legs by a fraction. He landed on both feet, then brought his blade down on Talon's back. It sliced through his leather tunic to draw sparks from a fine, chain-mail vest hidden beneath. Against an ordinary weapon, the mesh might have offered complete protection, but this sword's steel was of a higher quality. With ease, it cut through the metal links, to inflict a deep gash across Talon's shoulders.

A crazed expression entered Talon's eyes as his injury fuelled his desire to kill and maim. He brought up his weapon and wielded blow after blow. His strength, fired by pain and fury, bordered on the inhuman. Blind unthinking rage was as dangerous to him as it was to an opponent. Marazin was familiar with the reaction. It was something he had experienced. While Talon bled out and weakened, Marazin defended himself. Content to block, and thrust whenever an opening occurred, he bided his time. Although hard-pressed, his skills, honed to a high degree from his work with Karilyn, were more than adequate.

Blades flashed in the sunlight as the combatants fought in front of the mill. One minute they were on their feet, moments later they were rolling on the uneven pasture. Blows from fists, feet, knees and sword hilts connected as each attempted to gain the advantage. On the ground, Talon tried to gouge out Marazin's eyes. He grabbed Talon's wrist and forced away his hand, then head-butted him, breaking his nose. They broke apart, to circle while they caught their breath, then started again.

Karilyn and Willa watched from the side of the mill. The way Talon seemed to dominate the action, horrified Willa. The man was relentless in the brutality of his attack. Orvyn, who had claimed victory over his adversary, joined them.

"You must do something," Willa said. "Talon will kill your friend."

"No, he won't," Karilyn said. "Watch how he moves. He's letting his opponent exhaust himself. See how every time Marazin strikes, he inflicts a cut. Talon is bleeding from a dozen places. He weakens all the time. It will be over soon."

And so it was. Talon, temper back under control, knew what his enemy's strategy was. Without success, he had tried the same on Marazin. Talon's time was short. He could feel the strength draining from his body. He focused his mind on one final desperate assault. With the last of his energy, Talon launched a vicious attack. Driven back, Marazin collided with the mill wall. It gave way under his weight. He fell backwards onto the crumbling timber floor of the milling room. His sword flew from his grasp. It disappeared down the hole created when the millstones smashed through the floor.

Talon sensed victory; he leapt through the opening. Marazin pushed backwards, one hand seeking to pull his dagger from his belt. He rolled to one side, a fraction before a flashing blade smashed into the woodwork beside his head. Marazin kicked out against his opponent's knee. With a howl of pain, Talon collapsed on top of him. Marazin punched him in the face. With a horrible creaking and groaning, the rotten flooring fragmented. Into the chamber beneath, among the debris, both combatants crashed.

Chapter Forty Five

In the gloom below the mill, the fighters rolled apart. Talon, too, had lost his sword. Marazin leapt to his feet, then grasped the handle of his dagger. At a slight, upwards angle, he held it ready to strike. Talon could see his weapon, out of reach behind his enemy. He reached for his own knife. Marazin feinted to the left. Talon lunged forward to find his wrist caught in an iron grip. Marazin kept tight his hold. He forced Talon's arm back while he swept-up with his own dagger. Talon saw the danger, but was too late to stop the move.

A burning sensation ripped deep across his stomach. The knife-edge twisted and turned as it sliced through him. Marazin continued to stab. The wounded man's knife, strangely heavy, fell from his grasp. His legs gave way, and he sank to the ground. The victor, still holding Talon's wrist, laid his victim onto the earth. At least one blow had cut upwards, to slice into Talon's lungs. Out of breath, Marazin, ever watchful, dropped to his knees beside his dying opponent. Dust sparkled in the beams of light, which flowed through the open roof and gaping ceiling. His enemy had fought with great courage. Marazin would not leave him to die alone in this dank, dark hole.

Bright pink froth bubbled on Talon's lips. His eyes were feverish. In shock, he experienced little pain. He tried to speak. His voice was too faint for Marazin to hear. He moved closer.

"Who are you?" the dying man whispered.

"Marazin, heir to the Mastig."

"So, the Bearer of the Scraufin stands outside, and the heir beside me. The Mastig, does that exist too?" Weak from blood loss, he stumbled over his words.

"Yes, the object's in my possession," Marazin said. "Betlic's rule draws to an end."

Talon choked as a stream of froth and blood issued from his mouth. He became still. Marazin thought him gone, but, moment later, Talon's eyes opened. He looked at Marazin.

"The time's right for something new. Betlic was a good man, once, but..." Between words, his breath was rasping.

His voiced faded. Before he could finish, it gave out. Marazin spoke again though it was doubtful Talon heard him. The dying man sighed, his body relaxed. Marazin closed his opponent's unseeing eyes. There was little sympathy for him. He had done his best to kill Marazin. Had Betlic's adherent succeeded, he would have shown no remorse. Marazin wiped the blade of his dagger clean. After a quick search, he found his sword. With it replaced in its scabbard, he retrieved Talon's, the one that by right belonged to the king.

Something glinted from around the neck of his fallen enemy. Marazin bent down to look at it. On a chain, was an eagle's talon, mounted in silver. The victor removed it, then hung it round the reclaimed sword. If he was able return the weapon to its owner, the trophy should go with it. Amron had made known his mother's killer wore such an item.

Footsteps sounded behind him. Marazin whirled round, ready to defend himself. He lowered his sword when he saw Orvyn, with the youth at his side. With their heads bent low, they rushed towards him, along the channel under the mill.

"Are you all right?" Orvyn asked Marazin.

"A few cuts, plenty of bruises, but nothing serious."

Orvyn stared at the sword, and the pendant wrapped round its hilt. "Is that the weapon Amron accused you of carrying when you two first met?"

"It is! His majesty will welcome its return. I'm sure it'll give him equal pleasure to learn of Talon's death. Do you think it might be too much to ask that Amron leave me alone afterwards?"

"I doubt he'll be that grateful. He's slow to forgive. Forget him for now. Let's move outside, it stinks in here."

"Who's your friend," Marazin asked as they moved into the daylight.

"Sheply," Orvyn said. "The young shepherd I told you about, who helped me to find the first of the coded messages."

Marazin nodded. He offered his hand to the lad who took it shyly.

"I'm Marazin. It's good to meet you. If you're a friend of Orvyn, you can count on me, too. Come on, let's join the others. I'm curious as to whom the woman and child are, what they have to do with Karilyn, and how they came to be fugitives from Talon."

Orvyn climbed out of the channel behind the mill. He put out his hand to help Sheply, then Marazin, onto the level. Together, they turned the corner of the building towards where the women waited, away from the charnel ground at the front. To Willa's surprise, Karilyn ran across, to throw her arms round Marazin. As they kissed, Willa smiled in delight. Karilyn had found her man at last.

At their visible happiness, Willa suffered a pang of regret for her marriage. Her husband had treated her with kindness and adored their son. She lived a comfortable life, well provided-for in most material ways. Willa had wanted for nothing, except love. Her relationship had never developed beyond mutual respect. Her husband's death had upset her, but much less than that caused by Halwende's betrayal of his extended family. She could no longer picture her spouse's face. Scard had taken after her, so there was nothing in his looks to remind her of his father.

The boy was on his knees playing with a large dog. Despite its size and somewhat ferocious look, Scard showed no fear of it. After Karilyn had sent the pair out of Halwende's reach, they found the beast waiting for them at the side of the mill. Straight away, it moved to stand guard over them. Not until the fighting ceased did the dog relax.

Hand-in-hand, Karilyn and Marazin walked over to Willa. Karilyn blushed as Willa raised an eyebrow. Brief introductions were followed by more detailed explanations as to their simultaneous arrival at the mill. Orvyn was most attentive around Willa, even more so when he learned she was a widow.

Soon afterwards, Marazin and Orvyn went in search of the outlaw's camp. They needed to make sure no-one was left on guard, and to release the horses tethered there. In their absence, Willa was anxious to learn as much as she could about Orvyn. The men, before they returned, retrieved their own party's horses.

It was late afternoon. Visible for miles around, crows were circling above the mill. The more adventurous ones hopped among the bodies. If the survivors of the struggle wanted to avoid drawing attention to the scene, they must dispose of the dead. This was a task no-one relished. Scard remained under the watchful eye of Heardwine while the others carried the remains to the mill. Here, Marazin and Orvyn rolled them through the hole in the floor. The whole structure was unstable. With the use of horses and ropes, the building would collapse in on itself. Once buried under the wreckage, the dead would no longer attract scavengers.

Unsure what to do with Tedrick's body, they left it until last. Was he the traitor they thought him to be? Willa was positive he had delivered a message from Betlic to Talon. Yet, Tedrick did speak out when Talon told Halwende to kill her. The man was quick to trip Talon, too, and slay one of his other companions. It was a pity the blow had killed Tedrick. It might have been informative to hear his story.

In the end, Orvyn's words swayed his companions. During Tedrick's life, he had performed many dubious actions, but never those of a traitor. Whatever he was doing in the enemy camp, Orvyn said, it must have been at the command of the king. Nearby, was a ditch they could fill without too much effort. A shallow layer of water covered the bottom. With more reverence than shown the other bodies, they carried Tedrick to the dip. First, before they buried him, Orvyn suggested they demolish the mill. It might provide extra material to level the hole.

The timber uprights were crumbling. With the base of each of the mill's corner-posts roped to a horse, Marazin gave the command. The animals took the strain. The timbers creaked and groaned. With a crack, first one upright, then another, gave way. The roof imploded. In a cloud of dust, the whole building fell inwards. The rotten planks, holding the channel sides below, caved-in. In moments, the remains lay buried under a mound of rubble.

They put the horses to graze. Only Tedrick's body remained. Once they had buried him, they could leave. They wanted somewhere more pleasant to spend the night. Exhausted, Marazin was struggling to move. His injuries, suffered in the fight with Talon, were not serious, little more than bruising and several cuts to his arms. These latter stung with the sweat from his exertions. His back troubled him the most. It had pained him since he crashed through the milling room floor into the chamber beneath it.

Marazin winced as he picked-up a large stone, which had acted as a support for the mill floor. He turned, to carry it to where Tedrick's body lay. The stone thudded onto the soft ground. Marazin stared, mouth open. He ran towards the ditch. Tedrick, head in hands, was sitting upright. He groaned in agony. Orvyn reached him at the same time as did Marazin. Between them, they lifted the injured man and half-carried him to where

Karilyn and Willa were standing. This sudden turn of events shocked everyone. Both women had examined Tedrick earlier. His pulse had been too faint for them to detect. The shock of being lain in a cold puddle must have revived him.

Willa fetched water from the stream. She bathed the ugly cut, and the lump on the back of the injured man's head. His eyes were dull and unfocused. White-faced and sick, Tedrick was unaware of his surroundings, what had happened nor who he was. Too ill to move for now, His carers wrapped him in a blanket and left him to sleep.

Marazin and Karilyn's first duty was to the Mastig. In haste, they had to return to the rebels. Orvyn would not have hindered them. Neither would the inclusion of Willa, Scard and Sheply have made a significant difference to their progress. They could choose from the pick of the horses ridden by Talon and his men. A sick man was another matter. If his injury was serious, he could extend their journey-time for days, even weeks. The couple had to make a decision. Whatever conclusion they reached, delay was an option denied to them.

Marazin was building a fire, trying hard to keep his back straight. Orvyn, while he kept an eye on Tedrick, occupied Scard and Sheply with various riddles. Karilyn and Willa's chatter was constant. As they prepared a meal, their fall-out became a distant memory. Willa was in awe of Karilyn's accomplishments and the tenacity she had displayed to survive. It was difficult to associate the shy young girl Willa remembered, with the strong-willed, self-confident woman Karilyn now appeared to be.

In turn, Karilyn learned of Halwende's treachery, and the betrayal and murder of Willa's husband and her family. After her escape from the farm, the way Willa, with Sheply's help, had pitted her wits against Talon earned Karilyn's respect. To stay ahead of him for so long showed courage and determination. Willa, too, had discovered an inner strength that Karilyn found astounding.

They talked while they ate, then late into the evening. Exhausted, Scard was the first to fall asleep, followed soon afterwards by Sheply. Later, Marazin and Karilyn retired, to tend to Marazin's cuts and bruises. Willa passed no comment when, under the same blanket, the couple made their bed. For all she knew, they may have spoken their vows together. It was not her affair. She was much more interested in Orvyn. He cast frequent looks in her direction. Willa had known him only a few hours, but his face she would not forget.

At dawn, Marazin returned from watch. He rekindled the fire. Between them, Karilyn and he cooked breakfast. Willa had taken first watch with Orvyn, when the pair had talked until the early hours. Marazin shook him awake while, at the opposite side of the camp, Karilyn did the same to Willa. Scard and Sheply had finished their meal.

Tedrick's eyes were open. Orvyn took him a bowl of food. Although his physical state showed improvement after a night's sleep, it was clear he was unfit to ride. When Orvyn helped him to his feet, Tedrick was so unstable, Marazin came over to help set the man down again. The patient's condition made Marazin and Karilyn's decision easier for them. They must go on alone.

Tedrick's mind, unlike his body, was more alert after a night's rest. A mouthful or two of food left him better able to answer questions. Orvyn was most curious to know how he came to be riding with a band of Betlic's soldiers. Progress was slow. Tedrick's thoughts wandered. It was a while before disclosed everything, from his audience with Amron, his meeting with Betlic in the guise of Raulf's messenger, to the resultant movement of troops north. After initial shock, everyone reacted with anger to Amron's treachery, and Tedrick's part in it.

"You believed everything Amron told you?" Orvyn was furious.

"Don't let the king's petty, childish behaviour towards you and Marazin fool you," Tedrick warned. The pain in his head was unbearable. He was struggling to concentrate. "The man's no intention of giving up the throne, nor bartering it. Amron would rather die first. He's working to a plan of his own making. His majesty has kept much back from the High Council. Something's afoot, something he alone has full knowledge. He refused to tell me everything. If my mission went wrong, so he said, what I didn't know, I couldn't reveal under torture."

"What were the exact details Amron told you to pass to Betlic?" Marazin asked.

Tedrick took a sip of water before continuing. "By then, Betlic's men had entered the mountains. The king was most insistent Betlic knew how difficult it would be for his forces to breach the defences there. Amron wants the enemy to go north where it's easier for them to launch their main assault.

The king impressed upon me that no re-enforcements could reach him much before the start of autumn." The injured man paused. Exhaustion was blurring his vision. He felt nauseous.

Marazin was sure that either Amron had lost his senses, or his grasp of tactics was more advanced than anyone gave him credit.

"What else did he say?" Marazin demanded.

"I was to tell Betlic that, to be confident of success, he must strike, at the latest, by the month's end following the summer solstice. When I mentioned the Mastig, of which he'd spoken in the past, Amron said it was beyond anyone's reach. He was adamant that Betlic had killed the Scraufin bearer somewhere on route to join the rebels."

Karilyn looked at Marazin. The king had kept the bearer captive for several weeks. He knew she was alive. The timing, too, by which Betlic was to begin his assault, was close to that by which the couple expected to return. Information of which Hafter was aware. It was inconceivable he would not have told his majesty.

Marazin had an insight into Amron's plans. Once the bulk of Betlic's armies were together, the king was relying on the Mastig's arrival to counter the effects of the talisman. It was a dangerous plan. No wonder he kept it to himself. To prevent reinforcements from joining-up with Amron's forces, Betlic would have to speed-up his advance. This should bring him into line with the king's apparent deadline. Amron's estimate of early autumn for his allies to bolster his numbers, Marazin believed optimistic. He had discussed this matter with Hafter. The sage's assessment then had been that they would be lucky to receive any help before spring the following year.

Tedrick cleared his throat. He looked towards Marazin and Orvyn. "Thank you for saving me," he said. "You could have left me to die. You must know Amron once ordered me to find and kill you both. I disagreed with his reasons. That's why I ignored the signs I found of you at Hafter's summer home. Before I left, I told Amron this was my last mission for him. If anyone comes after you again, it will not be me."

The longer he talked, the fainter his voice became. He tried to speak further, but the thoughts slipped from his mind. He muttered, his words incoherent. As his eyes lost focus, Marazin eased him into his blankets where he fell asleep.

"What do you think?" Marazin asked.

Orvyn's inclination was to believe Tedrick. Before the king's arrival, Tedrick had the reputation of being a dangerous and ruthless man, one difficult to control. Despite that, what had never been in doubt was his loyalty to his country and to those he served.

"I believe him," Karilyn said. Marazin and Orvyn nodded in agreement. "Amron, apart from marriage, discussed many subjects while I was his 'guest'. Not once was there any suggestion he'd betray his followers, he's too much in love with power for that."

"I agree with Tedrick, Amron has something else planned. He can't rely on your return alone," Karilyn said to Marazin. "The Mastig may well counteract Betlic's mind games with the talisman, but his men still outnumber the rebels by a huge margin. If we knew what his plans were, we could work with them."

"I fear," Marazin said, "he wants to use the talisman and mantle against Betlic. That cannot be allowed to happen. Those objects must disappear; anything else is out of our hands. I hope he knows what he's doing."

Marazin knew now that speed was more imperative than ever. Had Tedrick not been with them, Marazin and Karilyn would still have had to abandon Willa's group. Orvyn, for their protection, would stay with them. By the constant glances that passed between him and Willa, Karilyn expected the task to be less than onerous for him.

It was a sad farewell for the women. After many years apart, they had been able to rekindle their friendship, only for circumstances to separate them once more. Each was aware that, over the coming months, the other's chances of survival were low. Karilyn and Marazin were about to ride into one of the most dangerous regions on earth. Between the pair and the man they sought, was the largest army in known history. Their mission to reach one person, among thousands, appeared hopeless from the start.

As for Willa, she and her party must find their own way to the rebel stronghold. They risked contact with the many other outlaw bands that roamed the land. Later, they would face crossing Betlic's busy supply routes, then risk discovery by his forces on this side of the mountain. Even if they made it through, it was uncertain whether they would have reached a place of safety. Should the collective efforts of Marazin and Amron fail to gain victory over Betlic, Willa's position would be worse than ever. She would be at the centre of the enemy's lair.

A forlorn figure, she waved farewell as Marazin and Karilyn cantered back up the valley, past the falls. She felt an arm around her. It was Orvyn. She looked up at him. She read his expression and saw the compassion in his eyes. Willa smiled, placed her arm round him and squeezed. Without hesitation, he responded. Could her luck have changed? Not since her capture had Willa felt so content and secure.

Chapter Forty Six

Amron strode from his chambers, into the large hall at the centre of his palace. In this room, for several mornings most weeks, he had sat in judgement on his subjects' grievances. Most nights, this space had resounded to the raucous sounds of merrymaking. The silence was eerie. Outside, the royal guard was mustering. Apart from the king, the building was empty, as was the township spread out around it. The surrounding lands, too, were still. Everyone had left.

Those able to bear arms were moving north, to a new stronghold, perched high above the valley floor. Until help arrived, Amron hoped his new fortress would protect his followers. Women, children, the elderly and infirm were long-since dispersed among the mountains. Many had sought refuge behind the fortifications in the passes.

It would soon be a month since word reached the palace that Betlic's army was moving northwards. Within the population, this news caused disquiet, which was slow to abate. Amron made several fine rallying speeches, which helped to calm the mood.

At the time, a majority of council members were unhappy. When were they ever anything else? They demanded a meeting. There was a belief among them, shared by many of his commanders, that someone was betraying them — which, in truth, they were. It was too soon for Amron to admit his part in this.

Then, as now, his confidence in his plan was absolute. It had to work. With so many threads still to converge, it was difficult to explain. Without clear evidence, Amron doubted the High Council would have the patience, or courage, to carry his strategy through to its conclusion. They would either strike too soon, or, once they recognised the overwhelming odds against them, try to escape over the western mountains.

Not that such strategies lacked merit. In the short term, they might even bring limited success. Amron relied more on his instincts than military logic. Legend said, he was the one to lead the world against the evil that Betlic represented. If so, then in its own mysterious way, the magic that surrounded the Mastig must guide his thoughts. That he believed.

If the rebels fled, Betlic would be relentless in his hunt for them. His armies would spread out across the lands. For Marazin to be most effective in his use of the Mastig, Betlic's troops had to be in one place, massed together. Amron had everything set for this to happen. One thing he could not afford, was for knowledge of his proposals to become common before he was ready. Raulf was untrustworthy, that he knew, but was he the only one among the leadership, or their advisors, of whom Amron should be wary. With Betlic on his way, Grogant's emissary had outlived his usefulness. The High Council gathering, Amron decided, would offer him a good opportunity to unmask Raulf and divert any suspicions towards him.

Three weeks ago, Amron had convened the oft requested meeting. The assembly was long and ill-tempered. Listening to the droning voices, Amron's mind had wandered. At length, Waldhere, one of his generals, spoke about the need for urgent action. When he moved on to talk of traitors hiding in their midst, his words turned into a tirade about inadequate leadership at the top. Alert now, Amron listened to the acerbic barbs, calculated to show him in a poor light. The general wanted all power removed from the throne. He thought he saw a chance to replace the king as rebel leader.

His majesty was fair game. His popularity was low. Waldhere knew the pressure under which council members laboured. He expected them to follow his lead. Too often, this upstart boy king had interfered with their plans. If it came to a choice between Amron and him, Waldhere believed his fellow generals, and most of the civilian council attendees, would support him. They had led the rebel cause for years without benefit of a monarch. They could do so again.

Amron remained impassive. He was aware of his general's ambitions, as Waldhere was soon to discover. Amron continued to observe as one or two heads around the table nodded in agreement. He was quick to note, however, that most attendees distanced themselves from the general's comments. Amron had heard enough. He waited until the speaker paused for a moment, then he intervened. It was time to assert his position and deal with his most pressing issues — traitors and tiresome commanders.

Amron stood. His chair crashed onto the floor behind. With sword drawn, he walked round the table, towards the speaker. Waldhere stuttered.

He fell silent. It came as a surprise to him, to realise that a contingent of palace guards lined the walls of the room. By the dim light of the candles, he had not seen them enter. These men, handpicked for the occasion, were among the king's most loyal.

"Sit!" Amron said. It was only a single word, but its tone was one of menace.

As Waldhere sank into his seat, Amron addressed the others. "Our esteemed general does have a point. Although why he has chosen to divert suspicion towards the throne, instead of its true target, is a wonder. Do you have something to hide, Waldhere? We shall discuss this later."

Waldhere spluttered and made to rise. The flat of Amron's sword slammed onto the table beside the general's hand. He fell back, his face white. The man was neither a coward, nor a fool. To attack the king, without being certain of the complete backing of his fellows, would be unwise. Waldhere watched his supporters. They looked away, as Amron fixed each of them, one-by-one, with a piercing stare. Shame-faced, many hung their heads, while others stared at Waldhere in contempt. His followers were fewer, or less courageous, than his ego wanted him to believe.

"This petty back-biting stops, now. Do you understand?" Amron demanded. "The enemy approaches our gates, while you waste your efforts in plots to undermine me."

Amron ignored the series of half-hearted protests that his last statement generated. The murmuring ceased as he talked over it.

"I hear complaint after complaint that I discuss matters behind your backs. I don't deny the accusation. Let me ask a question. How do you think I know about Waldhere's 'secret' agenda for this meeting? I'll tell you — because none of you can keep anything to yourselves. Discussions that are confidential should remain so, but, within the day they become common knowledge. This ends, now. Unless *I* wish it, the details of our conversations here, or in private, remain between those involved. My people need facts relevant to them, nothing more. Rumour and falsehoods, generated by loose tongues, serve no other purpose than to lower morale."

Amron glared. Heads nodded in agreement. His majesty's words were close to the truth. For a while, those wisest among his senior command had conceded that the king's methods, although unorthodox, were innovative and worthy of their support. His mountain defences, for instance, had shown great value. These more open-minded members had not convinced Waldhere and his close allies. After today, such support might be forthcoming.

"Now, let us consider the little matter of traitors. On this point, Waldhere, I fear you may be correct," Amron shouted into his ear.

Unnerved, the man shifted in his chair. He would never pass-on information to the enemy, but would Amron believe him? Only moments ago, Waldhere had tried to usurp the king. His majesty might consider his scheming general capable of anything. Waldhere's mouth was dry. His life was now at stake. Amron straightened again. He resumed his position at the table's head. Once there, he remained standing. He spoke to the Vretlianan emissary, seated nearby, who was observing the proceedings.

"Raulf," he said. "Please, assist me by helping this man inside," he pointed towards a doorway, at one side of the room.

In the dim light, a prisoner leaned against his guard for support. As Raulf drew nearer, he turned pale. He slowed, then stumbled to a halt. Only now did he recognise his agent. The prisoner's inquisitors had been thorough in their work. Amron had kept him alive for such a moment. The frantic emissary sought some means of escape, but to no avail. Armed men spread further along the edges of the room. At a sign from Amron, another man moved to stand beside the captive. Between them, the guards' half dragged, half carried their charge further inside.

Raulf backed away. In desperation, he ran towards the doorway. Powerful arms grabbed hold of him. Others stripped him of his weapons. He tried to speak, but someone thrust a gag into his mouth. Members of the High Council stared, speechless, as the scene unfolded in front of them.

"I believe most of you have met King Grogant's emissary, Raulf," Amron said. "Here's someone who does have a secret. Since his arrival, he has tried his best to betray us all. This is your traitor. We caught his errand boy," Amron indicated the original prisoner, "on his return from passing information to Betlic. The go-between has confessed everything. It seems, for a long time, friend Raulf has been working for the enemy."

The king was sparing with the truth. To divulge the messenger's capture had taken place on his outward journey was too much of a risk. It could expose royal involvement in the deceit. The prisoner was incapable of contradicting anything. Since his confession, his inquisitors had removed his tongue.

At a signal from Amron, the guards released their hold on the captive. Head bent, he sank to his knees. Amron motioned to one of the guards. He raised his sword high in the air. The blade glistened in the candlelight. Razor-sharp, the weapon flashed downwards. The sound was horrific as the head fell free. It rolled along the floor, to stop at Raulf's feet. He fainted.

A flagon of water, poured over his face, revived him. He cowered in front of Amron. Stunned, the council watched-on as the king sheathed his weapon. A guard presented him with Raulf's sword. Amron tested its weight. He half turned, then plunged the blade, straight through the traitor's heart.

After the removal of the bodies, under escort, Waldhere followed. The general might have been the chief instigator of the movement against the throne, but he had not acted alone. Within minutes, four of his closest allies, joined him. Away from the palace, they were fortunate to face a swift and torture-free death. Could Amron have trusted them again? No! Neither could he afford for them to become a rallying point, for opposition to his rule. The much-subdued meeting progressed, without further dissension.

Later that day, a horrified Tamin learned about the earlier events. Again, his son's actions showed a total lack of self-control. For once, Amron displayed no adverse reaction as he endured Tamin's tongue-lashing. Afterwards, the king took his father to a secluded area of the palace grounds, where no-one could overhear them, or read their lips. There, Amron confided his plans to Tamin, and the truth behind Betlic's advance north.

After a long and heated conversation, Amron was grateful to receive Tamin's grudging approval. At best, the king's plan was risky, at worst, suicide. The more he thought about it, the more Tamin became convinced of its viability. He knew, too, that luck would play a major part, but he accepted his son's strategy was the only one that could defeat Betlic. Tamin needed no telling to keep silent. He was aware of the consequences should the story leak out. Only if something happened to Amron, could Hafter become privy to this. In such a situation, it would be up to Tamin to persuade the sage to help carry through the plan to fruition.

03 80

Now, weeks later, the room was empty. Only the stains on the floor remained. For Amron, the events had produced the desired result. His generals no longer troubled him with petty complaints, nor schemed behind his back. The rest of the High Council followed their example. The lesson had been brutal. They knew beyond doubt the steel within the character of the man who led them. They were aware of the penalty for disloyalty. Never had their co-operation been so resolute.

The king completed his lonely wander through his empty palace. He wondered if he would see it again. Failure or success, he thought not. Here, he had come to terms with his heritage, and accession to the throne. To learn of his position had frightened him. Too long a fool, his antics had been a distraction. They diverted him from the responsibilities that, unasked for, had descended on his young shoulders.

When young, instead of guiding a plough, or tending to crops, his parents should have been grooming him for his future role. He understood his mother's reservations, but the decision was not hers to make. Because of that, since he had known about his royal-lineage, he had rebelled in the way he knew best, that of a petulant child. Tamin's dressing-down, after Karilyn's escape, had lifted some of the blinkers from his eyes. After Tedrick's departure, Amron, for the first time, looked on his followers as people, rather than irritants sent to plague him.

Tedrick's insistence he marry, and that his new wife want for nothing in his absence, surprised the king. That a warrior, like Tedrick, might have feelings came as a shock. It had not occurred to Amron that ordinary people might harbour hopes and aspirations of their own. Since then, he had paid more attention to their complaints and expectations. He came to understand that, although despised by many and feared by others, he was the one to whom everyone looked. The belief was everywhere; only the king could see them through the dark times ahead. The realisation was humbling. It was only then he understood his duty as monarch transcended everything. When the fighting was over, it would matter little to Amron whether his countrymen liked or loathed him. What he craved most was something he had never commanded — their respect. This intangible was an accolade he must earn. To do that, he would drive himself ever harder.

The royal standard no longer flew from the palace roof. In the courtyard, a company of men watched as Amron walked towards them. As he settled into his saddle, his bodyguard mounted their horses. At the centre of his escort, without a backward glance, he moved out.

From the rebel scouts who tracked Betlic's progress, Amron knew the enemy would be at the mouth of the valley within weeks. Everything was in place. Amron had stayed behind, only because he awaited more messengers. Yesterday, the last of these had delivered a note of confirmation to Amron from one of his allies. His majesty wished he could be as certain of Marazin and Karilyn. Where, he wondered, were they now? Without them, what Amron planned would be difficult, nigh impossible to accomplish. Thoughts of revenge against the pair were long forgotten. Of equal importance, all three had his or her own part to play in the struggle ahead.

Several days later, Amron rode into the stronghold he hoped would keep safe his people. This, and his mountain defences, had depleted most of his available fortune. His standard soon flew from the walls overlooking the valley. He had relocated most of his lowland army into the surrounding hills. The rest he split between the northern end and eastern flanks of the central lowlands. Once Betlic's men broke through, those along the valley side would use hit-and-run tactics to delay him. Amron's intention was to draw enemy forces into the forested uplands. Here, traps and ambushes awaited them. Unless unavoidable, he wanted to avoid direct, large-scale confrontation. Amron settled down to wait. Whatever happened next was out of his hands.

Chapter Forty Seven

For most of the day, after Marazin and Karilyn's departure, Tedrick hovered between sleep and consciousness. The rest aided him. His condition improved. By evening, he no longer felt so unwell. His headache persisted, with an intensity that, at times, was severe; but his vision was closer to normal. Tedrick's wits were recovering, too. With a start, he recalled what he had wanted to say that morning. Now he had gained an insight into Amron's plans, Tedrick's knowledge was of importance. He became agitated. In vain, the others tried to persuade him not to ride after the pair. Only when his second attempt to stand caused him to pass out again, could Orvyn convince Tedrick he was unfit, yet, to travel.

Tedrick's information might have been helpful to the couple. Over the past year, Amron had brought together those with detailed knowledge of the peaks. Between them, they devised a way through the mountains, which remained hidden from Betlic's forces. Should the need arise, the intention was for the rebels to use it to escape. Of greater significance, Marazin and Karilyn could have reduced their journey-time by travelling the route in reverse.

After much consideration, Orvyn decided against riding after them. It would have left his current companions without protection. Neither did he know what path Marazin and Karilyn might take. Since the trio's departure from the mine, Heardwine had guided them. The moorland, to which the couple had returned, was either rock-strewn, baked hard by the sun or covered in a layer of heather. Such surfaces carried few traces of people's passing.

Orvyn was skilful enough to track them, but, with a full day's start, he doubted he could catch them. He abandoned the idea. It occurred to him, too, that it might be for the best. Amron's plans, he suspected, relied on the Mastig's intervention at a particular time. If Karilyn and Marazin reached him too soon, from an unexpected direction, it could create more problems than it solved.

Instead, Orvyn turned his attention towards the horses they had inherited from Betlic's men. Tedrick would ride his own horse. From the others, Orvyn, with the aid of Sheply, selected another five he judged had the greater stamina. With two to use as pack animals, the group's means of transport, for themselves and their supplies, was more than adequate. Orvyn released the unwanted ones into the wild.

Tedrick expressed confidence he would be ready to ride the following day. As expected, after a good night's sleep, he showed much improvement. Despite the injured man's apparent recovery, Orvyn refused to start their journey. The blow to Tedrick's head had been severe. An extra day's delay was not critical. Before they subjected him to the rigours of the trail, the patient would benefit from the rest. To Orvyn's satisfaction, this allowed him to enjoy the company of Willa for the greater part of the day. During the morning, the pair kept watch high above the camp while Sheply and Scard explored the valley. Later, after Tedrick climbed up to relieve them, the couple returned below to make preparations for their journey.

The horses were large, powerful beasts. Their riders would need a firm hand to handle them. Orvyn had to be certain Sheply and Willa could control the ones chosen for them. Scard could double-up with an adult. In the past, Sheply had ridden his father's packhorses. To Orvyn's relief, the youngster showed no fear. He rode with confidence. It was plain the horses' previous owners had taken care in the selection and training of the animals.

Without use of a side-saddle, Willa understand now Karilyn's chosen mode of dress. Among the supplies acquired from Talon's men, Willa uncovered a clean pair of trousers that would fit her. As she carried them away from the camp, she cringed at the thought of who might have worn them. Out of sight of the others, she split the sides of her tunic. The trousers she pulled on afterwards. On her return, Orvyn nodded his approval. Willa found mounting and riding her horse was now easier, and much less revealing.

After a short ride round the area, Willa returned to camp. She reined in, then swung her leg over the saddle. As she leapt to the ground, Orvyn put out his hands to catch her as she landed. Their heads were close together. Everything went still. Their lips brushed. Willa's senses were on fire. Orvyn's too! Their mouths parted, their tongues met. Locked in a passionate embrace, they remained until, from behind, spoke a young voice.

"Mama, what are you doing?"

In haste, they separated. For a second, their hands touched. Flushed, they stepped back. Willa turned to her son. She wore a smile that lit her whole face. He could not remember his mother looking so happy. He ran over and put his arms round her.

"Nothing, Scard," she said, her expression one of innocence.

She bent and hugged him. Orvyn laughed as he walked away, a spring in his step.

☙ ❧

Soon after dawn, with Orvyn at its head, the travellers rode out. For weeks, they kept as near to a westerly line as they could. In time, the moon waxed, waned and began its cycle again. It was then Orvyn's group entered the foothills of the Mogallean Mountains.

Their journey had not been without event. Once the travellers left their camp, they followed the path of the valley south. Before long, it cut through an escarpment that bordered the northern edge of once well-tended fields. The party turned west, to follow the line of the cliffs towards the distant Plains of Zefreelah.

Four days later, they rode into an ambush for the first time. Trapped in a narrow ravine, Tedrick was slow to respond. His reactions were sluggish. Sheply, who had armed himself from the plentiful supply of weapons at the mill, had raced, with Orvyn, to fight at Tedrick's side. While Willa took care of Scard, the others fought off the outlaws. It was not so much that the intended victims won, but, after losing three men, the surviving intruders withdrew. Plunder was easier elsewhere.

After this attack, both Orvyn and Tedrick spent time training Sheply and, to a lesser extent, Scard. After setting up camp, the two experienced warriors would teach the basic skills of swordsmanship to the young ones. Both boys were quick to learn.

Several days later, another band struck. On this occasion, Tedrick was back to full fitness. While Scard remained with his mother, Sheply proved his worth alongside his mentors. This time, the lawless group paid the ultimate penalty for their assault. Injuries inflicted on the travellers were slight, so they were able to travel without interruption.

The closer the party drew to the mountains, the more the riders remained on alert. Dust, from Betlic's frequent supply trains, filled the air. Orvyn and Tedrick alternated between riding ahead and guarding their rear. Several times they took cover as scouts from the convoys approached. It was soon clear, those who guarded these columns sought more to deter potential raiders, rather than engage them in combat. From then onwards, it was with greater confidence the group advanced. Provided they maintained a safe distance from the supply wagons, the travellers could ride unmolested.

Not until they entered the foothills did the level of danger increase with any significance. Because of constant harassment by the rebels, convoys for Betlic's mountain forces were under much heavier guard. Armed patrols were a frequent hazard.

Although a close friendship may always have been beyond Orvyn and Tedrick, a mutual trust and respect developed between the pair. In the situations they faced, each learned he could depend upon the other without reservation. When conflict was unavoidable, they fought, side-by-side, back-to-back against groups of Betlic's men they encountered in the hills.

Tedrick led them north, into the mountains, away from Betlic's main thrust. Enemy patrols became fewer. Late one day, as the travellers rounded a bend in a narrow path, high above a winding valley, Tedrick found the landmark he sought. In the distance stood towering cliffs, into which millennia of wind and rain had carved an uncanny likeness to a human face.

By mid-morning the following day, the party was riding, dwarfed, beneath the rock face. From out of a wide slit, in the base of the scar, a river flowed. At the height of summer, as now, the waters were shallow and slow moving. Tedrick led his companions into the flow, to follow its path upstream.

Once they reached the entrance to the cavern, from which the river disgorged, the riders dismounted. With a tight hold onto the reins, the travellers led their horses into the darkness. Orvyn could see, in the distance, a faint glimmer. Tedrick took the lead. It was through this passage he had made his way through enemy lines, on his outward journey.

The glow, when reached, was a broad shaft of light, beamed down from the surface through a crevice in the rock. In total darkness, on they splashed. Sometimes the sound of their passing echoed as if they were in a vast chamber. At other times, the roof and walls closed in around them. Here, the water deepened, and the current flowed faster. Roped together, they waded knee-deep through the icy waters. Here, Sheply carried Scard on his back, while Tedrick took control of his horse. The darkness made the animals nervous. To calm them, the travellers talked to them in low tones.

The gloom ahead became less intense, their surroundings clearer. From beyond a bend, light was coming. Once round the corner they could see, through a gap, a sunlit ravine. Relieved, they increased their pace towards the open air. To their left, beside the river, was a grassy bank. They led their horses onto it.

The slope brought them to a narrow band of grassland. On each side of the gorge, cliffs rose high. In front of them, stretched-out between rock face and river's edge, the travellers faced a line of bowmen. The newcomers fell silent. Had Tedrick led them into a trap? He ignored the weapons. In a loud and clear voice, He explained who he was. It was fortunate that, since Tedrick's departure, the leader of the gorge's defenders was still in command at the post. The man recognised the speaker and, at a word from him, his archers lowered their bows.

Orvyn relaxed. This situation was one that should have occurred to him. Once Amron had established a safe route through the mountains, common sense dictated he would have to keep a strong presence to guard over it. What his people might use to escape, the enemy, if they discovered it, could employ to infiltrate the rebel base.

It was past noon. They had spent longer underground than Orvyn had realised. Inside the ravine, heated by the mid-day sun, the air soon dried their clothes. Scard and Sheply stayed close to Willa while Tedrick and Orvyn spoke with the captain. It was a short conversation. Further along the gorge, behind a newly built defensive wall, was a permanent encampment. With a guide to vouch for the new arrivals, the travellers continued towards the site. There they would stay the night. In the morning, with an armed escort, they would begin the final stage of their journey across the mountains.

Orvyn was unsure how warm would be his reception. Tedrick was less pessimistic. He owed his life to Orvyn and would allow nothing to happen to him. In truth, so Tedrick believed, Amron's concerns would focus on the Mastig's progress. Rather than revive old enmities, he would welcome, without reservation, the bearer of good news.

Chapter Forty Eight

Alongside his companions, Orvyn reached a high point on the trail. Each day, since leaving the rebel camp, the party had ridden hard. Once the travellers were safe within rebel-controlled territory, most of their escort had returned to base. Now, two weeks later, only a pair of guides remained with them.

At various strategic places along the route, the group had passed through defences that showed evidence of recent construction. Unlike the fortifications, which blocked the passes to the south, these were of earth and boulder mounds, topped with wooden palisades. Their purpose was to delay an advance, rather than halt one. These established camps provided good food and a bed for the night. Whenever convenient, the travellers stayed overnight at these sites.

The riders spread out as they came to a stop. For a moment, they paused to look down towards their destination. It would be another day before they reached the lower ground; but, in the bright morning light, the view lifted their spirits. The hills sank away to a valley far below, which snaked north and south. On the opposite side of this splash of green, distant peaks glowed in the sun's rays. Dark patches covered large areas of the valley bottom. From these, columns of smoke rose high into the still air.

"Betlic's men and their camp sites," their escort said.

The others nodded. The travellers had stayed overnight with a group of rebels, who brought them up-to-date with the latest news. With a part of his army, Amron had moved his court to a stronghold that overlooked the valley bottom. Since then, Betlic's armies had arrived. These had spread out to fill the low ground in front of the bastion. From Amron's citadel, his men mounted limited action sallies against the invaders.

Elsewhere, outnumbered as they were, the rebels used guerrilla tactics. In small groups, without warning, they engaged the enemy. After causing maximum damage and chaos, they retreated once more to higher ground. Back among the hills, any of Betlic's men tempted to follow, faced ambushes or traps. On most occasions, those in pursuit sustained losses much more serious than the raiders they chased.

In these raids, despite their targets being under heavy guard, the rebels destroyed, or damaged, large numbers of siege towers and mangonels under construction. Much against advice, Amron had taken charge of several missions himself. Although well-guarded, he refused to hide behind his men. He had triumphed in several skirmishes. While the people's respect for their king had risen, certain matters remained of concern to the High Council. In particular, Amron's reasons for choosing this place to make a stand. It was an ideal defensive position, but the possibilities of escape from it were few.

Amron seemed content to let weeks pass without a major offensive. His generals and the High Council were restless. Only those whose loyalty was beyond doubt had retained their places in the king's inner circle, yet even they found Amron's inertia frustrating. When pressed, the king would say, 'Everything would become clear in time, they must have patience'. These words did little to satisfy his senior followers.

By noon the following day, Orvyn and his party were descending a steep and winding track. Concealed by woodland from the valley below, the path led towards the base of the cliffs, beneath which Amron's stronghold lay. The closer the riders drew, the more a feeling of dread settled upon them. Although somewhat diminished by elements in the land, the talisman's power was still a significant influence on their minds. Orvyn could feel his willpower weaken as they descended. Somehow, the defenders below had survived. If they could endure, so could he. He prayed Marazin's arrival would take place soon. No-one, apart from him, could halt this debilitating assault upon their minds.

At barriers along the track, armed sentries waved through the party. Most recognised both Tedrick and Orvyn. Under the king's strict instructions, if either was to return, no-one should hinder their passage. Orvyn's concern about his reception lessened. One of their guides rode ahead, to warn of the party's coming. As a result, a group of riders gathered at the gates of the stronghold. When Orvyn saw them, he feared a trap.

Cyneweard, the man in charge, soon allayed his fears. "Tedrick, Orvyn, welcome back!" he said. He shook their hands. "We're here to keep away the curious, until the king's spoken with you all. He wishes to be the first to hear your stories. Please, follow me. We've quarters prepared for you both."

"What about our companions?" Orvyn asked.

"There are several rooms," Cyneweard said, "enough to accommodate you all. You may make whatever arrangements you like, once you reach them."

"Eadgyth, my wife, where is she? Is she safe?" Tedrick demanded to know. "I want to be with her. Our separation has been too long."

"She's in good health. As I said, Amron doesn't want your story to become public knowledge, until he's ready. She awaits you in your quarters."

Orvyn's eyebrows rose. Tedrick's outburst was a revelation. That he had taken a wife was news. From his expression, it was clear he was anxious to be with her. This new status might explain his reluctance to undertake any future missions for Amron.

"Where's the king?" Tedrick asked, as they rode at a trot round the edge of the fortress.

"He's below the cliffs, leading a raid against Betlic's men," Cyneweard said. "Overnight, they moved forward more siege weapons. The king hopes to destroy them before they can bring them into operation."

"When will he return?" Orvyn asked.

"It could be late this evening, or early in the morning. It depends on whether Betlic's men chase his majesty into the hills. Many times, we've ambushed the enemy there and inflicted heavy losses; it's rare now for them to follow."

The citadel, the newcomers found much larger than expected. On dirt tracks, they rode through a maze of huts and tented areas before they approached their quarters. Near to them, at the other side of the plateau, their path took them closer to the battlements that overlooked the valley. Orvyn studied them with interest. Only where they abutted the hills, at either side of the rear cliffs, did the defences have any significant height.

No taller than a grown man, the walls were rough-hewn and angled outwards. On the outer edges of the walkways, behind the ramparts, Orvyn observed two distinct types of openings. Most were slits, through which archers could fire their arrows downwards. In among those gaps, were channels for use with boiling oil, the majority of which were on either side of a large gateway. Should the enemy gain control of the roadway that twisted down the cliff side, those on the ramparts could pour the substance onto them.

Panicked cries of alarm came from the watch who manned the wall. Cyneweard turned his horse and raced towards the nearest sentry.

"What is it?" he shouted over the noise.

"It's the king's force," the man replied. "Betlic's men have them surrounded. His majesty's in grave danger."

Tedrick and Orvyn, who had ridden after Cyneweard, heard the news.

"What's the quickest way to reach the valley bottom?" Orvyn demanded.

"Through the gateway, then down the cliff road," Cyneweard answered.

"Open the gates," Tedrick commanded. "You," he ordered one of their escorts, "take the woman and children to their quarters."

As he drew his sword, Orvyn shouted to those keeping watch on the walls. "Quick, all of you, follow us."

Willa looked on in despair as Orvyn turned away his horse. The gateway swung open. He moved at speed towards the gap, followed by Tedrick and Cyneweard's group of riders. Against their escort's wishes, Willa, Scard and Sheply dismounted. They ran to the walls, which had emptied when the watch followed the riders. With the alarm raised, scores of soldiers hurried from their billets. A commander arrived to take charge. Most of the newcomers, he ordered to keep watch over the battlements. Several men, who came on horseback, he ordered to join the rescue party.

The siege weapons had been bait to draw out the rebels. At dawn, few guards were visible around the machines. Unknown to the king's men, under cover of darkness, dozens of others had placed themselves among the many dead that littered the ground. Once the raiders reached the weapons, the 'dead' had risen to surround the rebel band. To find Amron in command of the raiding party was a stroke of fortune for Betlic's men.

As Orvyn sped down the twisting path, he could see the mêlée around Amron's position. In the distance, a much larger enemy-force was converging on the scene. To Orvyn's relief, Amron was on his feet, though fighting for his life. The rescue party had to reach him before the enemy re-enforcements arrived, otherwise, his death was certain.

Once the riders reached the bottom of the cliff road, a thick, high wall obscured the events taking place on the valley floor. Those on guard rushed to lift the baton that secured the heavy wooden gates. The rescue party milled around at the gatehouse, while those on duty lowered a long ramp.

Before the platform touched the ground, Orvyn's horse galloped along the wooden planks. The animal leapt the short distance onto the hard-packed surface. The other riders followed. Behind them, along with the watch from above, the guard took up position around the entrance. At the first sign of movement towards it, the defenders would move inside, pull up the ramp and bar the gates. Anyone still outside, including his majesty, would have to take their chances. The stronghold's security took precedence.

The brief hold-up had allowed a dozen or more riders to catch up with the leading group. Within minutes, the enlarged party approached their beleaguered king and his men. The fighting was taking place within the confines of a small depression. The newcomers' arrival, over the rim, was without warning. Low in the saddle, the horsemen swept in, their swords wreaking havoc among Betlic's men. They swung round their horses, to attack again. Moments after this second onslaught, the riders leapt from their saddles and engaged with the enemy. Of the original rebel group, only Amron and three others remained. They were hard-pressed. Orvyn put into use everything he had learned sparring with Marazin and Karilyn. He fought his way to stand beside the king. Seconds later, Tedrick joined them.

Once Amron realised who his saviours were, the look of relief on his face was for much more than his unexpected rescue. If Orvyn had returned, the Mastig, too, must be near. With renewed hope, Amron launched himself at his opponents with a fury that was unstoppable.

More riders rode in from the stronghold. Soon, the sound of clashing swords fell silent. The fighting was at an end. A sudden whirr filled the air. Arrows thudded onto the lip of the hollow, at the edge furthest away from the cliffs. It was time to leave. Orvyn gathered up the reins from a horse, whose rider would no longer need it. He thrust them into the king's hands.

"Ride now, your Majesty," he urged, "before Betlic's men reach us."

A dozen men formed a guard round Amron as he galloped towards the cliffs. Orvyn looked back. White-faced, Tedrick was on the ground, a gaping wound in his side. Orvyn grabbed a cloak from a body nearby. He pushed it hard against Tedrick's injury to staunch the blood flow.

"Leave me," Tedrick whispered as Orvyn helped the injured man to his feet. "Save yourself, before Betlic's men arrive."

"No! Keep that cloth pressed against the wound," Orvyn said, as he half-carried half-dragged Tedrick towards his horse.

More arrows landed close to the pair. Strong arms came to Orvyn's aid. The last two remaining rescuers gathered up Tedrick. They threw him onto the back of his horse. Cyneweard, one of the men who had stayed, slapped the animal on its rump. Orvyn and the others leapt onto their own mounts, then dug in their heels. Once they cleared the hollow, they could see the wounded man was nearing the ramp. His horse had slowed to a trot, its rider swaying in the saddle. Tedrick was losing consciousness.

Orvyn tore after the man in front. More arrows followed the riders, but they were out of range. He risked a glance over his shoulder. A line of mounted men galloped towards them. They were gaining fast. Orvyn urged his horse to greater effort. Ahead, Tedrick had come to a halt. He slumped over in the saddle. Orvyn pulled up in a cloud of dust as he drew alongside the stationary animal. He leapt onto its back, then leaned forward to lock his arms round Tedrick. Cyneweard grabbed the reins. From the gatehouse, arrows flew overhead as the group approached it.

Behind the last rescuer, the ramp rose as Betlic's horsemen approached. A hail of arrows cut down the leaders. Their comrades retreated to a safer distance. Had not Amron insisted the way stay open until all his rescuers reached safety, the last group would have perished. Orvyn rode up the slope without stopping. He needed to find aid for his injured companion.

Orvyn dismounted. Willing hands helped him lift Tedrick from his horse. Orvyn turned as Willa ran to him. She threw her arms around him. With tears in her eyes, she held him close. Seconds later, Scard arrived. He, too, clung to Orvyn. Until that moment, he had not realised how much they cared for him, and he for them. He held Willa until she calmed. Sheply joined them. Together, their escort led them to their quarters. Of Tedrick, there was no sign. He was elsewhere, his wounds in need of urgent attention.

As Orvyn and his companions entered a large hut, set away from most others, a richly attired woman greeted them. A few years older than Willa, the woman's hair was a striking red and plaited. Crow's feet wrinkles around her green eyes were indicative of a more usual cheerful disposition. Now, her face expressed deep concern. Orvyn guessed this might be Eadgyth.

"Tedrick, my husband, where is he?" she demanded to know. "The people who brought me here said he'd returned. That disturbance, moments ago, what caused that? Was Tedrick involved? I ask question after question, but nobody will tell me anything."

"Betlic's men ambushed the king," Willa said, her voice soft and gentle. "Tedrick helped rescue him. In doing so, I'm afraid he's received a severe injury. When Orvyn brought him back, healers took him away."

Eadgyth's face paled, but she neither fainted, nor cried out.

"Thank you," she said, "for telling me." Turning to the man who had escorted the newcomers to the house, she pleaded, "Please, take me to my husband, now, I must see him and tend to his wounds."

"I'm sorry," he replied. "My orders are to keep everybody here."

"Well, my husband is elsewhere," Eadgyth's voice was rising with her anger. "His condition is grave and he's with strangers. I've no knowledge of what information these people bear, so I cannot pass-on any of it. I'm leaving. You can either take me to him, or I'll climb over you and find him myself."

"Take her, now," Willa said, an icy touch to her voice.

She stepped in front of Orvyn as his hand moved towards his bloodstained sword. The confrontation was in danger of escalating.

"Believe me," she said, "you don't want my man to force you to do this."

The escort looked uncomfortable. From the walls, he had watched the king's rescue and observed Orvyn in action. He capitulated. As she strode out, Eadgyth whispered her thanks to Willa.

Chapter Forty Nine

Despite the birth of a new day, the early morning darkness remained absolute. Inside a small, one roomed hut, several flickering candles relieved the gloom. Covered in a blanket of fur, Tedrick lay on a narrow bed, only his face visible in the wavering light. His condition was desperate. Hafter had not long-since returned to his quarters. Once aware of how serious was the wounded man's injury, Amron had summoned the sage. Hafter took one look at the gaping wound, then abandoned most of his array of potions and salves. For hours, he laboured over his charge. He was not hopeful. The internal damage was too severe.

For now, Tedrick was calm. Eadgyth was by his side, keeping a solitary vigil. She held his hand in hers. As the heavens lightened, her husband became restless. His eyes opened for brief moments. Each time, once his frenzied gaze found his wife, he settled again. A grey tinge appeared in the sky to the east. It lightened to the palest of blues. To the west, the tips of the highest mountains caught the first rays of the rising sun. Birds stirred. The patient regained consciousness. The dawn chorus had never sounded so beautiful to him. Tedrick looked up at Eadgyth. He was a lucky man. She returned his smile as she wiped away a tear. He squeezed her hand and whispered something to her. She bent down and, with great tenderness, kissed him on the cheek. Minutes passed, the final candle flickered. It died. In that moment, Eadgyth entered widowhood for the second time.

08 80

The previous afternoon, when Amron had visited Tedrick, the man had drifted in and out of consciousness. When awake, his speech was rambling and incoherent. It was clear to the king he would learn nothing from the patient that day. Instead, Amron knelt beside Tedrick, to thank him for his loyal service. It was doubtful the injured man heard or understood. Soon afterwards, Hafter arrived. He demanded everyone leave, so he could tend to the wound. Eadgyth, who had joined them, refused. One look at her worried face was enough for the sage to agree to let her assist him.

From there, Amron went to the cabin where his men had taken Orvyn. A guard ran ahead to announce the king's arrival. Amron dismissed his bodyguards' fears when he told them to wait outside the door. If Orvyn intended harm to his majesty, he would have left him to the mercy of Betlic's troops.

The king entered the room. Belongings lay strewn across the floor. In the midst of this chaotic scene, looking somewhat apprehensive, were the item's owners. Willa curtseyed, Orvyn bowed low. Sheply and Scard, unsure how they should react, copied Orvyn. They, too, bent their heads towards Amron.

"Your Majesty," Orvyn said, "you honour us with your presence."

"That is not so," Amron disagreed as he moved towards Orvyn. "I'm the one who feels honoured by yours."

The king held out his hand in a gesture of reconciliation. Orvyn reached out. The two men shook hands. Once Amron's firm grasp and its intent became clear, Orvyn's hesitation faded. He returned the welcome with enthusiasm.

"Come, let us sit down," Amron said, "then you can tell me everything that's happened, since you left with Marazin and Karilyn."

The king's lack of animosity, as he mentioned the couple, caused Orvyn to raise an eyebrow. He could not stop himself. Amron was quick to notice.

"I believe there might have been some, er, misunderstandings in the past," Amron admitted, after a brief awkward silence. "I now have a better understanding of my position, and the roles of others. Both my father and Hafter have made it plain how loyal you remained to the undertaking you gave me, the day we met and fought. It was I who went astray. I was unprepared for the responsibility. When this struggle is over, you and your friends have nothing to fear from me. You are free to come or go as you wish. Now, tell me; Marazin and Karilyn, were they successful?"

"Yes, your Highness. Marazin possesses the Mastig," Orvyn answered.

"Why aren't they with you?" Amron was desperate to know.

Orvyn explained how he and his companions had met with Tedrick, Willa and the boys. Before he related the full details of the fight at the mill, Orvyn retrieved something from one of his packs.

"I have a gift for you, your Majesty, from Marazin."

He handed the cloth-wrapped packet to the king. By its weight and shape, Amron knew at once it was a weapon. He pulled back the fabric. Underneath was a sword, similar to his own. It bore a remarkable resemblance to the one that had caused him to accuse Marazin of theft, and murder. It carried the same maker's mark as did the others but, as Tamin had said, it was shorter. Wound around the hilt was a chain with a silver mounted eagle's talon attached. Amron looked at the object with utmost loathing.

"The person who wore this trinket, and possessed this sword, what became of him?" demanded Amron.

"That was Talon, your Majesty, the man you've sought for many years. He refused to surrender. Marazin killed him in a fight. We buried Talon with his companions."

"Good," Amron said. There was satisfaction in his voice. "The return of my mother's sword will give my father great pleasure. At the earliest opportunity, we both shall thank Marazin. Please, continue with your tale."

Orvyn nodded. He explained how, because of the blow to Tedrick's head, Marazin and Karilyn had set off without knowledge of the hidden way through the mountains.

"How is Tedrick, your Highness?" Orvyn asked. His travelling companion's condition was of great concern. "When shall we be able to visit him?"

"His condition is critical," Amron said. "His wife and Hafter are at his side, tending to his injury. I saw him a short while ago. I was a hindrance, as you will be tonight. Wait until morning. If he survives the night, you may try then. If he doesn't, Eadgyth is with him. I believe he would prefer that above anything else."

Orvyn nodded. It would be better to leave them alone, until circumstances altered, either way.

"Marazin and Karilyn, where might they be?" Amron asked. He needed most an answer to this question. Everything he had been working towards depended on Orvyn's response.

"They can't be too far away. If not already at the entrance to the valley, they must be close by, a few days ride at most before they reach it."

A wave of relief flowed over Amron. It would be premature for him to inform the High Council, but that would happen soon. Then he would retaliate, with the might of all the forces at his disposal — forces much greater than anyone here could suspect.

Orvyn could tell the king only what Tedrick had revealed about his dealings with Betlic. As Amron was the person who had charged him with his mission, Tedrick felt it only right the king should hear the details first. Amron was not too disappointed. Betlic's men were inside the valley, at the time he needed them to be. To his majesty, this was sufficient proof that Tedrick's mission had been successful. Amron hoped the man lived long enough to appreciate the results of his work.

It was late evening before Orvyn had satisfied the king's thirst for knowledge. At his insistence, Orvyn repeated his tale several times. Willa's story, too, held much interest for Amron. The details of how she evaded Talon for so long delighted the king. Anyone who had the better of that devil deserved his majesty's respect. As Amron made to leave, Orvyn gave Willa a look of great fondness. A lift of his eyebrows seemed to ask an unspoken question. She nodded. Her face lit up as she smiled.

"Your Majesty," Orvyn said. "We wondered if we could ask one small thing of you before you go."

"Then ask! Anything, I'm in your debt!"

"It would be a great honour, your Highness, if you would bear witness to our marriage," Willa said, her voice quavering as she came to stand at Orvyn's side.

He took her hand. "We've seen what's befallen Tedrick and Eadgyth. If something similar happened to us, we would want to have shared a part of our lives first."

Amron looked at them in surprise. He smiled. This was unexpected. Others would have sought financial gain. These two had a less mercenary priority. For that, once his battles were over, Amron would bestow on them a handsome reward.

"Guard," he shouted.

They charged through the doorway, their swords raised.

"Put away your weapons," he said, "You're here to bear witness to this couple's marriage. Now, Orvyn and Willa, kneel, and speak your vows."

The pair knelt, facing each other, in front of the king. His men, with Scard and Sheply, encircled them. As was customary, Orvyn and Willa clasped each other's right hand in their own.

"Do you, Orvyn, take me to be your wife?" Willa asked.

"I do," Orvyn replied. "Do you, Willa, take me to be your husband?"

"I do," Willa said, a beaming smile on her face.

She leant forward to throw her arms round Orvyn.

"I bear witness to this marriage," Amron said, "as do these men. I wish you both a long and happy life together."

The couple stood as everyone congratulated them. The king stayed for a short while then excused himself. He took not only his guards, but Sheply and Scard went too. Amron decided the boys should spend the night under Tamin's roof, with him and Mildthryth. The door closed. Orvyn and Willa were alone. They embraced. Neither knew what the coming days and weeks might hold. They would treat every moment together as if their last, content in the delight of each other.

ೞ ೞ

An hour or two after dawn, Hafter returned to visit his patient. At the sage's advanced age, it was rare for him to sleep late. He wanted to see if Tedrick's condition showed any improvement — not that he expected any. The wound was too deep, the internal damage beyond his skills to repair. Hafter found it surprising that no-one had fetched him during the night. He tapped on the door. There was no answer. He tried again, louder this time. Concerned at still no response, he opened the latch and called out for Eadgyth. Silence! Worried, he looked inside. Apart from the shaft of light through the doorway, the chamber was in darkness. He hastened outside to throw open the shutters. Without a wasted moment, he hurried back.

Deep in shadow, at one corner of the room, Hafter could see the cot. Beneath the blankets lay the figure of Tedrick. Eadgyth was half-lying across her husband, her head resting beside his. In dread, Hafter moved closer. It was clear Tedrick had died. At first, the sage feared Eadgyth, in her grief, might have taken her own life. Hafter put out his hand. Her neck was cool, not icy, her pulse steady. At his touch, she stirred. Her eyes opened. Eadgyth's face, stained by the fall of many tears, stared at him, her expression blank. She allowed Hafter to help her to her feet.

Without haste, he led her from the building. With an arm round her, to prevent her from collapsing, he escorted her to the house of Tamin. There, after a brief explanation about what had taken place, he left the widow in Mildthryth's care. Amron's quarters were nearby; several guards were on duty outside his door. Hafter called on one of them to follow him. He made his way back to Tedrick where he confirmed the man was dead.

As Hafter covered Tedrick's face, he commanded the one who had followed him to break the news to Amron. Hafter had sympathy for the man's widow, but could summon little for Amron's lackey. In his opinion, Tedrick was no better than an assassin. As yet, the sage new nothing about the service the man had performed for his king, nor of his recent struggles at Orvyn's side.

His majesty arrived within minutes. He pulled back the blanket and gazed upon Tedrick's face. Amron replaced the cover. He bowed his head in silence for a short while before he turned to the sage.

"He was a courageous man, Hafter," the king said. "Please make arrangements for his funeral later today, one befitting a hero."

"As you wish, your Highness," Hafter could not keep the contempt out of his tone.

"Yes, I do wish. You've no idea what this man has endured for king and country. Until I make these deeds known, you've no right to judge him."

Amron spoke without rancour. Hafter had good reason to despise the fallen warrior. Soon he would learn details of Tedrick's mission, which might alter his opinion for the better. Before Hafter could respond, one of Amron's guards hurried through the doorway.

"Your Majesty," he urged. "Please, come outside, there's something you must see."

Curious, both Amron and Hafter followed the man. Out in the open, they looked to where he pointed. To the north of the plateau, along the edge of the mountains, a series of beacons was ablaze. Thin columns of smoke rose into the air. Amron felt his spirits rise. He had waited long for this moment.

"What is it?" Hafter asked. "Are we under attack?"

Like everyone else, he had no awareness of what these signals might portend. Only the king and those who attended them knew of their existence.

"It means everything." Amron's face carried a broad smile. "I will explain all, soon."

He summoned his guards, who he commanded to fetch every available council member, and Tamin, to the hall beside his quarters.

"Hafter, I wish you, too, to be present at this meeting. But first you must disturb the newlyweds. Orvyn's attendance is necessary."

"Orvyn? He's back? What newlyweds?" Hafter asked, confused.

Secrecy over the newcomers' arrival had extended to Hafter, more by default than intent. The sage's thoughts had been much too occupied on treating Tedrick's injuries. He had not thought to question the details of the man's sudden reappearance. Once finished with his patient, Hafter had returned to his quarters. As a result, he knew nothing about the events that led to Tedrick's wounding.

"Last night, your old friend Orvyn married Willa, the woman who arrived with him and Tedrick yesterday," Amron said. "Go. Offer your congratulations to them. Apologise for the interruption, but you must tear Orvyn away from her charms for a while. I need his support. Be gentle when you break the news of Tedrick's death to them. They fought their way to reach here, side by side."

In astonishment, Hafter stared after the king as he strode off towards his quarters. Amron's cares appeared to have diminished. For once, his majesty was cheerful. Hafter smiled. If Orvyn was inside the citadel, the Mastig must be near. Despite his advanced years, he skipped towards the hut Amron had indicated.

The door, barred from the inside, resisted Hafter's attempts to open it. He rapped on the wooden panels. After several moments, he banged again, harder. A muffled voice told him to wait. Soon, the sound of movement came from inside. The door swung open. An attractive young woman, flushed of face, invited him to enter. From behind her, into Hafter's sight, stepped a figure he knew well. It was true, Orvyn had returned.

Chapter Fifty

From out of the distance, two tiny dots appeared. As these drew nearer, they resolved into figures on horseback. They followed the route of the valley bottom. A large dog ran from the undergrowth to join them. Together, the three continued their approach. Lit by the glow of the setting sun, their shadows lengthened.

Concealed behind bushes, on top of the northern ridge, two men studied the riders' progress. In silence, the pair stretched-out on the warm ground, their bows beside them. A stream meandered through the valley. Its waters, below the men's position, had formed a pool. Here the travellers halted. The sun slipped below the horizon. In the gloom, their features were indistinct. Westward, the fiery orange and scarlet sunset faded to grey.

The watchers moved into a kneeling position. They had a decision to make. If those below were agents of Betlic, enough light remained to target them with an arrow. The riders dismounted. Snatches of their conversation carried up the hillside. It was clear, only one was a man. The watchers relaxed. Betlic's forward patrols rarely, if ever, included women. Neither were these two dressed in the uniform of the enemy. So, who were they? A few hours ride away, on the other side of the ridge opposite, stood the entrance to the rebel lands. Well-armed, the pair did not appear to be refugees. Despite their closeness to Betlic's supply routes, neither seemed nervous nor apprehensive.

The observers moved closer, to verify their suspicions. Moments later, the man took something from his saddle. Circular in shape, the article emitted a green light that flickered and sparked. The onlookers glanced at each other. They had their confirmation — a man, a woman, a dog, and a strange object. These were the ones for whom the watchers had waited. In silence, they withdrew from the hilltop to descend the slope behind the ridge. Several hundred paces away, they untethered their horses, then rode north.

By the time the riders reached their destination, darkness was complete. Without delay, the pair found themselves in front of their leader.

King Almeric looked up from his meal. His eyes were alight with expectation. He had sent observers to various locations, to watch over the many trails that led towards the rebel lands. These two were the first to return.

"Well, what news do you bring? Have you seen them?" The king was impatient for an answer.

"We believe so," Eglath, one of the pair said. Then, with help from Octha, his companion, he described what they had seen.

"Did you make contact with them?" Almeric asked.

"No, your Highness," Octha said. "We followed your orders. The couple wore swords. To have approached them in near darkness, so close to enemy territory, might have provoked an unwelcome response."

"You did well. If only a part of what I've heard is true, I fear you'd have been no match for them. However, it's their well-being that concerns us, not their demise. I have little doubt they are the ones we seek. Tomorrow, at first light, I shall meet with them."

He dismissed the two. Others, he sent to fetch his commanders. It was time to move out. Almeric, King of Vernalaka, his people known better as marshlanders, was ready. With thousands of his followers, he had come to play his part in Amron's plans. Almeric hoped the Xicaliman king's strategy was sound. As for a viable alternative — the marshlander had nothing less risky he could offer.

03 80

In the chill morning air, arms around each other, heads touching, Marazin and Karilyn watched as the sun rose above the horizon. Neither had slept during the short summer's night. It was more thoughts about the day to come, rather than desire that kept them from their slumbers, although that had helped to divert their minds. Today they embarked on the final stage of their journey.

Once they crossed the ridge and moved south, their lives would be in permanent danger from Betlic's patrols. The couple held each other in a tight embrace. For them there might be no tomorrow. They lingered long over one last kiss. With regret, they broke apart. Their obligations took precedence over their personal happiness. They untethered the packhorse and allowed it to roam free. The supplies it carried they abandoned. They were no longer of use. Their canteens, and the several days' food they needed, were of little burden to their own horses. Whatever happened afterwards, either they would be with friends, or dead.

Their preparations complete, the pair mounted. Both riders ensured their swords moved with ease inside their scabbards. A flicker of movement caught Karilyn's eye. She looked upwards, towards the northern ridge. She called out an urgent warning to Marazin. It was too late. Along the hilltop, as far as she could see, lines of horsemen had taken-up position. To the east and west, large numbers of them had ridden into the valley. Within moments, they had moved to surround the couple. The newcomers kept their distance. Cloaked in dark-brown mantels, their hooded faces remained deep in shadow.

On the northern ridge, the line parted. several men on horseback descended towards the pair. Karilyn had her sword in her hand, raised and ready. Although dressed unlike any adherents of Betlic's she had seen, she was suspicious.

"Put away your weapon," Marazin whispered. "These are marshlanders, allies of the rebels."

Karilyn was reluctant to do so. Her duty was to protect her lover, the heir, at any cost. She compromised, by laying the sword flat in front of her. No longer held in a confrontational manner, if required, she could bring the weapon to bear in an instant. Without warning, apart from the men who drew near, the surrounding army threw back their hoods. Uneasy, Karilyn shifted in the saddle. Marazin understood the message they sent.

"It's all right," he said. "Marshlanders remove their head coverings when going to war. Those coming to meet us retain theirs. They are letting us know their fight is with Betlic, not us."

Karilyn acknowledged Marazin's words, but remained unconvinced. Her sword stayed where it was, her hand clasped round the hilt. She relaxed more when she saw Heardwine wag his tail. The dog sensed no threat. The riders halted several paces away from the couple. Their leader nudged his horse a few steps nearer.

"Greetings," uttered a deep voice. "I am Almeric, King of Vernalaka. At war, or among friends, we go bareheaded. I hope to count you as the latter," he said as he lifted his hands and pushed back his hood.

Despite the regular covering of his head, his face was brown from extended exposure to the elements. Pockmarks from childhood illness marred the leathery cheeks. Long black hair, streaked with grey, fell to his shoulders. A braided leather band round his forehead kept the strands away from his face. Under bushy eyebrows, his eyes were brown, set deep over high cheekbones in a narrow face. His gaze remained steady. With a squat nose, thin lips and pronounced chin, the king was not the most handsome of men. His shoulders were broad, his hands massive. A powerful man, in both physical and mental outlook, he carried himself with the air of someone comfortable with his position. Marazin was glad they were not enemies.

"Greetings to you, your Majesty," he said. "I am Marazin. With my companion, Karilyn, we travel to join with King Amron."

"Yes, I know who you are, and what your intentions might be," Almeric stated. "Under Amron's direction, we have waited your arrival these last few weeks. We're here to escort and protect you for as long as we can. Amron has convinced me, along with many others, that you are the ones to defeat the tyrant's magic. The part of the allied armies is to distract Betlic and his men, until your work is complete, then defeat his leaderless armies. If everything goes well, we shall meet again when this war is over, to celebrate a great victory together."

"Your Highness, you speak of working under Amron's direction and his allies. What does this mean?" Karilyn asked.

"Amron knows, without the Mastig and the heir to wield it, triumph over Betlic is problematic. To continue to fight in small local campaigns, as has happened in other lands, makes it impossible to overcome the power of the talisman. Amron has enticed Betlic, and the bulk of his massed armies, into what his majesty believes to be a trap. Even without you, the men he has brought together might have a chance of success. But, once you use the object in your possession, Amron is confident we shall be victorious. Who else stands beside him, or where they are now, I have no knowledge. Amron, ever fearful that one of Betlic's agents learns of his plans, has kept them close to his heart. He's the one who will lead us into victory, so the ancient writings foretell. We can only pray the prophesy is not false. For now, we must let Amron know you're here."

"How do you propose to do that?" Marazin raised an eyebrow. "His palace is several weeks' ride from here, with an army in-between."

"Amron has moved north, to a new stronghold a few days' ride away. He'll have the news within the hour. As soon as I give the signal, a beacon will flare on the ridge ahead. The rebels have prepared other beacons, at high points along the edge of the mountains. The message will soon cross the peaks. Now, your king and his troops face their sternest test. They must keep the enemy occupied until we and his other allies reach them. So busy that Betlic cannot concentrate on anything else. Until we draw nearer to him, Amron's army must fight alone, against insurmountable odds."

"Once inside the vale, the Mastig's power will help the rebels. This beacon you spoke of, won't it alert Betlic's men between here and the mountains to our coming?"

"Large groups of my forces attacked before dawn. The land between here and the mouth of the valley, with the entrance itself, is clear."

Almeric signalled towards a small group of his men on the southern ridge. As those below watched, a column of thick black smoke rose from their position. The three spoke a while longer, before the king, with his escort, rejoined his followers. Marazin and Karilyn ascended the slope. As the couple cleared the hilltop, columns of smoke were visible in the distance. Below them, on the plains, they could see thousands of warriors on the move. Marazin and Karilyn felt a lift in their hearts. Without reservation, Almeric had committed to the fray.

By noon, with their protectors, the couple approached the ruins of the fortifications that once commanded the entrance to the valley. Using rubble from the walls, Betlic's army had widened and strengthened the road over the low ridge. Around them lay the bodies of the fallen, slain earlier in the day by Almeric's warriors. Ahead of them, a battle raged. Betlic had left a large contingent of men near the entrance, to guard his rear. These hostilities raged on until late into the evening. When Marazin and Karilyn descended onto the valley floor, the scale of the fighting was evident. What was clear, too, was the ratio of enemy to Vernalakan dead. It was true, what Orvyn had said — marshlanders were ferocious fighters. Rebel forces had swept from the mountains, to cut down any of Betlic's troops who tried to flee.

Inside the confines of the valley, the influence of the talisman was visible in the demeanour of the victors. Many held their heads in pain. Others walked as if they carried a great weight on their backs. For Marazin and Karilyn, their proximity to Heardwine, and the Mastig, protected them from the talisman's magic. Marazin believed it was within his power to remove this distress from his and Karilyn's protectors.

As the sky darkened, the army halted. It was time to make camp. Leaving Karilyn to care for the horses, Marazin walked away, whip in hand. It pulsed with light. As daylight faded, it glowed ever brighter. When Almeric's men realised what Marazin carried, they fell silent. In awe, they watched to see what would happen next.

At a distance, the warriors formed a large circle round Marazin. Alone, at the centre, he focused his mind. Over the past months, he had practised much. Earlier, he had reattached the cracker to the end of the whip. He was ready. Once he gripped tight the handle, sparks flew from the thong. In one rapid, flowing movement, he brought his arm forward. He flicked his wrist. The crack of thunder was deafening. A green glow lit the sky above him. It spread into the distance before fading to nothing.

Satisfied, Marazin took a deep breath and prepared himself. He leapt into action. For several minutes, he threw the whip, in many varied ways, forwards, backwards, sideways and around his head. The noise was horrendous. The atmosphere was alight for miles in all directions. In haste, Almeric's men moved to put greater distance between them and the creator of the disturbance. It was a matter of moments before they felt the results of the display. A great weight lifted from their minds. The talisman no longer held sway over them. At first a single voice called out, then more and more joined in. Within moments, the whole of Almeric's forces were roaring their appreciation.

Chapter Fifty One

Introductions and congratulations were, of necessity, brief. To his embarrassment, Hafter realised the sound of his knocking had drawn Orvyn and Willa from the pleasures of their marital bed. To their credit, they did not hesitate. In haste, they returned to their chamber to pull on more garments. Within minutes, the three were walking towards Tamin's rooms. Sheply, Willa feared, might have enlisted with the rebel forces. There were many his age who fought alongside the men. She wanted to reclaim Scard, but, first, she would help Eadgyth lay out Tedrick in readiness for his funeral. At Orvyn's side, the man had saved her life on more than one occasion. She owed him this last kindness. If able, Hafter would join them later.

Once Willa had left them, Hafter and Orvyn, with Tamin at their side, headed towards the hall. Guards ushered the trio into the meeting room. Seated, down the long sides of the chamber, were many of Amron's commanders and advisors, alongside members of the council. Others arrived from time to time, to fill the empty spaces. Orvyn's inclusion in the select group caused several raised eyebrows. As he was here at the king's express invitation, no-one opposed his presence.

Only those directing operations in the hills, would miss the meeting. After a short while, the final attendee arrived. As soon as he had taken his seat, Amron joined them from a side entrance. He indicated that the guards stationed at the main door should leave. As it closed behind them, its latch clicked into place. Benches, dragged in front of the doorway, allowed the council members to spread out.

At the head of the hall, opposite the main entrance, Amron's chair was in position, a pace or so away from the wall. Behind him, on a bench, sat Tamin, Hafter and Orvyn. On either side of them, two of Amron's bodyguard stood. Forewarned, they were ready for any trouble that might erupt. Behind one of them, a wall-hanging concealed another door. Amron was unwilling to take any chances. Beyond this opening, a contingent of his loyal retinue waited, in readiness to intervene.

It was time for Amron to reveal his plans, and what he had done to ensure their success. Once everyone settled, Amron took to the floor. He cleared his throat. The nervousness he once exhibited, when addressing such an assembly, had gone. Acceptance of his role had brought with it an air of authority. His face had matured; it had lost the look of indolent youth. Amron was no longer king in name. He was *The* King.

"Council members, commanders," he said, "now's the time to share with you many of the matters that have occupied my mind, concerning the defence of our nation."

"It's taken you long enough," muttered a voice from the shadows.

Much nodding of heads and murmurs of support followed.

"Why have you kept this information from us until now? Don't you trust us?" the speaker added, with more than a touch of bitterness, to a further chorus of accord.

"You forget Raulf?" countered Amron, his voice piercing the clamour.

"But you unmasked Raulf, months ago. You could have briefed us anytime since then," someone else spoke out.

"Can any of you say, with absolute confidence, no other traitor hides among us? No, I thought so," Amron answered for them. "Hidden among us could be any number of Betlic's agents. Much of what I have to tell you must stay within our circle. When I finish, I expect you to act upon my words. I will brook no hesitation. You must proceed as commanded. We have but one chance to be victorious. It's up to us to seize it."

Rallying speeches were a useful weapon for any leader under pressure. When spoken by Amron, it was rare for them to yield anything substantial. Whether today's rhetoric would be different was not yet apparent. The room fell into a non-committal silence. Although no-one wanted to believe one of their trusted followers could be another traitor, the possibility existed. Raulf's exposure had shaken their confidence. Amron sensed his advantage.

"A few hours ago," he said, "you saw smoke rising from beacons to the north. It meant nothing to you, but I have lived in hope of those signals," Amron paused a moment. "They tell me that, by nightfall, the heir to the Mastig will be inside our valley."

Amron's voice was lost in the uproar that followed this statement. Everyone was shouting questions. It was a while before he could restore order.

"On what do you base this story?" demanded Hrothwulf, one of Amron's more vociferous generals. "Everyone knows Betlic's men killed the Bearer of the Scraufin. The object's gone, forever. You've spoken of this tragedy many times. Without the Scraufin, there's no Mastig. The heir, if he exists, is powerless. There's nothing he can do."

"The bearer lives," Amron said. He added, with a slight variation of the truth. "For a while, before embarking on her mission, she was a guest at my palace. She left, earlier in the year, with Marazin. *He* is the heir. Orvyn, who sits behind me, accompanied them on their mission to find the Mastig."

"Marazin, the heir? The bearer, a woman?" Hrothwulf was incredulous. "Impossible! This is the great plan on which you've laboured for months — a dead bearer, a missing Scraufin and a non-existent magical object. This is madness you speak! Have you lost your senses?"

"The King's correct," Hafter stepped into the argument. "The bearer is a woman. Her name is Karilyn. Late last year she arrived at the palace. I spoke with her many times. During this period, I entertained Marazin and Orvyn as my guests. She *is* genuine. I will swear against any oath you wish. I have documents, too, that prove Marazin is the true heir."

Tamin came to his feet and stood between Hafter and his son.

"It's all true," Tamin confirmed. "Then, Raulf was in attendance at court. To protect the bearer, his majesty kept her existence secret. Betlic had to remain ignorant of her survival. As long as he believed she was dead, her chances of a successful mission were much greater."

"How do we know she and Marazin succeeded? A puff of smoke, this tells you everything?" Hrothwulf asked. He was sceptical. "Orvyn, as we can see, has returned. He appears to have lost Marazin somewhere along the way. Instead of the heir, he brings with him your lackey, Tedrick, some damned woman and two children. Now, I suppose, you're going to tell me that pathetic creature is the bearer?"

Orvyn bristled at this slight against Willa. "That 'damned woman' is my wife. She's not the bearer, but her courage and tenacity are beyond question. I will not have her spoken of in this manner. What I can tell you is the true bearer's mission was successful. I've seen the Mastig. It exists. Marazin and the bearer's path took a different course from ours. Two cycles ago of the moon, after we had released Tedrick from Betlic's men, the couple left us. Be thankful that, at our time of need, the heir draws near with his charge."

Even Hrothwulf was starting to believe. The mention of Tedrick being with Betlic's men did not escape his attention. To allow such a remark to pass without comment was against his nature.

"Tedrick, a prisoner of Betlic's forces, how did that happen? The last time I asked after the man, you said he was working for you, your Majesty, in the mountains. If it's taken him this long to reach here after his rescue, either the hills have moved or his assignment differed from what you told us."

Amron coughed, now he was nervous, proceedings were about to become even more fraught. "He was not a prisoner," he said. "I persuaded Tedrick to replace Raulf's messenger. Tedrick was working on my behalf alongside Betlic's forces."

Hrothwulf stepped back, his mouth open in astonishment. For once, although his lips moved, he could not find the words.

"Why else do you think Betlic found his way here?" Amron asked. "He was certain to discover the most indefensible way into our valley. I took the necessary steps to ensure his arrival was at a time that was to our advantage."

"So, it's you who betrayed us," Hrothwulf shouted, his voice restored, but strained. "You were the traitor, not Raulf."

"Of course Raulf was the spy," Amron roared back. "I replaced his messenger with Tedrick. He was privy to specific information, items I wanted Betlic to know and believe. Raulf's envoy had much more damaging information he would have passed to the enemy."

Hrothwulf stopped listening. His fury mounted by the second as did that of several others. The condemnation was far from total. Many refused to believe the king guilty of treachery. His earlier revelations about the Mastig gave a small majority reason for doubt. Before making final judgement, they would listen to his story in full. Discussion between those with opposing views became fractious. Both sides exchanged blows. It was a close decision, but, with order once more restored, they agreed to hear out Amron.

"I make no apology for concealing these matters from you," Amron said. "Secrecy was my concern. You must believe me when I tell you Tedrick was unhappy with his task. Whatever he's done in the past, his allegiance to our cause cannot be in doubt. Because of his loyalty, he allowed Betlic's men to capture him. A little of what happened afterwards, he told Orvyn.

"When taken prisoner, Tedrick faced interrogation. It was fortunate for him, and for me, he could convince his inquisitors and, later, Betlic, he was

Raulf's messenger. I needed Betlic here in the valley, at this time. I'd already discussed with Hafter when we could expect the heir's return with the Mastig."

"But why bring Betlic here? We could have joined battle with him out on the plains, beyond the mountains?" came a voice from the crowd.

"Why? Because, along with much of his army, he might escape, to rally and fight again," Amron replied. "It could take years, and bring about the death of thousands, before we gained victory. Here, in this valley, we have Betlic trapped. The earth reduces the effect of his magic and…"

"Trapped!" Hrothwulf interrupted, the idea was preposterous. "With respect, your Majesty, how, might I ask, is Betlic trapped? He outnumbers us at least twenty to one. He can ride out of this valley whenever he wants. Even if the heir neutralises his power, how can you say we have ensnared him? We stand alone, a child against a raging bull."

"Have I said we're alone?" Amron asked. "The signal we received this morning did not originate with the heir and his companion. The first beacon was lit by King Almeric's men. He and his army have awaited the heir's arrival these past few weeks. Marazin now has the forces of Vernalaka to protect him. As we talk, they advance in our direction."

"What, a few men, a raiding party?" Hrothwulf scoffed.

"No. The king brings with him all his forces," Amron countered.

"Oh! Good!" Hrothwulf said. "Now they outnumber us nineteen to one. Victory is ours!" There was no attempt to disguise his sarcasm.

"If you'd allow me to finish," Amron snapped, his voice like ice. "Why do you think I was last to leave my palace? It was because I awaited the arrival of several messengers, of whom Almeric's was only one. In the mountains opposite lie the armies of Vretliana, Mystiannia, Vussak, Hunsale and many others. They, as has Almeric, have brought the bulk of their men. For several weeks, they have been moving into position and preparing for this moment."

Amron now had his audience's full attention. This news was most unexpected. For the first time, a faint spark of hope gripped them. Might they survive? Amron did not wait for further interruption.

"Outside, a huge beacon is under construction. Soon, its smoke will rise high. This is the signal to our allies to advance but, because of the distance they have had to keep, it will be several days before they can reach here. For us, we have to keep Betlic occupied until they arrive. When you leave here, those commanders among you will lead your men, and all our reserves, against Betlic's army. Make him believe the beacons signal our offensive against him. Where possible, draw his men into the hills, or, if not, fight him in the valley. It is our lot to deflect him from the truth. I am convinced that Marazin will soon bring into action the Mastig. Although, that aids us, it also serves as a warning to Betlic. He'll try to find and eliminate the heir. But, that is Almeric's task to safeguard the chosen one, not ours. Against us, Betlic will redouble his efforts."

"Our losses will be high," Hrothwulf said. This time it was more a statement, less a criticism. Amron had convinced him.

"So be it," Amron declared. "Betlic must concentrate his energies on us. If he learns of our allies too soon, he will be ready for them. Our casualties will be greater, victory much less certain."

The meeting was lengthy. Before it ended, Hafter left to help in the preparations for Tedrick's funeral. It would proceed when Amron and the High Council agreed their strategy. Amron told the ensemble he expected their presence, too, at the ceremony. Earlier, he had detailed the circumstances of Tedrick's death, how he had sacrificed himself for his king. Amron had been the target of the sword that killed the warrior. Tedrick had leapt between him and his assailant, to take the full force of the blow.

Hafter had heard this disclosure before he left the meeting. The full story had surprised the sage, but not engendered any sympathy in him for the dead man. Hafter would always think of Tedrick as a ruthless killer. Although, it did prove it was possible to find some good in people, no matter how small, or how deep they buried it.

The sage looked across the stronghold. True to Amron's words, a beacon was burning. What had they added to it? Hafter was unsure. One moment the thick smoke was black, the next pale grey. The breeze was minimal. High into the afternoon sky, the column spiralled. Hafter turned away and hurried towards the room where Tedrick's remains lay.

Hafter arrived too late to help. Others had washed, anointed and redressed the body in clothes befitting a noble warrior. His sword lay at his side. Eadgyth knelt beside her husband. She was alone as requested. Willa had collected Scard and returned to her own quarters. Sheply, as feared, had left the stronghold. He was riding to join one of the rebel groups in the hills.

Eadgyth stirred in irritation at the intrusion. She relaxed, when she saw it was Hafter.

"A pyre is ready," she said, her eyes dark ringed, tears ready to spill. "I say my farewells later. The king, so Willa said, will attend. Where's my Tedrick been these past few months? No-one will tell me, nor any details of how he came to die. Whatever he'd done, he'd returned safe. Now he's gone."

Her anguish, made worse by her need to know, was heartrending. Hafter paused for a few moments while he selected his words. He told Eadgyth as much as he could, about Tedrick's mission and his last act of heroism for his king. Hafter admitted there was little, yet, he could disclose. Once he was free to do so, she would learn the truth of everything. Gratified, Eadgyth listened. She thanked Hafter for his help. At her request, he left her alone with her husband's body, until it was time for him to make his final journey.

☙ ❧

It was late evening. The meeting between Amron and his commanders, which followed the departure of the civilian council members, had ended. Each one had his orders. Everyone knew what was at risk, and what was expected of them. If called upon to do so, each commander was ready to sacrifice himself and his men. They would do everything in their power, to divert Betlic from learning the truth about the rebel's re-enforcements.

The sun was behind the western mountains, although, at the edge of the plateau, enough light remained for the crowd to watch the ceremony. Tedrick's body, wrapped in a shroud of white, lay on top of a large pile of logs and kindling. Eadgyth was grateful for the large numbers of council members and senior officers in attendance. Many of the plateau's inhabitant, too, had come to pay their respects.

Amron gave a eulogy. It moved many to tears. Orvyn spoke last, then, with a flaming brand, he walked towards the pyre. Within moments, the fire took hold. The blaze was fierce. Eadgyth's legs buckled. To everyone's astonishment, the king stepped to her side. With his arm round her, he held her steady until she could stand unaided.

With heads bowed, the crowds remained for a while. As the flames died down, towards the north an eerie green flash lit up the sky. The strange light faded. No sooner did it disappear when more flashes lit the whole northern sky. It glowed brighter and brighter. In silence, everyone turned their heads to watch. The phenomenon lasted only a short while before the lights faded again.

A murmur of voices began. On faces, illuminated by the flames, glimpses of fear were visible. Was this another of Betlic's tricks? The clamour was deafening. At the king's insistence, Orvyn stood on a piece of raised ground, ready to address the throng. From Marazin and Karilyn, he had learned the visual effects of the Mastig's use.

Before Orvyn could speak, a rushing noise, accompanied by a gust of wind, sent the flames from the pyre streaking sideways. The sound of distant thunder pealed and echoed along the valley. By the time it ceased, the outlook of the multitude had changed beyond recognition.

Most had forgotten the sadness behind their attendance. No longer did the weight of Betlic's magic rest heavy on their shoulders. Released from his mental shackles, people danced, sang and shouted in relief. Amron beckoned Orvyn to step down, there was no need for explanations. The Mastig was within range.

With broad smiles, the king's commanders left. Amron returned to his quarters. In small groups, the crowd melted away, their minds on other matters. Soon, only Eadgyth, Hafter, Orvyn and Willa remained. Mildthryth had taken charge of Scard once more. The four stayed until the fire had consumed all and only the smouldering ashes remained.

As a new dawn broke over the land, they escorted Eadgyth to her rooms. Willa promised Hafter that, for a while, she would keep a close watch over the widow. They took their leave of each other. Hafter walked away. Orvyn and Willa returned to their quarters.

He closed the door. Moments later, Willa crept into his arms. Orvyn looked into Willa's worried eyes. It had taken him all his life to find her. He loved her above everything. Somehow, he must survive the coming days and weeks. The thought of Willa in Eadgyth's position was unbearable. For her sake, he must live.

Chapter Fifty Two

Betlic had changed, but not for the better. The past few days had been brutal to him. If he had given it a thought, he would have struggled to remember when last he slept. Unwashed, hair dishevelled, his face drawn and haggard, he staggered from one crisis to another. His grip on the minds of others decreased with each mile the Mastig drew closer. When first he had seen the columns of smoke from the beacons, Betlic was unsure of their meaning. Later in the day, the rebel's response had billowed skywards from their stronghold. Then, that evening, the northern sky had lit up.

From the thunderous sounds that followed, and the affect of these events on his followers, Betlic knew the impossible had happened. The bearer was not lying dead in a mountain pass. She had found the heir and, between them, recovered the Mastig. The wretched object was close and coming closer. The where and how of its discovery was of no consequence to him now. What concerned Betlic most was how his enemies had deceived him and the Eye while they accomplished this feat. That night, he had been in shock.

At dawn, the following morning, came the first of a barrage of attacks launched by rebel forces. Amron's warriors, suicidal in manner raided up and down the valley. Betlic understood, now. The beacons were as much a signal to attack as they were to announce the Mastig's arrival. From the start, Betlic realised he could no longer influence the minds of his enemies. The ferocity and confidence of their attacks were proof of this. Despite this, his initial reaction was to persevere. The hours of concentration he spent over the talisman exhausted him, but to no avail. As his own men became disheartened, he abandoned the struggle. Instead, he concentrated on rebuilding their morale.

No sooner did Betlic attempt this when unrest stirred among his conscripted followers. Most of those adherents had joined his forces under fear of death. Through the talisman, Betlic had controlled their minds. Unable to resist, they had followed his commands without question. Now, with the Mastig to undermine his efforts, it took more and more effort, to prevent his conscripts from deserting and to keep his loyal supporters strong.

Day after day, peals of thunder rolled over the land. For now, the nights remained silent. Although more visible in the early morning, and late into the summer evenings, eerie green lights lit up the northern skies. The time between flash and sound decreased each day. The Mastig and its bearer must be close. While Betlic became weaker, the heir grew stronger.

Despite his difficulties, the forces loyal to Betlic, and their resources, were vast compared to those of the rebels. Daily, Amron's men suffered losses at a level unsustainable for long. The Mastig was a distraction, a serious one, but Betlic was hopeful he would end its threat soon. Several companies of battle-hardened warriors were searching for the heir. For now, none had returned. The Mastig still roared out its thunder while distant lightning flashed. Had fatigue not clouded Betlic's wits, it might have occurred to him to question whether the heir was receiving assistance.

ɞ ʖ

It was the fourth day since the Mastig first lit the evening sky. High above the valley, in his stronghold, Amron was holding a meeting with his commanders. This time, there were much fewer attendees sitting round the edges of the hall. Many were out in the field. Others, along with their men, were among the dead or missing. Those in attendance were weary; few were without minor wounds. Bloodstains, sprinkled front and back, stained Amron's own tunic. A few spots were his, most belonged to his enemies. His right eye was half-closed and blackened. A deep cut seeped beneath a cloth, wrapped around his head.

The news was neither encouraging nor bleak. As forecast, casualties were high. Amron's northern forces had joined with Almeric's men. Their combined strength, along with Marazin and the Mastig at their centre, had brought them to within a day's fighting of the rebel stronghold.

The valley side of the plateau was no longer safe. Betlic's engineers had redesigned his mangonels for height rather than distance. Placed close to the cliffs to be effective, and in range of rebel archers, those who operated the machines risked death at all times. Large rocks and boulders rained down, on and beyond the defensive walls. Rotting bodies, of both men and horses, fell with the stones. The prospect of disease was a serious consideration inside the rebel stronghold.

Amron's own machines, although smaller in size and number, returned as many of the projectiles to their senders as they could. The enemy brought siege towers into use. By necessity of a great height, these cumbersome constructions were, with minimal effort, easy to overbalance. So far, the rebels had repulsed attacks from these sources. The onslaught was relentless. Amron feared, unless his allies arrived soon, his men would succumb to the overwhelming odds against them. Despite the huge losses among Betlic's men, it seemed to have made little difference to the massed ranks of invaders spread out across the valley.

Amron did his best to raise the morale of his commanders. Although, without assistance from more than Almeric's men, Amron knew as well as they did, they could measure their survival in days. It was to the council's credit that few expressed their doubts about the long overdue arrival of their allies' promised support. In private, Amron shared their misgivings. He was close to losing hope. Help should have been here by now. How long could it take to ride to his aid? Two days, a half longer at most, from where his allies were to muster in the mountains. Amron feared the relief forces, on seeing what lay ahead, must have turned and fled.

As he gazed around the room, at the strained faces of his men, Amron felt a great sense of failure. Something had happened to him these past few months. His people had put their faith in him. The weight of that responsibility lay heavy on his shoulders. Now they must believe he had failed them. Had someone told him, a year ago, he would feel this way, he would have laughed. Damn it! He had done what he believed was right. What did he know? He was an ignorant country boy, come late to the trappings of power and command. If alone, he would have wept with frustration.

For a moment, pre-occupied with their own thoughts, each member of the meeting fell silent. With a tremendous crash, the outside door, opposite to Amron, flew open. Everyone leapt to their feet, hands ready on their swords. In the entrance, Hafter stood, eyes staring, white hair tangled by the wind. There was neither apology, not explanation for his interruption.

"Come!" he roared at them. "Follow me!"

Without further utterance, Hafter turned and ran from the hall. For a man of his age, it was a rare sight. The doors swung in the breeze behind the sage. The ensemble stared at each other. What was wrong now? With looks of consternation, the whole roomful rushed outside, then raced towards the walls.

There were huge gaps in the defences where boulders had smashed through the battlements. Few of the nearby abandoned buildings remained standing. Only when the runners reached the edge of the cliffs, did they catch up with Hafter. He had halted, at a place where damaged stonework had collapsed. The men spread out. With an uninterrupted view of the valley, they studied the ground far below. They could see nothing that might warrant the urgency of Hafter's outburst. Amron turned to the sage, his expression one of bafflement.

"What is it Hafter?" the king demanded. "What's the problem?"

Hafter lifted his arm and, with shaking finger, he indicated an area beyond the outermost reaches of Betlic's camps and men.

"Look!" was all the sage said.

Amron and his commanders raised their eyes. At first, they were unsure. Then a few smiled. Others followed. As one, they cheered. In the distance, beyond the sight of those below, galloped lines of horsemen. Dozens deep, the rows spread out, from north to south. In huge divisions, different coloured uniforms and standards became visible. Help was at hand.

With his eyes shielded from the mid-day sun, Amron watched the advancing tide. There were thousands of riders moving towards them. A sinking feeling came over the king. Only thousands! Much too few to make any difference. They faced ten, twenty times that many. He had hoped for so much more. Amron had gambled with his nation's future and lost. He swayed, his eyesight blurring with the moisture that pricked his eyes. Hafter's hand, strong for a man of his age, grabbed hold of the king's arm. The sage had seen the expression on the king's face and sensed his disappointment. He leaned over and whispered into Amron's ear.

"Faith Amron, faith," Hafter said. "Look beyond. Can't you see what follows."

Amron steadied himself. He blinked and wiped his eyes. With his gaze redirected, he concentrated on the distance. It was a moment or two before he realised what Hafter meant. A few thousand paces behind the riders, the whole ground was on the move. The dark shadow he thought cast by a cloud, was a sea of people. Countless thousands were racing into war. The horsemen were the vanguard. His allies had come through for him. Every man, able to lift a sword, spear or club was there.

"Go to your men," Amron shouted. "We ride now. The time's come to fight our final battles. Let us pray for victory."

As one, they turned and ran for their horses. There was a tremendous flash, followed moments later by a peal of thunder, louder than ever. Was the heir aware of what was taking place? The rebels' spirits lifted higher. No-one doubted their king anymore. Nothing could stop them now.

CB 80

In a building, at the rear of the plateau, Willa looked up as Hafter entered. It was a large room, fifty paces by a hundred. It was one of many. Everywhere, the wounded lay, on cots, in-between cots, along the aisles and in every nook and cranny that their carers could put into use. With the onset of heavy fighting, Orvyn had returned to the king's service. Willa was happy to leave Scard under Tamin's watchful eye. The king's father was too infirm to fight. With Mildthryth, Willa organised the care of the injured. Her friend, Karilyn, had a talent for fighting; with Willa, it was healing. Her energy endless, she worked alongside the others, tending those who might survive, and comforting those who would die.

Hafter relayed the latest information to Willa. Thoughts of her husband in peril soon tempered her relief at the arrival of the allied forces. Only for brief periods had they seen each other since the night after their marriage.

"And Orvyn?" she asked, eager for news. "Have you seen anything of him?"

"I glimpsed him with the king's party, as they left, moments ago. Orvyn's well, and looks to be without injury," Hafter lied.

Hafter had caught sight of a bandage around Orvyn's arm. The man appeared untroubled by his wound, but to know about it would have added to Willa's worries. Before she could question him more, Eadgyth called her away. The widow had put aside her own grief to help. A new arrival needed their ministrations. Hafter looked around — so many young men and women, injured, crippled or dying. He hoped their sacrifices would prove to have been worthwhile.

Chapter Fifty Three

The allies' intervention from the west had shocked Betlic as much as the Mastig's arrival. With the rebels isolated in the east of the valley, he had concentrated his efforts there. Once his campaign intensified, without any reported signs of the enemy in the western hills, he withdrew his patrols to take part in the battles against the rebels.

The initial onslaught by mounted warriors, followed soon afterwards by swarms of foot soldiers, had decimated huge swathes of his army. The ensuing fighting had driven his men back. Now, trapped between the rebels and their allies, they were close to the cliffs beneath the rebel stronghold. Once Betlic's hold over the waverers in his army had gone, many defected, or turned on their commanders. Man for man, it was without doubt he still outnumbered the forces ranged against him. Was it enough? With the talisman no longer as effective, his troops were unable to match the enemy for ferocity. By dawn, the following day, it was clear to Betlic his position was perilous.

As he looked out of his hastily repositioned tent, a flash of green light lit up the morning sky. The delay between that and the sound of rolling thunder that followed was slight. The heir and the Mastig, along with the fierce fighters who surrounded them, must be close. Betlic now knew the reasons why his men had been unable to kill, or capture his adversary. An army of marshlanders protected him.

One option did remain open. It was something that should guarantee his victory, or demise if he was careless. If he did nothing, his death looked more certain each hour that passed. To his tent, he called his generals, much fewer now than once they had been. In brief, he outlined his intent. They nodded their agreement. Not that Betlic needed it, but he did want them to keep fighting.

The prospect of defeat was a concept new to them. Apart from suing for peace, there were few other options open to them. The forces they faced would be unlikely to want to negotiate a treaty, certainly not one that allowed the enemy-hierarchy freedom. As did Betlic, his commanders knew death awaited them at the hands of Amron and his allies. If caught alive, their ends would be neither quick, nor painless. If Betlic could do something to bring them victory, his generals would do everything they could to help.

A group, selected from the most loyal members of Betlic's men, formed a cordon round their leader's position. For this undertaking, Betlic could not be distracted until he had finished. Total silence would have been preferable. The clamour of battle, along with those infernal peals of thunder, denied him such luxury. His commanders returned to the field. The clouds, which brought showers of rain overnight, had moved away. Once the sun cleared the peaks, it would be another hot day.

Inside his tent, Betlic covered the entrance. A volume of ancient manuscripts lay open, at the page he needed. It was time to perform the ultimate spell. To succeed, he must utter the words without error. The enchantments, hidden deep within the talisman and its Eye, would then transfer to him. Provided he retained the talisman about his person, he would become invincible, or so he believed. This was the darkest of all the charms handed down from the object's creator.

Omitted from the manuscript was something that, had Betlic been aware, might have cautioned his actions. Karilyn had feared this result, but she knew only a part of the story. The use of magic to define your own destiny comes with a penalty. Should Betlic succeed with the spell, the essence of the sorcerer, the talisman's creator, would return. At first, Betlic would receive the objects' powers. But later, as the hours progressed, the dark mind preserved within the Eye would join with him, until it subjugated his entire being. As a person, Betlic would exist, but only as a fragment of the enchanter's consciousness, to use or discard at will.

Oblivious to this, Betlic moved towards the book. Inside the tent, it was gloomy under its heavy covering. He lit several candles, large ones that would burn for hours. Betlic reread the script, as he had done many times. The words had long-since been committed to memory. Until now, to speak them aloud had been unnecessary. Tension compelled him to read them again. If he made one mistake, he would not live to regret it.

With the talisman outside his tunic, hanging from its chain round his neck, Betlic sat cross-legged on a rug. The mantle, he settled over his shoulders. On the mat, in front of him, was the Eye. When the time was right, it would return to its resting place, at the talisman's centre. In a circle enclosing the Eye were a dozen dishes, filled with various oils and potions. Each one was required, in turn, at a specific part of the proceedings.

Betlic slowed his breathing. A low humming noise issued from his lips. He concentrated his mind on the sound. Extraneous distractions faded as Betlic allowed it to replace the outside clamour. He focused his thoughts. It was without conscious decision he replaced the hum with speech. Faultlessly, the words flowed.

The minutes passed. The Eye lifted from the ground and floated towards Betlic. It came to rest, an arm's length from his face. It emitted a pale blue ray of light that reached out, to enter his eyes. Its brightness dazzled him. Unblinking, he was unable to remove his gaze. The glow held him captive.

Inside Betlic's head, something strange happened. His brain felt to be in the process of rearrangement. This sensation was not one that engendered fear in him. The opposite was nearer the truth. He was finding a clarity of mind beyond anything experienced.

A dish rose upwards. It floated towards Betlic. As it drew near, it started to tip. The oils it contained flowed over his forehead. Soon afterwards, another container came towards him. Betlic's head fell backwards. The contents of this silver bowl poured into his mouth. He swallowed. His head straightened. The piercing light from the Eye, again shone into his eyes. This time, the colour had changed to a deep ruby red. Betlic's brain seemed to be on fire, his muscles paralysed. Beads of sweat came together. In rivulets, they ran down his face.

There was no lessening of activity. In-between these occurrences, Betlic's voice uttered the words he had learned. At regular intervals, bowls floated round him. From some, the contents poured over his head, while from others, liquid flowed into his mouth. Each time the ray of light from the Eye changed colour, so did Betlic's body temperature. One moment hot, the next he was shivering from the cold, then hot again.

The whole of Betlic's being was changing. Pains shot through him as bones clicked and groaned from hidden pressures. The longer the spell took, the more a dark energy invaded him. The talisman was glowing now. It too emitted a ray of light, this one aimed towards the Eye. Something passed between the two objects, which the Eye transmitted to Betlic.

The last page of manuscript faded from Betlic's mind. The incantation was at an end. The talisman and Eye dimmed. Each bowl was empty. The Eye lifted from the ground to spin, faster and faster. It moved away, to the edge of the tent. The spinning slowed, then stopped. For a moment, the Eye hovered, waist height above the ground. It hurtled across the room, to embed itself inside its slot in the face of the talisman. The impact sent Betlic reeling backwards. He smashed through the tent flap, out into the open.

His eyes were red. During the ceremony, blood vessels had leaked. His appearance was demonic. He rolled several times before coming to a halt. The sun was high in the sky, past its noon position. Betlic shook himself, then stood. He had survived. A red glow flickered down his arms as he moved. His mind filled with a million thoughts. He was omnipotent. With hands outstretched, he bellowed out a roar of triumph.

The echoes faded. Betlic became aware of an unnatural silence around him. The distant noise of strife still sounded, but he was at the centre of a stillness that surprised him. For the first time, he took note of his surroundings. As instructed, his guard had spread out, in an extended circle round his tent. None of his men, he realised, were standing. Their torn and lifeless bodies seemed to mock his newfound power. Betlic raised his gaze. Several hundred paces away, an army of brown cloaked warriors were sitting astride their horses. He was surrounded.

A large man, with a pockmarked face, shouted a command. The sky darkened. A cloud of arrows arched, then floated towards Betlic. Without thinking, his hands lifted. A feeling unlike anything he had experienced took control of his body. Flames shot from his fingertips, the arrows incinerated. Their ashes floated down, to land at his feet. Betlic looked at his hands. This unexpected ability fuelled his sense of power, he was unstoppable.

He fixed his gaze on the leader of the mounted men. He shuffled in his saddle, but held his position. Slowly, to the north of Betlic, horsemen began to move their horses apart. A way opened. On and on it went, further and further into the distance. It must have been a thousand riders deep. The parting proceeded to lengthen. It reached the last of the horsemen. A gap appeared at the end. Betlic thought they were offering him a way out. The fools, had they no understanding? He was going to destroy them all.

Betlic felt his eyes drawn towards the distant opening. At first, he could distinguish nothing; the distance was too great. Everything came into focus.

Two riders appeared at the centre of the gap. The pair grew large in his sight, as if in front of him. He possessed the Eye's powers. The two on horseback were a man and a woman. At the side of the man's horse stood a large dog. Something shimmered in the rider's hand. It produced a bright green glow. Betlic knew who it was. The heir had come to claim him. This was to be their battle. Only one would survive. With his newfound strength and abilities, Betlic's confidence was supreme. Nothing could stop him.

The riders nudged their horses. The animals began to walk, the dog at their side. No longer was speed a priority. For a moment, Marazin and Karilyn looked at each other. Last night they had spent in each other's arms. They needed no words to express what they meant to each other. They prayed they might survive this ending to their quest.

On either side, Almeric's warriors turned to face them, their swords raised in silent honour of the riders. The noise of distant fighting faded, to leave only the sounds of creaking leather and the soft tread of horses' hooves. Behind the couple, the ranks of marshlanders refilled the gap. Marazin fixed his eyes on Betlic. The heir was unwavering in his approach. The Mastig, the whip of green light, rested in his right hand.

As they reached the empty circle, Karilyn moved ahead of Marazin. Betlic waited. He had grown in stature. His mind was afire. He swung his arm. A ball of fire, aimed at Marazin, hurled across the gap. Before he could bring the Mastig into use, the flames were upon him. Shadowy shapes flew in front. He glimpsed Karilyn's face. A blinding flash robbed him of his sight. A smell of burning flesh pervaded the air. The sound of something heavy, hitting the ground, followed. Karilyn had performed the ultimate sacrifice.

Marazin cried out in despair. It felt as if a giant fist had smashed his heart in two. His whole body shuddered. Somehow, he stayed on his horse as it bucked in fright. He went beyond anger and sorrow. As his vision returned, he dug in his heels. His horse leapt forward. Without a backward glance, Marazin threw the whip. It uncoiled. Lightning flew from its end. Thunder rolled. A shimmering green light flowed along his arm, across his shoulders, before rising to circle his head. As it faded, Marazin's mind cleared. Rage no longer blinded him. His emotions were under control. All tension left his body. Marazin had transcended to a higher level of consciousness. Betlic would die.

Chapter Fifty Four

Trapped and delirious, Orvyn was in grave trouble. Yesterday afternoon, at Amron's side, he had ridden from the stronghold. An hour later, they joined forces with a rebel group fighting in the hills to the south. Together, they launched a series of frenzied attacks on Betlic's positions. Late in the day, Amron's party had strayed too far into the valley. Surrounded by Betlic's men, only with great difficulty had the main group battled their way to safety.

To aid the king's escape, Orvyn, with a dozen others, fought an intense rear-guard action. When a flurry of arrows killed many of their fellows, those who remained had broken out, to ride to more secure ground. During this struggle, a lance, aimed at Orvyn, missed him, but brought down his horse. In its death-throes, the beast rolled onto its rider's leg. Orvyn's ankle snapped. At the time, he was unaware of his predicament. His head had struck the earth with force. He was unconscious.

Betlic's men, believing the fallen man dead, raced off in pursuit of the king. The battle had raged backwards and forwards. When Vretlianan riders came to the rebels' aid, Betlic's followers retreated north. Apart from the many bodies, the area round the horse's remains was now empty of friend and foe alike.

When Orvyn awoke, it was dark. He felt nauseous, his head pounded, and he was unable to move. In desperation, he struggled to free his leg. The horse's weight was too much. He was going nowhere. From the angle of his foot, he suspected a broken bone. Soon, it rained, a steady downpour. The dip, in which he lay, filled with water. His neck rested on the lip of the depression. He was in no danger of drowning, but his body was soaking. As the temperature dipped near dawn, the cold was relentless.

In a dream-like state, Orvyn passed the morning. He drifted in and out of consciousness. During his lucid moments, he caught the sound of voices, sometimes close, other times far away. He had no way of telling on whose side they belonged. His leg had swollen. The sun dried the land, and those upon it. It was too late to stop Orvyn from spiralling downwards into sickness. By noon, his temperature was high and rising. Visions of Willa appeared to him. In his heart, he doubted he would see her again. Here he would die, pinned beneath his horse. Green lights lit up the sky to the north. Thunder pealed overhead. Whether it was real, or the result of his high temperature, Orvyn was beyond caring. He was developing a racking cough and his body was burning with fever.

He thought he heard voices. His attempt to shout started him coughing. The land seemed to be spinning. Someone was talking, much closer this time. He could not understand what they were saying. Orvyn felt himself falling into a hole, so deep it had no end. In the darkness it was cool and comforting, a place without pain. So this was what death felt like? Willa's face floated in front of him. A great yearning overcame him. He tried to touch her lips. The vision faded. His mind became blank.

"Over here," a voice called. "I thought I heard something."

A man strode among the remains. Another joined him.

"There's no-one alive," the second person said, as its owner wandered around the bodies. "We're wasting our time here."

"Look, that one under the horse. He's a rebel fighter. I'm sure he twitched a moment ago," the first speaker pointed in Orvyn's direction.

The two men moved towards the body.

"Quick, he's breathing," the second one cried. He was kneeling beside Orvyn.

The man cast around him. Nearby, a long-handled battle-axe lay. He wedged the axe-head beneath the horse, a hand's width from Orvyn's trapped leg. The first newcomer placed a stone under the handle.

"Press down hard, while I pull him clear," the man on his knees said.

Within minutes, Orvyn was free. Strong arms lifted him. Between them, the pair carried him away. Late that afternoon, he was under the care of healers, men and women who had accompanied the Vretlianan forces. To them, he was another, unknown patient, one among thousands. After they tended his wounds, they laid him out in the open, beside his fellow injured, to recover or die. The bandage on his arm, which Hafter had noticed, had covered a deep scratch from an arrow. The wound was raw and inflamed. Many archers coated arrowheads in noxious substances.

Orvyn's fever grew worse. Whether it was caused by a night in the wet, poison from his wound, or both, no-one could say. Not that it was of any consequence. There was little expectation of survival. Had the healers' time to dedicate to reducing his temperature, the outcome might be different. It was unfortunate, but many others needed their attention — others with futures more certain.

A group of horsemen picked a path through the lines of wounded men. On seeing who rode at the party's head, those who could, bowed low. King Grogant acknowledged their homage, but his thoughts were fixed on matters that concerned him more. Lightning displays to the north had ended earlier, with a contest between a new, red light and the original green. What they signified, he could but guess. After a final enormous red flash, both it, and the green light, that for days had given hope to everyone, had been absent. Grogant feared Betlic might have triumphed over the heir.

The young soldier who rode at the king's side had risen far since his original mission to the rebels with Marazin. Sherwyn was now a senior aide to Grogant. He took more interest in the injured than did his master. As Sherwyn passed the rows of wounded, he glanced at each patient, his keen eye taking in every face. One looked familiar but, in the man's current condition, Sherwyn struggled to place him. The party reached the end of the row before he remembered.

"Your Majesty," he said, "please, wait a moment."

Sherwyn leapt from his mount and ran back, to kneel beside the injured man. He was tossing and turning, mumbling words that made no sense. But no doubt remained in Sherwyn's mind. This was the person who had saved Sherwyn and Marazin from Amron's wrath. This was a debt Sherwyn must repay. Still mounted, with increasing impatience and irritation, the king glared at his aide. Sherwyn sprinted to Grogant's side.

"Finished?" Grogant asked, annoyance raising his tone. "May we now proceed?"

"Please, your Highness, if I could speak to you for a moment? That injured man, he's important to me."

"Continue," the king commanded, as he saw the look of concern on Sherwyn's face.

The king's aide was a good man. If Sherwyn thought this person was of significance, Grogant would listen — albeit briefly.

"That wounded man, it's Orvyn, the rebel who saved the lives of Marazin and me."

"The warrior Amron humiliated? They tried to hunt him down, didn't they?"

"Yes, your Majesty, he's the one."

"Then we must save him," the king decided. "He did our nation a great service."

Grogant demanded to see the healers, to whom he made clear he would hold them to account if Orvyn died. After a further short discussion with his aide, his majesty ordered that knowledge of the wounded man's whereabouts stay hidden from all but him and Sherwyn. In the belief that Amron still wished harm to Orvyn, Grogant thought it safer for the patient. Concealed inside a covered wagon, they would escort the injured man away from the battlefield. As soon as his healers believed him well enough to travel across the mountains, they would transport him to safety in Vretliana. With Orvyn's identity a secret, Amron's personal grudge against the man would remain unfulfilled.

CB 80

In the rebel stronghold, a few hours ride north from where Orvyn lay, Willa, ashen-faced, attempted to stay positive. Earlier in the morning, Hafter had brought news that her husband was missing in action. The details the sage knew were few. Yesterday, separated from Amron in the heat of battle, Orvyn disappeared. Not all of those who fought beside him had returned. The most that any survivor could say, with certainty, was Orvyn's horse had fallen, its rider with it. Whether he lived was unknown. At Amron's command, a search party sought for the absent man.

The sky lit up, a brilliant flash of red. A cold chill ran through Willa. She grabbed Scard by the hand. Together, they hurried towards the walls. No sooner had the red light faded when the heavens glowed green. Thunder rolled across the valley. What followed was a confusing mixture of red and green flashes. On and on they went. The barrage of sound was deafening. Breathless, she reached the battlements and fought her way through to the front of the crowd.

To the west, within a circle of horsemen, a mounted man galloped towards a figure standing in front of a tent. Green streaks of lightning flew from the man on horseback. From the hands of the other combatant, orbs of fire swept towards the horseman. A long way behind the rider, another horse stood, as if waiting for its master to return. Nearby, a black shape lay on the ground, smoke rising from the object. Whatever was taking place, by instinct, Willa knew this was the final act of Betlic's bid for absolute power. Rooted to the spot, in silence she watched, to see what would be the result.

Beneath the cliffs, on the valley floor surrounding the arena, combat stopped. Everyone turned to face the commotion. Weapons in hand, the antagonists stepped apart. Transfixed by the sights and sounds, they waited for what would happen next. The nearer to the centre of action they were, the less intense became the fighting. Further away, the battle continued unabated.

Chapter Fifty Five

Whether it was the pounding of the horse's hooves, or the blood racing in his ears, Marazin was conscious of little more than the beat. It urged him ever faster. Around him, the whip lashed through the air. Streams of energy streaked towards the defiant figure in front, deflecting or exploding the glowing orbs it sent hurtling in the rider's direction. Explosions of green and red lit up the sky. Betlic, for it could be no other, was only strides away, when Marazin reined in and leapt from his horse. It turned and galloped to safety.

Alone, at the centre of the circle created by the expectant watchers, the two men faced each other. A flashing sphere of red exploded in front of Marazin. Visible only to the participants, a green aura had spread from the Mastig to surround him. It deflected much of the explosive force from the orb. Despite that, the blast hurled him to the ground.

On his face, he skidded over the soft earth, until the long grass halted his progress. He twisted onto his back. Another glowing ball slammed into the spot where moments earlier he had been. Marazin brought up his knees as he rolled back. With hands on the turf, beside his head, he kicked out. Almost in the same instant, he pushed hard. The Mastig remained in his grasp as he leapt into the air. Propelled upwards and forwards, he landed, upright, on both feet. He raised his arm and flipped the whip's handle. The end of the thong streaked outwards.

This time, Betlic crashed onto his back, thrown by the force of the energy unleashed against him. He grimaced as he stood. Wary now, the opponents circled as each attempted to gauge the other's strengths, or find a weakness. The respite lasted no more than a few seconds before the participants resumed hostilities.

Almeric's men moved further out from the centre. Several of Betlic's wayward spheres of fire had landed close to the watchers, scorching those near the front.

Waves of sound erupted as each of the adversaries, with the enchantments they possessed, tried to gain an advantage. The brightness of the noonday sun diminished in comparison to the brilliant flashes that accompanied the contest. First one participant, then the other, would push back his rival with the ferocity of his attack.

In the battle of power and wills, neither could achieve dominance. Time moved on, its passage rapid. As it did, Marazin detected a pattern in Betlic's movements. He alternated between arms as he issued a barrage of flaming orbs, two dozen, or more. Before he could start again, he would pause a moment, to recoup his energy.

It was a while before Marazin, concerned with his own survival, realised what happened in that instant. Later, as he flicked aside the final orb from another series, something caught his attention. As Betlic's arms fell idle, the reddish aura that surrounded him diminished. At first Marazin considered this observation insignificant. After the third time of seeing, Marazin wondered whether this apparent weakness might be useful to him.

What if, when Betlic's aura dimmed, the protection it afforded also faded! If so, Marazin believed he had a way to defeat his opponent. He would have the one chance. If it failed, forewarned, Betlic would take precautions against further challenges.

For several minutes, they maintained their struggle. Again, for brief moments, Betlic paused his attack. On each occasion, either Marazin was out of position, or his opponent's stance was wrong. Marazin remained patient. Betlic unleashed another barrage of orbs. Marazin twisted and turned as he defended himself with more throws of the whip. As one final, flaming sphere hurtled towards him, Marazin dropped to his knee beneath it. Betlic lowered his arms. He was facing his opponent. Marazin, anticipating the diminishing of Betlic's aura, was already throwing the whip. It ran true. The tip of the thong wrapped itself around the chain suspended from Betlic's neck, the golden thread that held the talisman.

With a flick of Marazin's wrist, a wave pulsed along the length of the whip. Flashes of green flew in all directions. The links snapped. The talisman lifted clear of its possessor. In the same moment, the mantle's cord became unknotted. The garment slid to the ground. The thong was high over Marazin's head. He flicked the handle again. The tip of the whip unravelled. The talisman, set free, landed in the thick grass, some distance behind him.

Betlic was far from defeated. If that was Marazin's expectation, it would remain unfulfilled. In fury, Betlic roared at his opponent, but his attempts to launch more orbs failed. Without the talisman on his person, his ability to create fire had ended. Despite this, he retained other aspects of the charm. His aura returned, now much stronger. Betlic grabbed his sword. With both hands on the hilt, he held it high. He raced towards Marazin. The blade crackled. Blood red sparks dripped from along its length. Marazin released his hold on the Mastig. It coiled itself round his waist. He drew his own weapon. It was fitting. Betlic should die as he had lived, by the sword.

With ease, Marazin sidestepped Betlic's blow. A shower of red and green embers covered both men. Betlic stepped back. He raised his weapon again. Marazin moved at lightning speed. He turned and swept his sword towards his opponent's exposed body. Betlic saw the danger. Without difficulty, he blocked the blow in time. Again, sparks flew in every direction.

In a manic fury, the combatants fought. They parried blow after blow, deflected others or smashed them back. In desperation, Betlic tried to push Marazin to where the talisman had landed. Betlic twisted and ducked beneath a thrusting sword, then attempted to slice through Marazin's legs. He leapt sideways, to avoid certain amputation. With his opponent off balance, Betlic should have tried to finish him. Instead, the lure of the talisman was too strong. Head down, he shoulder-charged his adversary. As Marazin hurtled to the ground, Betlic ran on, convinced the prize was his.

Before Marazin hit the grass, the Mastig had uncoiled itself from his waist. As his sword slipped from his grip, the Mastig's handle dropped between his open fingers. Marazin clasped hold of it, rolled over and threw the whip. The end of the thong wrapped round Betlic's legs. Still several paces from the talisman, he landed with a thud, winded. Jagged red flames leapt from the object, stretching towards Betlic. They fell short. He turned as, in desperation, he struggled to uncoil the rope that bound his legs.

With a quick movement of his hand, Marazin flicked the whip. The end came clear and, as he gained his feet, it returned to him. Again, the thong coiled around his waist. He had already released the handle and snatched up his sword. Betlic was slower to stand. Before he could move towards the talisman, Marazin was upon him. Betlic was a tough, seasoned, brutal and dogged fighter. Marazin was younger. His skills were greater, his reactions faster, and he was the more agile of the combatants.

Betlic swung a blow. Marazin arched backwards. He felt the breeze from the blade as it passed in front of him. As Betlic fought to bring his heavy weapon back into play, the heir struck. In a two-handed grip, he brought up his sword, then spun round at speed. The razor-sharp edge sliced into Betlic's throat. The blow carried such force, it almost cleaved his head from his neck. Blood spurted. He collapsed. The head, wearing an expression of disbelief, bounced as it hit the ground. When it came to rest, Betlic faced towards the object he had tried so hard to reach.

A ray of intense red light flowed from Betlic's open eyes into the talisman. A flash, greater than anything seen that day, erupted from the Eye. The beam faded. The talisman glowed for a moment longer. Once it had fallen dormant, Marazin lay down his sword. The Mastig, again, appeared inside his grasp. He picked-up the talisman with his left hand. The whip coiled itself around the object until a deep green glow was all that he could see. Weary, Marazin staggered towards the mantle. He scooped up the garment to roll it into a tight bundle. With the whip's remaining length, he bound together both objects.

Exhausted, he sank to the ground where he sat, head in hands. Now the action was over, his grief at Karilyn's loss overwhelmed him. The pain was unbearable. He wished himself dead, too. Without her, life was meaningless. Around him, silence was absolute. Almeric and his men were motionless, stunned by the events they had witnessed.

Minutes passed. In his imagination, a hand touched his shoulder, a gentle touch. It brought back memories of the previous night. Damn this madness. He concentrated on something else. The feel of the hand was no more. A strange sensation came over him as though someone knelt at his side. Two soft hands clasped hold of his. He raised his head, his eyes opened. Beyond his tears, Karilyn's face swam into view. He was dreaming. She was dead. It was his fault. He had been too slow with the whip. To save him, she had leapt in front and taken the full force of Betlic's fire in his stead.

Hands let go of his. With tenderness, they caressed his cheeks. His vision cleared. Blood trickled down the face in front of him, the hair surrounding it was singed and tangled, but it was that of the woman he loved. How she had come to him, he neither knew nor cared. She threw her arms around him. He clung to her, terrified she might disappear. From the depths of despair, Marazin had risen to be the happiest man in the land.

From a distance, Almeric watched the couple as they embraced. He smiled. Their part in the battle was at an end. They had earned their time together. He turned to one of his aides and issued a string of instructions. Soon afterwards, he led away his army, to continue the fight. There would be many fanatical supporters of Betlic who would rather die than surrender. A group of warriors detached themselves from the departing men. They formed a protective circle round Marazin and Karilyn.

Chapter Fifty Six

Willa's anguish was clear for all to see. Ten days had passed since Orvyn's disappearance. The search party, sent by Amron to find him, soon discovered the remains of Orvyn's horse, but, of its rider, there was no sign. The searchers combed the area and scoured dozens of Vretlianan campsites set up to care for the wounded. Each patient received a visit, but Orvyn was nowhere. It was with reluctance the king halted the search. With the defeat of Betlic, Amron had other, more pressing matters that needed the redeployment of his men.

Across the fields of battle, in their thousands, the dead littered the ground - too many for individual burials to take place. The weather was hot, the stench horrendous. Where fuel was available, they burned the remains, friend and foe alike. Elsewhere, work-details dug mass graves. Along the valley, hundreds of low mounds appeared. Amron was of the opinion Orvyn's body was burned, or interred in one of these burial mounds. It was probable the location of the man's remains, as with thousands of others, would remain a mystery.

Considering the chaos across the land, most, with regret, would have accepted his majesty's assessment. Willa was not such a person. She refused to believe her husband was dead. Determined to find him, and against Hafter's wise council, Willa insisted on continuing the search, by herself if necessary. Because the land was still unsafe, Amron was sympathetic enough to provide her with a small escort.

The day following the defeat of Betlic, Marazin and Karilyn came to the stronghold, to meet with Amron and Hafter. Overnight, while they recovered from their ordeal, they had remained under the protection of Almeric's forces. Neither had suffered serious injury, but, in his battle with Betlic, Marazin's use of the Mastig had exhausted him.

Before the couple left their battlefield, they performed one last duty. With great sorrow, they laid to rest their faithful companion, Heardwine. Karilyn owed her life to the dog. As she had leapt from her horse,

Heardwine's powerful hind legs had launched him from the ground. Coming up behind Karilyn, its giant paws, pummelling into her back, had thrust her over the front of Marazin's horse. An instant later, Heardwine's body had absorbed most of the energy from Betlic's fiery orb. The flash, and her heavy landing, had stunned Karilyn. When she awoke, beside Heardwine's charred remains, Marazin's fight with Betlic was close to the end.

The couple's meeting with Amron, though somewhat reserved on both sides, was cordial. No-one spoke about Karilyn's time at the king's palace. It was better for such matters to remain unsaid. It was Hafter who mentioned Orvyn's disappearance. Once freed from further commitments, Marazin and Karilyn went in search of Willa. Down in the valley, her despair had deepened the longer her search remained fruitless.

Over the following days, the allies reclaimed the whole of the valley from the remnants of the invading army. Almeric's men had taken Betlic's body with them. Under a flag of truce, they met with the late ruler's generals. With their master dead, his body as proof, the heart went out of them. Several of his commanders appeared bemused by their whereabouts, as did many of their men.

From the moment Betlic first put on the mantle, while holding the talisman, he had exercised extensive control over the minds of his followers. To many, it seemed as though they had awakened from a dream. Those who had joined him, since the invasion of their lands, were most affected. The months, sometimes years, between then and the present were vague uncertain memories to them.

What to do with the prisoners? This matter provoked much discussion between the allied leaders. Almeric and Grogant, along with many rulers whose lands had remained free, favoured executions. The heads of those countries that, alongside Xicalima, had suffered under Betlic's occupation, too, inclined towards a policy of retribution. In private, Amron and Hafter had discussed this matter. It was time for Amron to make the final transition, from country boy to statesman. To everyone's surprise, he spoke at length in support of an amnesty. After the years of suffering his own country had endured, everyone had expected him to be the most ruthless of all in his opinions.

Over the coming months, he said, everyone would want to return to their own kingdoms, to reclaim and rebuild. Betlic was gone. Although, the bulk of his advancing army was dead or disbanded, large forces of occupation retained a stranglehold on the conquered nations. If leaders of these countries were to regain their own lands, first they must evict its keepers. To accomplish that, they would need an army. Held captive, in the valley below and high in the mountains, were thousands of Betlic's men. Many of these were skilled warriors, whose origins were a cross-section of most of the subjugated nations. These men no longer held any allegiance to Betlic. His power over them was through the talisman. That had ended with his death.

Betlic had sought only the best. If the assembled leaders wiped out the elite of their fellow countrymen, what would remain for them to rule? A strong nation needed strong people to rebuild it. Amron was adamant, if his fellow leaders spared the lives of their prisoners, those affected by this act of mercy would reward them with a lifetime of loyalty.

It was Amron's passion that swayed the leaders of the other realms it was time to move forward. Over the coming weeks, he would become the driving force behind a series of negotiations. These would lead to a peace treaty between nations that would last long beyond Amron's lifetime. Afterwards, the heads of the free territories would return to rule their own lands. Each would leave a large contingent of men to help liberate the occupied countries. They would reclaim Xicalima first. The other lands, that Betlic had oppressed, would follow, one-by-one. Only when the last one was free would the final warriors return to their homes.

But that was yet to come. In the valley, Willa was in tears. Karilyn did her best to offer comfort. She had long-since lost hope. Even so, until Willa accepted the inevitable, that Orvyn had gone, Karilyn would help her search. Marazin was absent. Amron had recalled him for another meeting. The heir would return later in the evening. Willa's face was pale. She had lost weight, her garments hung loose around her. She gazed at Karilyn.

"Thank you," she said, as she wiped her black-rimmed eyes. "I know you think Orvyn's dead, yet you've not let that stop you from helping me. I pray you're wrong, but fear you may be right. Can I beg of you to search one more day? If we find no sign of him by tomorrow night, I'll return to Scard. He must be missing me, I know I miss him."

"I'll stay for as long as you want Willa, you know that. The decision is yours."

She knew, if Marazin disappeared, her actions would differ little from those of her friend. It was late, time to make camp. The two men, who remained as escort, fetched wood for the fire. Willa prepared a meal. Karilyn refrained from helping. The work took her friend's mind off her troubles. Later, Marazin rejoined them.

"What did Amron want?" Karilyn asked, once their escorts had retreated to their own tent, leaving the trio free to talk in private.

"It was to ask me what my plans might be. He and the rebels will march on Xicalima soon," Marazin answered. "Hafter was there, too. He's been researching my history. It seems a large estate still stands, and a house that belongs to me. As we knew, my family were of high status. I have a few distant cousins, none of whom has a claim to the land. Amron was most insistent we are welcome to settle there. I heard too, from Hafter, that the king's infatuation with you is no more. A young lady, of noble birth, has caught his eye and, once he becomes established in Xicalima, they'll announce their marriage."

"What did you say?" Willa asked. "I expect you two will settle in Xicalima."

There was a wistful intonation to her words. She had nowhere to go. Her old home was no more, destroyed by Halwende and his 'new friends', as was her extended family. Her new husband, so everyone believed, was dead. A destitute widow, with a young child to care for, would face a daily struggle to survive.

"I told him no, of course," Marazin said. "I asked him to share the land and property, equally between my cousins."

"What!" Willa said. "You've done what, Marazin? After everything you two have been through to free Xicalima! Karilyn, you can't let him throw away his inheritance."

"It's all right." Karilyn smiled. "We've already discussed what we want from our future. The lands in Xicalima are a pleasant surprise, but we could never live there."

"Why not? Isn't this one of the things you fought to achieve?"

"Over the coming months, Karilyn and I have much travelling to do," Marazin said. "We have to conceal the talisman and find somewhere else to hide the mantle. Not until that's done can we take the Mastig back to its place of creation, to return it to its original state."

"But, I don't understand," Willa interrupted. "Why can't you live in Xicalima once everything's done?"

"I'm the heir, and Karilyn is the Bearer of the Scraufin," Marazin said. "If we settle in Xicalima, everyone will know us for that."

"We'd live under the constant threat of kidnap or worse," Karilyn added.

"You think Amron untrustworthy, is that it? You believe he's not changed and intends to harm you," Willa thought she understood their fears. "But, that can't be true, he's shown such kindness towards you both."

"No, it's not Amron," Karilyn said with a quick laugh. "The king has seen what the talisman can do, how it changes people and takes over their minds. He accepts the dangers involved, and this has cured him of any temptation towards it. Despite that, it's doubtful whether we could ever trust him. Once in Xicalima, adulation and power could turn his head again, leading him to believe we are a risk to his sovereignty. It's others from who we'll be at greater risk. To them, the lure of the talisman will prove irresistible. They'll try anything to find it. If we settle anywhere where we are known for what we are, we'll become targets for those who want the object's power."

"Karilyn's right," Marazin said. "We have to settle somewhere where we're unknown. Our first-born," he added, as Karilyn blushed, "will be the future heir. Another of our children will become the bearer. Never before has an heir and bearer continued together, the line of each. To give our future children a chance of survival, we have to disappear."

Willa turned to Karilyn. "So, I'll never see you again? This is too much to bear. After all these years apart, you tell me circumstances must separate us again." The upset was clear in Willa's tone. It was with difficulty she held back her tears.

"You and I will be friends forever," Karilyn said, leaning over and putting an arm round Willa. "Marazin and I would be happy for you and Scard to live with us."

"At the southernmost tip of Vretliana lies a fertile valley set in rolling hills, close to the sea. It's a place where we could all live, hidden away from the world," Marazin said. The area boasts several cottages, a large house and, apart from that, few neighbours. It belongs to King Grogant. It's too remote for him, he has visited it only once. After everything I have done for him,

I'm confident, in secret, he'll deed it to me. I was unable to meet with him today because he was out in the field."

"I appreciate your kindness," Willa said. She understood the spirit in which he had made the offer, but was too proud to accept it as it was. "But I can't live off your rewards. If I join you, it'll be as your housekeeper, or in some other position."

Both Marazin and Karilyn stared at her in amazement.

"You'll be no servant of ours," Karilyn said, annoyed at the idea.

"Willa," Marazin's voice was gentle, "Orvyn has done great service to the king. He saved his life and helped me and Karilyn bring the Mastig here to defeat Betlic. Amron owes him a huge debt. He was going to bestow generous rewards on Orvyn. Now, instead, these belong to you and Scard. In the next few days, you'll be an independent woman, a person of considerable wealth. A servant you'll never be."

Willa sat back. It was a while before she could take in what her friends had said. If only Orvyn could be here to reap his rewards. She burst into tears, relief and sadness mixed. Marazin slapped himself on the forehead.

"I almost forgot. I've some good news," he remembered. "Sheply's alive."

"He is? Is he all right?" Willa demanded to know. She was fond of the young shepherd. Scard thought of him as a brother.

"He's lost a couple of fingers on his left hand," Marazin said, "and several other wounds. None is too serious; he recovers well. He asks after you constantly. I do believe he's adopted you as his replacement mother," he added with a grin.

"I'd be proud to be so considered." Willa smiled for the first time in many days. "I trust there'll be room for him, too, with you."

Marazin nodded. The land he had in mind for them to settle would make for good grazing. If Sheply wanted to join them, he would be master of his own flock.

It was late. They settled for the night. Marazin had agreed to spend another day in search of Orvyn. As did Karilyn, he believed his old friend dead. He also knew that only if they found his body, would Willa have closure.

Chapter Fifty Seven

With Karilyn and Marazin's help, Willa was able to widen her search for Orvyn. Now, during the final hours of their quest, they were several hour's ride from where they had started. As had the original party sent out by Amron, the three had scoured the rows of wounded, inside the makeshift camps set up for them. Orvyn was not among them, nor would anyone admit to seeing him. A few days earlier, the searchers entered the Vretlianan camp where his rescuers had taken him. Under strict instructions from their king, they kept knowledge of the injured man's existence and whereabouts to themselves.

A long convoy of covered carts rolled over the trail, taking Vretlianan casualties back to their homeland. The three riders moved to one side as the wagons reached them. They weaved in-between the moving carriers. At each open flap, they studied the wounded passengers. None of the faces was familiar. At the rear, the final cart appeared laden with barrels and sacks of food. After a cursory glance, the riders continued on their way. It was time to return to Amron's stronghold and for Willa to decide upon her future.

CB ᙏ

Near the front of a wagon, Orvyn stretched-out. Supplies, piled high at the back, obscured his view of the world. His fever had broken a few days earlier, but he remained seriously ill. The swelling of his arm was reducing daily. On several occasions, his carers had drained poison from around the arrow scratch, before coating it with mashed Yarrow plants. This treatment reduced the inflammation until the wound no longer wept. His ankle remained in splints.

No matter how he lay, the cart's movement caused him discomfort. A potion, created from various herbs, eased his pain, but made him drowsy. Orvyn drifted in and out of consciousness. He thought he heard the sound of voices. One of them, so pleasant, reminded him of Willa. He stirred and tried to call out, but his voice was too weak for anyone to notice. The mixture took effect. He fell into a deep sleep.

Much later, when he awoke, the convoy was in the foothills. A vague memory of hearing Willa's voice came to him, but he dismissed it as a dream. No-one would tell him where he was, nor to where he was going. He tried to ask those who cared for him, but they were too busy to listen. They had their orders. This man must remain hidden until they were high in the mountains, far away from any rebel forces. It was of no concern to his carers what he wanted. When he was well enough to ride, and travel unaided, he was free to do whatever he desired. Until such a time, he stayed with them, under their protection.

03 80

Willa bade her tearful farewells to Eadgyth and Hafter. For the past few days, since Marazin and Karilyn's departure, Willa had prepared for her journey. Sheply was to join her and Scard in their new life. As Marazin had foretold, she was now a wealthy woman, although, without Orvyn it meant little to her. In truth, she would have exchanged it all to be with him. She had decided to move to the valley that King Grogant had deeded to Marazin and Karilyn. At their suggestion, a hunting lodge and surrounding land, which bordered the green swathes, the king gave to Willa.

Marazin, unaware of Grogant's interest in the missing man, only thought to mentioned Willa as a recipient deserving of his majesty's generosity. Grateful, but in a hurry, the king would have agreed to almost any request Marazin put before him. Grogant, his mind on other matters, had forgotten the connection between Marazin, Orvyn and Sherwyn. His aide was absent on a mission, so there was no-one to remind the king.

Despite public assurances that she accepted Orvyn's death; Willa refused to believe he had gone. If he was dead, she felt sure, somehow, she would know. The passion they had shared, in their few private moments together, was unlike anything experienced with her first husband. Whenever she lay down and closed her eyes, she imagined his hands caressing her. Orvyn must be alive.

One thing was indisputable; there were no sightings of him among the rebels, nor their allies. The more she gazed towards the mountains, across the valley, the more she felt drawn to them. This region she had yet to explore. If her husband lived, his injuries must be severe. Otherwise, nothing would have prevented him from returning to her. Ever hopeful, she prayed she would find the answers to her questions, somewhere on the slopes of the distant hills.

Eadgyth wore a robe of black. Willa refused to do the same. She would not mourn Orvyn until she saw his body. Willa embraced Hafter, then shook hands with Eadgyth. Tedrick's widow was a revelation to the sage. She had a keen wit, and an intellect that more than equalled his. For many years, he had sought someone to continue his work. In Eadgyth, he found that person. She, in return, delighted in his dusty manuscripts and vast array of potions. Here was a vocation to stimulate her mind. More organised than her mentor; this was something that, on occasion, would cause friction between them.

Willa mounted her horse. Sheply was already astride his while Scard sat upon a small pony. Behind them, several wagons stood, most filled with the wealth bestowed on her and her friends by Amron. Their drivers awaited her signal to move out. A large escort of warriors, provided by King Grogant, would accompany them until they reached their destination. Another wagon, laden with supplies, pulled in front of the others. Sitting beside the driver were a young maidservant and a cook. Willa had employed both — one, orphaned, the other widowed in the recent conflict. On the bench behind was Swanhild. She had begged to come with Willa, so, in time, she could return to the service of her mistress, Karilyn.

With a last wave, the group took their leave. Once on the valley floor, their guide rode ahead. For several weeks, they followed the trail into the mountains, climbing, it seemed, forever. It would be months before they reached their new home. Willa knew it would be even longer before she saw Marazin and Karilyn again. It was odd, the higher Willa climbed, the more a feeling of anticipation came over her. For what, she could not explain. She lost her drawn and haggard appearance. Her appetite returned and her figure filled out again. For some strange reason, she was happy.

☙ ❧

Frustrated by his situation, Orvyn was irritable. His state of health was much improved, his crutches thrown away. With the aid of a stick, he could hobble. His strength increased daily. Rest, good food and, now he was stronger, exercise, all played their part in his recovery. He received sympathy from his carers, but no support for his wish to return for Willa. They were sorry about his continued separation from his wife, but their king's instructions were specific. Orvyn's guardians refused to deny them. Until he was fit to travel alone, he must stay with them.

The wagons had come to a halt. In the fading evening light, food roasted over an open fire. A flat-sided slab of rock rested beside the path. Orvyn hobbled over to it. He picked-up a pebble. In large letters, he scratched the word 'Willa'. Beneath it, he drew an arrow, to point in the direction in which they would travel the following day. The act, he was aware, had accomplished nothing practical to improve his situation, but afterwards, when he looked at his work, he felt more positive in his outlook.

Next evening, Orvyn did the same thing, on a cliff face at the trail's edge. These marks turned into an obsession. To begin with, others thought him mad. He was oblivious to their comments. The change in Orvyn's attitude was clear to all. As the days passed, he became much more optimistic and less ill-tempered. Other members of the group joined him in his task. Soon, at every opportunity, someone would scratch 'Willa' on a rock, with an arrow pointing the way.

ᛦ ᛉ

The air was chill, the sky threatening. Willa was thankful the highest part of their travels lay behind them. A fresh layer of snow already brightened the tops of the peaks. She feared a heavy snowfall might trap her party. Her wagon drivers, of the same opinion, ensured their descent was rapid. They travelled hard and long, to make the most of the shortening days.

"Look, Mama," Scard called out to her. "Your name again," he pointed to a rock at the side of the trail.

Willa moved her horse, to stand beside her son's. When she saw the first message, a week or two before, she had been afraid to trust her eyes. Later, they found other, similar, scratched directions. To begin with, they noticed one or two marked rocks a day, but now, they were everywhere. The earlier ones seemed to be the work of one person, but, latterly, several hands were identifiable.

Willa had exasperated her guide when, at a fork in the trail, she refused to follow the path he indicated. At the side of the way, a dozen inscriptions pointed towards the other direction. It might add a week or two to their journey-time, but Willa had no concerns. Others tried to point out that use of her name was widespread. She ignored their well-meant advice. Nothing they said convinced her otherwise. She knew, somehow, these messages were meant for her.

It was clear, from the freshness of these latest scratches, Willa's party were catching up with the writers. These new marks, unlike their surroundings, were free from the muddy coating left by the runoff from recent rains. Her escort and wagon drivers sensed her urgency. They responded by quickening their pace. The following morning, they rose before dawn. At first light, the party was moving down the trail.

All afternoon, they caught glimpses of a convoy of wagons, travelling ahead. Willa dug in her heals. Soon, she was a long way in front of her own group. Half a dozen members of her escort galloped after her. They had found it unproductive to argue with Willa. Determined and headstrong, she was the one in charge. But, because she treated everyone with equal kindness and respect, her companions held her in high regard. The men would follow Willa anywhere, her safety their main consideration.

Under a setting sun, the riders rounded a bend in the trail. Ahead, a few hundred paces away, the group they chased had pulled up for the night. Willa brought her horse to a halt. Fires blazed at the edge of the camp. People, some on crutches, milled around as they waited for their meal to cook. To one side, a solitary man with a slight limp, stick in hand, walked towards some boulders nearby, opposite to the campsite. He leaned forward as he took something from his tunic. With care, he scratched on the surface of the rock.

For Willa, the world stood still. She could only stare. The lone person was in silhouette. Its outline forever embedded in her memories. Scarcely able to breathe, she eased her horse into motion. Willa drew closer. The sound of hooves reached the ears of the bent figure. He paused in what he was doing. Supported by his stick, the man straightened. He turned towards the newcomer. In the last rays of the dying sun, the rider's face glowed. No-one had ever looked more beautiful to Orvyn.

Chapter Fifty Eight

Bitterness tinged Marazin's thoughts. He turned his gaze towards Karilyn. His expression softened. It was sadness, now, that showed in his face. Neither had suffered an injury, but here they would die — today, tonight or tomorrow! It was small compensation they would be together. He could see no other positive outcome for their situation. Trapped, high on a narrow ledge, there was nowhere for them to go.

Not long after dawn that morning, as they prepared to ride out, the sound of rushing horses took them by surprise. When the outlaw band fanned out, it left but one route for the couple to take. Had they known it was a dead-end, they would have stayed below to fight their final battle.

Behind them and over to their right, a rock face rose high to end in a wide overhang. It was impossible for them to surmount. A low rocky outcrop sheltered the pair's position from those on the valley floor. Beneath them, the cliff face was vertical. The only viable way they could descend, was by a narrow pathway to their left, the one they had raced up, hours earlier. Their attackers were aware of the couple's predicament. In the rocks, at the base of the slope, the enemy waited.

The sun's heat beat down on the pair. Below, their horses grazed on the lush grasses that covered the fertile floor of the narrow valley. To taunt the trapped couple, the outlaws tethered the animals in full sight of the ledge. Water bottles, filled to the brim, hung from the saddles. As intended, these served to increase the couple's thirst. At regular intervals, one of the watchers would stroll into view. With exaggerated movements, he would drain his own leather-canteen, only to refill it from the nearby gushing spring. The assailants knew they could wander with impunity. Tied to the saddles, too, were the pair's bows.

Earlier, the outlaw band attempted a direct assault. The bloody stains on the narrow pathway attested to the futility of such a move. The slope was wide enough for only one person to attack at once. The defenders' skills were too great to succumb so easily. After another day without water, in this hot weather, they would not be so agile. Their strength would have weakened.

With plenty of food and fresh water, their attackers could afford to wait. They knew who their intended victims were. This group of stragglers from Betlic's army would wait, forever if necessary, to avenge themselves on the man and woman they had cornered.

Fired by the enemy, spent arrows in abundance covered the ledge. Because of these, the couple now had shelter of a kind. Marazin had removed his tunic, which he hung over several of the missiles pushed into cracks in the rock. The fabric provided protection from the sun's rays, but did not prevent the build-up of heat, which was relentless. Side by side, the couple discussed their options.

It was a month or two short of a year since the pair had said goodbye to Willa. Since then, they had travelled far and wide. Prior to leaving, they met with King Grogant. His majesty had been generous towards the man, whom, so long ago, he sent in search of the mantle. It was a pity Marazin would be unable to take advantage of his rewards.

Until this morning, the couple's travels had been uneventful. They had separated the Eye from the talisman, then concealed each segment in separate locations, in different countries. When Marazin released the talisman from the Mastig's protective coils, the pull of the dark charms was intense. In haste, he had buried the talisman deep underground, in a barren mountain range. They dropped the Eye into a narrow, funnel-shaped hole, below cliffs on the northern coasts. The object had sunk, far below the level of the incoming tide. In a cave, high in the side of a cliff surrounded by open desert, Marazin thrust the mantle deep into a crevice. He covered it with rocks and sand.

The Mastig, its usefulness now over, they returned to its place of inception. In another ceremony, similar to the first, the whip's core unwound, until all that remained was the Scraufin. It had saddened both participants to see the small pile of brown hair, which separated out from the silver thread. Life was emptier without Heardwine's company. The dog's energy had been boundless, and its loyalty unfailing.

In the months afterwards, the pair followed a winding route. It took them past the mill where Talon lay buried, and onto the Plains of Zefreelah. From there, they rode southwest, towards the southern edge of the

Mogallean Mountains. During this period, they met many diverse groups of former refugees, most returning to their homes. The majority were friendly, while others posed little threat. Not until the couple reached the trails, to the east of the mountains, did they sense any unease.

With the defeat of Betlic's main army and the scattering of his forces elsewhere, trade routes had reopened. Lines of wagons moved north from Xicalima and south from the Marshlands and coastal regions. Near the bottom of the Mogallean Mountains, other routes going east or west formed a crossroads. A sprawling town had sprung up around this meeting of paths. Filled with huts, newly built for the wealthy, and tents for those yet to make their fortunes, it was a wild and somewhat lawless place.

Marazin and Karilyn were quick to notice the wagons they passed were under heavy guard. The goods they carried would be a magnet for outlaws. As the couple approached the new town, a Vretlianan patrol surrounded them. The area was neutral territory, so Grogant had taken responsibility for keeping it safe for travellers. Once the members of the patrol recognised the pair, they escorted them to their base. If only they had taken the advice of the people there, he and Karilyn would not be in their current predicament.

The garrison's commander had warned about bands of marauders, roaming loose. He was clear that, until Marazin and Karilyn reached Vretliana, they would be at risk. Made up of remnants from Betlic's original army, the renegades would do anything to wreak vengeance on the pair for what they had done. The couple acknowledged the danger, but rejected the offer of an escort. They believed that, by travelling alone, they would attract less attention. That had been one of the few, unwise decisions the pair had made, a lapse in judgement that was about to cost them their lives.

Marazin and Karilyn had a simple choice to make. They could wait until, too weak to defend themselves, the outlaws took them prisoner. Neither was under any illusion as to their fate then. Their end would be long and agonising. The alternative was to attack and die fighting. They decided on the latter action. But not yet! When it happened, they would pick the time. Instead, they waited out the day, ignoring the shouted insults and obscenities directed at them.

From the number of horses picketed higher up the valley, the couple estimated there were at least thirty in the band they faced. Despite the couple's formidable skills, these odds were too great.

In whispers, the two spent their remaining time in idle chatter. What they said was inconsequential. There were no regrets. What they had shared would have taken others several lifetimes to achieve. What mattered most was that they were together. As darkness fell, the temperature dropped. Marazin retrieved his tunic.

Later, when the moon rose high into the night sky, the couple took hold of each other's right hands. They spoke the same vows as had Orvyn and Willa. Witnesses were unnecessary. The pledges were as binding. Until today, it had not seemed important. Now, on their last night on earth, it was somehow appropriate.

With their backs against the rock face, their arms round each other, they waited for the moon to disappear below the horizon. Not that it would matter. The enemy must realise that, if their prey was to attempt to break out, they would choose that time. That short period of darkness, between moonset and sunrise, was the only one in which the couple could descend unseen. Around the base of the path, the outlaws would be waiting.

The moon sank lower. Distorted by its proximity to the horizon, it appeared to grow larger. The distant howl of a wolf sounded. Another, much closer, answered it. The land erupted in a series of howls. The sound sent shivers down Karilyn's spine. She snuggled closer to Marazin. Her dread was irrational. She knew how rare it was for wolves to attack humans. Despite that, she feared, later, they may feast from her broken body. For several minutes, before quiet returned, the dreadful sounds persisted.

The moon dipped beneath the horizon. The land darkened. It was time to move. In silence they stood. They eased their swords in their sheaths. For a moment, they held each other. They stepped apart. As one, they turned towards the end of the ledge and their final walk. Light from the stars was sufficient to guide their way.

Marazin placed a foot on the path. The slight sound of movement reached him. Someone, something, was ascending the slope. He put his hand out to caution Karilyn to wait and stepped back. His sword was in his grasp. It looked as though their enemies had become tired of waiting. Marazin and Karilyn were ready. High on the cliff, they would take many more of their foes with them.

A dark shape leapt over the last, stone covered length of path. Marazin sprang backwards. He knocked into Karilyn, who swayed perilously on the edge of the ledge. She steadied herself, then stared over Marazin's shoulder. In the pale starlight, she gasped at the sight. They were face to face with the largest wolf either had seen.

The beast sat at the end of the path and fixed them with an unblinking stare. Karilyn looked round, then grabbed Marazin's arm. She whispered in his ear.

"Look, across the valley," she said, her voice betraying the unease she felt.

With reluctance, Marazin turned his gaze away from the wolf. In the faint afterglow left by the moon, vague shapes were moving along the hilltop opposite, to disappear as they dropped into the darkness below the skyline. He rubbed his eyes. What was happening? Marazin looked back at the beast. It had remained without moving. It neither snarled, bared its teeth nor threatened in any another manner, but it did block their way.

Marazin was cautious. To take advantage of the night, they needed to move, now. But, to do so, they must dislodge this full-grown timber wolf, something that was certain to make a considerable noise. Their only hope of survival, faint though that was, was the element of surprise. They must arrive unannounced. Any hint of a struggle and that chance would have gone.

Marazin took a step towards the beast, his sword ready in his hand. Any hope of the creature's retreat disappeared. From out of what seemed to be the depths of the earth, a rumble started. Marazin moved forward another half-step. The growl deepened. It turned into a snarl. Without hesitation, Marazin stepped backwards. He knew that if the animal leapt, it could take him and Karilyn over the ledge. The noise stopped. The wolf relaxed.

"Keep still," Karilyn whispered. "If we wait a moment, it might leave."

"I don't understand what's happening," Marazin said. "What makes such a creature so unafraid of us, and what were those shapes?"

"More of its kind," Karilyn said.

Before Marazin could say anything more, the beast raised its head.

"No, shush," Karilyn hissed at it, but it was too late.

The howl pierced the silence of the night. Beneath them, others took up the call. Within seconds, a confusing mixture of sounds, movement and frightened cries filled the air. With screams of agony, bodies thudded to the ground. In the darkness, sparks flew as thrashing swords smashed against rock.

Throughout the clamour — snarling, slavering, flesh tearing noises prevailed. Karilyn's skin crawled. The sound of people running came to the listeners. Horses' hooves pounded as they carried their grateful riders away. Moments later, the wolf-pack gave chase. The pitiful sounds, which later reverberated along the valley, caused both Marazin and Karilyn to shudder.

The noises decreased. Peace descended over the area. The wolf, its gaze unwavering, remained motionless. From the hillside opposite came another howl. This differed from earlier ones. Unlike those, it echoed throughout the valley. The beast, at the end of the ledge pricked-up its ears. It stood. With what could have been a nod of its head it turned, then disappeared down the pathway, as silently as it arrived.

Shaken, Karilyn fell into Marazin's arms. He felt little better. If what had taken place below was what he believed it to be, it was something beyond his darkest nightmares. In the distance, the wolves called to each other. Their howls became fainter. They faded altogether. The couple were alone. Their instincts told them this was so. No longer did they sense danger.

They stayed on the ledge. Nothing could have persuaded them to leave until daylight. Whatever lay below, it was not something to wander through in darkness. With their backs against the rocks, they huddled together. As the stars faded, the pair slept. The sun rose. The couple stirred. Their throats were dry, but, as their memories returned, their pangs of hunger disappeared.

Ever cautious, Marazin and Karilyn descended towards the valley floor, their swords in their hands. It was soon apparent the need for weapons was over. Both averted their eyes from the surrounding sights. Each had witnessed the aftermath of battle. Nothing then could have prepared them for the carnage here. Swarms of flies filled the air, attracted by the sickly-sweet smell. Their horses had bolted. The couple fled on foot. As thirsty as they were, neither would drink from the polluted spring. There would be clean water further along the vale.

The sun rose higher. The snort of a horse and the sound of hooves alerted Marazin and Karilyn. They drew their weapons and, in the shelter of a rocky outcrop, they waited. Marazin parted the leaves of a bushy plant, growing from a crack in the stone, he watched the trail ahead. Moments later, he sheathed his sword. Together, the pair stepped into the sunlight. Walking towards them were their own horses. What made the wolves spare them, the couple could not imagine. They took hold of the reins and mounted.

Later that day, high on a hill, a huge dog basked in the afternoon sun. Lazily, from its vantage point, the animal watched as two riders, side by side, rode over a low ridge. The shaggy beast had a familiar look. The dog was young, around three years old, but there was no doubt who its father had been.

As they began their descent into the valley beyond, the riders linked hands for a moment. The dog stood. It stretched. Nearby, a large timber wolf waited for its companion to move. At a distance, the animals followed the trail left by the horses. Only when the travellers reached safety, would the dog release the wild creature from its spell.

Other Fantasy novels by Brian R Hill

The Shintae (2nd Edition)

After recovering The Shintae, an ancient relic of mystical properties, the Maraen warrior, Kaer, is surprised by the enemy and left for dead. After recovering from his injuries, Kaer is once more charged with retrieving The Shintae. With his companion, Angharad, he travels into the Cantaen Mountains in search of the object. Together, the pair face great danger, natural disaster and all-out war before they can hope complete their arduous task.

Standing in Kaer and Angharad's way is Sartae, an antagonist whose evil ambitions know no bounds. A leader, whose cruelty and hatred is legendary. As the mission progresses, Kaer and Angharad must use all their skill and knowledge to stay alive. As the venture races towards its explosive climax, even this may not prove sufficient.

"The Shintae, a mysterious stone with magical powers, is entrusted to the forest-dwelling Maraens. The Cantaens, the Maraens' enemies living in the mountains, steal the stone to use against them. The Maraen hero, Kaer, manages to get the stone back but is ambushed by a group of Cantaens and loses the Shintae to them. The race is on to retrieve the Shintae before the Cantaens learn to decipher the words that will set free its incredible power. Brian R. Hill's fantasy tale is richly told. His characters are strong, determined and dedicated to their tasks. They face many obstacles yet refuse to yield to any of them. Mr. Hill's story takes the reader on an incredible journey..." Patricia Perry - Author.

Shadows from a Time Long Past

The stranger, to whose aid Nerian comes, is young, beautiful and mysterious. Why is she so insistent he accepts the gift of a Crook? It is a decision he soon regrets when he finds himself the target of a manhunt by the forces of the merciless Lord Sigeberht. Instead of saving himself, Nerian risks his life to find the woman and return to her the object?

Held captive within the tyrant's castle, Naomi, the Crook's Guardian, awaits her opportunity to escape. When Lord Sigeberht fails in his attempts to obtain the object, external forces take control of his mind, driving him blindly towards disaster.

While Nerian searches for Naomi, unknown to him the Keeper of the Gauntlet also seeks her. What links the Gauntlet and the Crook? Why are Naomi's childhood games important? Released from confinement, Shadows of evil spread across the land. What is the significance of Gabrielle, the Keeper's kidnapped daughter? As a weapon against the forces of evil, the innocence of a child should never be underestimated.

Shadows from a Time Long Past is an action-packed story that will keep the reader absorbed from the first page to the last. It is filled with memorable characters such as the devoted Almund, Keeper of the Gauntlet, who searches for Gabrielle, his kidnapped daughter; and young Nerian who is drawn into the conflict because of a chance encounter with Naomi, the Guardian of the Crook. The merciless Lord Sigeberht seeks not only the Crook but the Gauntlet because combining the two will grant him unimaginable power. Will he succeed? Mr. Hill's rich settings, remarkable characters and well-crafted story make this a must read. Patricia Perry - Author.

A MODERN-DAY POST BREXIT THRILLER.

Love, Lies and Treachery

WITH YORKSHIRE AND THE DALES AS ITS BACKDROP,
FROM THE START, THIS NOVEL GRIPS THE READER'S ATTENTION.

Young, naive and idealistic, all Nathan wants is to change the world for the better. Involved in the affairs of the Party for National Unity, from its inception, Nathan's progress is rapid. After the party seizes control of the country, his own ruthless actions bring him to prominence. Then, over a matter of days, his life falls apart. Arrested, brutally interrogated, his loyalty questioned, within days he becomes an outcast without family or friends. Now, he knows the true nature of the monstrous regime he helped to create.

Uprooted, Nathan is resettled in a city many miles from his hometown. Alone and under surveillance, he has time to reflect on his past deeds and on the increasing brutality of the ruling party. Before he can hope to atone for his past deeds, he must regain the trust of his masters. To his horror, he learns of a new and deadly threat to the population by the government. Soon, he discovers all he needs to know about love, lies and treachery. Dictatorship, abduction and insurrection are a heady combination for anyone to handle.

This story is especially relevant in today's world, where governments want to capture more power and control over their populations. The characters are strong, the action is exciting. The author has created a frightening situation that makes the reader stand up and take notice. Patricia Perry - Author.

"...a novel that twists and turns and is extremely poignant in the present political climate..."
Ronnie Brown – Singer/Song Writer.

The above novels by Brian R Hill are available on Amazon as Paperback editions, and on Kindle as Digital Downloads.   www.amazon.co.uk/Brian-R-Hill/e/B0034P3WCQ/

Made in the USA
Middletown, DE
18 August 2017